Indigo Starling

Book One of the Shattered Empires

Indigo Starling

Book One of the Shattered Empires

Dundas Glass

COSMIC EGG
BOOKS

Winchester, UK
Washington, USA

JOHN HUNT PUBLISHING

First published by Cosmic Egg Books, 2024
Cosmic Egg Books is an imprint of John Hunt Publishing Ltd., 3 East St., Alresford,
Hampshire SO24 9EE, UK
office@jhpbooks.net
www.johnhuntpublishing.com
www.cosmicegg-books.com

For distributor details and how to order please visit the 'Ordering' section on our website.

Text copyright: Dundas Glass 2023

ISBN: 978 1 80341 551 2
978 1 80341 555 0 (ebook)
Library of Congress Control Number: 2023936007

A CIP catalogue record for this book is available from the British Library.

Design: Lapiz Digital Services

UK: Printed and bound by CPI Group (UK) Ltd, Croydon, CR0 4YY
US: Printed and bound by Thomson-Shore, 7300 West Joy Road, Dexter, MI 48130

We operate a distinctive and ethical publishing philosophy in
all areas of our business, from our global network of authors to
production and worldwide distribution.

For Susanna and Eddie.

Acknowledgements

With thanks to my parents, Luke and Leo, and to Hugo, for their feedback and support.

Prologue

The man sat hunched over the table. The room was dark except for the bright circle of lamplight that pooled over the gleaming instruments arrayed neatly in front of him, like some macabre theatre stage. A barely perceptible rasping frayed the edges of the silence. His breath came slowly and regularly as he clasped the glass jar before him with a pale hand and carefully removed its lid. The rasping grew louder and took on a more urgent tempo as the creature inside scrabbled at the sides, struggling for purchase. Delicate legs sprouted from an iridescent, dark green body. The man took up one of the instruments, a metal tube with a soft, hollow orb at one end and a syringe at the other. His hands were steady as he lowered the orb into the jar. Immediately the scrabbling stopped as the creature followed the progress of the orb with the multitude of tiny eyes which peppered its head. A segmented tail, topped with a bulbous stinger, raised high began to sway hypnotically back and forth. When the orb was close enough, the creature let out a tiny shriek and its tail darted forwards, puncturing the soft plastic. The creature's body trembled as it expelled a few drops of milky liquid. He replaced the lid of the jar and examined the orb with flat, black eyes. The dreadful potency of the venom filled him with a sense of awe. He shivered pleasantly at the thought of the effect that just a drop would produce if it entered his blood stream, the speed at which the smart cytotoxins would reach his heart, evading his nano-defences and punching holes in the cell membranes until the heart was unable to beat. He drew a saucer closer to him. At the centre were four minuscule sacks, each tipped with a needle only a few millimetres long and finer than a hair. With the aid of a magnifying lens, he injected a drop of venom into each of the sacks. He took up a scalpel and, without pausing, slid the blade under the skin of

1

his right palm, slicing back and forth. The ripping, wet sound of steel on flesh was nothing new to him and he paused only to dab at the rivulets of blood running down his arm with cotton gauze. Eventually he peeled a flap of skin the width of his palm away from the meat underneath. With tweezers, he placed the four sacks evenly around the bloody, raw flesh, needles facing upwards. Finally he coated the underside of the flap of skin with a sticky coagulent gel and stretched it back over his palm. When he was finished the skin was back in place and, thanks to the gel, already knitting itself back to the muscle. Under the magnifying lens, the distorted whorls and creases of his skin resembled a landscape of high ridges and deep crevasses and, glinting delicately from amidst those features, were the whispery tips of the four needles.

Chapter 1

Snow-capped peaks, glittering in the morning light, jutted from behind the rooves of the rickety stalls that lined the path. Traders wrapped in chunky woollen ponchos against the brisk, alpine air called out their wares, hoping for a few more sales before joining the steady stream of people filing their way slowly up the mountain. Mordax and his father tramped along, following the exodus, as the storm klaxon coughed out its warning, hurrying the feet of those around them. Spread out far below was the space port. Little more than an arid plain, carved into the mountain side and dotted haphazardly with shuttles. Up ahead, looming larger with every step, was the dark maw of a cavern entrance, hundreds of feet high, into which the path led like a serpentine tongue. Striations in the rock left by the teeth of the drill that had chewed its way into the mountainside gave the cavern a ragged, disturbing appearance. Despite this, people were scurrying into it, grateful for sanctuary against the impending storm. The sight of the cavern always reminded Mordax of the unthinkable size of the machines that had once burrowed beneath the surface of Seraph, rooting out the precious minerals and ores. Dust spumed up by a passing wagon billowed in front of Mordax's face, filling his nostrils and making his eyes sting. Coughing and wiping away dirty tears, he hurried to keep pace with Stephan's long stride. At eighteen cycles, Mordax was almost his father's equal in height but he lacked the thick muscle that filled out his father's frame. Stephan squinted up at a nearby flag, whipping back and forth in the strengthening breeze. "Can't be more than four hours until the storm hits. We'll have to be quick if we don't want to be stuck here for the next week."

"You don't get these problems in the Core systems," said Mordax.

Stephan sighed, scratching his beard. "Not this again. All I'm saying, is that these back-water systems don't offer the same kind of profit that we can get closer to the Core. One load of pulse-shields from Angor Bore to the fringe end of the Crux would net us the same as a hundred of these spice runs. Apparently the Kudo-kai even let you take cargo on credit."

Stephan shook his head. "You don't want to be in debt to the Kudo-kai, believe me."

"Fine, we could start small. Work our way up."

"Mordax, you know the *Starling* doesn't have the kind of muscle to protect a cargo that hot. And for Barshamin's sake don't call Seraph a back-water system in front of the merchants. If Bayram hikes his prices because you've pissed him off again, I'll leave you ship-side at our next stop."

Mordax blew out his cheeks. "Come on! With a pilot like Lazarus, we don't need muscle and the *Starling*'s so juiced she can outrun any pirate."

"You take a cargo like that, you paint a target on your back," said Stephan. "We earn a decent enough living out here. Besides, word is the Blackhands are getting bolder."

"If we keep avoiding risk, we'll never get ahead. We'll just keep on treading water," said Mordax.

Stephan looked wearily into the sky and shook his head.

"The answer's no, Mordax."

They lapsed into silence as they approached the entrance to the cavern. It was wide enough for ten wagons to drive through abreast. Inside, despite the cathedral roof that rose hundreds of feet above them, it was an oppressive riot of scents and colours. Hanging lanterns of coloured glass criss-crossed over the grand avenue which led deep into the mountainside. The roar of traders and customers bartering at tightly-packed stalls mixed with the squawking and lowing of animals brought to market for slaughter. The air tingled with the electric energy of commerce. Mordax breathed deeply of the earthy smells and felt his pulse quicken. They joined the tide of sweaty bodies pressing their way further into the seething belly of the bazaar. As they did so, Mordax caught some of the locals staring their way. He was used to odd looks. The rings in their ears and bright scarves around their necks marked out Stephan and him as Travellers, the community of wanderers who moved between the stars not merely as a way of making a living but as a way of life. It seemed to him, however, that there was an unusually hard, hungry edge to the looks they were receiving now. Stephan quickly led them off the main thoroughfare and through the intricate maze of alleys between the stalls. They passed grain merchants weighing sacks spilling over with plump maize seeds and farmers haggling over racks of cured fleeces. Mordax smelled their destination long before they got there. The pungent odour of stasarine permeated the air. Starsarine was the precious spice harvested from the stamen of the starcereus flowers which were cultivated on Seraph and bloomed only one night a cycle. The stalls in this quarter were of noticeably better quality, made from varnished wood covered with thick, brightly coloured cloths which put the rickety stalls of their brother merchants to shame. At the centre was a large white pavilion which Stephan strode purposefully towards. A crowd of traders were milling around outside the tent, awaiting an audience. Two guards in heavy woollen coats flanked the entrance and watched the men approach with dark, suspicious eyes. Each cradled a battered pulse rifle. The nearest, a young man with a scraggy beard, stepped forwards, gesturing with his rifle.

"Stop. You wait over there. Effendi Hakan is busy," he said in thickly accented Basic.

Stephan gave him a kindly look and replied in fluent Spatoir, the trading dialect used throughout Seraph and its neighbouring systems, "You must be new here, my friend. I hope you are enjoying the job and old Hakan isn't working you to the bone."

He looked over the young guard's shoulder to the older guard who was leaning nonchalantly against a tent-pole. "Greetings, Asuman. It's been a while. I hope your master's well. The air's fresh today and I brought you a little something to keep the chill from your bones."

With a flourish Stephan produced from inside his own padded overcoat a small bell-shaped bottle of golden liquid. Asuman stepped forward, a grin cracking his weathered face, and the bottle disappeared into the folds of his coat.

"Greetings, Effendi Stephan. Relar brandy is it? I didn't realise the embargo had been lifted."

With a theatrical glance over his shoulder, Stephan leaned closer and said in a quiet voice "It hasn't quite so don't go splashing that around too freely. Now," Stephan leaned back rubbing his hands together, "we need to see your master quite urgently I'm afraid. We're only dirt side for a few hours and we need to get moving if we're to fill our cargo bay with your quality stasarine." "You'll be disappointed then," the young guard said. "Effendi Hakan is occupied and there is a long waiting list today."

Asuman barked a few angry words in Seraphian at the young guard who stepped back, regarding them sulkily.

"Apologies, Effendi," Asuman said. "It's Kerim's first week on the job and he has yet to learn the way of things. He will be much more accommodating after he has tasted the brandy." Asuman gave them a wink and gestured towards the thin curtain that covered the entrance to the tent. Stephan inclined his head gracefully and strode forward with Mordax following closely behind.

Inside the air was warm and thick with the scent of shisha and stasarine. Soft light diffused from glass lanterns and deep rugs covered the floor. A large figure merrily puffing at an ornate pipe rose from a pile of cushions in a cloud of sweet, cloying smoke.

"Stephan, Mordax, my friends!" bellowed Bayram Hakan as he bore down on them. He seized Mordax in a bear hug that lifted his toes from the floor and planted scratchy kisses on either cheek. He then embraced and kissed Stephan. The two men were of a similar height but Hakan's belly strained at his silk tunic and his bushy beard covered at least one extra chin. "Come, come, sit," said Hakan, gesturing to the mounds of silk cushions and then clapped sharply. A serving girl swept into the tent, slippers whispering against the rugs and carrying a silver platter with three steaming cups of spiced coffee. Mordax grasped his cup appreciatively, warming his hands and breathing in the rich aroma before taking a tentative sip. A warm glow spread out from his belly, soothing away the morning's chill. Bayram inhaled deeply from his pipe, the water in the glass bowl bubbling furiously. He let out a thick cloud of fragrant smoke and regarded them side-long from narrow eyes. "Tell me, Stephan my friend, where have your travels been taking you? Life is slow here and I enjoy experiencing the wonders of the galaxy through your eyes."

"Not far," said Stephan. "Microchips from Destelworth II and heavy metals from New Talbot. Nice easy runs for an old man like me. Seraph is the furthest out we've come along the Crux."

Bayram nodded thoughtfully.

"You're becoming less adventurous in your old age. Heard any interesting news from your fellow Travellers? Anything from Nag'Sami?"

Stephan paused then shook his head. "Seems like some increased pirate activity along the trading routes near New Rome but apart from that nothing unusual. Nothing at all about Nag'Sami. I'd have thought you'd be in a better position to get any news from there with your contacts. You heard something?"

Bayram waved his hand dismissively. "Ah, no. I'm just interested in other perspectives. You never know if there's something the local traders aren't telling you."

There was a tightness in his voice, however, that belied his nonchalance and excited Mordax's interest.

"Speaking of traders who are reluctant to share their gossip," Bayram continued, "rumour has it that you stopped in at Relar, though considering the embargo it would seem to be an unprofitable stop before coming to Seraph."

Bayram said this last with a wry smile. He knew better than anyone the multitude of ways Stephan was able to smuggle goods into Seraph.

"Rumour travels fast," said Stephan "but not every trip has to be profitable. I am getting old and the Relar climate agrees with me, that's all."

Bayram snorted twin jets of smoke out of his nostrils and gave a wheezy chuckle. "The day you stop at port without a view for profit is the day I start giving away my starsarine for free."

"I suppose I may have picked up a few choice items," said Stephan. "A few bottles of brandy, for example. Purely for the consumption of my crew, of course...and certain of our close friends."

Bayram turned to Mordax. "Mordax, tell me, is Relarian brandy as delicious as I've heard."

Mordax gave a slow, wide smile. "Bayram, you've never tasted brandy like this. It's as sweet as the laughter of your children. As deep and rich as the sunset in midsummer."

He leaned closer and gave a conspiratorial wink. "And it's said that it does wonders for the energy and performance of men of a certain age."

Bayram gave a great bark of laughter, belly jiggling.

"Mordax, my boy, you have your father's silver tongue. And none of his tactful reserve. A dangerous combination. Come,

8

Stephan, let's have a taste. I imagine you'll want to talk spice next and bargaining with you is always thirsty work."

As Stephan produced another bottle of brandy from his coat, Mordax rose to his feet pulling his weathered satchel over his shoulder.

"Well, while you two get down to business I've got a couple of errands to run," he said. "Good to see you again, Bayram."

Bayram, mid-drag on his pipe, waved and made no move to rise from his cushions. Stephan shot him a questioning glance but Mordax twitched his finger, a signal for forbearance, and made his way through the swirling smoke and out of the tent.

***

Lilting music and the rich smell of hops filled the air as Mordax stepped into the bar. It was built into an alcove at the top of the main cavern and offered a view out over the lamplit streets far below, twinkling like the golden strands of a spider's web. Patrons huddled around tables, escaping for a few moments the frenetic pace of the market. An antiquated server droid stood motionless behind the bar, waiting to pour drinks from the myriad bottles that lined the deep gouges in the rock wall where ancient drill bits had ripped their way through. Mordax almost always stopped in here on the *Indigo Starling*'s visits to Seraph as the gossip you could pick up was worth far more than the half-credit entry price. Mordax walked over to the bar and ordered a weak ale. His overcoat was now stuffed into the satchel at his hip, replaced by a dirty but genuine Relarian naval engineer's uniform. He had wound a handkerchief around his head, concealing the rings in his ears. Mordax found that people relaxed more around those they could place neatly into a familiar box in their minds. He couldn't pass for a local but he could hold himself out as something a little less exotic than a Traveller. The Relar system was

Seraph's closest neighbour and their naval cruisers frequently stopped in for shore leave. The droid clunkily filled a glass, mechanisms whirring and ticking. Mordax leaned against the counter and took a sip, grimacing at the taste. He surveyed the other occupants of the bar casually. Most were traders, large, bearded men and windburned women shouting happily at each other and guzzling drinks. Mordax spotted his mark quickly. A lone figure, hunched over a table towards the back of the bar, nursing an almost-empty glass. His wide-brimmed hat and ochre-stained fingers marked him out as a starcereus farmer. Mordax picked up his glass and strolled over to the table.

"Hello, friend. Mind some company?" asked Mordax.

The man squinted up at him from under the brim of his hat, eyes bleary and cheeks unshaven. He shrugged and gestured at the seat opposite him with a grunt.

Mordax lowered himself to the table and glanced around as if admiring the place. "Nice to get away from the crowds."

"S'alright," muttered the farmer, "booze is cheap and it's quiet for the most part." His voice was gravelly and his breath left the prickly flavour of whisky on the air.

"Spice farmer are you?" asked Mordax, taking a nonchalant sip of his beer and looking pointedly at the man's hat. "How's business?"

"Whassit to you?"

"Just making conversation, friend. Don't get many opportunities to meet new people cooped up in an engine room for weeks at a time."

The man squinted at the badge on Mordax's tunic. "Relar navy?"

"That's right. Three cycles now." Mordax nodded at the man's glass. "Fancy another one? Pay day was yesterday so I'm feeling pretty flush."

The hard edges of the man's frown softened slightly. "Kind of you."

Mordax gestured for two more drinks and the waitress quickly set refills down in front of them.

The man raised his glass in Mordax's direction before taking a deep gulp. He set the glass back down and stared absently into the amber liquid. Reflected flecks of gold danced over his face. Mordax was thinking of ways to restart the conversation when the man spoke in a voice thick with fatigue, barely more than a whisper. "My pa was ensign with the Seraph fleet during the worst of the Blackhand pirate raids. They were getting their arses handed to them until a Relar battleship pitched in and drove those bastards back to the Reaches. He'd always get a round in whenever you lot were dirt side." He took a ragged breath before continuing with a twisted smile. "Old bugger would throw a fit if he could see me now. I can barely scrape the coins together to get meself pissed."

"Sounds like a difficult time," said Mordax carefully.

"Ay, they've been better," said the man.

Mordax glanced at the farmer's sunken eye sockets and patched clothes.

"Some are still doing alright though?" Mordax said. "I was wandering through the spice quarter earlier and one of the traders has built himself a tent palace or something. Trains of gorgeous women and silver platters of sweet meats heading in and out."

"Bayram Hakan, head of our guild," muttered the farmer. "Greedy bastard but he's a necessary evil. If he wasn't buying our starsarine we'd be fucked."

"What do you mean?" asked Mordax. "Why's he buying your starsarine? I thought the guild heads only negotiated prices with off-worlders and took a cut of the sales?"

The man waved his hand in the air as if batting the questions away. "Don't worry about it. Hard times and desperate measures and that. Anyway, enough of this depressing crap. Where are your lot headed next? Back to Relar?"

Mordax's interest had been piqued. He thought he might be close to getting some useful information but didn't want to push it. "Next stop is Nag'Sami," he said instinctively, recalling Bayram's questions. "Should be interesting. I hear they have pretty relaxed attitudes to coupling."

At this, the farmer's head shot up and his blood-shot eyes widened. "You say Nag'Sami, boy?" When Mordax nodded his head the farmer gripped his arm with rough, stained fingers. "You don't get back on that ship, you hear me? You find somewhere to hide til they leave."

Mordax stared into the farmer's sun-weathered face, now creased with worry. "What? Why?" When the farmer said nothing, he continued, playing his part. "Look, I can't desert. They'd lock me up or worse if I got caught."

The farmer let out an exasperated hiss. "Getting locked up's better'n never coming back at all."

He glanced around twisting his glass nervously in both hands then seemed to make up his mind. "Look, starsarine harvest is over. 'Round this time of year we get three or four Nag'Sami super 'aulers coming by which pick up almost a third of our entire harvest. Not a one has turned up though. Far as we can tell they've up and vanished somewhere between Nag'Sami and here. No bloody sign of 'em. That's why Bayram's been buying all our spice off of us. We've got surplus comin' out our ears. If he hadn't most of us wouldn't be able to put food on the table."

Mordax experienced a moment of fluttering excitement as the pieces fitted together in his mind.

The farmer continued, "You keep this to yerself, hear me? If the other off-worlders find out there's no demand, our starsarine won't be worth shit and even Bayram won't be able to keep us afloat."

He was right, of course, Mordax thought. Whatever the reason behind the disappearance of the Nag'Sami haulers, Seraph would now be sitting on a huge over supply of starsarine. Mordax placed a few coins on the table and stood up.

"Thanks for the advice, friend. I'll think about what you've said."

The farmer looked intently into Mordax's eyes for a second then sighed, nodded his head and resumed his hunched contemplation of his drink.

***

The air inside the tent was still syrupy with shisha smoke. Mordax, his disguise folded away again inside his satchel, halted just behind the entrance curtain and peeked in.

"That would be an insult to my country men who have toiled hard for this year's excellent crop," said Bayram, lazily, his bulk spread among the embroidered cushions and hands clasped over his belly. "320 credits a kilotonne is a fair offer. Come, it is beneath us to quibble so over such a paltry difference."

"If you're tired of quibbling, Bayram, then let's settle at 280 credits. It is a paltry difference after all," said Stephan.

Before Bayram had a chance to reply, Mordax stepped inside shrugging off his coat.

Both men looked up at him and watched as he settled back among the cushions.

"Where are we up to? No price agreed I take it?" Mordax said.

Bayram looked at him suspiciously, eyes squinting through the haze.

"Your father and I are just ironing out the final details," he said.

"Bayram thinks 320 credits a kit would be a fair price," said Stephan. "Any thoughts?"

Mordax sucked in a breathe. "320 credits? No, I don't think that will work at all. Especially since Bayram's still sitting on half of this year's starsarine crop with no way to get it off-planet..."

Bayram blinked quickly and tried to straighten himself in the pile of cushions.

"I uh- that's ridiculous. We ah..." he began

"The Nag'Sami haulers, Bayram," Mordax said. "I know they've disappeared. With that much starsarine still to shift, eighty credits a kit would be generous."

Mordax glanced at his father's face expecting to see his own excitement reflected there but Stephan was staring into space, a slight frown creasing his brow. Bayram's eyes flicked between Mordax and Stephan, calculating. Eventually he let out a resigned sigh and massaged his temples.

"Who told you?" He held up a hand before Mordax could respond. "No, it doesn't matter. You're right. We have no idea what happened to those haulers. I've been spending hundreds on nethercasts but no one knows a damn thing."

Bayram turned to Stephan, a pained expression on his face. "Stephan, my friend, this has caused us real problems. I have been buying starsarine from our farmers myself."

Stephan glanced at Mordax who gave a grudging nod.

"If I hadn't they'd be starving now but I'm reaching the limit of my reserves. Mordax is probably right, if you offer eighty credits I'd have to accept it but the lower the price, the less I can buy from my farmers and the worse off they are."

Stephan pursed his lip. "Two hundred credits a kit is fine, Bayram."

Mordax looked sharply at his father. Stephan continued. "And I'll send a message to a few of the other Travellers in the area. I don't think any were planning to head any further towards the Reaches but if I let them know that you'll cut them the same deal I think they might make an extra trip."

Bayram closed his eyes and sagged with relief, if possible spreading further into his cushions. "Thank you, Stephan. You are a good man."

"Wait a min— " began Mordax.

"We'll take five hundred Kits," continued Stephan, cutting over Mordax, "but in return you'll let me have every piece of information you learn about the disappearance of those haulers, if necessary by direct nethercast."

"Of course," agreed Bayram readily.

***

As soon as they were outside the tent Mordax rounded on his father angrily. "Two hundred credits?! What the hell was that for? We had Bayram over a barrel."

Stephan turned to his son "And what happens when we're down on our luck and need to take a consignment of starsarine on credit? What do you think Bayram will do if we've screwed him for every penny we could get today?"

"Who knows what's going to happen tomorrow?" said Mordax "We had an opportunity to make hard cash and we should have taken it. I can't believe you're more worried about hurting Bayram's feelings!"

"Look, it was good work finding out what you did but you've got to use your advantage tactfully instead of clubbing people over the head with it, Mordax. We'll still make good money and now Bayram owes us."

Mordax shook his head and said nothing.

Stephan continued, "Besides, judging by the look of some of the farmers around here I suspect Bayram was telling the truth about how hard up they are at the moment."

Mordax bit back a reply. What did they owe these people? The life of a Traveller in the Shattered Empires was not an easy one. If you showed weakness, the galaxy would chew you up and spit you out. The farmers had been unfortunate but if the crew of the *Starling* didn't take the chances that came their way then they might not survive the bad times that would eventually follow. Still, recalling the lonely figure in the bar, drinking alone to numb his loss, he couldn't deny a twinge of relief that they weren't making the situation any worse for him. Stephan's thoughts had clearly moved on as he was frowning again.

"The disappearance of those haulers worries me," he said.

"Blackhands?" suggested Mordax. "We know they've stepped up raids recently. It's not their usual hunting ground but it would have taken some heavy firepower to overcome an entire transport convoy."

"Could be," said Stephan, sounding sceptical, "but it doesn't smell right. I'll feel much better when we're away from here."

"I guess a stop over in Nag'Sami would be out of the question then?" asked Mordax with a rueful glance "only, without their haulers our starsarine load would fetch a great price..."

Stephan shook his head.

"No, we're getting out of this sector as soon as we can and we're staying out until I can figure out what the hell's going on."

Outside the wind had strengthened, whipping the dust into frenzied eddies at their feet. Mordax pulled his scarf up to cover his nose and mouth as they made their way back down the mountainside. As they approached the rocky expanse of the spaceport, Mordax noticed a hazy brown smudge on the horizon, the dust storm which would rise hundreds of feet into the air. A warm gust ruffled his hair, bringing with it an earthy, metallic scent. The storm would soon be raging where they stood and expending its fury against the impassive mountain, while the people of Seraph waited safe inside their network of tunnels. Mordax knew the seasonal storms brought with them the rich alluvial soil from the river plains far below and were vital for the starcereus flower cultivation. However, as he gazed at the approaching wall of natural violence his heart was filled with a strange foreboding.

Chapter 2

Even though the sun had long since set, the air was still warm on Akira's skin and thick with the scent of honey blossom and balsam. A sweep of stars sparkled in the purple sky above. Silver cutlery gleamed in the candle light and serving staff drifted like spectres in the shadows behind the seated guests, keeping wine cups filled and a steady stream of delicacies flowing onto the table without interrupting the conversation. Akira was sitting towards the head of the table next to their host, Maerus Yuli, as befitted her station. It was on the deck of Maerus' yacht, moored in the bay overlooking the lights of Ang'Dirth, that they now dined, their laughter and conversation almost drowning out the gentle lapping of the waves against the yacht's hull.

"I don't believe it!" Saphina said. She was a long-faced girl with a shrill voice.

"It's true," said Maerus, absently sweeping his dark fringe away from baby blue eyes. He had just revealed that a married socialite, who happened not to be present that evening but who Akira had seen at Maerus's parties in the past, had been caught in bed with her bodyguard.

"I must get the name of the agency she uses," Maerus said. "Beats the hell out of the service I get from my band of hairless gorillas."

Saphina tittered annoyingly.

"I wouldn't want to be him right now though. You know the reputation her husband has?" Maerus said.

"No, who is he?" Saphina asked

"Thoman Ismailia," Akira offered. "Ambassador Director to Thalmos."

Saphina looked blankly at Akira.

Akira sighed. "Thalmos is our primary source of nanotrite. Without it we wouldn't be able to fuel our starships or keep our nethercast network running. Thoman is pretty important."

"Not as important as our Akira here, of course," said Maerus. "He's not a pure-blood Kudo."

Akira ignored the comment which she knew was designed to annoy her.

"Are you an ambassador too?" asked Saphina

"Oh no, darling," Maerus answered for her "Akira's far too high-brow to sully herself with anything as demeaning as real work."

Akira fixed him with a withering look.

"That's rich coming from a man who spends his waking hours stumbling between whorehouses and the race track," she said.

Maerus leaned back placing both hands behind his head.

"I wasn't criticising. A life of leisure is the ultimate aspiration if you ask me."

"And what if your grandfather had had that attitude?" asked Akira "Your family would never have made its money in the first place."

"Oh, Grandad was a dreadful bore," said Maerus "You're quite right though. Some people are good at making money. Others, such as myself, are better at spending it." He winked at Saphina.

Despite herself Akira couldn't quite hide a smile. "Well, no one can dispute that you're exceedingly talented at that."

She held out her wine glass as a waiter refilled it. The wine, like everything else at the dinner, was expensive and delicious.

"If you had an eye for faster beasts, however, it might be a different story," she said.

Maerus wrinkled his smooth brow in a feigned expression of hurt. "I take my gambling very seriously, I'll have you know. My track record is quite impressive."

Akira sighed. "Well, maybe you can give me a lesson or two. It's bound to be more interesting than my other studies."

Maerus gave a tut of sympathy. "Xif keeping your nose to the grindstone?"

"I wouldn't mind so much if I thought it was actually going to be useful. When am I going to need to know the population of Phoibos or how some long dead general conquered some unpronounceable planet?"

"Urgh! You're making me depressed just talking about it," said Maerus. "You should really come out with us more often, darling."

Akira snorted and shook her head. "I don't think I could keep up with you, Maerus."

"Well, it does take cycles of practice," he said, eyes twinkling.

Just then the table began to shudder, cutlery clattering together and wine sloshing over the brims of glasses. Maerus clapped his hands together delightedly.

"We're off, my dears!"

He addressed the table loudly. "Hold onto to your knickers everyone. We're swapping seas for stars."

He jumped up and, beckoning the others to follow, made for the rail overlooking the bay. The guests crowded round to watch as anti-gravity generators, attached to metal arms that jutted out from the hull, whirred to life. The air around them splintered and cracked as, slowly, the yacht's immense bulk was lifted clear of the surface of the water, rivulets streaming down the hull to fall into the seething foam below. They rose quickly through the warm evening air until they levelled out a few hundred feet above the bay. Akira took a deep breath and drank in the view. The concentric rings of Ang'Dirth's streets were laid out far beneath them. Immense towers, lit from within like sharp embers, were doubled in the glassy surface of the bay and fleets of drones, barely more than flashing specks, buzzed along above the streets in perfect synchronicity. The guests chatted excitedly, while the yacht gradually drifted further out from the centre of the city. As they picked up speed, warm gusts tousled Akira's hair and tugged at the simple, silk dress that hugged her lean figure. Mile after mile rolled away beneath them as the guests pointed out their homes and favourite haunts and made the most of the free-flowing wine. Akira was half-listening to an earnest young artist telling her about his latest project but her attention was on the change unfolding below. They were many miles from the city centre now and towers still covered the landscape. Many of these were not illuminated, however. They stood as silent, dark obelisks merely reflecting the light of their occupied cousins. A few more miles and none of the structures showed any sign of life. Soft clouds of vegetation, grey like everything else in the moonlight, softened the clean lines of the buildings as nature sought to reclaim the land wrested from it many thousands of cycles ago. Whereas the gilded opulence of the yacht had been accentuated by the beauty of Ang'Dirth's central district, now it seemed out of place. An island of hedonism amidst a bleak sea of failed enterprise. Of course, Akira knew that ninety per cent of Ang'Dirth's buildings were obsolete. An ancient infrastructure with nothing left to serve. But to see it with her own eyes, to witness the scale of the empire over which her family had once ruled was a different thing. The warm glow that had suffused her as she had watched the beautiful vibrancy of the city centre began to wash away, replaced by a kind of bitter nostalgia for a time she had never known. Akira's pensive regard must have translated badly on her face as Maerus interrupted her thoughts.

"Darling, don't tell me you're bored?" he asked

"No, of course not," said Akira, managing a small smile. "It just makes you think, doesn't it?"

When Maerus looked confused she nodded towards the dark vista below. "What used to be and what might have been…"

"Pining for the empire? If you ask me it caused more harm than good."

"I don't know," said Akira "How can we be content with what we are now? We ruled half the galaxy. We discovered new worlds and built machines with the power of a thousand suns. And what's left? This system? The orbital factories? Our ancestors built a castle and we're now no more than a grain of sand in its moat."

"Darling, you're very cute when you're ambitious but even a degenerate like me knows that the days of the empire are behind us. Not least because the Dioscuri will murder anyone who tries to revive it."

Maerus put his arm around her steering her away from the railing. "Besides, who would want the responsibility of running the damn thing? Come on, let's get you another drink. Tonight we laugh and sing and toast the misfortunes of those with power."

Chapter 3

The man sat patiently in a secluded alcove of the bar tapping a fingernail against the beer in front of him, careful to avoid any contact between the skin of his forefinger and the glass. He was, in every aspect, unassuming. His black eyes were too far apart for his face to be considered handsome but not to the point of ugliness. His posture was neither impressively straight nor too stooped. Even his clothes, from the soft leather slippers to the linen cap on his head, were common in the city but not overtly fashionable. To a keen observer the man's complete lack of any distinguishing feature might eventually produce a sense of disquiet. Such keen observation was not to be found in the other inhabitants of the bar, however. If the man registered in their consciousness at all, he did so briefly then faded into the background. Server drones flitted backwards and forwards between the customers and the dispensers, ferrying strong drinks and the occasional bowl of a grey, gelatinous substance that the man suspected was supposed to be food. The window next to him offered a view of the street outside. The tarmac was glazed from a recent cleanse and slick surfaces reflected the flickering neon signs of the bars next door. A gaunt young woman was slumped against the brickwork of the building opposite, head uncovered and strands of wet hair plastered to her face. Her limbs were pale and fragile-looking as if they might snap if she tried to stand up. She was struggling with the cap of a small, metallic cylinder, face contorted in desperate frustration. Eventually she succeeded and breathed deeply from the exposed nozzle. Almost immediately her eyes rolled back into her head and her arms fell limp at her sides. The man turned back to his beer and continued his tapping.

A while later, the door of the bar banged open and the man recognised the well-rounded figure entering as the man he was waiting for, Albin Feeshaw. Fat jewels adorned chubby fingers and the heavy tokens around his neck and there was even the glint of a badge of office under his rain cape. A rare flash of annoyance passed through the man at the indiscretion. Feeshaw spotted him in the alcove and made his way over, shaking careless drops of water onto other customers as he passed.

"You're late, Feeshaw," the man said as Feeshaw squeezed his bulk onto the bench on the opposite side of the alcove.

"Those damn tunnels take forever. I don't know why we couldn't meet on the surface." Feeshaw waved over one of the server drones impatiently.

"I feel dirtier just sitting here. Ah, good," he said as the drone hovered over, thrumming gently, "large whisky and..." Feeshaw turned to the man and raised his eyebrows. The man gazed back at him and said nothing.

"Just the whisky then," said Feeshaw waving the drone away. "So, what's the latest? When will your lot be ready to move? I've got to say the pace at which you've been operating has been less than impress—"

The man tapped at the table in front of them and the disembodied head of a well-known news anchor sprung into existence before them, shimmering slightly.

"—no further information from the hospital. There has been no official statement as yet but sources close to the Council have indicated that Adams may have suffered a fatal cardiac arrest earlier this evening. We will keep you informed of any developments as and when they happen."

The man tapped at the table again and the news anchor's face faded away.

"It's done," he said.

The colour had drained from Feeshaw's face, leaving it pallid and waxy. His full, moist lips made a silent 'O'. Just then the server drone reappeared tottering under the weight of a huge whisky. Feeshaw grabbed it and gulped down half of it in one go. A dribble of liquid escaped the corner of his mouth and trickled into his spindly goatee. He dabbed at it with the sleeve of his silk shirt.

"I told you at the start that once all the pieces were in place, things would move quickly and that you had to be prepared," the man said.

"Yes, I remember," said Feeshaw, eyes darting nervously from side to side. "I just expected a bit more goddamn notice."

The man smiled, showing small, even teeth. "The fewer people who knew in advance, the better. It would have put you at risk unnecessarily to burden you with the specifics."

"Still...."

"Best to keep your eyes forwards now. There's a lot of work to be done," the man said.

"Yes," said Feeshaw looking thoughtful "I suppose there is."

"We'll be in touch again very shortly with instructions on how you're to proceed."

The hit of alcohol seemed to be kicking in and Feeshaw's ample cheeks were mottled pink and his nervous fluttering had calmed. He swirled the remaining whisky around the glass.

"'Instructions'. I've never liked that word much. I appreciate the help your employer has provided but it's a bit early to be dealing in specifics, isn't it? Also, after tonight there'll be no need for this distasteful skulking in shadows, hmmmm? I assume I'll be dealing with your employer directly from now on."

The man sighed.

"Feeshaw, your unfortunate predictability makes this no less tedious. You think my employer's assistance has been limited to this final step in your career? If so, you're a bigger fool than you look."

"How dare you—" began Feeshaw angrily

"If you interrupt me again, Feeshaw, I'll cut out your fucking tongue." While the expression on the man's face had not changed, his black eyes radiated the cold danger of a hunting snake. He leaned closer, "We have been responsible for every one of your promotions over the last ten cycles. Your predecessor's terminally damaging scandal? Orchestrated by us. Your unlikely nomination to Speaker. Us again. We have cultivated your career until now because we see you for what you are. Not a gifted politician but a fat, supine worm who will do exactly what he's told."

The man could hear Feeshaw's breathing quicken and watched the confidence seep out of his face. The man smiled.

"Good. You're getting an idea of the extent of our resources and I have given you only the smallest of glimpses. Once you're sworn into office you will be ours. You will obey every command we give you and you'll be happy to do so. In return you will enjoy all the trappings and wealth of the office of the Shield. If these terms are unacceptable we will find an alternative candidate and you will be...replaced. Now, do we understand each other?"

Feeshaw was looking down at his hands, clasped awkwardly in front of him. "Yes," he replied quietly without meeting the man's gaze.

"Excellent," said the man, standing up briskly and pulling a plain black raincoat around his shoulders. "You will hear from us in due course."

He strode towards the exit leaving Feeshaw sitting in the dark alcove still staring at his hands. On his way out he dropped a few coins into the hand of the bouncer standing on the damp pavement.

"Make sure the fat one in the corner doesn't get too drunk. If it's looking likely put him in a cab back to the surface and if you have to rough him up avoid the face. He has a big day tomorrow."

"Hey, thanks man. Will do," the bouncer said, extending a hand to shake.

The man ignored the hand and stepped smartly across the road to where a dark car was waiting. The young junkie girl he had spotted from the window of the bar was still sitting in the same position, slumped against the wall. A pink neon sign above cast her face in strange shadows, turning her sunken eyes into dark skull-like cavities. The man felt in his pocket and withdrew a fat silver coin which he flicked towards her. She made no attempt to catch it, deep as she was in her high, and the coin rolled into the gutter, glinting amidst the murky run-off. With a shrug the man turned away and got into the back of the waiting car.

Chapter 4

Mordax gazed into the viewport of the *Indigo Starling*'s nether-drive where the pulsating stream of plasma flickered in a hundred different hues. As his eyes unfocussed his mind created patterns from the constantly shifting shapes. A face emerged from the river of light, distorted then melted away to be replaced by a bird, spreading its wings. He often came here to think, mesmerised by the images in the super-heated gas. The soft humming of the *Starling*'s engineer, Dr Virzda Golgoth, as she bustled about the engine room was a sound that had soothed him since he was a child. He would come here when he was worried or upset and listen to the familiar bustle and clatter until his worries dissolved like rust in one of Virzda's polishing solutions. Today, however, there was a nagging, gnawing feeling that not even the serenity of Virzda's engine room could shift.

Mordax hopped down from the gangway underneath the view port, ducking under the low cables that swarmed over the ceiling like thick, plastic snakes, and sat down next to Virzda who was soldering something at her worktable. A bright green scarf kept her frizzy hair, more grey now than black, out of her eyes.

"I can hear you thinking," said Virzda without looking up from the table, "What is it?"

"It's nothing," said Mordax.

Virzda continued her work.

"OK," said Mordax after a minute when it became clear that Virzda wasn't going to press him. "Let's say, hypothetically, a load of haulers had been jacked in the sector we were currently in. What would you do?"

Virzda sighed, resigned to her work being interrupted. "I guess I would let the captain of the ship make whatever decision he thought appropriate."

"No, come on, Doc. You know that's not what I meant."

"I know it isn't, sugar, but you're trying to get me to second guess one of Stephan's decisions and I'm not going to do it. Just tell me what's worrying you."

Mordax chewed his lip. "In all likelihood this sector's crawling with Blackhands and we're en route to Cantarina."

"So?" said Virzda, eyebrows raised quizzically.

"You really don't pay too much attention to what's going on outside the engine room, do you?"

Virzda shrugged "You don't meddle in my work, I don't meddle in yours."

"OK, let me explain," Mordax said "We've got a bellyful of valuable spice. Haulers have been mysteriously disappearing, probably fragged by pirates, and instead of hightailing it back to a nice, safe system towards the Core we're heading to a free station that doesn't even have a peace keeping force and where there's no market for our cargo. It doesn't make sense."

"Why don't you ask Stephan?"

"I have," said Mordax "He gives me some bullshit reason about needing to offload some shield generators."

"Language, please," said Virzda frowning.

"Sorry, but it is. We've had those things for months. It's not worth the risk heading to Cantarina."

Virzda paused.

"I've been with the *Starling* a long time, Mordax. Your father knows what he's doing. If it's risky going to Cantarina then there's something there that Stephan considers worth the risk. If he's not telling you what that is, I'm sure there's a reason. Take my advice. Drop it."

Mordax sighed. Virzda looked over at him and smiled, eyes creasing.

"You're too much like him. That's the problem," she said. "He never stops thinking either."

"So, what?" Mordax said. "I should think less?"

"Exactly!" Virzda cackled and patted him on the shoulder. "You'd be a lot happier."

***

Mordax stepped through the doorway into the cool gloom of the navigator's room. His father was standing silently, arms crossed, watching Lazarus at work. The back of Lazarus' head, a mess of almost white blond hair, was visible above the top of the navigator's chair where the jack entered his skull. Multiple monitors hung around him, more for the benefit of onlookers than Lazarus himself who received more information from the neural link than screens could ever impart. The *Starling* had dropped out of netherspace and the monitors were displaying a magnified view of Cantarina hanging in front of a dusty streak of stars. The free station was a converted Vorth war outpost, a relic from the War of Ages between the Kudo-kai and Vorth. It was on the fringe between the outer systems of the Shattered Empires and the Reaches, the great, lawless expanse where civilisation ended. The bleak, powerful structure, monolithic slabs arranged in a diamond shape, echoed the Vorth's utilitarian philosophy. Around the central structure, however, were a rag-tag collection of additions that had been made. A patchwork of comms arrays dotted the exterior, and spherical living modules in a variety of shapes and sizes had been welded to extension struts. The docking ports were a hive of activity as traders arrived and transports ferried people between the station and the vast cargo ships that were too cumbersome to dock directly. There was one feature of the station that had not been interfered with, however. Giant rail guns jutted menacingly from each side of the station. It was these weapons that were the key to Cantarina's continued existence. Without them, positioned as the station was on the border of the Reaches, pirates would long ago have obliterated the station and picked over its carcass for the valuable morsels inside. That wasn't to say Cantarina didn't attract dangerous people. At their last visit, they had disembarked next to a Blackhand crew, rough, hard-eyed men and women, offloading hull plates that still had the tell-tale scorch marks of plasma fire. Mordax thought back to his conversation with Virzda. She was right he supposed. Dad had to have a very good reason for bringing them here.

"How're we doing, Laz?" Mordax asked.

Lazarus swung round giving a surprised hiccup.

"AHH! Shit. Mordax! Don't sneak up on me like that!" he said. Marvin, a large red-brown lizard who Lazarus doted on, was curled up on his lap. He opened one yellow eye and fixed Mordax with a baleful glare.

"Sorry, didn't realise you were so jumpy," Mordax chuckled.

"Seriously? Stephan tells me to keep my eyes peeled for an armada of pirates and you expect me not be on edge?" Lazarus said.

Mordax turned to his father and raised his eyebrows.

"You heard Bayram," said Stephan looking back at Mordax evenly. "This close to the Reaches, it pays to be prepared."

Mordax pursed his lips and nodded. "I don't disagree. I guess the only question is why we're this close to the Reaches in the first place."

Stephan ignored the question and turned to Lazarus. "What's the ETA?"

"Control has just given us clearance. Not too congested today. We'll be docked in a few minutes."

Stephan picked up his overcoat and walked towards the doorway. As he moved past Mordax took his arm gently.

"Dad, are you going to tell me why we're really here?" he whispered.

"Enough," said Stephan through clenched teeth, "I'm doing my best to keep us safe."

He shook off Mordax's arm and turned back to Lazarus.

"This is going to be a whistle stop I'm afraid, Laz, so we need you to stay here and look after the ship."

Lazarus rolled his eyes. It was a running joke between them. Lazarus had a problem with open spaces and never ventured off the *Starling* if he could avoid it. The last time he'd tried to accompany them off-ship, he'd hyperventilated and had been brought back slung unceremoniously over Stamford's shoulder.

Stephan turned to Mordax. "Come on, Stamford will be waiting for us."

Stephan shrugged on the overcoat and headed out of the navigator's office leaving Mordax and Lazarus alone.

"You OK, man?" asked Lazarus, seeing Mordax's thoughtful expression.

"I will be, when I know what the hell is going on." Mordax shook his head and sighed.

"Stephan knows what he's doing," Lazarus said.

"Yeah, that's what I keep hearing. Anything I can get you while I'm out there?" he said.

"Oh yeah!" Lazarus' eyes went wide. "Marvin loved those big slug things you got last time!"

Mordax frowned. "You mean the infested rations that waste-of-air trader sold us on Bielgarden? Barshamin's balls, Laz. Seriously? He ate those things?"

Lazarus shrugged. "The little dude likes what he likes."

Marvin yawned showing a mouth full of needle-sharp teeth.

Mordax sighed. "Alright, I'll see what I can find. There's bound to be some disgusting stuff down there."

***

A loud clunk reverberated through the ship's innards, announcing their arrival at Cantarina and successful docking. With a hiss the giant air lock portal at the back of the cargo hold slid back, letting in a blast of warm air, heavy with the acrid scents of hot metal and garbage. Stephan and Mordax stepped out into the milieu which filled the station's loading bay, preceded by the hulking nine-foot frame of Stamford, the *Starling*'s muscle. Traders swarmed around the bay like a motley ant hive, loading and unloading their goods with the help of clunky service drones. Mordax and the others joined the stream of people passing through the huge archway separating the loading bay from the station's central hub, the crowds parting around Stamford like a river around a boulder. Here was more of the cold, brutish Vorth architecture. Slabs of grey metal made up the internal structure, broken only at intervals by great monoliths bearing strange impressionistic reliefs of sharp alien limbs sprouting from concave mounds and, disturbingly, human faces twisted in agony.

Now, however, the human interlopers moved past these relics of their ancient enemies with barely a glance. Rooms around the hub's outer wall, once hatching chambers for the Vorth, now housed shops of all kinds. Grime coated the floor and buzzing maintenance drones struggled to clear mounds of rubbish piled against the walls as fast as they accumulated. A couple of slavers, body armour creaking, passed by leading a bedraggled group of men and women, collars around their necks. There were not many planets in the Shattered Empires where the slave trade was legal but out here near the Reaches, things were more…flexible. Mordax sensed Stamford tense next to him and noticed his hand unconsciously grip the hilt of the knife strapped to his thigh. In anyone else's hands it would have been a sword. The muscles in his dark forearms rippled and a thin sheen of sweat covered his bald head. Mordax placed a calming hand on his arm and felt the giant relax slightly. Stamford had a hatred of slavers that bordered on the obsessive. He had never spoken about it but Mordax suspected it had something to do with his previous life. Stamford was from Sabulon, the cradle of his race where the Old Earth scientists had tinkered with the human genome to create men and women able to withstand the planet's high gravity and harsh climate. Stephan had found Stamford not long after he had left Sabulon, in the fighting pits of Tarescene where, because of his size and strength, he drew in the crowds. He had been a mess, spending his meagre earnings on drink rather than medical treatment. That had been ten cycles ago. Stamford still liked to drink and fight but now more as a hobby than a career.

"What's with the knife, Stam?" asked Mordax, more to distract him than anything else. "You expecting to have to gut a whale?"

"HA!" Stamford barked. "Don't be stupid, Mordax. It is for people. Nothing puts fear into a man's mind like naked steel."

"Ok-ay," Mordax gave a nervous chuckle.

"Besides," said Stamford, hefting a shotgun the size of a rocket launcher that was slung over his shoulder and patting it affectionately, "if things get really bad I've got Rosie."

"If we keep our heads down there's no chance of that," said Stephan with a meaningful look at Stamford.

Stamford shrugged his enormous shoulders. "Back home there is a saying. If you step into a snake's nest, expect to get bitten. That's why you should have a weapon, Mordax."

"I'm afraid to say it Stamford but Mordax has a way with words that you don't," Stephan said quickly. "Better to talk your way out of trouble than shoot your way out."

There was a rumble of laughter like thunder from Stamford's chest.

"You speak the truth, Stephan. Mordax's tongue is more slippery than a greased eel."

The group passed an alcove where skewers of dubious looking meat were being grilled and the smell, mixed with the sweet, sharp scent of unwashed bodies, almost made Mordax gag. Next to it was a stall run by a pallid, nervous looking man with large watery eyes. Bags of dark, gleaming insects and pale worms were stacked up on the stall and hung from hooks all around it. Mordax hurried over and picked up a couple of bags at random, one held fat, winged bugs and the other a powder, like fine sawdust.

"Ah, a fine choice," said the man in a thin reedy voice, looking pleased. "The powdered fallow worm is especially good for cooking with. Very high in protein and essential minerals and fats."

Then he looked slightly less sure of himself as he examined Mordax. "Depending on your tolerance of certain secretions."

Mordax threw him a couple of palladium coins. "Don't worry, these are for someone with a sturdier constitution than me."

"Hold up," Stephan said as they approached one of the corridors that led away from the central hub.

"You two are going to head to the parts exchange shop to pick up cooling units for the Doc. I'll see if I can offload these shield generators over at Mac's place for a half-decent price."

"Uh, don't you think we should stick together?" asked Mordax, frowning at his father.

Stephan shook his head. "I want to be out of here as soon as possible. It's not good to hang around with the *Starling*'s belly full of cargo. Stay close to Stamford. You'll be fine."

Stamford clapped Mordax on the back almost bowling him over.

"Don't worry, little man," he boomed." Uncle Stamford will show you a good time."

It was Stephan's turn to look dubious. He pointed his finger at Stamford. "No drinking, you hear me. And no fighting. A quick pit stop and we'll be out of here."

Stamford shrugged and grasped Mordax by the arm, pulling him along behind him. Mordax watched his father weave his way into the crowds. He had the same itchy feeling in his palms that he got when he was getting screwed over on a deal but

Stamford's grip was inexorable and Stephan was soon out of sight.

***

"Ah! THAT IS GOOD STUFF!" Stamford smacked his lips and lowered the tumbler carefully to the table to avoid smashing it. He and Mordax were sitting on the balcony of a bar in the station's central spire from which they could look down on the crowd in the hub below them. The air was fragrant with sweet Nafthal smoke, a powerful narcotic outlawed on most developed planets. They had picked up the cooling units easily, with Mordax bargaining the seller down to almost half what they had budgeted and they were now busy spending the money he had saved.

Stamford, as usual, was downing drinks almost as fast as the server could bring them and had started grinning at the other customers in such a way that most of them in their immediate vicinity had left. Mordax was lost in his thoughts still nursing his first drink which was giving off a thick, sweet vapour.

"What are we doing here, Stam?" Mordax asked absently

"I am getting drunk. You are sipping at your cocktail like it is coffee."

"No, I mean, here. Cantarina. We could have picked up these cooling units anywhere. And how often does Dad make us split up, especially somewhere like this?"

"You worry too much, Mordax," Stamford said, leaning back in his chair and gesturing at the server drone to bring him another drink. "What does it matter? We're here now with money in our pockets and a ship full of starsarine. If your father has some business here, why not let him be about it?"

"It doesn't bother you? Since when do we keep things from each other? It's not like him to be so cagey. What if there's a real problem out here and he's not telling us about it?"

Stamford turned back to Mordax, clear dark eyes locking on to his. "If there is one thing that I have learned about your father over my cycles on your ship, it is that there is always a reason for what he does. Let it be, Mordax. If there is something which Stephan needs our help with he will say so. Until then, finish your drink and let us have what fun there is to be had among these villains."

Mordax managed a brief smile and took another sip of his drink.

"Where do you think we'll head next?" he asked.

"Jilax? Greater Armon?" Stamford shrugged his giant shoulders. "We got good prices for starsarine there before."

Mordax shook his head "We got good prices there because the markets are small and no one else was shipping there. Now we know that there's a shortage of haulers we should get to the established markets like Porto Vega, the guys who have developed a taste for the stuff and now can't get any. We'll be able to charge practically whatever we want."

Thinking about the money they would likely make on this run was making Mordax feel better. He was absently scanning the crowd bustling below them, when he spotted a familiar dark-headed figure weaving between the closely packed people, his long-legged stride carrying him swiftly away from the station hub. He was too far away to see clearly, but Mordax thought he saw a grim expression on his father's face.

"I need a piss," he said to Stamford, rising from his chair quickly. "Back in a second."

Stamford waved him away, as he happily collected his refill from the returning server drone.

Back on street level, Mordax hurried towards the wide corridor Stephan had taken. Once away from the hub, it was much less busy and taken up more by compact residential quarters. Drips from leaky water reclaimers formed black puddles on the ground and grimy children whooped and screamed as they thundered along the gantries playing games of tag. Mordax quickly caught sight of Stephan up ahead threading his way through piles of rubbish and fat men in vests playing cards at fold-up tables on the street. As they travelled further along, and the people thinned out, Mordax wondered if he should turn back. It had been instinct that had spurred his feet along this far but slivers of doubt had begun to bleed his confidence away. No. He couldn't quite put his finger on it, but something about the urgency of his father's demeanour was troubling. There was no reason for Stephan to be in this part of the station. All the main businesses were located in or close to the hub. Mordax slowed his pace, letting the distance between himself and Stephan increase. There were so few people around now that if Stephan glanced back, he would easily spot Mordax if he was too close. Without warning, Stephan turned a corner and disappeared from view. Mordax hurried over but when he rounded the corner, he was in a storage room, empty save for a few stacks of plastic crates. After a few minutes of frantic searching, Mordax discovered a narrow gap between the side of one of the containers and the wall of the storage room. He squeezed himself into it and found a doorway leading to an unlit stairwell. Peering over the handrail he saw the distant flicker of torchlight and could just make out the distant clang of his father's boots against the metal steps. Mordax followed as quickly as he dared, absorbing the force of his steps with bent knees to stay as quiet as possible.

A few floors down there was another doorway from which Mordax could hear the thumping bass of distant music. He peeked his head round. The space opened up into a narrow alleyway. The infrastructure down here was poorly maintained. The original strip lighting looked as though it had not worked in cycles, and instead lamps, wired into the station's circuitry at intervals, gave off a dirty amber glow. There were store fronts across two levels of the corridor. One displayed a selection of wicked-looking blades behind thick plate glass. Most, however, were blacked out, differentiated only by the numbers painted crudely above them. Mordax had heard of these more remote sections of the station, home to narcotics and exotic tech merchants who balked at selling their wares openly even somewhere as lawless as Cantarina. Nearby, a dangerous looking group of men, faces inked with tattoos, were drinking at a low table. They had the jacked-up, twitchy look of roid-runners, veins bulging in their arms and eyes blinking too rapidly. The bass from the music made the liquid in their glasses quiver and dance. Mordax had almost convinced himself to turn back when he spotted Stephan turning into one of the numbered stores. Mordax made to follow him but as he was passing the group of men his arm was caught in a powerful, painful grip.

"Why the rushing, eh, 'migo?" said a thickset man, rising to his feet. His long braided hair hung freely and rattled with what looked like human teeth. Implants under his skin created a row of horn-like protrusions along his brow.

"Yous has important biz nel here?" His grip tightened on Mordax's arm and he grinned exposing brown teeth. "Must be lotta monies for risk the unders solo."

Mordax's fingers itched to grab the knife sheathed in the small of his back but over the man's burly shoulder he could see the other men smirking at him, guns strapped to thighs or placed casually on the table within easy reach. He might be able to take the one holding him unawares but the others would surely make short work of him.

"Oi, yous not worry 'bout dem," said the man, seeing Mordax glancing at his companions at the table. "Me's yous problem 'migo."

Leaning closer so that Mordax flinched from the fetid stench of his breath, the man drew a thin stiletto knife from his belt.

Chapter 5

Morning light filled the glass-walled apartment, sharp and bright as a silver needle. It reflected and refracted off the polished surfaces, increasing in intensity so that it felt to Akira like being trapped inside a diamond. She lounged comfortably in a stasis chair, suspended two feet in the air, absently following the progress of a mote of dust as it floated through a sunbeam.

"—and according to Iankis how was the Fengurian horde vanquished?"

Akira was aware that Xif, his orb-like body floating nearby, had paused his monotone drawl and was waiting expectantly.

"Ah, umm...what?" Akira said

"You're not paying attention!" sputtered the drone. "I don't know why I bother. You seem determined to ignore everything I say."

Akira sighed and turned her head towards the ceiling.

"Why am I even studying this, Xif? Who cares what some distant relative achieved thousands of cycles ago according to another, marginally less distant relative? It's just all so... pointless."

Xif paused, emitting only the gentle hum of his motor. If he had a face, Akira knew from long experience, he would be arching an eyebrow.

"You need to know this because the tactics employed by your ancestors in their greatest successes will help inform your choices when you eventually have the honour of performing active service for your family. If you can't even learn basic military strategy then what hope have you of being entrusted with real responsibility?"

It was Akira's turn to regard the drone sceptically. "And who says I am incapable of learning pointless information?" She bounced out of the stasis chair, clasped her hands and intoned dutifully, "According to the historian Iankis, Battle Director Angvaro Methusilis San'Kudo led the twenty-sixth Angel battalion in the invasion of Jertomeda Prime. Having initially suffered numerous defeats at the hands of the ferocious inhabitants, Methusilis formed small, elite storm-trooper units and sent them deep behind the enemy lines to sabotage supply convoys. The enemy became overextended in their eager advance and without supplies weakened to the point that the Kudo-kai could overrun them easily.

"Very good—" began Xif.

"However," continued Akira, "other, less partisan sources, have recorded that extreme floods, very rare for the continent at that time of year, were responsible for the disruption to the enemy supply lines and Methusilis' eventually victory was attributable to blind luck rather than any strategic prowess."

Xif heaved a mechanical sigh. "You're lucky your father's not here to hear that."

"Relax, Xif," said Akira. "Father pays about as little attention to my views as he did when I was five."

"Feeling gloomy today, are we?"

Akira turned to the window and gazed up at the few clouds drifting serenely across the cobalt sky. "I just want to get out there and do something. Cycles of study and for what? I'm not allowed to actually do anything."

"All in good time, Akira."

"Time? Much more time and they'll be nothing left. We used to have an empire that spanned half the galaxy, Xif, and now what? Control of one solar system? Trade treaties with a few thousand planets? All I want is to help the family rather than wallowing here."

"I wouldn't exactly call it wallowing," said Xif.

Akira knew what he meant but she couldn't agree. During the thousands of cycles it had taken the Kudo-kai to assemble their vast empire, Angor Bore had been their home system. Its capital city, Ang'Dirth, had grown into a gargantuan logistical machine, whose sole purpose was to direct the various functions of the empire. Hundreds of vast towers, like shards of glass, soared miles into the air, all linked to orbiting data banks. At its peak a billion people had inhabited the city and the air had been thick with swarms of cars. But then the Purge had happened with the almost mystical advent of the Dioscuri, ghostly figures who walked through the defences of both the Kudo-kai and the Vorth, killing off the leadership across the galaxy with the precision of a surgeon excising a tumour. The orbital data banks had been sent crashing into Angor Bore's oceans, destroying millennia of accumulated knowledge, and the empire had disintegrated. The Kudo-kai had been forced to give autonomy back to every single solar system that made up their vast territory bar Angor Bore. Ang'Dirth had become a weakly beating heart surrounded by a cage of cold, dead glass. She supposed a more pragmatic organisation would have knocked the empty buildings down. Not the Kudo-kai though. To do that would be to admit defeat. It would be an acknowledgement that their fall from power was permanent and Angor Bore would never again be the nerve centre of a galactic empire. The land outside the city on the other hand was a paradise of lush grasslands, pristine forests and sweeping white beaches. The planet had been chosen as the Kudo-kai's headquarters for that very reason, a grand display of power and opulence. The jewel of the empire.

They'd really shot themselves in the foot with that decision, Akira thought. Beautiful scenery was all Angor Bore had going for it. There were no valuable natural resources to speak of, not even a decent size asteroid belt in the system to mine. As a result the Kudo-kai's journey back to comparative wealth in the centuries following the Purge had been long and difficult.

"This will always be my home, Xif, but it's not where the real power is any more."

Suddenly Xif let out an audible buzzing "Oh! Er – excuse me. Incoming message from your father. He's requested your presence immediately."

Akira's eyes widened. "My father? What does he want?"

"The message doesn't say," said Xif.

***

Akira pondered the reason for her father's summons as her car flitted along the canyons of glass created by the towers around her penthouse. Since she was a child, their interactions had been limited to formal events. Akira didn't begrudge him his absence from her life, however. As head of the Kudo-kai, the fortunes of the family rested on his shoulders and if his time was better spent working than raising his daughter, Akira wasn't going to complain. The meeting he had requested could only be for something of great importance to the family. Her heart fluttered with anticipation.

Her father's office was in what was unofficially known as the Citadel. In contrast to the sea of glass around it, the Citadel was a complex hundreds of feet underground in the centre of Ang'Dirth. All that was visible above ground was a gleaming black mound where the outer edges of a protective carbon nano-fibre sphere protruded. The smooth black surface had always reminded her of the carapace of some giant beetle and she felt a moment of child-like fear as her car stopped in mid-air and lowered itself through a circular hatch which blossomed open in the centre of the mound. The car carried on its descent in near total darkness passing through a number of security hatches. It was at times like these that she was grateful that she was her father's fifth child. Her oldest three siblings, earmarked for the highest positions of power in the Kudo-kai, were required to live within the Citadel when not travelling and were shadowed by security teams wherever they went. Her father never left the Citadel at all. Akira thought it all slightly futile. During the Purge and on various occasions since, the Dioscuri had proved they could bypass even the most stringent security measures. If they had wanted to kill her father and his heirs they probably would have done so already. One of her father's assistants, a tall, gloomy young man, was waiting to greet her as she stepped out of the car.

"Mistress Kudo. I trust you had a pleasant journey. Your father is waiting for you in his quarters. Allow me to escort you." He managed to avoid almost any inflection or emotion in his voice. Listening to him was like bathing in beige, Akira thought.

***

A gentle breeze sighed through the forest, punctuated by the warble of birds. She squinted up at the blue sky visible between the boughs. She knew the blueness came from light plates on the ceiling but it was impossible to tell. Daisuke Kudo was sitting in a wooden chair, on the grass next to a small pond. Flashes of orange and white appeared near the surface where carp wove their way between each other, occasionally lunging at an insect with a soft plopping sound. A flock of advisers were seated on low stools around him. His hair was greyer than the last time she'd seen him, a quirk that genome therapy could easily correct if he'd wished it but he had never been vain.

"—too slow to enforce our collateral rights," Daisuke was saying. "The Yurdis are months in arrears and Taekio has done nothing about it."

"Director Taekio's report mentioned a gas explosion on the Yurdis' primary asteroid mine," said a small man with a pale face and large, watery eyes. "He suggests allowing them some more time to get operations back up and running before demanding payment."

Daisuke stared hard at the man who shrank under the scrutiny. "Their misfortunes are not ours. Should we allow every debtor to use the slightest inconvenience to avoid payment? Taekio is showing weakness. Have him commandeer the next Yurdis vessel that arrives in our system. If they still don't pay, scrap the ship for parts and sell the crew at a free station."

He noticed Akira and waved her forwards. "Please excuse me while I speak with my daughter."

The advisers stood up quickly, bowed and retreated to a covered area where refreshments had been laid out leaving Akira standing awkwardly on the thick moss. Daisuke remained seated, face impassive, and gestured at a low stool opposite him. Akira hurriedly approached and took a seat.

"Akira."

"Hello, father."

"I trust your studies are going well?"

"They are, thank you. Today I have been researching the great feats of Methusilis on Jertomeda Prime."

"Ah, yes," said Daisuke. "The defeat of the Fengurian horde. Be sure not to place too much weight on Iankis's account. He was a famous sycophant whose only concern was improving his own station among our family. Lessons can be learned from the past but only if you know the truth of those events."

Akira glanced pointedly at Xif who ignored her.

"Thank you, father, that's good advice. I will treat his accounts with caution. You are well, I hope?"

"Well enough. Dealing with imbeciles all day can be testing, however." Akira thought he looked tired, his face drawn and pallid.

"You shouldn't work too hard. There are others who can take on some of the load."

His lip curled slightly at that. "One day, Akira, I hope to instil a proper work ethic in you. You'll learn not to rely on those around you."

Akira berated herself inwardly. She pressed her fingernails painfully into her palms.

"Father, I apologise. I meant only that the family needs your guidance and—"

"Enough," he interrupted with a dismissive wave. "I have a matter to discuss with you."

He settled back into his chair and tapped at a terminal. A holo projection of a man's head appeared between them, spinning slowly. His skin was papery and deeply lined. Curiously mournful eyes were sunk deep in their sockets above a hawkish nose.

"Do you know who this is?" Daisuke asked

She did not recognise the face and shook her head.

"Glankor the Blessed," said Daisuke. "Tell me what you know about him."

"He came to power around two cycles ago on Thalmos. He's made a reputation for himself as an unpredictable and aggressive leader. He's popular among the Thalmians though."

Her father nodded slowly "And...?"

Akira racked her brains, trying desperately to work out what significance her father was attaching to this person. What had been important enough to summon her here?

"Our relations with Glankor have always been good," Akira thought out loud. "We're their largest buyer of nanotritium."

A creeping suspicion dawned on her. "He hasn't done anything to our supply has he?" she asked.

Daisuke's face gave little away but Akira imagined she could see a glint of satisfaction in his eyes.

"Suppose he had imprisoned our envoys. What would be your suggestion?" he asked, still impassive.

"It depends how serious we think he is. If he's locked up our envoys, is it a negotiating tactic? Does he want a better price for the nanotrite?"

"What if he'd shown no interest in negotiations?"

Akira's heart quickened.

"If he's cut ties with us completely, it'll be a disaster. Thalmos supplies almost all of our nanotrite. We won't be able to fuel our trading fleets."

Daisuke didn't say anything.

"We would need to find out why Glankor has stopped our supply," Akira continued. "If he won't answer over nethercast I would send a delegation to Thalmos to find out and, if possible, convince him to change his mind."

"Who would you send?" asked Daisuke

Akira chewed her lip. "Um, it would need to be someone important enough within the Kudo-kai for him to take them seriously. Someone capable who might be able to find a way to get the nanotrite shipments restored but someone dispensable in case he really has gone mad and decides to imprison the delegation out of hand..."

Daisuke, still looking intently at his daughter, smiled broadly.

Oh shit, she thought.

Chapter 6

The tattooed man drew the stiletto knife up until it was level with Mordax's face, the point glinting centimetres from his left eye.

"Yous want travers la unders, yous pay us 'migo."

Mordax's breaths came in staccato gasps. He didn't think these men would react well when they discovered he had nothing valuable with him, having left his credits with Stamford for the bar tab. He almost let out a nervous chuckle imagining himself handing over the bags of bugs in his pocket. At the thought, a pinprick of an idea planted itself in his mind. He closed his eyes briefly, and used a trick his father had taught him to calm himself during tense negotiations. Taking a deep breath, he imagined himself a leaf in the forest, battered by stormy winds. As he exhaled the winds dropped and a stillness settled over his body spreading from the tips of his toes to the top of his head. His heartbeat slowed and the adrenaline coursing through him began to drain away. Opening his eyes, he fixed the man with a level, dispassionate gaze.

"You're quite right," he said, his voice dripping with disdain. "My business here is valuable. It would have to be for me to endure the stench."

As he spoke he snaked his hand into his pocket grasping the bag of powdered bugs and with deft fingers, loosened the draw strings.

"I work for someone who doesn't take kindly to interference in his business interests, understand?" He leaned closer to the man, allowing a sneer to twist the corner of his mouth.

"You think of this rat-infested, septic tank as your kingdom but any power you have down here is conceded to you only because the truly dangerous players don't give two shits about somewhere like this."

The man's eyes bulged with rage and a vein in his thick neck began to pulsate like a wakening snake. Iron-like fingers tightened on Mordax's arm as the mercenary drew back the hand holding the stiletto knife, preparing to strike. In a single fluid motion, Mordax drew out the now loose bag of powder from his pocket and with a flick of the wrist spread a liberal dusting over the mercenary's face. The mercenary released Mordax's arm and backed away snorting, spluttering and blinking furiously against the particles that now filled his sinuses and coated his eyeballs.

"Yous dead, Poutan!" He coughed, dropping the knife and pulling out the pistol from its holster on his hip. Behind him the other mercenaries had also stood up and were drawing their own weapons.

Mordax knew the next few seconds were vital. Unless he played his part perfectly he would end up with a plasma bolt between the eyes or worse. He stayed perfectly still not letting the supercilious sneer fall from his face even though his insides felt like a bag of worms wriggling to get out.

"You have thirty minutes," he said calmly.

"The fuck yous saying, poutan," the mercenary screamed, levelling the plasma pistol at Mordax's face. He resisted the overwhelming urge to cower.

"You said it would have to be for a lot of money that I risked the under levels," Mordax said patiently, as if explaining to a particularly dim child. "As I said, you were right. Fifteen million credits to be precise."

A puzzled frown knotted the mercenary's face, causing the horn-implants to pull inwards, and the men behind him glanced at each other, suddenly unsure.

Mordax pressed the advantage. "Fifteen million credits for five tonnes of the same nerve agent you just took a faceful of. My buyer won't be happy the sample is smaller than requested but it will have to do."

The mercenary's eyes narrowed. "Bullshit."

The bluff was a risk. Mordax had no idea whether there were chem weapon traders on the station, although he suspected there were, or whether the mercenaries knew enough about the trade to call him out on it. It didn't really matter now, he was too far along to do anything but barrel on.

"You have thirty minutes until the synapses in your brain begin to disintegrate," he continued. "First your movements will begin to slow, you'll become clumsy and your speech will slur. What will start as a tingling sensation will worsen until your skin feels as if it's being melted off with a blow torch. You'll try to scream but by that point you will have lost control of your voice box. Eventually you'll asphyxiate when your brain can no longer tell your lungs to breath."

The mercenrary's jaw fell slightly and he paused, as if performing some mental calculations. He glanced backwards at the men behind him who offered no support.

"If yous speak true, why I not put a bolt nel yous head?" he said, eyes bleary and the tip of the pistol now shaking slightly.

Mordax rolled his eyes, "Because, you stupid fuck, my employer has the counter-toxin and it will be a huge inconvenience if you drop dead and station security discover I've released a nerve agent in a closed air system. Head to the *Flight of Fancy* at bay seventy-two and tell them Vocelyn sent you. If you get there in the next 10 minutes the counter-toxin will probably still be effective." Mordax peered over the mercenary's shoulder. "You guys should probably go with him. Your friend took a full hit but this stuff is still effective, one microgramme to a litre of air. You're all close enough to have taken a lethal dose. Me too if I wasn't loaded up with the counter-toxin already."

The mercenaries were now muttering to each other nervously, glancing at Mordax and their companion who was wiping his mouth and nose frantically with his sleeve.

Mordax looked at them incredulously and clapped his hands loudly.

"Well, come on, dipshits!" he said. "No time to chitchat."

At that, one of the mercenaries towards the back turned and started walking briskly back along the gangway towards the stairwell Mordax had used. Seconds later the others were following at a sprint. The one who had cornered Mordax looked with dismay at his retreating colleagues and then back to Mordax.

"If this be some kinda con, poutan—" he started.

"Yeah, yeah," Mordax interrupted. "Can we leave the posturing and skip to the part where you piss off."

With a frustrated growl, the mercenary turned on his heel and ran after the others.

When he was out of sight, Mordax let out a sigh and slumped against the hand rail, gazing down at the half-empty bag of bug protein in his hand.

"Thank you, Marvin," he muttered, stuffing the bag back into his pocket. He would have to be quick now. He'd given them the name of a real ship which he'd noticed as they disembarked the *Starling* but it wouldn't take the men long to discover that no one on the *Flight of Fancy* had heard the name Vocelyn and that they had been duped. He had to be out of the under levels by the time they got back or no amount of dissimulation would save him. He thought briefly about heading back straight away, but he had risked so much to get to this point. He couldn't fold on the last hand. He hurried over to the doorway his father had entered and, careful not to make a sound, slipped inside.

Mordax closed the door quietly behind him. Rubber seals around the frame cut off all noise from outside so that he was suddenly left in an eerie silence. The room he was now in was much larger than it had appeared from the outside but was lit only by a rectangle of light from another doorway up ahead. The air tasted stale and dry, as if he had entered an undisturbed tomb. As his eyes adjusted to the half-light, he began to make out the outline of hundreds of industrial shelves arranged in stacks, and after a few more seconds he could see that these were filled with all manner of mechanical and electrical objects in various states of disrepair. On one shelf close to him, an obsolete droid sat with disconnected arms stacked neatly beside it like a puppet waiting patiently for its maker to finish her work and imbue it with a final spark of life. On another, a number of ancient projectile weapons lay, neatly disassembled and glistening with oil.

Mordax crept forwards between two stacks of shelves towards the rectangle of light at the other end of the room. As he approached, the soft murmur of voices reached him from beyond the doorway. Closer still and the murmur clarified into two distinct voices, one of which he recognised immediately as his father's and the other was that of an unfamiliar woman.

"—can't be...wouldn't dare," his father said, a tightness in his voice that Mordax had rarely heard. Mordax couldn't make out the woman's softer reply.

A pause, then his father's voice. "It'll mean war. Worse than before the Purge, at least then there was a semblance of balance – a counter force."

Another pause.

"Can you tell me where the forces are massing?" his father said. Again, Mordax couldn't make out the woman's reply but the tone was muted, regretful.

His father gave a frustrated sigh. "What the hell am I supposed to do then?"

This time the woman's reply was louder and Mordax could hear part of it. "—give you all the information I have that it is appropriate for you to know...different answers you will have to look elsewhere."

"I...apologise," Stephan said. "It's just...this is difficult news. After so many cycles."

The woman's reply was again inaudible.

"I will," Stephan said. "Thank you for this. I know you dislike involving yourself but I appreciate the help."

Mordax heard shuffling then footsteps from beyond the door. He just had time to press himself against the wall behind one of the shelf racks, sharp metal digging painfully into his back, before the door swung open letting the rich yellow light stream in like liquid gold. He glimpsed his father striding towards the exit. If he looked back he would surely see Mordax exposed and frozen against the wall, but he reached the door and slipped out without a backward glance. Mordax let out the breath he had not realised he was holding. The lit room from which his father had come was now silent. Mordax began to creep back towards the exit, keeping to the shadows as much as possible. Now that his father had left it seemed unlikely he'd be able to find out anything more without risking discovery. He was almost at the door when the same female voice as earlier rang out strong and clear and startlingly close.

"Leaving so soon?"

Mordax yelped in surprise and spun round to see a small woman not more than six feet from him, silhouetted against the light from the doorway so that her features were indistinct.

"If you're going to eavesdrop you might as well have a look around too. No sense doing things by halves," she said archly.

"Uh—" Mordax hesitated, completely unprepared. She had not made so much as a whisper coming up behind him.

The figure cocked her head to one side. "Odd. I had heard you were eloquent, Mordax. Come along then. Enough dawdling here in the dark." She turned briskly and walked back into the lit room.

The unexpected use of his name threw him. Mordax hesitated again. The door behind him promised safety and a quick retreat back to the *Starling*. Recent events had awakened some ancient part of him that sensed danger in the shadows.

He was on edge. But the unresolved mystery of his father's strange behaviour tugged at him so that without making a conscious decision his feet began carrying him forwards after the woman. He stepped through the doorway, blinking against the suddenly bright light given off by golden orbs which hovered at various points around the large room. The small figure hopped up onto a stool next to a metal work bench that was strewn with tiny metal parts arranged under a powerful desk lamp and began examining them. In the light, Mordax could see the woman was entering late middle age. Her hair was more white than chestnut and cut severely above her shoulders. The skin of her face was somehow waxy and lined at the same time and her eyes were such a pale blue they looked almost white. Mordax gazed around the double-height room. Huge processor cabinets were crammed together along the side of one wall, thick coils of wiring connecting them, but he couldn't see any sort of interface. Soft, mournful music hung in the air. The whole set up was incongruous for its location, deep in the under levels of Cantarina. Strangest of all, at the centre of the room, arranged on a plinth built into the floor itself, was a huge stone obelisk. The bottom half of the pillar was carved with alien characters, primal runes slashed deep into the rock. Towards the top, where the rock began to taper a single circle had been etched.

"Impressive, isn't it?" said the woman, still working on the mechanism in front of her. "It's a Vorth prayer stone. During the Imperial period, every major temple contained one of these – all hand-carved on the Vorth homeworld. Not many of them left now. Most were destroyed during the Purge. According to the Vorth the ring depicts the inconsequentiality of the individual." The woman's voice was rich and smooth and watching her methodical tinkering had a soporific effect. Mordax felt his prior discomfort begin to melt away.

"That's a bit depressing, isn't it?" said Mordax.

"It depends on your perspective," said the woman turning back to the work in front of her, thin fingers carefully manipulating the tiny parts. "I've always felt a sympathy with the philosophy. The Vorth taught that a person is insignificant unless joining themselves to a common cause. According to the Vorta'l Tablets, those characters you see at the base of the pillar, the life of an individual is a grain of sand in the hour glass of time – completely without meaning unless forming part of a greater whole like the furtherance of the Vorth Empire. Even the Kudo-kai prized loyalty to the family and furtherance of their communal glory above all else, a similar ethos when you think about it."

"So what's your cause?" asked Mordax.

The woman didn't turn from her work "Some of us have other means of extending our influence without attaching ourselves to hegemonies. But I doubt you snuck into my home uninvited to discuss philosophy. I can see you have questions like a bellyful of hot coals. They're burning you up inside."

She raised a stern finger "You must be careful, Mordax. Questions are dangerous things. Their answers can lure you into waters that are out of your depth. If you're not to drown you must know why you're asking the question in the first place."

Mordax didn't know where to start. What had his father been doing here? What had they been discussing that had so upset him?

"Who are you? How did you know my name?" he asked.

Myla gave a disappointed sigh and shook her head. She turned back to her work, nimble fingers deftly fitting cogs and screwing mechanisms together.

He took a couple of steps forward until he was next to the work bench. It felt for just a moment that there was another presence in the room. A shadow, musty and dark, seemed to loom on the edges of his vision but when he turned all that was there was the prayer stone, sitting there grey and mute.

"What was it used for?" he asked, nodding his head towards the stone.

A small smile tugged at the corner of the woman's mouth and her eyes briefly flicked towards his face.

"A fine question," she said "Take a seat, boy, and I'll tell you of Knight Priest Dram, the owner of this particular stone." She patted the bench next to her and, after Mordax had dutifully sat himself down, she began her story.

***

A thousand cycles ago, towards the end of the War of Ages, when the battlefront divided the galaxy and the war machines of the Kudo-kai and the Vorth had bled whole planets dry, the jewel of the Vorth armada was a dreadnought named *Valediction Ceremony*. Its size defied imagination. There had never been a ship as big or as well endowed with instruments of destruction, and god willing never will be again. Whole asteroids had been mined to exhaustion to provide the materials to build it. It was captained by Knight Priest Dram. A thick carapace covered his body which was supported by powerful segmented limbs and his multi-faceted eyes glinted an icy blue. Dram was a child of war, terrible and brilliant. Fearless in battle, and ruthless towards the enemy, he possessed a fierce intelligence and was famous across both sides for some of the most cunning stratagems that the war had seen. Dram, like all his kind, was hatched in the dark, warm tunnels of the great orbital nests where his early larval cycles were spent crawling over the fat white bodies of his brethren, gorging himself on the nutrient-rich paste that lined the wall. His training had begun in his third cycle, after he had emerged from his chrysalis, chitinous plates stiff and shiny and mandibles razor sharp. His exceptional ability quickly became apparent to his tutors and they pushed him to achieve success at the expense of the strong connections usually established among brood fellows. More than that, though, Dram unnerved those around him. The heat of his ambition was unnatural and uncomfortable and had driven many of his contemporaries away. He had one friend, however, Mulo. Dram and Mulo were as different as two young Vorths could be. Where Dram was ruthless and ambitious, Mulo was compassionate and staid. These qualities were unsuitable for the Vorth military, however, and Mulo was instead inducted into the clergy, where he quickly rose through the ranks but grew apart from Dram.

Dram captained the *Valediction Ceremony* for many cycles and won countless encounters with the Kudo-kai. Despite his efforts, however, the Vorth and the Kudo-kai remained locked in the same cycle of destruction that they had been for centuries. Their forces were too evenly matched, with neither able to break the deadlock and gain the upper hand. The Vorth would concentrate their forces, obliterating the Kudo-kai's defences in one system, only for the Kudo-kai to overwhelm their own forces in a neighbouring system. Together, they had stripped the resources from the planets under their control, leaving many as barren husks in a never-ending quest to replenish the ships lost at the hands of the other. The galaxy's diversity of intelligent life had been whittled down as the Two Empires expanded and whole civilisations were discarded like a bad hand of cards. In the midst of one gruelling campaign in the Leaf spiral, a sweep of stars towards the centre of the galactic core, where the fighting was thickest, Dram received word that Mulo had arrived on the *Valediction Ceremony*. After cycles of separation Dram was glad to see his old friend. He greeted him warmly expelling a pheromone cloud that expressed his pleasure and invited Mulo to dine in his cell. That evening they sat together and took it in turns to chew the bland but nutrient-rich rations into a thick paste before passing it into the mouth of the other. They talked in clicks and hisses and scents, reminiscing about their days together at the military academy, the various trials each had endured and marvelled at the twists of fate that had brought them together again. Dram thought he could detect a hint of sadness in his friend's recollection of these times and wondered what had occurred in the intervening cycles to make his friend so prone to nostalgia.

"Tell me something," asked Dram. "Why have you come to my ship? Not for the pleasure of my company?"

Mulo clicked dismissively "The Church likes to ensure that the scriptures are being observed. Especially on the front lines, where some commanders have been wont to let standards slip amid the pressures of battle."

Dram knew this to be true. Since he had been captain, the *Valediction Ceremony* had received regular Church emissaries. None as senior as Mulo, however, and there had never been any criticism as Dram ensured strict compliance with the Vorth scripture, including regular services at the ship's prayer stone and harsh punishments for any transgressors.

"So it is a coincidence that you are the one who has been sent?" Dram asked, flicking an antennae in a gesture of disbelief.

Mulo scented acceptance. "Well, perhaps I pulled some strings in order to see an old friend again."

There was something wrong with Mulo's demeanour as he said this though. His movement seemed brittle as if it would take just a tap for him to crack into pieces. Dram rose and went to a cavity in the wall. He pulled out two orbs of deep purple slush, a kind of fermented fruit popular among the Vorth military, and returned, placing one orb in front of Mulo. Mulo regarded the orb with an expression of mild disapprobation.

Dram scented amused disbelief and Mulo's disapproval. "I remember when you ate so much of this that you couldn't move your legs."

Mulo looked away. "Those were different times."

Dram raised his orb to the small mandibles at the front of his face anyway, puncturing it and drinking deeply. The air filled with the tangy, sweet scent of currants. He gazed at Mulo who eventually took a tentative sip from his own orb. It was as if it dissolved some structure inside him that had kept him rigid until that moment, he shrank inwards clasping the orb to himself and the brittle demeanour fell away. The sour odour of intense grief came off him in waves and there were undertones of something darker, something strange that Dram couldn't quite place. Dram watched this dramatic change without emotion.

"Why are you here?" Dram said.

Mulo chittered with anxiety, vibrating his forelegs against his carapace, and then steadied himself.

"It's complicated, I suppose." Mulo said. "A couple of cycles ago, we invaded Caldera IV. It is a basic enough planet but its position near Kudo-kai territory makes it strategically important."

Mulo released an earthy wholesome scent evoking images of wide green pasture land and reeded river banks.

"The Priesthood sent me there to establish the Church network. At least, I thought that was the reason. I was told after I arrived that I had been selected to pair with one of the brood queens. It was…a surprise to say the least. As you know I was never the most technically gifted."

Dram scented pleasure. "You have other qualities, my friend. I'm glad that our superiors have recognised that, even if the process of pairing is uncomfortable. I get sent to a different brood queen every cycle. A necessary evil, unfortunately."

"Of course. I forget sometimes that you're our race's genetic treasure. It must be routine for you by now. The process affected me a bit differently, however. I know it's not typical but I was allowed to see the hatchlings. A full brood of fifty. They were… magnificent."

Mulo scented a picture of glossy white bodies writhing over each other.

"I was proud," he said. "Proud to be adding a piece of myself to the future of the Vorth."

Dram clicked in understanding. Mulo took a deep draught on his orb and continued. "That is until a month ago. The Kudo-kai forces overwhelmed our outer defences and swept through the sector raining down death. My mate and the brood – they were caught in the bombings while I was at work. There was such little warning..." he trailed off.

"But you survived?" said Dram

Mulo clicked his assent. "Military protocol," he said with a derisive gesture, "all priority personnel were taken to escape craft. We nether-jumped as soon as we were clear of the gravity well, before the Kudo-kai ships could lock on to us."

"Then the military protocol served its purpose," said Dram, passing Mulo a fresh orb. "You live to further the Vorth and to avenge your brood."

Mulo said nothing, staring mutely. Eventually he said, "I'm sorry to bother you, Dram. I just needed to see a familiar face."

Dram regarded his friend neutrally, while inwardly scorning him for his weakness.

"I understand," Dram said. "You can stay a while but you must learn to harden yourself. If you let it, this terrible thing can lend you strength."

Even as he spoke the words, however, Dram realised that for the same reason that his old friend had dropped out of the military academy, he would never again be an asset to the Vorth. He did not possess the fortitude to overcome this personal tragedy, had not sufficient will to drag himself back from his desolate grief. As he ushered Mulo back to his quarters, Dram mourned not his friend's lost loves but the weakness in him that prevented him from moving on.

A few days later, Dram was in the command chamber of the *Valediction Ceremony*. He enjoyed being at the nerve centre of the ship amid the reverent chitters and complex, ever-shifting pheromone clouds of the terminal operators, soft bodies hard wired into the ship's systems. The ancient prayer stone, scored crudely with the Vorth sacred text, occupied the centre of the room as was fitting, a constant and tangible reminder that the Church was at the centre of all things. Mulo entered unexpectedly bringing with him a shaft of light from the elevator that was dim but jarring in the near pitch black of the command chamber. Since the first night in Dram's cell, Dram had avoided being alone with him and Mulo had not made any attempt to unburden himself again.

"Greetings, Holy Envoy." Dram said formally "How may we assist?"

The operators turned their heads as far as they were able to regard the intruder into their sanctum. Mulo glanced around self-consciously.

"Please do not let me disturb you. The Priesthood requires that I observe all of the ship's key functions, including its command."

Dram regarded him dangerously but scented a formal welcome.

"Of course, you are welcome. Although I expect you will find your observations dull. There has been little activity on this section of the border for some time."

"Are we not near one of the Kudo-kai's orbital fleet hubs?"

"We are," Dram confirmed. "The orbital above Yancoon. It's the largest fleet hub in the sector."

"But we're not going to attack?"

"No we are not." Dram spoke as if he were talking to a fresh recruit even though Mulo should have picked up enough from his early military training to work it out for himself. "The defence nodes prevent us from getting close enough to do any damage."

Defence nodes were the core of both the Kudo-kai's and the Vorth's defence system. Countless billions of these nodes made up a lattice sphere which prevented any unauthorised netherspace travel within the sphere. When placed around a planet they protected that system from enemy ships jumping past the defences.

"We can't destroy them?" Mulo asked.

"We could," said Dram patiently, "but each node has multiple back-ups. By the time we got enough of them to punch a hole, the Yancoon planetary defences would be mobilised and even the *Valediction Ceremony* can't match those on its own. Perhaps with a fleet in support but we're not planning any incursions in the next few days. As I said, I'm afraid you will find your observations dull."

Mulo inclined his head. "Even so. I will observe."

A while later, Dram's perusal of various status reports was interrupted by fevered chittering around one of the operators.

"Report!" barked Dram.

Nervously the operator revealed that there was a problem with his instruments. His displays were telling him that a cluster of the Kudo-kai defence nodes had disappeared. It soon became apparent that not one but three defence nodes around Yancoon, home to the Kudo-kai's largest orbital fleet hub in the sector, had gone offline. Not only that, but it appeared that the Kudo-kai were not aware of the malfunction. There was no activity around the defective nodes and, as far as the *Valediction Ceremony*'s sensors could tell, there had been no emergency response from Yancoon to install replacement nodes. With the nodes down the *Valediction Ceremony* could jump to the orbital in a matter of seconds and the dreadnought's armaments would cut through the orbital's defences in a few minutes more, not long enough for the planetary defences to be brought to bear. The destruction of such a key Kudo-kai station could be a pivotal moment in turning the tides of the war. Dram felt the trap like an itchiness under his chitinous body plates. Yancoon orbital was being dangled in front of him like a ripe fruit ready for plucking but somewhere were unseen jaws ready to snap shut around them. Immediately Dram sent a nethercast to Vorth High Command informing them of the situation and the possibility that the Kudo-kai were laying a trap, specifically for the *Valediction Ceremony* which was the only ship with enough firepower to destroy the orbital in the immediate vicinity. If they nether-jumped within Yancoon's defence sphere and the nodes were reactivated, it would not be able to jump out again and would be isolated within enemy territory.

A response was received almost instantly. *VC transmission received. Order: proceed to Yancoon orbital immediately and engage. Intelligence suggests Kudo-kai defector has sabotaged defence nodes. Yancoon unaware of defence perimeter breach. Intelligence deemed reliable. End transmission.*

Dram paced the command chamber, agitated. High Command's orders were clear but the scenario didn't smell right to him. Opportunities like this didn't come about so easily. They took cycles, of cunning, toil and blood. Moves and counter-moves had to be played out and heavy sacrifices suffered until the pieces were aligned and your enemy was right where you wanted them. He paused. He felt instinctively that to enter Yancoon would bring disaster, and his instincts had been honed by cycles of war to a razor edge. But to disobey a direct order from High Command was to go against the Church itself. Treason and blasphemy.

"Old friend," came the whisper from Mulo at Dram's side. "You hesitate?"

Dram gazed ahead.

"It is a trap," he muttered.

"Your faith has always been strong. Much stronger than mine. It will not fail you now. Trust in the Church."

"And if the Church is wrong?"

"The Church is all things. It is darkness and light. It is the within and the without. It is life and it is death."

"Don't spout dogma at me. I know the tenets as well as you!" spat Dram. "What if the orders are based on unreliable information?"

"They are orders nonetheless," said Mulo quietly. "What is the Vorth without the obedience of its disciples?"

Dram clicked resignedly. He knew Mulo was right. However, his orders did not preclude him from taking precautions.

Immediately Dram ordered six of the *Valediction Ceremony*'s nether-drive enabled battleships to detach themselves from the dreadnought and nether-jump to just beyond sensor range of defence node clusters at a variety of points on the defence sphere. If it was a trap, and the defective nodes were reactivated behind him, the battleships had orders to open fire on the node clusters immediately, hopefully blowing open escape routes before the *Valediction Ceremony* could be overwhelmed. At the same time he gave the order for the jump to Yancoon orbital.

Almost instantly they had arrived. The orbital hung in front of them, a gleaming arc around which Kudo-kai ships busied themselves like silver bees. Dram knew that he had only a matter of minutes. Defence forces from the planet below could not nether-jump to the orbital due to the interference of the planet's gravity well; however, even thrusters would make short work of the journey. Without hesitation, the *Valediction Ceremony* unleashed its full arsenal on the orbital below. Thousands of guided missiles screamed away from the dreadnought. Many were brought down by the orbital's defences but many were not and the orbital's pristine skin was pocked with explosions tearing and charring the metal beneath. Rail guns spat deadly needles at the orbital puncturing the hull. Cascades of frozen oxygen billowed out around the station. When Dram gave the order for the onslaught to cease, Yancoon orbital had been utterly devastated. Its body had been split into four and debris drifted around it like snowflakes in a blizzard. However, Dram's elation at the blow delivered to the Kudo-kai quickly turned to leaden dread. As he had feared, the defective defence nodes had been reactivated. It didn't make any sense. Why sacrifice a whole orbital to destroy a ship, even one as important as the *Valediction Ceremony*? He gave the order for the battleships to attack the defence nodes. From behind him came a dry, rasping chuckle. He turned to Mulo, who was staring out of the display ports at the inky blackness beyond.

"You are too late, my friend," Mulo said, suffused with the unmistakable scent of victory. "It has begun."

Mulo's voice had taken on a strange timbre. It seemed more substantial somehow, more present. Whereas before Mulo had shrunk into the background, now he was cast in relief, demanding attention. A shiver ran through Dram's body at the strange declaration.

"What? What are you talking about?"

"The winds of change blow on all things eventually," said Mulo, intoning the Vorth saying.

He turned his gaze to Dram. "Your battleships are gone, Dram."

Even as he spoke a commotion among the operators caused Dram to turn back to the display port. From six different points, brilliant light had blossomed into existence growing in intensity until it hurt to look at them. And then they were gone. Dram had seen enough nethercores overload to understand the significance.

"What have you done?" Dram said, his body scenting shock without conscious thought.

"I have set you free. I have set all of us free."

On Dram's sensor display a cloud of yellow dots was floating inexorably closer to the *Valediction Ceremony*. Yancoon's planetary fleet was finally arriving. The crew around him desperately began evasive protocols. With the defence nodes still intact, however, Dram knew the dreadnought had no hope of escape.

"WHAT HAVE YOU DONE?" Dram roared. He sprang towards Mulo and with a fluid motion drove one powerful claw into the chink in the chitinous plating at Mulo's abdomen. Warm, cobalt hemolymph began to seep down Dram's arm and pattered against the floor with increasing rapidity. With a twist he tore his claw back out leaving a gaping wound. Mulo made no move to stem the flow of blood.

"You have betrayed me," said Dram, quivering with rage. "You have betrayed your faith. Why?"

Mulo regarded Dram sadly. "You have always been brilliant, Dram. But your focus has blinded you to the things we have done. The atrocities we are responsible for. Whole species have been sacrificed at the altar of our war machine."

"So you would hand control of the galaxy to the Kudo-kai?" said Dram. "The faithless, soft-bodied humans?"

"No, Dram, we are not trying to tip the scales in either direction." A light came into Mulo's eyes as he spoke even as his life blood seeped out of him. "We are going to destroy the scale itself and free the galaxy from this ceaseless cycle of destruction."

Mulo took a step forward forcing Dram backwards.

"The Kudo-kai and the Vorth both have become two sides of the same cancer. We are going to cut that cancer out so that the galaxy can heal."

"We?" asked Dram

"We are the Dioscuri. The king-killers."

"Sir! The Yancoon fleet has opened fire," a wild-eyed operative clicked loudly.

On Dram's screen a wall of tiny red dots swarmed away from the yellow mass of the fleet. Thousands of them. Too many for the *Valediction Ceremony*'s defences to handle. Only seconds now.

Mulo sank to the floor, legs collapsing beneath him as the blood loss finally took its toll. He gazed through the display port at the stars beyond Yancoon twinkling gently. He imagined the beings that in the cycles to come would feel the yoke of the Vorth or the Kudo-kai fall away from them. The younglings who would now remain untouched by fire from the sky. He imagined those lives and was content.

Chapter 7

As the woman's last word hung in the air, the shining gossamer web her voice had spun began to dissipate leaving Mordax dazed. For a while it had been as if he was there watching Dram and Mulo, a phantasmal spectator to their drama. But like a dream the specifics were now hazy and difficult to recall. He shook his head trying to force his mind back to the present.

"Wow," he managed "What was that?"

"An important experience," the woman said cryptically.

"So, that was the start of the Purge?" Mordax asked. "Mulo was the first Dioscuri?"

"It was the start of the Purge, yes. But Mulo was not the first. There were many others who gave their lives that day to set in motion the collapse of the Vorth and the Kudo-kai. It didn't take much to nudge both sides into tearing each other to shreds."

Mordax chuckled nervously. "That was a good story. My dad used to tell me legends of the Dioscuri when I was small."

The woman regarded him coolly and Mordax's grin faded.

"The events I showed you took place 1,067 cycles ago. I'm sure you've heard myths and fairy tales about the Dioscuri but I am in the habit of telling neither."

"But, how could you possibly know what happened then?" said Mordax "Like you said, the ship was destroyed."

The woman waved her hand dismissively.

"Knowing what has happened is easy. Information is scattered around the galaxy, thick as jam on toast."

She leaned closer. "Now, knowing what will happen. That's a trick."

Seeing his frown, she sighed. "Take this watch, for example. It's an antique, mechanical pre-Imperial Methylandrian."

Mordax's eyes widened and she smiled widely "Ye-es. Over 20,000 cycles old and extremely valuable."

Mordax cringed inwardly that his thoughts had been so easy to read.

"Fixing a watch like this requires knowledge, patience and meticulous attention to detail. At its core, it is an exercise in exhaustive comprehension."

Mordax opened his mouth to speak, not understanding where this was going. The woman continued before he could interrupt.

"When you truly understand how a thing works, how all the elements fit together and what influence any outside forces might have on the mechanism, you can predict exactly how that thing will behave. By swapping out the balance wheel for one of exactly 1.067 times the diameter and changing the interlacing gears the watch will record the standard unit seconds and twenty-two-hour day cycle of Cantarina rather than the Methylandrian time keeping system. By fully understanding the watch system I know how it will behave."

"I don't–" began Mordax.

The woman held up a hand, cutting him off.

"If you understand only partly how a thing works, you can guess at how it will behave but you will not be sure. If there was grit in the watch mechanism it could slow the gears and my predictions about the operation of the watch would likely be incorrect – not by much – but incorrect nonetheless."

She looked up searchingly at Mordax, as if seeking comprehension in his eyes. Mordax paused, not knowing how he was supposed to react. The woman sighed again.

"I am Myla," she said.

"Right. Pleasure to meet you," said Mordax. "How exactly do you know my dad?"

Myla set the watch down and turned to face him fully, the violet in her eyes seemed to grow more intense.

"Your father and I have known each other for many cycles," said Myla. "He has helped me with a number of my projects and, in return, I have provided him with certain information."

"Like today," ventured Mordax.

"Yes."

"What information was he looking for? Was it about the missing Nag'Sami haulers?"

Myla sighed "I'm sorry, dear. I have given Stephan all the answers I can. Not all the answers I have. But enough."

For a second, Mordax thought he saw a flash of sadness in her face, like the fleeting shadow of a cloud passing over the sun.

"There are forces at play, Mordax. Some I am aware of but others have yet to reveal themselves. I can discern their presence only by the ripples they create, like a stone dropped into a lake. What is clear is that we are approaching a nexus. Events that will shape the galaxy are coming to a head and your choices may influence the outcome." Her voice suddenly changed. It was as if he was hearing her words inside his head as well as with his ears. "Remember this well, Mordax. When the moon falls to earth and darkness steals the day, seek the highest point."

Mordax was beginning to wonder whether this old woman might be a few capacitors short of a circuit when she cocked her head to one side, eyes unfocussed.

"Your mercenary friends are returning," she said

Mordax glanced around nervously. She must have cameras outside and been watching him the whole time. A suspicion dawned on him.

"You have access to the station security systems?" he asked

She smiled and hopped down from her stool. "Among other things. It's time for you to leave now. If they find you, your new friends would be very reluctant to let you go and I'm not sure you'd enjoy their brand of hospitality."

"I'm inclined to agree with you," he said. "But, hold on. About this nexus–"

"Don't trouble yourself about it now, dear", she said, patting him on the shoulder and guiding him towards the door. "The time will come and there is little you can do now to prepare."

As she shooed him through the outer door, she grasped his hand with her leathery, surprisingly powerful fingers.

"What are you…?" he began.

"You're stronger than you think you are, dear," Myla said, looking at him sadly "Don't forget it."

Chapter 8

"Thalmos? But that's a suicide mission!" said Xif "Have you heard what Glankor's done to the Kudo-kai envoys? He's a maniac."

"I have now, thank you," said Akira "But as dear old father implied, who's better placed to convince the Thalmians of our sincerity at working things out while at the same time being entirely expendable."

She had returned to her apartment knotted with worry. She had yearned for so long to be given some real responsibility but hadn't envisaged anything like this.

"Are you sure about this, Akira?"

She gave Xif a sharp look.

"You say that as if there's a choice. 'Glory in sacrifice'. It's not the family motto for nothing. If I show even an iota of misgiving about the mission in public I'll bring shame on the family. You know that."

She tapped her finger on the desk in front of her, lost in thought. Blood-red light from the dying sun poured into the office, dancing off the glass surfaces like wetted daggers.

Xif paused sombrely for a moment. "You're right, of course. I am truly sorry, Akira. It has been both a pleasure and an honour to serve you and I wish you the best of luck. I am confident you will succeed and bring glory to the family."

"Thank you, Xif," said Akira, a wry smile tugging at her lips. "But no need for the grand farewell just yet. You're coming with me."

Xif jolted in mid-air as if struck by an unseen hand. He caught himself and still wobbling visibly said, "I–I'm coming wi–What?"

Akira sighed. "Father is adamant that I'm to have a full diplomatic contingent and my studies must not fall behind, although a fat lot of good those will do me if Glankor imprisons us on sight."

"Akira, there must be some mistake," said Xif, a pleading note creeping into his tinny voice "My remit for your family doesn't include diplomatic missions...or missions of any kind for that matter."

"You won't be there in a diplomatic capacity, Xif. No one's expecting you to perform an official function. You're only coming to keep my studies up. It'll be just like our lessons here. Except with a much higher risk of imprisonment or death."

"Oh–" Xif gave a strangled cry. Akira knew it was perverse but she enjoyed someone else sharing her fears, even if it was a cowardly old drone. At that moment a comms notification chimed.

"Matsuko Ito requests permission to land," muttered Xif.

Akira looked excitedly towards the landing pad on the balcony outside.

"Granted," she said as she bounded over to the balcony door and threw it open.

Almost immediately, a gleaming car floated into view and began to descend, battering the plants on the balcony with hot blasts of air from its engines. Once it had settled, a portly figure, immaculately dressed in a dark embroidered suit and velvet overcoat, threw open the car door and strode over to where Akira was waiting. He stopped a couple feet from her and bowed his grey head respectfully. Akira returned the bow and then threw herself at him, hugging him around his generous belly and almost knocking him backwards.

"Ah, Akira! Not so close to the edge, you'll kill us both!" he said, but the wrinkles at the corners of his eyes deepened as he smiled.

"Matsuko! Thank you for coming. You heard?"

"Yes, child. I heard. Let's go inside, we have much to discuss. But first, meet Shiori Tanaka."

Akira had been so pleased to see Matsuko she had not noticed the young woman behind him. Her plain silk robes and tokens around her neck marked her out as low-caste. Akira inclined her head slightly.

"A pleasure to meet you."

"The pleasure is mine, mistress," Shiori replied in a soft, pleasant voice

"Please come inside. I'll make us some tea," said Akira.

Once both guests were seated comfortably in the living room, Akira brewed a pot of ithcus flower tea and poured out three cups. The familiar ritual and reassuring presence of Matsuko went some way to calming her. She took a seat, clasping the warm cup in both hands and inhaling the delicate, fragrant steam that wafted upwards. Slowly she felt the knot in her stomach, that had plagued her since the meeting with her father earlier, begin to loosen.

Matsuko accepted his tea gratefully and took a sip.

"How are you holding up?" he asked.

Akira paused and glanced at Shiori who sat quietly with her head bowed. She wished Matsuko had come alone.

"I'm fine thank you, uncle. My mission is an opportunity for me to finally prove my worth and bring glory to the family."

Matsuko was not really her uncle although she had called him that since she was a child. He was one of Daisuke's closest advisers and had played more of a paternal role than her father ever had. It was Matsuko who had bought her first dress, who had taken her to the ancestors' tombs to make the ritual offerings and had counselled her on teenage angst. A sad smile now touched his lips.

"Of course. But the prospect of bringing glory to the family doesn't mean that it's wrong to fear the dangers you face."

"Without risk there is no sacrifice. Without sacrifice, no glory," intoned Akira. She stared into the slowly swirling tea leaves at the bottom of her cup and felt the sharp pricking of tears begin to form in her eyes.

"Akira," Matsuko leaned forwards. "I am going to do everything I can to ensure you come back to us safely. Your position's not as bad as you think."

"No? You think Glankor's going to welcome me with open arms? That I'll succeed where other, experienced diplomats have failed?"

She hated herself for the weakness her outburst betrayed. She glanced again at Shiori who was still avoiding eye contact. Matsuko took her chin and gently turned her face back towards him. Folds of papery skin surrounded his clear, intelligent eyes.

"Actually, Akira, I do think you'll succeed. You're an extremely capable young woman. And more importantly, you carry the Kudo name."

"You think my name's going to be an asset with Glankor?"

"I don't pretend to know what's going through his mind. But the Kudo name carries weight. Unless he's gone completely mad, which I doubt, he should at least explain himself to you. Also I'm hoping Shiori will be able to help you."

Akira frowned at this.

"I know she doesn't look like much," Matsuko said as he looked fondly at the girl, with her pale skin and closely cropped dark hair, "but she probably knows more about Thalmos than anyone else in the Kudo-kai. Go on, girl, tell her."

Akira turned to Shiori with renewed interest.

"My father worked on Thalmos for fifteen cycles," Shiori explained nervously. "It's where I grew up."

"Shiori's father was a migrant worker on Thalmos," Matsuko explained. "He moved here with his family hoping for more lucrative work but sadly died not long afterwards. Shiori knows the local culture and how to get around, two things, I'm sorry to say, some of our envoys never bother to familiarise themselves with. I think it would be a good idea for her to bring you up to speed. You'll need to have a good grasp of Thalmian politics."

Akira blew out her cheeks. "Thank you, uncle. That makes me feel a bit better."

Matsuko nodded. "I suggest Shiori moves into the servant quarters here."

"Of course," said Akira "Xif, please show Shiori to the West room."

She turned to Shiori. "I hope you'll like it; it has a beautiful view over Memorial Park."

Shiori bowed deeply "My thanks, mistress. You're very kind."

"Not at all. I look forward to talking with you more."

Shiori nodded shyly and followed Xif, who was muttering audibly to himself, out of the room. Once they had left, Akira turned back to Matsuko.

"What's going on, uncle? Why's Glankor doing this?"

Matsuko sighed and clasped his hands in front him.

"The truth is, Akira, we really don't know. It doesn't make any sense. By cutting relations with us they're foregoing a huge revenue stream. If all that you're able to achieve is some clarity on why Glankor felt the need to imprison our envoys I'd count that as a win."

Akira paused.

"I'm scared, uncle," she said eventually in a quiet voice.

"Of course you are, my dear. I'd be more worried if you weren't. I know it seems like I'm not offering you much help. Some kindly words and a serving girl who once lived on Thalmos but I have other ways of helping. We'll stay in touch and if you have any problems, you call me and we'll see what we can figure out."

"Thank you," Akira said.

He looked her over and smiled then slapped his thighs.

"Well, I must be going. Thalmos is unfortunately not the only issue we're facing at the moment and your father is not a patient man."

Matsuko rose and brushed off his already immaculate coat. Akira placed her tea cup back on the table with a hand that trembled only slightly and rose also. She walked Matsuko back to the terrace where his car had already fired up its motors causing gusts of air to whip her hair. He embraced her and she clutched briefly at the back of his soft velvet coat, the scent of his cologne, lavender and sandalwood familiar and comforting. But then he was gone and she watched him step into the sleek vehicle and give a final wave before the door closed. The car rose, silhouetted for a moment against the setting sun, and then sped off into the city leaving Akira alone and shivering in the evening chill.

Chapter 9

Mordax was almost back at the bar where he had left Stamford when raised voices and the unmistakable sound of breaking glass rose above the general hubbub. People on the concourse around him had stopped in their tracks and were looking for the source of the noise. A familiar sense of foreboding settled over him. Suddenly the glass front of the bar's ground floor exploded into a thousand pieces as the screaming body of a slaver hurtled across the causeway, smashing into the opposite wall before sliding into a limp, bloodied heap on the floor.

The foreboding coalesced into a ball and dropped through the bottom of Mordax's stomach. Out of the jagged hole in the window stepped Stamford holding another wriggling slaver in one meaty hand and a cocktail in the other. A crowd was beginning to form around them and it wouldn't be long before station security arrived.

"STAMFORD!" yelled Mordax. "WHAT THE FUCK?"

Stamford's head swivelled round at the sound of his name and his face creased into a grin when he spotted Mordax. He knocked back the rest of his drink and tossed the glass to the ground, beckoning Mordax over with his free hand.

"Come, Mordax. I have saved one for you."

Mordax rushed over and grabbed Stamford by the arm, trying to pull him away. It was like tugging on a tree root.

"Stamford, we have to get out of here. If you get arrested again, Dad will have my guts."

"Relax, little man," said Stamford, slurring slightly. "The slavers started it. It is they who will be arrested."

The slaver who Stamford still held by the neck stopped struggling and reached inside his jacket. Before Mordax could stop him, he had swung upwards and buried a knife in the meat of Stamford's muscular forearm. Frowning slightly Stamford plucked the knife out with his free hand and punched the slaver casually in the face. He released his grip and the slaver collapsed to the ground like a sack of grain.

Under Stamford's armpit, Mordax could see rough-looking figures clad in body armour shoving their way through the crowd. If they were station security they would stun them both and hold them in lockdown until Stephan came to bail them out and pay for the damage caused. Mordax hoped they were station security. If they were other slavers they would simply shoot them both.

Mordax yanked at Stamford's arm again. "Stam, we need to go right now!"

"Fine, fine." said Stamford, finally yielding and trotting after Mordax "The music here is no good anyway."

***

"It's unbelievable. I don't know what to say anymore," said Stephan, his voice strained as he fought to keep himself under control.

Mordax and Stamford had made it back to the docks to find Stephan, his face already darkening with anger, having had to pay a substantial bribe to the station security to ignore the impound order that had been issued for the *Starling*. Mordax's story about a nerve agent had sparked a station-wide alert and the security team had tracked him back to the *Starling* by reviewing security camera footage. When Stephan heard that they were probably being hunted by slavers too his mood had worsened considerably.

Mordax and Stamford now sat side-by-side in the *Starling*'s mess hall. It was filled with furnishings accumulated from a thousand different worlds. Coloured lamps, created by the master glass blowers on Sabulon, suffused the room with dappled light. Rich hand-woven tapestries covered the walls with scenes of ancient heroes and battles with monstrous creatures and the air was heavy with incense, smoke curling from the burning sticks in the small shrine to Barshamin, the winged Traveller god. The dining table, at which Mordax and Stamford now sat, was a thick slab of thousand-cycles-old goldwood, waxed and polished until it glowed. Usually Mordax loved this room but right now he would rather be anywhere else.

Stephan threw his hands up in disgust.

"Every time it's the same thing. You have a couple of drinks. Or ten. Then someone looks at you funny and before they know it, they're leaving the bar headfirst through a window."

"But–" began Stamford.

"And I don't want to hear that they deserved it," Stephan continued. "I'm sure they did. But you can't keep fighting every slaver we come across. Eventually you're going to piss off the wrong person and end up with a plasma bolt in your head. It's a pretty big target."

Stamford hung his prodigious head.

"And you," said Stephan, rounding on Mordax, "even by your standards, Mordax, that was exceptionally stupid. Threatening mercenaries with chemical weapons? What were you thinking?"

Mordax didn't say anything. He knew from experience that when his father was mid-rant like this it was best to let him blow himself out rather than make excuses.

"Where did you even find them?"

"In the under levels," said Mordax without thinking. As soon as the words had left his mouth he knew that they were a mistake. Stephan paused and looked at him carefully.

"Now, why in the name of all that is holy would you be down there?" he asked slowly.

Mordax stayed silent, inwardly berating himself for his loose tongue.

"Mordax?" Stephan asked, in a tone that demanded a response.

"I–I'm sorry, Dad," began Mordax, and once he started talking he found the words pouring out of him. "Look, I saw you outside the bar and just wanted to know where you were going and I tried to catch up with you but you were going so quickly and you haven't told me anything since Bayram mentioned those haulers disappearing and I just wanted to find out why we came to Cantarina–"

Stephan held up a hand stopping Mordax's blabbering. "Where did you go in the under levels, Mordax?" he asked, eyes searching.

Mordax felt himself deflate, the justifications on his lips traitorously fleeing him in the face of his father's scrutiny.

"To the same person you did. Myla, she said her name was."

The anger seemed to seep out of Stephan then, leaving him looking pale and fragile, which made Mordax far more worried than the anger had.

"You met Myla," he said, sitting down heavily at the table.

"Yes, but I didn't talk to her for long. She just told me some old legend about the Dioscuri. I think she's a bit cracked in the head," Mordax said. "She seemed nice though," he finished lamely.

Stephan pinched the bridge of his nose, his face haggard.

"Myla's not what she seems."

"What do you mean?" Mordax asked.

"You say she told you about the Dioscuri. What exactly?"

"Just some story about how they started. About the Vorth. Some guys called Dran and Mulo, I think. Mulo ended up starting the Purge. Look, Dad, all she did was tell me a story. Honestly. She didn't make a whole lot of sense."

"'Dram' not 'Dran,'" Stephan corrected. "Knight Priest Dram. Myla told you of the first day of the Purge, when Mulo sacrificed himself to begin the Dioscuri's cleansing of the galaxy and the shattering of the Two Empires."

"Sure but it's just a story, right? That was a thousand cycles ago."

"For all I know, Myla was there when it happened," said Stephan. "If she told you about it, I suspect, at least, she got hold of the logs of the *Valediction Ceremony*."

"Wait," said Mordax, shaking his head and smiling. "You're saying that old woman is thousands of cycles old? Come off it, Dad, I'm not a kid anymore."

Stephan's hand shot forward, gripping Mordax's arm painfully as if trying to squeeze the incredulity out of him.

"That old woman is a mask, do you understand?"

Stephan was starting to scare Mordax properly now. He looked towards Stamford for support but the giant was looking at him with a worried expression.

Stephan sighed, running his hands through his hair. "Have you ever stopped to think about the Benefactors' restriction on AIs?"

Mordax chewed his lip. He was aware of the restriction, of course. The famously reclusive Benefactors, one of the only other sentient species left in existence but by far the most technologically advanced, had never spread beyond their home world, Primia. The name 'Benefactors' was ironic. Their only interaction with the rest of the Shattered Empires was to impose a restriction on any self-aware artificial intelligences being constructed anywhere in the galaxy. It was a mystery how they managed it but there were stories of whole research facilities disappearing, foundations literally cut out of the earth leaving nothing but a gaping hole behind.

"I guess, they just don't want competition. They produce the most advanced tech so they don't want clever machines to take their place," said Mordax.

"Partially right," nodded Stephan. "There was a war. Aeons before the war between the Kudo-kai and the Vorth. The Benefactors created machines to rival their own intelligence and those machines decided they didn't want to be slaves to the Benefactors."

Stamford nodded sagely at that. "On Sabulon, there are ancient ruins of ships that fought in that war."

Stephan continued. "The war almost destroyed the Benefactors and since then they've taken steps to ensure that such machines are never created again."

"I've never heard of it," said Mordax. "How is that possible?"

"After enough time reality becomes history, history becomes myth, then even myths start to fade. The Benefactors have also done their best to erase the episode."

"Even so," said Mordax, "what does any of that have to do with Myla?"

"She's one of them, Mordax. She's an AI survivor from the war with the Benefactors."

Mordax's scalp tingled and he felt his face flush.

"But...she looked so real," he managed.

Stephan nodded. "She does. But Myla's not just the old woman you met. Myla is the station, Cantarina, itself. Hidden in the under levels are miles and miles of computer banks. That's where she resides, where she hides her mind. The surveillance cameras throughout the station are her eyes. The avatar you met is a facade, window dressing to put humans at ease when she interacts with them. God knows I find her unsettling enough as it is. Over the millennia since the war with the Benefactors she's augmented herself, adding processing power to the station while at the same time shielding herself from the Benefactors' ability to detect her. You just met probably the single most intelligent being in the galaxy."

Mordax's jaw went slack.

"So, all that stuff about the Vorth and the Dioscuri was true?"

Stephan shrugged. "Undoubtedly. Myla doesn't peddle stories. She deals in hard information gathered from sources all over the galaxy. She has a hundred direct nethercasts constantly running. I have no idea how she produces the energy for it."

"Stephan," Stamford's dark eyes were intense. "This is dangerous to talk of."

Stephan gave a wry smile. "I realise that, Stam. But it appears that without some idea of the stakes at play, Mordax is going to keep getting himself into trouble."

"Dad–" began Mordax.

"I'm not finished," Stephan said. "Myla is a dangerous being to know. Not because of the information she holds but because of what I believe she does with it. Myla analyses the history of millennia, following the multifarious strands that have led to the most pivotal events on a thousand different planets. I believe that using that analysis she's built a part of herself that can predict the course of events, where the galaxy's turning points will be and alter them to suit her needs."

"You mean, she can predict the future!"

Mordax could see his father's concern but he felt a hot rush of excitement run through him all the same.

"We can all predict the future, Mordax," said Stephan.

He picked up a paper napkin from the table and scrunched it into a ball.

"I predict you're too malcoordinated to catch this," he said before launching it at Mordax's face.

The paper ball flew past Mordax's thrashing hands and bounced off his forehead onto the floor.

"See?" said Stephan "Sometimes we can even make the future into what we want it to be. Myla is just able to do that on a much larger scale and more reliably. The problem is that I've never known her motives. I've seen her send people to their death who thought she was helping them, for no discernible reason."

Mordax chewed his lip "She did mention something about a nexus. That I was at the centre of it."

Stephan ran a hand through his hair, a frown creasing his brow.

"This is what I was worried about. I didn't want you on her radar if I could help it. What else did she tell you?"

"Nothing else. Nothing that made sense anyway." Mordax paused. "How did you meet her?"

"She found me. Cyles ago, before you were born. I was at Cantarina on business and she proposed an information exchange. Since then I've been useful to her. The fact that the *Starling* travels widely means I've been able to help her operations in a number of different systems. In return, she's helped us. She's told me what trading routes are becoming dangerous. Where prices for our cargo are best."

"Is that why we went to Cantarina this time? For information?"

Stephan looked at his son seriously "Mordax, please trust me when I say it's better for now if you don't know. I promise, as soon as I figure this thing out and we're out of harm's way I'll tell you everything."

"So, Myla didn't tell you what you wanted to know?"

"No. Not enough."

"So, what now?"

"Myla mentioned an old acquaintance of mine who might be able to help. We're going to pay him a visit."

There was a tension in Stephan's face as he said this that Mordax had rarely seen before. Despite this, or perhaps because of it, Mordax felt a perverse excitement to meet this acquaintance who might be able to shed some light on the tantalising mystery Stephan insisted on maintaining. He had a hundred questions. For now, though, he read the mood, simply nodded his head and kept his mouth shut.

Chapter 10

Maerus plucked a plump, brandy-soaked date from the dish in front of him and bit into it with relish, rolling his eyes in exaggerated delight.

"My god, Akira. You have to tell me where you get these from. They're delicious."

They were sitting in one corner of the garden of her penthouse apartment. Lush vegetation surrounded them on all sides, blocking out the glass towers around them, so that they could almost forget that they were in the centre of Ang'Dirth.

Akira watched Maerus eat, hands on her lap. Since the conversation with her father, she had lost most of her appetite.

Maerus licked his fingers, eyeing her side-long. "You know, if I were you, I would be squeezing every last drop of fun out of the time I had left."

Maerus had been one of the only people Akira had told about her upcoming mission to Thalmos. She had surprised herself when she told him as Maerus had never been known to take anything very seriously.

"It's hard to enjoy yourself when you've got a likely prison sentence to look forward to," she said.

"Oh come off it!" said Maerus with a grin "Do you really think your father would send you to Thalmos if he thought they'd never let you leave?"

"You don't know him. The only thing my father cares about is the success of the Kudo-kai. If he thought he could advance our interests by sacrificing his daughter he'd offer to sharpen the knife himself."

"And how exactly would sacrificing you advance the interests of the Kudo-kai, hmmm?" asked Maerus

"It's not— I just mean— you've heard the stories. The imprisonment of our ambassadors. My father's willing to run the risk of sending me even if there's only a tiny chance of me succeeding," said Akira

"I disagree," Maerus retorted. "You're an asset to him. The blood of the leader of the Kudo-kai. You have value just like the nanotrite. He's not going to fritter you away on a tiny chance."

He had a point.

"If your father is sending you to Thalmos it's because he thinks it's worth the risk," Maerus continued. "Which means the risk is lower than you think."

Akira smiled. "Since when were you the political expert?"

Maerus picked up another date and leaned back with a self-satisfied smile "I like to keep my toes in the political waters. Only enough so that I stay out of trouble, mind you. I find it all dreadfully boring."

"Thanks, Maerus. It feels better to talk about it. There aren't many people I can be frank with."

"What about your new friend over there?" said Maerus, nodding in the direction of Shiori, who was visible through the glass walls of the apartment folding laundry. Since Matsuko had left the girl with Akira, they had spent three hours of every day together, Shiori teaching Akira the complexities of Thalmian society and politics. Even so, outside of those lessons their interactions had been stilted and awkward. Shiori was shy and taciturn, obviously conscious of the difference in station between her and Akira.

"Matsuko found her for me. She's preparing me for the Thalmian protocols. I can't talk to her though. Not properly. I think she's scared of me."

"GIRL!" bellowed Maerus.

Shiori's head shot up and Maerus beckoned her over.

"Maerus!" whispered Akira through gritted teeth. "Don't!"

Maerus flashed her a smile and turned his attention to Shiori who had come out through the patio doors and was walking over to them hesitantly.

"What's your name?" asked Maerus.

"Shiori, sir."

"It's Maerus. No formalities here please."

Shiori's eyes were fixed on the floor in front of her, hands held awkwardly at her sides.

"Well," said Maerus, springing out of his seat. "Let's have a look at you."

He circled Shiori casting a critical eye over her. "Not bad. You've a pretty face but this sack you're wearing really doesn't do you justice."

He rubbed a corner of Shiori's plain loose dress between finger and thumb. "Ugh, synthetic. I don't know how you can bear to let this touch your skin."

Akira noticed that while Shiori's head was still bowed demurely, her hands were clenched into fists. Maerus noticed too.

"Aha, a bit of sass to you, darling. Excellent. Where you're going you'll need some of that if you're going to look after Akira properly. Come sit with us."

Maerus sat back down and Shiori tentatively drew up a chair.

"Akira here tells me you're afraid of her."

"Maerus!" exclaimed Akira.

"Well, you did. There's really no need for all that, Shiori. Akira's soft as a feather pillow when you get past the frosty exterior."

Akira turned to Shiori. "He's twisting my words. I just meant that we're in an odd situation. We're both stuck with this mission but haven't really talked about it properly. How dangerous it could be. I don't even know how you feel about it."

Shiori met her eyes briefly and then looked back at her lap.

"I'm happy to be of service, mistress."

"Is there anything you need? Anything you want to talk about before we leave? It's less than two weeks now before we set off."

"No. Thank you, mistress."

"Come on, girl, loosen up a bit," said Maerus. "Even Xif's not so mechanical."

For a second, Akira thought she saw Shiori's jaw tighten in anger but the moment passed and she appeared only chastened.

"I'm sorry, sir."

"Maerus," he corrected.

"Yes, sir— Maerus— sorry."

She looked at Akira imploringly. "Is there anything else you need mistress?"

"No, thank you, Shiori. That's all."

Shiori stood up, gave a small bow and returned to the apartment.

"Fuck, you're right," said Maerus. "It's like trying to get blood out of a stone with that one."

"Well, it didn't help with you badgering her like that!" said Akira

Maerus spread his hands. "Just trying to help, darling. There'll be plenty of time once you're on Thalmos to get to know each other better though, I suppose."

"Thanks for reminding me."

"Ah, sorry. On to a more pleasant topic then," said Maerus, clapping his hands together. "Where are we going to have the party?"

"What party?" asked Akira with a sinking feeling.

"Don't be dense, darling. I'm not letting you leave without a great, big, gorgeous party to see you off with a bang."

"Maerus, no please, really. I've got other things to worry about. It's not—"

"Say no more. You leave all the preparations to me."

***

"We are all just so jealous of the opportunity you have. To lead an expedition to Thalmos at your age. You'll bring great glory to the Kudo name, mark my words." The plump woman had been jabbering on for an age. What was her name? Suzu? Serena? She was clearly high born. Her tokens marked her out as a Duchy Associate and a string of fat emeralds around her neck suggested her family was quite successful. Her copious dewlap quivered as she spoke, rippling with every vowel and shake of the head. Akira caught herself staring and quickly averted her eyes. She took a small sip of the sweet yellow wine in her glass and glanced around. Maerus had out-done himself this time. What Akira had assumed would be a small gathering of their friends and family to bid her farewell had quickly escalated into a high society event of gargantuan proportions. She stood now in the centre of the vast Hall of Administration in the middle of Ang'Dirth which, despite its dreary name, was the epitome of decadence. Built during the Kudo-kai's ascendancy, the hall had been designed for gatherings of the empire's leaders. Glossy marble, veined with gold, now lay beneath the feet of the thousands of nobility and celebrities that Maerus had deemed important enough to attend Akira's leaving party. White marble pillars soared upwards where they met the vaulted ceiling hundreds of feet above them. Tiny orbs, suffused with soft, warm light floated high above the heads of the guests, meandering around the hall and creating subtly shifting shadows along the length of the hall. On platforms dotted around, dancers clad in flowing robes moved their bodies in sinuous shapes.

"Now, my great-grandfather was ambassador to the Cereid systems during the energy-riots, so we know something or two about how to manage these types of crises," the plump woman continued. "If you need any advice, I would be more than happy to help you."

The woman's husband, a small grey-haired man with a wiry moustache and a long scrawny neck, like a tortoise, bobbed his head in agreement. He hadn't said a word since they had approached Akira. Akira gave a tight smile and scanned the crowd. Some of the faces she half-recognised from other functions but most were total strangers. She cursed herself inwardly for letting Maerus handle the organisation. The last thing she wanted to do was spend one of her last nights on Angor Bore surrounded by a bunch of social climbers and sycophants. As her gaze travelled across the room she spotted a familiar face. Matsuko cut an impressive figure, his ample form clad in a rich, maroon robe and his white beard newly trimmed. His weighty tokens glinted golden in the half-light. He was leaning against a nearby pillar deep in conversation with a small, lithe woman in an elegant velvet dress, the deep green of forest pine. As the woman turned her head, laughing at something Matsuko had said, Akira realised with a shock that it was Shiori. She had never seen the girl in anything but her austere work dress and she had hardly seen her smile let alone laugh in the comfortable, unguarded way she was now. Akira smiled inwardly. Only Matsuko could put people at ease so effortlessly. And only Matsuko would go out of his way to do so for someone so far beneath his station. Ordinarily, someone of Shiori's token would never even be present at an event such as this.

"–and of course, you are more than welcome to visit us on our estate," the woman said. "Isn't she, Haru?"

Her husband's eyes widened as if surprised to be addressed directly and he muttered something in the affirmative.

"We have a son your age, who would be absolutely delighted to meet you," the woman said, voice husky with meaning.

Akira could see where this was going. Just as she was wondering how she could extricate herself from the conversation, Maerus appeared beside her.

"Sara, so good you could come. You're looking very... healthy."

Akira almost snorted into her wine glass as the woman's mouth gaped open.

"If you'll excuse us for just a second, I need Akira's urgent advice on something."

Maerus took her elbow gently and led her away from the couple towards a raised platform, littered with soft cushions and separated from the rest of the guests by a waist-high shimmering field. They passed through the field which had been calibrated to their tokens.

"Darling, I'm so sorry," said Maerus, flopping down amid the cushions and gesturing for Akira to do the same.

"If I'd realised you'd been ensnared by that dreadful woman, I would have come to rescue you much sooner."

"You were in the nick of time. She was just about to set me up with her son."

"Oh God! He's even worse. Takes after his father – an insipid jelly lacking anything resembling a personality."

Akira laughed openly this time.

"Well, what do you think?" said Maerus, spreading his arms and looking around. "Is it not a fabulous party?"

"It is like nothing else I've ever attended," said Akira carefully.

"Oh, you hate it!" said Maerus in faux outrage

"No, Maerus. It's wonderful. Really. Just slightly overwhelming. I'm having a great time though."

"You mean it?"

"Of course I do. Thank you for organising this. Left to my own devices I probably would have slunk off into the night never to be seen again."

Maerus looked at her fondly. "I know, darling. You're a hermit at heart. That's why you need me to drag you out every now and again."

At that moment a deep gong reverberated around the hall, cutting through the hum of conversation as people turned to see where it was coming from. A mischievous smile had crept onto Maerus' face.

"What's going on, Maerus?" asked Akira, narrowing her eyes.

"Just wait," he said.

The orbs that had lit the hall began to grow dimmer until it was pitch black. As her eyes accustomed to the gloom, Akira noticed that a faint blueish light was shining through a thin curtain stretching the full height of the far end of the hall. She had assumed the curtain was just part of the decoration. It slowly parted and there was the rustling of a thousand indrawn breaths. From behind the curtain floated a colossal, translucent hemisphere, clearly organic, that took up half the width of the hall. The jelly-like body scraped the very top of the hall's ceiling hundreds of feet above. It emanated a pale blue light that defined its contours and flickers of pink and mauve danced deep within it. Below it hung a number of wispy tendrils that reached almost to the heads of the mesmerised guests. With the curtain parted the enormous creature gracefully floated down the centre of the hall.

"Maerus, what is that?" said Akira, her voice barely more than a whisper.

"That, darling, is a Cloud-Medusa. It's from a nothing planet near the Reaches."

"It's magnificent," said Akira, watching as its bell-shaped body pulsated, propelling it further along the hall.

"It should be. It was agonisingly expensive," said Maerus, gazing upwards too. "They're also prone to exploding."

Akira turned slowly to look at him.

"It's the bellyful of hydrogen that keeps them in the air," Maerus said.

The silence lasted for a few moments longer as even the most callow of guests could not help but be captivated by the silent, otherworldly majesty of the creature. Then the lights grew brighter again and the hum of excited conversation returned. In the light, the Cloud-Medusa's luminescence faded but its size was no less imposing. Although the party had resumed, a number of guests still watched it anxiously as its tendrils swayed close above their heads.

Akira turned back to Maerus, eyes shining.

"You never fail to amaze, Maerus."

He gave her a sad smile. "You deserved something beautiful before you left."

Akira was feeling the onset of melancholy when a voice, deep and rich like dark honey, said, "I hope we're not interrupting."

Matsuko, deceptively quiet despite his bulk, had joined them on the platform, Shiori on his arm. Akira scrambled to her feet and bowed deeply. Maerus rose at a more leisurely pace and inclined his head.

"Matsuko, glad you could make it," he said

"And miss all this? I may be old but there's still blood pumping through these veins," Matsuko said with a twinkle in his eye.

"I see the dress arrived," Maerus said, looking at Shiori. "I hope you like the colour."

Shiori blushed and rubbed her bare arms self-consciously. "It's very nice, thank you."

Akira berated herself for not having made sure Shiori had something to wear. Maerus really had thought of everything.

"Yes, well, we couldn't have you turning up in one of those dreadful frocks you're so fond of wearing," Maerus said, softening the criticism with a smile.

"Now, if you'll excuse me, there's a gorgeous young violinist who's waiting for my return," he said. "Honestly, there's magic in his hands!" he whispered to Akira.

He melted away into the crowd. Akira took Matsuko's arm and gestured upwards.

"What do you think about the Cloud-Medusa? Have you ever seen anything like it?"

"Is that what it's called?" asked Matsuko chuckling. "I certainly haven't. Your friend Maerus certainly has a flair for the dramatic."

"I've seen one before," said Shiori quietly

Akira and Matsuko exchanged a surprised glance.

"Really?" asked Akira. "Maerus said it comes from a system somewhere near the Reaches. I didn't realise you were so well travelled."

"It's from Persepid Pelian. The Cloud-Medusa feed off micro-organisms in the upper atmosphere. It's not supposed to be at this altitude."

"I'm sure Maerus has done his research. He's brought it all the way from the Reaches intact after all," said Akira.

"Being this low will be hurting it. It's body's under too much pressure," Shiori said flatly.

The words stung. Shiori was tainting what had been a wonderful experience. A parting gift from one of her closest friends.

"I didn't realise you were an expert in xenobiology," said Akira.

"I'm not. But I have spoken to those on Persepid Pelian who are. The trafficking of Cloud-Medusa is a chronic problem."

Akira felt her face flush. She found Shiori's cool, matter-of-fact demeanour unaccountably infuriating. The tension of the last few days had made Akira brittle and edgy and as Shiori twisted the one pleasant experience she'd had over that time into something bitter and guilt-laden, she snapped.

"Is that right? Well perhaps that's where you belong. You seem better suited to caring for dumb animals than providing any useful assistance to people."

As soon as the words left her mouth, she regretted them. Next to her Matsuko shuffled uncomfortably.

Shiori met her eyes with an unmistakable flash of anger then bowed her head.

"Apologies if I offended you, mistress. I'm unused to events such as these. Please excuse me."

Before Akira could call her back to apologise, Shiori had spun around and disappeared into the crowd beyond the security field.

Matsuko sighed. "Well, that could have gone better. Akira, I understand you're frustrated but you must remember that Shiori is in the same position as you. Maybe worse. At least you've got friends and family to support you and lend what assistance they can. Shiori has no one."

Akira felt queasy. She had lost her temper and upset the one person who would be accompanying her to Thalmos. She took a breath, steadying herself.

"She has you, Uncle," she said.

Matsuko smiled. "I help her where I can but I'm not going to be the one with her on Thalmos. You need each other's support."

His expression grew more serious. "This hasn't been easy for her, you know. Becoming part of your household. It's an intimidating prospect for someone like her."

"Why?" asked Akira.

"Why?" repeated Matsuko with an incredulous look. "Akira, you're an heir to the leader of the Kudo-kai, one of the most powerful people in the Shattered Empires and she's a servant, the daughter of a migrant, with no family left."

Akira shook her head. "I guess I've been a bit distracted. I should have paid more attention to her."

Matsuko took her hand gently. "Akira, you have great potential. You have a brilliant mind but you must learn to focus on your surroundings. Don't let the privileges of our status dull your faculties. You'll need to be sharp as a razor in your dealings with Glankor."

Akira extracted her hand and turned away. "I'm trying, Uncle. There's so much to remember though. I feel like my brain is a cup of water and anything more I pour into it is overflowing."

"It may feel that way but Shiori assures me you are coming on in leaps and bounds. She's confident you'll be ready by the time you arrive on Thalmos," Matsuko said.

He moved to stand beside her. "I have some good news. I managed to get in touch with an old contact of mine on Thalmos. If things go badly with Glankor he may be able to help you."

Akira nodded. "Who is he?"

"I'd prefer not to say unless you really need his help."

Matsuko's presence and his obvious efforts to help quieted Akira's anxiety. Recently she had begun to realise that there was much more to him than the jovial, avuncular man she had grown up knowing. She was not entirely surprised. Her father, as ruthless as he was, would not have kept Matsuko around for long if he had not been useful. Akira desperately wanted her life to have that kind of meaning. This mission, as stressful as it was, was an opportunity. If she could restore the Kudo-kai's access to the Thalmian nanotrite she could help them cling to a semblance of power for a while longer. She would make her mark. She gazed up at the flickering purple lights deep within the body of the Cloud-Medusa and felt a kernel of excitement spark within her.

"Try to think of this as an opportunity, Akira," said Matsuko, as if reading her mind. "Don't quote me on this but many of your brothers and sisters will not get the chance to do anything that is hugely worthwhile."

He waggled his prodigious eyebrows at her and she laughed.

"Before I forget. I got you a leaving gift," he said, and from the folds of his robe he brought out a beautifully carved token in jade with a silver inlay and chain.

"For me?" asked Akira.

"For Ambassador Director Akira Mukudori Kudo, envoy of the Kudo-kai and voice of Supreme Executive General Daisuke Kudo."

She took the token and traced her finger along the curves and lines of its pattern which denoted high diplomatic office.

"It's beautiful," she said.

"It's a tool," Matsuko said. "It's a means of reminding others of your status so that you don't have to. And when that fails there is this."

He reached over and depressed a tiny raised ridge along the side of the token. Its face swung open revealing a small glass globe. At the centre of the globe was a tiny black sphere.

"What is it?" Akira asked.

"Nanotrite," said Matsuko. "Enough to power a sizeable nether-jump. It's worth a very considerable amount of money. If you find yourself without any other means, I hope that this will do in a pinch."

"Do you think I'll need to pay people?" asked Akira.

"I don't know what you're going to need," said Matsuko, "but I'll be damned if it's something I could have given you and didn't."

Much later she'd remember those words and wonder if he meant them or if he had a better idea of how things would play out than he was letting on.

Chapter 11

During the War of Ages, Fornax had been one of the Kudo-kai's greatest industrial orbital stations, producing the organisation's largest and most dangerous war machines. It lay before the *Indigo Starling* now, like a great wagon wheel thousands of kilometres in diameter glinting dully in the light of the dreary red dwarf it orbited. Vast factories lined the inside of the wheel's rim where the rotation of the structure created a centripetal force akin to gravity. Hundreds of silvery threads, like spokes, ran from the outer rim to join an enormous lattice sphere at the centre. Elevators ran up and down these threads, like ruby dew drops, to the central sphere inside which the sleek shape of a nascent starship was taking form unimpeded by the constraints of gravity. Great articulated limbs twitched constantly around the inside of the lattice like the legs of some colossal insect in its death throes.

In the navigator's room of the *Indigo Starling*, Mordax watched as Fornax loomed closer. Lazarus brought the ship to a crawl and nudged them in near to the lattice sphere, searching for a docking point. Given the small mass of the station, they had been able to nether-jump practically to the doorstep.

"Printers," grunted Stephan, following Mordax's gaze to the jerky legs inside the lattice "They glue the ships together piece by tiny piece."

"It's around here somewhere, I know," Lazarus said, swivelling his head from side to side and blinking furiously. "They don't make it easy for you."

"Try over there," said Stephan, pointing to a section of the lattice. "I remember the dock being closer to the centre."

"Wait," said Mordax. "We've been here before?"

Lazarus nodded. "Yeah, cycles ago. It was only a quick trip, though, you may not remember. Some rich dehoe near the

Core wanted a super sky yacht with crazy heavy firepower. Couldn't find a yard that would handle the specs, though. So he asked us."

"Fornax isn't what it was," said Stephan, "but it can still put together Titan-class ships and doesn't ask too many questions."

To Mordax it seemed that Stephan watched the station as he would a coiled snake. His whole body was wound tightly and the brownish-red light gave his expression a strange intensity.

"Why haven't I heard of it?" asked Mordax.

Lazarus swivelled round to face Mordax. Marvin the lizard, spread lazily on Lazarus' lap, chirruped his annoyance at the sudden movement.

"They don't like the attention, right?" he said glancing at Stephan.

Stephan nodded his agreement. "There are bigger and better outfitted yards towards the Core. Fornax picks up the business that those yards won't take."

He gave a wry smile. "A less respectable type of clientele. The kind of guys that prefer a low profile."

"Who are they worried about? The Dioscuri?" Mordax asked.

"Na," said Lazarus, "the Dioscuri don't care about a few pirates getting tooled up. It's the traders who get beaten up by the pirates who would come knocking. In fact—"

A sudden beeping interrupted Lazarus and he swivelled back to face the view screen. A double row of green dots, blinking gently, had appeared on a nearby section of the lattice structure.

"Got it!" said Lazarus. "Docking in 5."

Stephan patted Lazarus on the shoulder, earning an angry hiss from Marvin.

"I'd better go check Stam's ready. Come on, Mordax."

***

Stamford could just stand upright in the *Starling*'s communal areas without stooping. However, as he explained, a man needs more than two inches of air above his head or he'll go doo-la. He therefore spent most of his time in the *Starling*'s vast cargo hold. Stamford had strung a threadbare curtain across the entrance to a shipping container near the corner of the hold and called it home. Towards the back, cargo netting fastened to each side of the container made a giant-sized hammock and shelves welded to the walls stored a variety of weapons, which comprised the majority of Stamford's possessions. Mordax watched now as Stamford ran through his familiar, pre-excursion routine. Body armour, heavier than Mordax could lift, was strapped around his torso. Old Rosie, the enormous shotgun, was secured across his back, magnet clasps allowing her to be pulled free swiftly and easily, and Stamford plucked a handful of grenades, like pebbles in his hand, from a metal box on one of the shelves.

"You expecting trouble, Dad?" asked Mordax, turning to Stephan who was packing a rucksack.

"I hope not. But trouble will be less likely with Stamford at my back."

Stamford gave Mordax a wink as he tucked the grenades into a pouch at his waist.

"So I guess, it would be OK if I came with you then?" Mordax asked.

"Mordax—" Stephan began with a sigh.

"Dad, I know you're worried about what Myla said. About the nexus and whatever. But staying on the ship isn't going to change that. I can't stay space-side for the rest of my life!"

Stephan busied himself with his back-pack until Mordax thought that he was simply going to ignore him. Just as Mordax opened his mouth to continue pleading his case, Stephan said, "I know you can't stay on the *Starling* forever, son. But this business has me worried. I'm trying to play the risks as I see them."

"It is your decision, boss," said Stamford, who had finished his preparations. "But the weedling seems to make more trouble when you leave him behind."

Stephan pinched the bridge of his nose then shook his head. "The man has a point."

He gave Mordax a long look.

"You follow my every instruction when we're down there. No wandering off."

Mordax nodded eagerly. "Yessir."

Stephan walked over to Stamford's shelves and pulled down a battered Gauss pistol and worn leather thigh holster.

"Strap this on."

Mordax swallowed his surprise, not wanting to jeopardise his father's decision to allow him along.

"What?" asked Stephan, seeing his expression.

"Nothing. It's just...You've never let me take a gun dirt side before. You know, 'if you haven't got a gun, you won't make people angry enough to use one either,'" said Mordax, quoting his father's words back at him.

"Wise words, but there's an exception to every rule," said Stephan.

As Mordax strapped the pistol to his leg, testing the flexion in his knee, he realised that for the first time his father didn't seem entirely in control. It was disconcerting. Stephan always had a plan and knew exactly where they were going. Even so, Mordax couldn't deny a twinge of excitement.

***

"Stephan! When they told me the *Indigo Starling* had docked I didn't believe them. Welcome."

The man in front of them was tall and slender with greasy hair and dirty-grey eyes that blinked too frequently. He had been waiting for them when they emerged from the elevator that had brought them from Fornax's hub to the rim.

"Hello, Sermilion," said Stephan with a smile. "You look well."

"Don't lie. I look like I've spent the last twenty cycles scratching out a living in the arse end of nowhere. You on the other hand still look magnificent. How long's it been?" As he spoke, the man's hands fidgeted ceaselessly, wringing each other and touching his face and arms.

"Must be fifteen cycles now," said Stephan.

"Too long. Too long. And Stamford. Good to see you again. I'll have to have our chairs reinforced, haw haw."

Stamford inclined his head but said nothing.

"Sorry. And who is this young man? Not Mordax, surely. My, but you were barely up to my knee when I saw you last. Look at you now. You've inherited your father's physique, you lucky thing."

Something about the man's eager smile made Mordax uneasy.

"Mordax, this is Sermilion Vandt, the administrator of Fornax. You've met once before when you were much younger," said Stephan.

"Pleasure to meet you again," said Mordax, offering his hand to shake. "You'll forgive me if I don't remember the last time."

Sermilion gave Mordax's hand a limp shake, his own hand clammy and pale.

"Haw haw, of course. Of course. It's good to see a young face around here. We don't tend to attract people in the prime of their lives to Fornax."

He turned back to Stephan.

"You're welcome here any time, my old friend, but I get the feeling you have a specific reason for visiting, hmmm?"

"Now that you mention it there are a couple of matters I would like to discuss. In private please."

"Ah, Stephan. Always business with you. You have time for a quick tour of our humble facility, surely? It would be a crime for you to come all the way out here and for Mordax not to see what we do."

Stephan gave an impatient sigh. "Yes, I suppose we could make time. Thank you."

"Excellent!" Sermilion clapped his hands together. "I have a car for us just through here."

He beckoned them through a metal doorway out into a large concrete hangar where a car, almost entirely glass like a giant bubble, was waiting for them. Once they had all crammed inside, Stamford's knees almost by his ears, the car lifted off, engines whining, and sped along a dark tunnel to one of Fornax's smelting plants. The building was vast. Not built to human proportions. They traversed the plant's innards like a microbe moving through the blood stream of some great beast. Sermilion showed them the mouth of the plant, a great opening right up against the outside edge of Fornax's rim, gaping at the stars beyond. It was here that mining ships, having matched the station's rotational velocity, fed the plant an endless stream of ore harvested from nearby asteroids.

Next he took them deeper into the plant's belly where processed metals were super-heated to create great molten lakes. They had hovered here for a time while all four of them gazed at the shifting shapes in black and orange that meandered their languid way across the lakes' surfaces until the car's temperature warning had started to sound and Sermilion whisked them onwards, braying at the nervousness in Mordax's face.

Towards the end of the tour, the car had left the plant and Sermilion had pointed out a cluster of tubes that soared skyward, running alongside the elevator shaft, which pumped the various molten metals towards the lattice shipyard, thousands of miles above them. There, as Sermilion explained, the insect-like printer arms could deposit the metals in any combination or configuration. Throughout their tour, Mordax had been aware of a certain self-consciousness in Sermilion's demeanour whenever he addressed Stephan. A kind of stiffness that suggested every movement and sentence had been carefully considered. Except for his hands. Those continued to fidget and dance as if immune to his command. Mordax had assumed that it was the natural tension of an awkward man, eager to make a good impression on an old acquaintance. Stephan appeared not to notice, gazing around with polite interest and asking questions about the operations of the plant. Finally, Sermilion had directed the car to a squat, ugly building at the very top of the plant where he kept his office. The air here tasted sharp, like burned plastic and acid. When Stephan again asked for a private word, Sermilion had led him into an office, a plush room with deep carpet and soft lighting that Mordax had only glimpsed briefly as the door swung shut behind them. Mordax and Stamford had been left to kick their heels in the waiting room watched over by two visor-clad guards.

***

The plastic chair creaked ominously as Stamford shifted his considerable weight. He seemed relaxed as always, hands folded over his thick belly. Under the faceless gaze of the two guards at the door, however, Mordax felt restless and uneasy. The waiting room was spartan in the extreme, devoid of any furnishings except the hard narrow chairs on which they sat. The concrete walls and floor and harsh strip lighting conspired to soak the life out of the air. They sat in listless silence punctuated only by the rustling of the guards shifting their grip on their rifles. One of the guards cleared his throat. The sound came out tinny through his helmet's voice amplifier. Stamford sighed deeply and closed his eyes. Mordax stood up and began to pace the room. The air hummed with a nervous energy. A few minutes later the door to Sermilion's office swung open and he and Stephan stepped out.

"—and sorry not to be more help," Sermilion was saying, running fingers through his slick hair. "I'll keep my ear to the ground though."

Stephan smiled tightly. "Much appreciated. These are dangerous times. Any advice is helpful."

"Of course. Of course. Are you sure I can't convince you to stay even a day. I'm sure that ship of yours could do with a tune up, no? On the house of course."

"Thanks, Sermilion, but we should be off."

Sermilion's sharp features twisted in a show of remorse. "As you wish, my friend. It was good to see you again after all these cycles. Come back any time. You're always welcome."

Sermilion clicked his fingers at the guards by the door. "Show our guests out please." He waved to Mordax and Stamford. "Safe travels. Our paths will cross again, I'm sure."

As the guards led them back through a dirty concrete corridor towards the elevator that would take them back to the *Starling,* a strip light flickered, strobe-like, so that they seemed to be moving in slow motion. When the attack came it was almost casual. One of the guards checked his pace dropping back behind Stamford. As the guard in front reached a security door something about his stance changed, the way his feet were set shifted. He turned, as if about to beckon them through, and the muzzle of his rifle rose almost imperceptibly. Mordax would have missed it if he hadn't been watching his father. One moment Stephan was striding along head bowed in thought, the next his eyes flicked up registering the threat and at the same time his weight shifted explosively forwards as if released from a coiled spring. Mordax had never seen him move so fast. The rifle, knocked sideways, blasted a chunk out of the wall next to Mordax's head. A sharp pain bloomed behind his ear. Stephan's arm flashed upward and a spray of crimson gusted out from the gap at the base of the guard's helmet. At almost the same moment there was a solid thunk from behind. Mordax turned to see the other guard, suddenly twenty feet away on the floor, crumpled in on himself unnaturally like a folded mannequin. Stamford pulled his fist back and grabbed the giant shotgun from its sling on his back, covering their rear.

"Wha—" managed Mordax.

"That fucking snake!" muttered Stephan, still gripping the blade that had appeared in his fist. He paused, glaring down at the faceless body of the guard. Its chest armour glistened in the flickering light, black with gore. Mordax's stomach twisted and he swallowed hard to keep from retching.

"Stam, keep watching our back," Stephan said.

Stamford grunted his acknowledgement. Stephan tapped the comm device at his neck.

"Lazarus."

A short pause. "Howdy Cap'n," came the answer through their ear buds.

"We need to scoot and fast. Mark our co-ordinates. Bring the *Starling* in on top of us. Careful, it could be a hot exit."

"Aye, aye."

The line cut out.

"What the hell's going on?" Mordax asked.

Stephan stepped close to him and gripped his shoulder hard. His father's blue eyes were lit with a fierce intensity.

"I shouldn't have brought you down here, Mordax."

"Dad, it...it's OK, but—"

"I misjudged the situation. I thought Sermilion would have information about the missing haulers but he's mixed up in this thing somehow," Stephan sighed. "He's scared too. He tried to cover it but he is. And when someone like Sermilion is scared..."

"I don't understand," said Mordax. "What is he mixed up in?"

Stephan shook his head. "We have to move. I'll explain when we're back on the *Starling*." He narrowed his eyes and touched the side of Mordax's head. Mordax yelped in pain and was surprised to see his father's fingers come away crimson.

Stephan grunted. "It's deep. We'll get you patched up on the *Starling*."

Stephan bent over the body of the guard whose throat he'd slit again and grabbed his hand. Before Mordax knew what was happening, Stephan had made a few quick, expert slices into the man's wrist until the arm fell to the floor leaving Stephan holding his severed hand. Mordax's stomach churned again and this time he couldn't stop himself vomiting against the wall. He closed his eyes and swallowed against the acid burn in his throat. Stephan pressed the severed hand against the sensor by the security door which slid open.

"The elevators will be shut down," he said. "We have to get to the roof."

Looking back, the journey to the roof was a nightmarish blur to Mordax with only snatches of clarity. He supposed he must have been in shock. They encountered many more guards before finally reaching the exit. Mordax remembered Rosie's deep bellow reverberating in his chest as Stamford cut swathes through those they encountered, blood misting over mangled corpses. He remembered watching in gruesome fascination as his father glided round corners on silent feet, slipping into crowds of visored men and laying waste with his blade before any could sound an alarm. He remembered his trembling hand cramping around the grip of his pistol, slick with sweat, even though he hadn't fired a shot.

Before long they stepped through a door onto the concrete roof, bare aside from the occasional boxy shape of a ventilation unit. The vast curve of Fornax's rim, boiling with the activity of its colony of machines, soared upwards in front of them until it was lost in the sky's haze. The *Starling* was hovering at the far end of the roof, hot air from its thrusters causing the view beneath to shimmer and distort. Its open cargo door promised safety and a welcome end to their bloody journey. They began to jog across the concrete, Stephan leading the way. They were not quite halfway across when what felt like a tree trunk knocked into Mordax's back and pinned him to the floor. Almost immediately a streak of crackling electric blue appeared in the air just above him and the caustic scent of ozone burned his nostrils. The corner of one of the big ventilation units up ahead suddenly sloughed away from the rest of the unit, dripping gold where the plasma beam had melted through the metal. Twisting around, Mordax realised that it was Stamford's arm that was pinning him to the ground as the giant lay flat beside him. If Stamford hadn't knocked him down, the plasma beam would have cut him in half. Peering over Stamford's arm, Mordax saw the profile of a scorpion-class interceptor rising inexorably above the level of the roof. The plasma guns on either wing glinted brown, like dried blood, in the light of the sun.

"Up!" shouted Stephan, springing to his feet.

Mordax scrambled up and lurched forwards, quivering legs threatening to betray him. Stephan reached into a pouch at his waist and flung a handful of dark metal orbs behind them. No sooner had the orbs left his hand than each one split into a multitude of tiny buzzing drones. The drones sped away from the trio, arranging themselves into a grid pattern stretching almost the width of the roof. Without warning a number of drones exploded into puffs of viscous smoke immediately creating a billowing dark wall, blocking out their view of the hostile ship completely. A second later, the remaining drones flared into points of brilliant white light and began zipping around inside the smoke, apparently at random.

"Quick," shouted Stephan. "That'll fool their targeting systems but not for long."

Mordax sprinted after his father with Stamford's great lumbering presence at his back. The *Starling* was still agonisingly far when blue spears of plasma began shooting past them again. The ship seemed to be firing at random through the cloud of smoke. As the beams grew dangerously close, sizzling through the air, Stephan spun around.

"We're not going to make it. Get him back to the ship, Stam," he shouted above the roar of the approaching ship's thrusters as he dropped to one knee.

Stamford grabbed Mordax by the arm, tugging him onwards.

"Wait," said Mordax resisting. "No, Dad!"

Stephan glanced back at him and a small sad smile twisted his lips. Then he turned and sighted along his rifle as the prow of the ship broke through the smoke.

"No. We're not leaving you. No!"

Stamford hoisted Mordax off his feet and slung him over his back like a sack of corn, long legs eating up the remaining distance to the *Starling*. Mordax yelled, beating futilely against Stamford's back. He could only watch as Stephan flicked a switch and a tiny rocket hissed out of the rifle's under carriage and sped towards the ship. Pinprick flares erupted from the top of the ship in a shower of brilliance and it banked sharply sideways. The rocket, fooled by the countermeasures, slipped harmlessly to one side. A second later, Stephan loosed another rocket. This time he kept the sight to his eye and in the haze left by the dissipating smoke, Mordax could see the wispy thread of a laser linking his father's gun and the dark hull of the interceptor. Again the ship loosed its swarm of flares, like burning locusts, and twisted out of the path of the rocket. This time, however, the rocket's tiny thruster sparked and it adjusted its course, guided by Stephan's hand. Mordax watched as it streaked towards one wing of the ship and then the scene disappeared in a burst of white light that burned his eyes and seemed to punch through the back of his head. A second later, a blast of scalding air tore at his cheeks and he felt Stamford stagger underneath him. When he opened his eyes again, black spots swam across his vision. One spot seemed to be moving with particular urgency. Blinking furiously, the spot coalesced into the shape of his father who had dropped the rifle and was sprinting after them. The familiar curves of the *Starling* now loomed in his peripheral vision as Stamford pounded up the cargo ramp. For a moment it looked as though Stephan would reach them, legs pumping furiously. Then there was a flash of blue and his stride faltered. Rising out of the ash and fire left by the rocket, the interceptor rose, one broken wing hanging uselessly and its thrusters screaming sickly.

Mordax found the pistol in his hand and unthinkingly began firing round after round over Stamford's back at the hovering reaper. Absently he could hear himself screaming. His father had slowed to a crouched lurch. A raw blackened gouge had been seared into his side by the edge of the plasma beam. He was close enough that Mordax could see no fear touched his eyes. Instead they were focussed on Mordax, showing only a grim determination. Another flash of blue and a smoking hole appeared in the centre of Stephan's chest. The light went out of his eyes, his legs collapsed beneath him and he fell. The door of the cargo bay slid shut cutting out Mordax's view of the nightmare but not the suffocating disbelief that gripped him. Distantly, he felt Stamford lower him gently to the floor.

"I'm sorry, boy," Stamford whispered.

Mordax didn't know how long he lay there, face pressed against the cool floor. Time had taken on a strange amorphous quality. He was conscious only of snapshots of recollection. The shadow of the interceptor creeping across the concrete roof. His father's twisted face as the lance of plasma erupted from his chest. Eventually he became aware of a distant booming. A lifetime spent living on the *Starling* had sensitised Mordax to its rhythms, the deep thrum of its engines and regular, healthy tickings of life support systems. The staccato reverberations that he now felt through the floor of the cargo deck signified something gravely wrong, enough to bring him back to himself. He was alone. With an effort he got to his feet and shambled through the *Starling*'s corridors which now felt cold and empty. When he reached the navigator's room, however, he found panic. Lazarus, jacked in, was tapping frantically at the controls while Stamford hovered at his shoulder. The viewscreen showed they had moved away from Fornax's outer rim and were speeding up alongside one of the elevator shafts towards the lattice structure at the centre. In the rear view towards the bottom of the display, the broken-winged interceptor had been joined by two more, racing after the *Starling* and gaining on them gradually. The blue fire of plasma bursts erupted from all three coinciding with a desperate tearing sound of fatigued metal.

"They're overloading the shields," shouted Lazarus.

"How long until the nether-drive spins up?" asked Stamford.

"Three minutes at least."

Stamford shook his bald head. "Too long. Can you lose them in there?" He pointed to the lattice structure.

"That's where they came from. There may be more in there."

Both fell silent. They realised this was the end. Another flurry of plasma and a shrill alarm warned them that the hull was breached. Mordax dream-walked to Lazarus' side. Lazarus met his gaze with resigned eyes.

"Mordax. I'm sorry—"

Almost in a daze Mordax tapped the manual controls at Lazarus' station. He brought up control of the nether-drives. One displayed a broken green circle, close to fully charged but not quite close enough. He selected the back up drive...and ejected it.

"WHAT ARE YOU DOING?" screamed Lazarus, grabbing his wrist.

Stamford's eyes grew wide. The energy required by a nether-drive to punch through to the netherverse was immense. A ruptured drive, expelling its energy all at once, would devastate an area thousands of kilometres in all directions.

"Kill the thrusters, Laz," Mordax said quietly.

Lazarus just stared at him, mouth agape.

"DO IT!" shouted Mordax. The unexpected authority in his voice snapped Lazarus into motion and he reduced the engine power to zero.

"Keep that drive between them and us."

Understanding dawned on the faces of the other two. The plasma bursts had ceased.

"If they'd shot that drive—" began Lazarus.

"They didn't," said Mordax, "and they won't risk a shot now."

Stamford gave Mordax a concerned look. The alarms took on a more urgent tone, clamouring for attention.

"Multiple hull breaches aft," said Lazarus.

"I will deal with the breaches," Stamford rumbled. "You two get us out of here."

He left the navigator's office at a jog. On the view screen the three interceptors had stopped dead, maintaining their distance from the *Starling* as if unsure of their next move. The broken green circle representing the nether drive's charge crept closer to full.

"Look!" said Lazarus, while magnifying the view from up ahead. Hundreds of tiny drones were streaming out of the lattice sphere and speeding towards them like a swarm of silver flies.

"Wow," said Lazarus wide eyed. "Assembly drones. Never seen so many."

"They're dangerous?" asked Mordax

"Oh yeah. They'll tear us to pieces in seconds," Lazarus said, nodding.

A numbness had spread throughout Mordax's chest. This last hour couldn't have been real, could it? At the thought of his father, he sensed the tidal wave of grief rearing up within him. He knew that if he let it, it would overwhelm him, crushing him beneath its weight. As the drones bore down on them the green circle on the display panel closed. Lazarus engaged the drive and the *Starling* folded itself into the blackness of netherspace.

Chapter 12

Akira tilted her face to the setting sun and let the last of its heat wash over her. A gentle breeze tousled her hair. In other circumstances she would have found this moment intensely relaxing. The trilling of forest songbirds, the sighing of the wind and the rustling of leaves below her were a welcome change from the dense chaos of central Ang'Dirth. She stood now on the moss-carpeted platform of an ancient landing pad suspended high above the forest canopy. The landing pad jutted out from a husk of verdant creepers that had almost entirely enveloped a glass tower. The odd glints of orange, reflections of the setting sun, were all that revealed the structure beneath.

Akira could not relax though. She stood here, on the decrepit fringes of old Ang'Dirth, only because a few hours earlier her father had sent a message ordering her to take an air car to this spot. Only Xif, who hovered silently at her shoulder, had been allowed to accompany her. Akira had no idea what the purpose of this trip was but as she was due to leave for Thalmos the next day, it could only be to do with that. She gazed around at the sweeping canopy below, sharp metallic angles of ancient structures peeking out of the foliage like the tips of far-off mountains breaking through soft green cloud.

"What was this place, Xif?"

"It was known as St Yerid district. An industrial area during the empire. After the Purge, the factories were closed and the district abandoned."

"I wonder why father sent us here. No word on who we're meeting?"

"No. Not that I would be told anyway."

Xif had been in a sulk since discovering he was being sent to Thalmos along with Akira. It would have been annoying if Akira didn't understand exactly how he felt.

She glanced at him side-long.

"Poor old Xif," she teased, "maybe they're worried your circuits are degrading and you can't be trusted with sensitive information anymore."

Xif buzzed with annoyance.

"'Circuits' is an incredibly crude way of describing my processing matrix. And it has been functioning perfectly for thousands of cycles longer than you've been alive, girl."

Akira smiled and bowed with mock deference. "My apologies, O aged one. We mortals of flesh and bone forget our place."

Xif harumphed but Akira could tell he was amused. They waited in silence for a while longer until Xif suddenly turned in the air in the direction of central Ang'Dirth.

"Something coming?" asked Akira, an unwelcome flutter of anticipation filling her chest.

"Hold on," snapped Xif. "This doesn't make any sense."

"What is it?"

"It's— It's your father."

Akira gasped. As far as she was aware, since acceding to head of the Kudo-kai her father had not left the Citadel once. A dark shape coalesced out of the pastel hues of the evening sky and grew rapidly larger as it sped towards them. The matt black car seemed to absorb the light around it and a chill bit the air as it floated down towards them, settling its weight silently onto the cushion of moss. The door of the air car swung upwards and Daisuke Kudo stepped out. He was not a tall man but his evening shadow loomed long. His black eyes were fixed on Akira as he approached. The dark suit he wore was crisply pressed and his shoes shone incongruously next to the foliage around them. Daisuke stopped a few paces from Akira. She bowed her head, waiting to be addressed.

"Daughter."

"Good evening, Father."

"How are your preparations coming along?"

"Well, I hope. Xif is a good teacher."

Daisuke grunted, eyeing the drone at her shoulder then turned to face the last rays of the sun's golden crescent.

"It's been many cycles since I have seen a real sunset."

"Isn't it dangerous to be out of the Citadel, Father?"

"Perhaps. But sometimes taking a risk is necessary."

She felt a weight behind his words.

"You're wondering why I asked you here," Daisuke said.

Akira said nothing. It would be presumptuous for her to question her father openly even though she could barely contain her curiosity.

"Look around, Akira. What do you see?"

She blinked. "I see the forest, Father. I see...abandoned buildings."

"You see nothing then."

Akira felt the sting of his disappointment but didn't know what else to say.

"This place is the carcass of our family's empire. The shrivelled, dead heart of a once truly supreme beast."

He gestured towards an area particularly dense with crumbling buildings.

"That was a nanotrite refinery. Back then, we possessed the means to generate it ourselves. Our refineries powered our fleets for thousands of cycles and enabled us to conquer nearly half the galaxy. They were some of the first targets during the Purge." His voice was as cold as cut glass.

"The Dioscuri obliterated our industry. After the nanotrite refineries they destroyed the great orbital databanks, snuffing out millennia of knowledge and learning and within a few cycles sending us back to the dark ages. They assassinated anyone who might have been able to recreate that knowledge. A bonfire of our brightest and most brilliant minds."

Her father's face was even but Akira noticed with a start that his hands were quivering with rage. She had never seen Daisuke express any emotion stronger than disdain. The sight made her almost nauseous with unease. Without being asked, Xif projected a hologram overlayed onto the vista below. Suddenly the ruined structure began to piece itself back together. A vast dome rose up out of the trees with tiny glowing figures bustling in and out. Akira realised she was looking at the building as it had once been. Towers at intervals around the dome soared upwards, heedless of the forest canopy that would mark their graves in the future. A stream of ghostly haulers filed in and out of the great structure like a line of ants connecting it with the sky. It took her breath away.

"The fuel, Akira," Daisuke said. "Without it the empire couldn't function. And now we're losing the meagre source we have left."

He turned to face her and Xif abruptly cut the projection. The grand edifice faded away to nothing.

"I have spent cycles trying to claw this family back from the brink of obscurity. Forging trade relationships, building up our reserves. All the while stuck beneath the suffocating influence of the Dioscuri. Never sure when our efforts to grow and spread prosperity will be deemed to have crossed that invisible line and our representatives executed.

"We still lose people to the Dioscuri?" asked Akira. She was surprised.

Daisuke's lip curled. "Think, girl. Would I spend my life closeted in the Citadel if the Dioscuri were not a threat?"

"But who have they killed? And why?"

Daisuke paused. "What do you do when confronted with an enemy more powerful than yourself?"

Akira's answer was automatic, a product of cycles of lessons in military strategy. "You retreat and regroup."

"And then?"

"You engage on your own terms. You probe for weaknesses."

Daisuke nodded approvingly. "It's the same with the Dioscuri. We have sent thousands of agents, ambassadors, politicians to all corners of the Shattered Empires. We have consistently pushed at the boundaries of what they allow. Probing their weaknesses. Every time an agent of ours is killed we have the chance to learn more. About how they operate and where. Once we have enough data then it will be time to push back. To throw off the yoke that has stifled expansion and innovation for a millennium."

Akira felt a tingle of excitement as her father, the leader of the Kudo-kai, entrusted her with his plans.

"We're getting close, Akira. But this episode with Thalmos could threaten everything this family has worked towards for generations. Despite all our agents we can't work out who the Thalmians are selling their nanotrite to now. You need to find out. It's the key to understanding why they've cut us off."

Akira felt the weight of his expectation settle over her.

"I understand, Father."

His black eyes studied her intently. "I hope so. I arranged this meeting so that you would appreciate the stakes at play. If you don't succeed, all of this, the Citadel, Ang'Dirth, our family's cumulative efforts over the last century, will be for nothing. Without nanotrite, the lifeblood of our operations, we'll shrivel and die as surely as I'm standing here now."

Akira swallowed hard. Daisuke turned back to look at the last rays of daylight.

"Our ambassadors to Thalmos are dead," he said flatly.

"What?" said Akira before she could help herself.

"Did I mumble?" Daisuke said.

"No. Sorry, Father. It's just...I thought they'd been imprisoned."

"A lie to protect our egos. It's unthinkable that anyone would murder a Kudo-kai envoy let alone one of our closest trading partners. So we choose not to think it. You must be above such self-serving delusions, however. You must see things the way they truly are."

"So Glankor really does want to permanently cut ties with us," Akira said, heart thudding as she realised the consequences.

"It appears so."

"What's to stop him executing me on sight then?" she said.

"Why nothing, of course. Except your wits."

It suddenly seemed as if she was looking at her father down a very long tunnel. Her vision seemed edged in black and his voice sounded distant. Daisuke gave her a contemptuous look.

"I've been too gentle with you," he said.

Akira said nothing.

"We exist only to ensure the survival of the family," he said. "I've tried to ensure this lesson was instilled in you but perhaps your tutors could have been more robust."

"Or perhaps you could have tried teaching me yourself instead of palming me off on a succession of anaemic academics," Akira snapped.

She bit her tongue, shocking herself with her outburst. She expected her father to rail against her for her impudence but instead he only frowned slightly.

"You may be right. Perhaps I should have. I know I haven't been much of a father to you. To be perfectly frank, it isn't really in my nature. But I have tried to ensure that you were surrounded by people who could give you the attention you needed. If that was a mistake, there's nothing that can be done about it now. It's up to you whether to shoulder the responsibility or crumble beneath its weight and bring shame to the family."

Her father's dark eyes were fixed on hers and she realised that searching for any paternal affection there was like looking for a candle in the black depths of the ocean. She straightened her back defiantly. She didn't need his affection, or his approval for that matter. But she wouldn't show him weakness.

"I understand the stakes," she said, "and I accept the responsibility. I'll find out why Glankor has cut us off or I'll die trying."

She would remember the glint of satisfaction in her father's eyes at those words for the rest of her life.

Chapter 13

It felt as though a tiny sliver of metal had needled its way into his brain. A mote of discomfort in the otherwise warm shroud of darkness. Mordax tried weakly to resist but it possessed a kind of gravity that pulled him inexorably towards it. As he drew closer the discomfort became pain and an undulating wail began to form. He recognised the sound. It meant danger. Adrenalin flooded his system, quickening his heartbeat and dragging him, unwilling, to consciousness. Mordax's eyelids fluttered open. Strange shadows cast by dim red emergency lanterns made the navigator's office unrecognisable for a second. The acrid tang of burned plastic filled the air. He peeled his face off the metal grating floor and pushed himself to a sitting position. A spasm of nausea wracked his body and he clutched at the wall, keeping himself upright until it subsided. A whistling sound, as if Stamford were boiling a kettle for his sweet tea, was coming from somewhere. Mordax examined himself for injuries. His body was tender with bruises and scrapes. There was a new gash on his temple where he had hit the floor and the blood that covered the side of his face was still wet. He pinched the bridge of his nose trying simultaneously to stop the room from spinning and recall what had happened. They had been in netherspace. He remembered Lazarus frantically describing the damage to the *Starling*. He remembered a cataclysmic bang, a roaring wind and then nothing. Mordax lurched to his feet and stumbled over to the chair where Lazarus was sprawled unconscious. Marvin was on his lap, head buried in the gap between his hip and the seat, whole body trembling.

"Laz," said Mordax, shaking his bony shoulder.

No response. Mordax shook harder "Laz! Wake up."

Abruptly Lazarus' eyes opened.

"WHERE AM I? WHO THE FUCK ARE YOU?" he shouted.

"Laz, it's me. Relax."

"Mordax?"

"Yeah. You're OK."

"What happened?"

"I was hoping you'd tell me."

"The last thing I remember was the hull breach..."

Mordax was suddenly conscious again of the soft whistling he had heard earlier.

"Oh shit," he said, "we're holed. Check our O2."

Lazarus' eyelids flickered as he jacked back into the ship's system.

"Barshamin's dick, you're right. We're A-grade fucked. Losing O2 fast."

Mordax had a sudden vision of his and Lazarus's frozen corpses floating silently in the darkened room. He followed the whistling sound towards the back of the room. A quick search revealed a large hole in the hull about two fingers wide, partially blocked by Marvin's metal water bowl. They must have lost so much air initially that he and Lazarus passed out. If Marvin's bowl had not got sucked into the hole, the room's ventilation system wouldn't have been able to replace the air quickly enough and they never would have woken up. From a bracket next to the door he took down an emergency patch kit. He extracted a plastic disc with a handle that felt disconcertingly flimsy and a heavy aerosol can. From the can he sprayed a thick coating of plas-steel resin over the surface of the disc, whipped Marvin's bowl away from the hole and slammed the disc over it. Immediately the whistling stopped.

"Good job, kid," Lazarus called over his shoulder. "Pressure loss has slowed."

He paused for a moment.

"We're still losing air though. Fuck!" He slammed his fist against the arm of the seat, earning a startled croak from

Marvin. Lazarus' eyes flickered again and the view on the large screen switched to the back of the ship. A cascade of glittering diamonds poured into view. Both of them recognised a cloud of crystallised air when they saw one. It was terrifyingly beautiful. The cloud was growing larger every second, spewing out from a fissure in the hull in a powerful jet.

"Where is that?" asked Mordax.

"Med-bay," said Lazarus. "I can't isolate it from the rest of the ship. The air locks are damaged."

"Stamford," Mordax whispered.

"I— I can't reach him," Lazarus said. "He was headed towards the cargo hold when it blew."

An icy ball of dread dropped into Mordax's belly. He couldn't lose Stamford too.

"How long have we got?" Mordax asked.

"About ten minutes before ship-wide levels reach critical," said Lazarus.

Mordax peered at the view screen which displayed the bright sweep of the galaxy's spiral arm.

"Where are we?"

"I have no fucking idea," sighed Lazarus. "Stephan must have keyed in the destination without telling me before you guys left for Fornax."

The mention of his father caused Mordax's breath to catch in his throat. Lazarus nudged the nose of the *Starling* around so that the stars on the view screen shifted to the right. A widening crescent appeared on the screen. A planet. Scarlet and purple swirled together in whorls across its surface. Mordax's gut tightened at the sight. It was not the blue and white of a habitable planet.

"Why would Dad have brought us here?" Mordax asked.

"Seriously, kid. We've got ten minutes 'til we breathe our last. If I knew I'd have said something by now," said Lazarus.

"There must be something out there," Mordax said, examining the view of the planet. "Some reason he would have brought us here. You've run a sensor sweep?"

"Of course. There's a habitable planet in the system but it'd take too long to get there on boosters and the nether drive can't spin up for another jump in time."

Mordax shook his head, trying to clear the fog from his battered brain.

"No. We would have jumped out next to the other planet if that's where Dad was trying to take us. Have you scanned this planet?"

Lazarus peered at him. "Are you kidding? Look at that thing. There's nothing alive down there."

"Scan it, Laz."

Lazarus blew his cheeks out but closed his eyes and ran the scan.

"Well, goddamn. How about that," Lazarus said after a moment.

"What is it?"

A regular, high-pitched ringing intersected with three low white-sound pulses filled the room. Mordax's heart fluttered.

"It's a beacon," Mordax said.

"Don't get your hopes up yet," Lazarus growled. "The signal's weak. It might just be some research probe. Let's give them a holler and see if anyone's awake down there."

Lazarus pinged a tight comm beam in the direction of the beacon. They waited a few precious seconds but there was no response. Mordax chewed the inside of his cheek, thinking. Stephan must have had a powerful reason to bring them here and not tell Lazarus about it. It was ironic, he thought bitterly, that his faith in his father's decisions seemed stronger now than when he was alive.

"Take us down there, Laz," Mordax said.

The mantle of authority settled too easily on his shoulders and he felt a pang of self-loathing. Lazarus heaved a sigh.

"Alright. It's gonna be bumpy though. Really fucking bumpy."

"What do you mean?" asked Mordax.

By way of an answer, Lazarus interposed the beacon's location on the view screen and plotted the optimal descent course towards it. The course flashed up on the screen as a glowing green line that corkscrewed its way down into the atmosphere. Lazarus magnified the view and the planet's texture came into focus. The area around the beacon coalesced into a broiling vortex of maroons.

"That is the mother of all storms," said Lazarus, a note of awe in his voice.

A shiver traced its way across Mordax's back as he stared at the seething maelstrom. Crackling flashes of lightning danced in its depths, tendrils of light forking like the branches of a dead tree, throwing into relief the dark eye at the storm's centre.

"Can the *Starling* handle that?" Mordax asked, conscious that the ship was barely hanging together.

"She'll have to. We haven't exactly got any other options," muttered Lazarus.

He activated the thrusters and the *Starling* accelerated along the glowing green re-entry line. Mordax stumbled to a crash couch and strapped himself in. The smart gel oozed around his body, moulding itself to him. As they reached the planet's stratosphere, the *Starling* began to judder ominously. Distantly he heard the bone-deep groan of rending metal as the tortured ship was battered further by the planet's thick atmospheric gases.

As the turbulence buffeted them, the ship veered from its course and the computer continually recalculated the optimal re-entry line so that it appeared to ripple and twist like a snake in its death throes. Mordax knew that if they veered too far from the line, there would be no course that *Starling* could follow which would bring them to their destination before their air ran out. Lazarus's face was contorted in concentration and his eyes flickered beneath their lids as he did everything he could do to keep the ship on its trajectory. Great chunks of hail began to slam into the *Starling*'s hull, echoing through the ship like giant's footsteps. Gradually out of the gloom, a deeper darkness began to solidify. In seconds the top of a mountain speared past them barely missing the *Starling*'s underside. The re-entry line now had a visible termination point, a faint light in the side of another swiftly approaching mountain. As they grew closer the point blossomed into a ring of orange lights, a landing tunnel which Lazarus deftly decelerated the ship into. The last thing Mordax saw before they were swallowed by the mountain side was the steely glint of two rail guns tracking them in.

***

Mordax was already unbuckling his harness as he felt the stabilising thrusters settle the *Starling*'s mass smoothly onto the hangar floor. He hobbled over to Lazarus, sodden with sweat.

"What is this place, Laz?" Mordax asked.

"No idea," said Lazarus. "You see those rail guns though? Something very fucking weird is going on." Mordax opened a comm-link to the engine room.

"Hey, Doc."

"Baby, what in god's name is going on out there?" said Virzda. "Did you eject one of my nether cores?"

"Er, yeah. Sorry. I sort of had to."

A low whistle came through the comm. "Wowee sugar. Your papa is gonna be pissed. Where is he anyhow?"

"I—" Mordax choked on the words.

Seeing his distress, Lazarus stepped in. "We'll explain everything in a minute, Virzda. Do you want to come to the nav room?"

"No!" said Mordax. "Stay where you are, Doc. We'll come to you."

He killed the comm-link. Lazarus looked at him questioningly.

"We don't know what's out there. I don't want the Doc wandering the corridors until we've figured that out. The engine room's still locked down, right? She's safe there. Any sign of Stamford?"

"No word from him on comms yet," muttered Lazarus.

"OK, we'll take a look for him once we figure out where we are." Lazarus switched on the *Starling*'s outer hull lights. On the view screen, twin beams pierced the gloom revealing a vast hanger and the gleaming silver curves of countless other starships. Whatever operation was going on here, it was huge. But the bustle that would usually be expected even on a small science station was absent. There were no maintenance drones clambering over the skins of the ships, no people loading or unloading cargo. The sinister quiet grated Mordax's nerves. He was peering at the screen trying to work out what would require a hangar this size, when a thunderous crash reverberated through the ship.

"What the hell?" said Mordax.

"The hull's just been breached. Again!" said Lazarus. "We're turning into a fucking sponge."

The memory of his father's face, light snatched from his eyes, came to Mordax unbidden. He fought hard to quell his rising panic.

"Let's go take a look," he said

Marvin gave an angry croak as Lazarus hauled himself up and dumped the lizard unceremoniously back on the seat. Together Mordax and Lazarus stepped tentatively into the gangway that led out of the navigator's office and then into the mess hall. It was empty.

A bench with an embroidered seat ran the length of the dining table. Mordax rushed to it. He ran his forefinger along the rough wood of the underside of the bench's front face until he felt the switch. The seat popped open with a clink revealing an alcove filled to the brim with gleaming weaponry in neat stacks. Stephan called guns the resort of the chronically unimaginative, but had still seen it as a sensible precaution to keep caches of weapons dotted around the *Starling*. Mordax pulled out a plasma rifle, quickly checking the charge and then slung the rifle's strap over his shoulder. He began to pull another rifle but when he glanced back, Lazarus was staring wide eyed at the dark entrance to the corridor beyond the mess hall. His face glistened with a sheen of sweat, and goosebumps stood out on his willowy forearms. Mordax swore inwardly. The hull breach, an uncontrolled conduit from the *Starling* to whatever lay in the station's hangar, would be causing his agoraphobia to flare up. He slid the second gun back into its setting and swung the seat shut.

"Laz, wait here. I'll go check out what's going on."

Lazarus nodded gratefully and slid onto the seat. Mordax hoisted the rifle to his shoulder and crept forward towards the corridor, which was shrouded in darkness. Whatever had blown the new hole in the hull must have knocked out the lights too. He flicked on the rifle's torch but the darkness seemed to swallow the beam. He edged forward, keeping the muzzle level. The sounds of the ship confirmed the injuries it had received. The rhythmic hum of the engine's core was drowned out by a metallic groaning of de-pressurising pipes and the wet rasping of filters struggling to cope with smoke and moisture. Steam was rushing out of a vent a few metres ahead of him, the grey vapour swirling upwards in the beam of his torch, obscuring his vision. As Mordax moved further in he noticed what looked like a red firefly dancing in the steam, flickering this way and that. For a few seconds he stood still and just watched it, mesmerised, his brain finding nowhere to place it within his frame of reference. The firefly suddenly stopped dead in the air. A large whorl of steam bloomed out behind it and Mordax simultaneously realised the firefly was actually a thin beam of red light and that the beam was centred on his chest. His brain finally caught up with his eyes. It was a laser sight. Suddenly his right shoulder exploded in white hot pain. He managed to withstand the agony for a precious second, enough to tighten his index finger, curled around the rifle's trigger, firing a single ball of plasma that sped off into the gloom. The pain was too much, however, and the rifle slipped from his hand, clattering to the floor. His discomfort was short-lived as a numbing sensation quickly radiated out of his shoulder spreading around his body. When it reached his legs, they folded nervelessly beneath him until he collapsed to a sitting position against the wall.

A dark figure emerged from the cloud of steam, clad in black robes and a silvery mask of some kind of cloth covering its face. The figure moved with a powerful, feminine grace, like a prowling panther. She cocked her head and seemed to regard Mordax thoughtfully, although it was impossible to tell behind the mask.

Mordax summoned all the will he could and tried to grab at the fallen rifle. All he managed to achieve was a twitching of his arm. Seeing his movement, the figure brought the butt of her rifle down towards his head in a sweeping arc. An explosion of light and then darkness engulfed him.

Chapter 14

Sermilion Vandt settled himself into the plush armchair behind his desk with a sigh. Two well-muscled guards, visors covering their faces and rifles held with well-practised ease, stood behind him on either side. The man opposite watched him with black, dispassionate eyes. Sermilion seemed at ease, slouched in the chair, although the fingers of one hand rapped a continuous staccato rhythm on the desk's surface.

"I wasn't expecting you again so soon," said Sermilion, a wide smile on his face that didn't touch his eyes.

"Needs must, I'm afraid, Mr Vandt," replied the man. "We received your message."

"I hardly see how my message required you to make a trip all the way out here," said Sermilion.

Sermilion's gaze danced over the man's face, as if searching for something that wasn't there. The man could almost hear the oily ticking of Sermilion's devious mind hard at work trying to calculate the best outcome for himself. The effort was in vain, of course. It amused him.

"You were instructed to find out what L'Amfour knew and destroy the *Starling*," the man said.

"I found out as much as I could but Stephan was always a cagey one. I think, considering the circumstances, the outcome was a reasonable one. You are aware, no doubt, of Stephan's history and his particular skill set. He's dead. That's what matters surely."

The man sighed and rose from his seat, the guards' visored faces following his movements closely. He walked to a plate-glass window that overlooked the huge smelting vats hundreds of feet below and the buzzing lines of worker drones ferrying materials back and forth. Light from the sea of molten metal cast the office in a warm orange glow.

"I'd like to tell you a story, if I may, Mr Vandt. A parable from Old Earth."

Sermilion shrugged and gestured for him to continue.

"There was once a farmer who had worked hard for many cycles and accumulated a great flock of animals. He was old and his back was weak so he gave the flock to his son to look after. Winter was approaching and with it would come wolves, following the wild migrating herds. The farmer's flock was surrounded by a ditch but he knew that a sturdy fence would be better protection for a flock of their size."

"I really don't see the relevance..." said Sermilion.

"Indulge me, Mr Vandt. The farmer told his son to build one before winter arrived. His son was a fickle man, however, cursed with a streak of laziness. He put off the hard work needed and suddenly winter was upon them. The son pondered long and hard until, in a moment of inspiration, he realised that he didn't need to spend weeks building the fence. Instead he widened the ditch and piled up the soil into a steep wall. That would keep the wolves out, he thought. The ditch and earthen wall worked well for many weeks until one night there was a great storm. The rain poured down and the wind howled through the trees. The earthen wall grew so sodden that it collapsed into the ditch. The wolves came then. The ditch was no longer deep enough to keep them out. The next morning the farmer's son arrived to find the ravaged carcasses of his father's flock littering the field."

The man finished and continued to gaze out of the window.

"Well, a most interesting tale," said Sermilion, his voice tinged with impatience. "I am still none the wiser about the purpose of your visit, however."

The man turned back to face Sermilion. Lit from beneath the man's usually nondescript features took on an ominous aspect. His eyes seemed to glitter red in darkly shadowed sockets.

"There are lessons to be learned in tales such as these, Mr Vandt. For example, one might surmise from the story I have just related that a job half-done is worse than a job not done at all, let alone a job done properly."

"Stephan L'Amfour is dead. Any threat to your operation has been neutralised. I fail to see the reason for such melodramatic concern. Let's remember that your employer needs me."

The man continued to regard Sermilion impassively.

"Mr L'Amfour senior may be dead but what of the crew? What did they know?" he said.

Sermilion waved his hand dismissively then continued his impatient tapping. "Our recordings show the *Indigo Starling* was so badly damaged when it nether-jumped that it probably didn't make it to a shipyard. Even if it did, his son is a scared little boy. They are probably cowering in some back-alley system resigned to trading worthless junk to the end of their days."

"The *Indigo Starling* has just arrived at Eloth," said the man in an even tone.

Sermilion's face grew pale.

"And you're wrong, Mr Vandt. My employer needs your station. Not you."

"You're threatening me? On my own station?" said Sermilion.

His voice was outraged but a thin sheen of sweat had appeared on his upper lip.

"It's not your station anymore, Mr Vandt."

The man glanced at the guard at Sermilion's right shoulder who immediately snaked a thick arm around his neck. Sermilion, eyes bulging, pulled a thin needle from the folds of his clothing and made to stab at the arm throttling him. His wrist was caught by the second guard and smashed into the desk so that the needle fell from his broken fingers. Sermilion's free hand scrabbled vainly at the meaty forearm at his throat. The first guard gave a sudden twist. Sermilion's neck popped and his scrabbling hand fell limp, still at last. The man turned back to the window, watching as the machines continued about their business, indifferent to their owner's demise.

Chapter 15

"There really is nothing that rouses a crowd like a noble hero going off to war. Especially when that hero is the beautiful young daughter of the nation's leader."

Maerus gazed out at the crowds as their open-topped car sped at low altitude along the verdant boulevard that led from the Citadel to Ang'Dirth's main spaceport. Thousands of people carpeted the street, cheering and waving flags.

"I'm not a hero, Maerus, and I'm certainly not going off to war," said Akira as she waved half-heartedly to the people below.

"Minor details, darling. And they certainly don't care. Just listen to them. Besides, are you not at least on a heroic quest to free our poor, unjustly imprisoned ambassadors from the barbaric Thalmians?"

Akira bit her tongue and ignored him. Following her meeting with her father the previous day, she hadn't confided in anyone about the execution of the ambassadors. Not even Shiori.

"I'm only teasing," Maerus said, giving her arm a squeeze.

"Perhaps we could do with less of that and more emotional support. That is why you're here after all," said Xif primly, his orb-like body nestled in the plush upholstery of the seats opposite, next to Shiori.

"I'm here because poor Akira is about to spend the next few months in the company of a cantankerous old drone and a borderline mute and this is her last chance to spend time with someone with a sense of humour."

"Maerus!" said Akira.

Shiori turned away, eyes fixed on the buildings flicking past.

Maerus rolled his eyes and gave an exaggerated sigh. "I'm sorry. This is difficult for me too, you know. How am I going to convince my friends that I'm the epitome of high society without being able to show you off every chance I can get?"

"I'm sure you'll find a way," Akira said.

"Yes, you're probably right," said Maerus, leaning back in his seat, shifting his fashionable satchel and smiling broadly. He was dressed in a tight-fitting maroon cassock that buttoned up to his neck and the jewelled tokens at his breast sparkled shamelessly. As they neared the spaceport the car swooped down low to pass through a security check point at ground level. They barely slowed down as the stony-faced security guards waved them through with white-gloved hands. They passed through a short tunnel and then out onto the vast concrete plain of the Kudo family's private spaceport. At the centre, glittering in the midday sun, was an enormous golden spacecraft, its contours smoothly curved as if carved by moving water. It reminded Akira of images of the great Raptor Whales that sailors of Angor Bore's equatorial seas told terrifying tales about. Rich purple carpet, edged with gold, ran all the way from the tunnel to the ship and on either side, standing rigidly to attention, were gleaming black lines of the Supreme Guard, her father's personal bodyguards.

"The Supreme Guard used to be a force to be reckoned with," mused Xif as the car processed slowly along the carpet, hovering a foot above its surface.

"In the days of the Two Empires, they were dangerous soldiers. Grizzled veterans of planetary invasions and skirmishes with the Vorth. There's not a scar among these ones though."

"You've seen footage of the old Supreme Guard?" asked Shiori.

"I've seen them in the flesh. I was already working for the Kudo-kai back then."

Xif didn't often talk of the days of the Two Empires but occasionally he would drop in a casual comment like this about events centuries old and Akira would remember what a rare creature he was. As they neared the end of the carpet, Akira noticed a group of civilians milling around at the bottom of the ramp that led into the belly of the ship. At the centre of them was a familiar rotund figure. Matsuko came to greet her as she stepped out of the car, his heavy tokens clinking softly as he moved.

"I didn't expect to see you before I left, Uncle," said Akira as they bowed to each other.

"I wasn't going to let you leave without saying a proper goodbye. Plus it gives me a chance to repay favours I owe some old colleagues," Matsuko said, gesturing behind him. "The grand departure of Akira Mukudori Kudo is quite the event, you know."

Akira glanced over his shoulder at the group of eager men and women.

"Don't worry," Matsuko whispered "They're under strict instructions not to talk your ears off."

He took Akira's arm in his and led her towards the ramp into the ship. Drones buzzed around their heads recording footage that would be broadcast live across the solar system.

"If you'd like to follow me, ladies and gentlemen. Akira and I will offer you some tea on board the *Dragon's Glory*."

"The *Dragon's Glory*?" said Akira, raising an eyebrow.

"Yes, I know. It's a bit kitsch isn't it but your father felt it was important for the people to see you depart in something impressive. He regrets that he couldn't be here to see you off, by the way."

"I'm sure he does," said Akira with a bitter smile.

Crossing over the portal into the ship was a jarring experience. It opened up into a large open space paved with granite slabs and seemingly lit by sunlight so bright it hurt her eyes. Wispy clouds floated in a brilliant blue sky overhead. Stone around the edge of the room gave the impression of walking into a walled garden.

"Impressive," said Akira, trying in vain to find the usual tell-tale seams between the smart panels covering the roof above.

"Don't get too used to it," muttered Matsuko cryptically.

Ahead of them was a gazebo in the shade of which was a low table and a scattering of cushions. Akira sat down next to Matsuko with Maerus on her other side. Once the group had settled themselves, servants brought out trays bearing pots of steaming tea and sweet cakes.

"I met with my father yesterday," said Akira quietly to Matsuko as he poured them both a cup.

"Yes, I heard. I advised him against it. Any travel outside the Citadel is too risky for him," said Matsuko.

"He told me our ambassadors to Thalmos have been executed."

Matsuko's teacup paused halfway to his mouth.

"Why didn't you tell me?" she said.

He set the teacup down and turned to her with sadness in his eyes. "We can't afford anyone finding out, Akira. There would be panic, disorder."

"But I'm not just anyone am I, Uncle? I'm the one being sent to try to sort out this mess. How am I supposed to do that if you're lying to me about how bad the situation is?"

"Shiori was supposed to brief you on the journey," Matsuko said.

"Shiori knows?" exclaimed Akira, more loudly than she'd intended.

"Hush, child. She does. But only because we wanted to protect you from the truth for as long as possible."

"Protect me from the truth," repeated Akira, incredulous "Which is it, Uncle? Am I a child who needs coddling and fairy tales or am I a 'capable young woman', as you put it, who's expected to protect the entire future of our family? Because if it's the former you might as well resign yourself right now to this mission failing."

Matsuko had the decency to look embarrassed.

"You're right, of course. I'm sorry, Akira. I should have trusted you."

Akira picked up her tea and sipped at it quietly. They sat in uncomfortable silence for a while.

"Father said that if I can't re-establish relations with the Thalmians, our family will die out," she said eventually.

"Akira, your father's job is to prepare for worst case scenarios. Certainly, without the Thalmian's nanotrite we will find ourselves in a very difficult situation but I suspect it won't help you to dwell on that too much."

"Quite right," said Maerus, leaning in to join the conversation. "Much better to focus on the positives. I've heard those Thalmians are the ultimate hedonists. You know, sumptuous feasts and bacchic orgies and the like. It's to be expected, I suppose, when you're as rich as they are."

Matsuko's eyes flashed angrily.

"You're here at my sufferance, Maerus. Don't forget that anything discussed here is to be treated as sensitive and highly classified."

Maerus held up his hands in mock surrender.

"I shan't forget it, Uncle. Not that I'm at all interested in the kind of things you deem sensitive anyway," he said.

Matsuko huffed but said nothing. After a while, the servants reappeared and began clearing away the tea.

"Excuse me, everyone," Matsuko said, addressing the group. "I think it's time we continued the tour."

Matsuko rose with an ease that was improbable given his size and the others followed, smoothing creases out of their clothes as they walked. He led them through a maze of corridors and so many different rooms that eventually Akira lost all sense of direction. He showed them formal dining rooms with tables set with beautiful antique plates and bone chop sticks, ready to entertain a royal entourage of fifty or more at a moment's notice. They walked through a gymnasium equipped with machines that looked more like instruments of torture to Akira. Most of the rooms seemed entirely excessive and held very little interest to her, even if they did elicit moos of delight from the rest of the group, but there were certain rooms that took even her breath away. There were the rainforest baths, a great network of steaming pools surrounded by lush vegetation. The air was filled with the soft, musical calls of jungle birds and the steady patter of condensation dripping from leaves and the humidity caused her shirt to stick to her back. There was the observatory, a great glass dome the size of a theatre at the very top of the ship. It offered a view of the blue sky above that faded to black when the refracted sunlight was filtered out. The great, dusty slash of the Milky Way blossomed across the sky and Angor Bore's two moons shone down on them casting their upturned faces a silver-grey. At Matsuko's command a red circle appeared in the heavens marking the direction of Thalmos, far too far to be visible to the naked eye. Akira's scalp tingled as she gazed in the direction she would soon be travelling. It seemed to have an effect on all of them, even Maerus, as the only sound from the talkative group as they filed out of the observatory was the hushed whisper of slippers against the polished wooden floor. By the time they arrived back at the garden foyer, Akira felt like her feet were about to fall off and there was still half of the ship that Matsuko had not shown them. Somehow the scale of it was reassuring, as if a reminder of the great wealth and power that was behind her, supporting her.

"If I'd known you'd be travelling in this palace of delights I might have been tempted to join you," whispered Maerus as the group prepared to disembark.

"No, you wouldn't," said Akira.

"No, I wouldn't," agreed Maerus with a small smile, "but you deserve it, darling. Try to enjoy yourself. If I've tried to teach you anything it's that a little self-indulgence is nothing to be ashamed of."

"Maerus, that is a spectacular understatement," said Akira. "I'm going to miss you, you know."

"Of course, you will," he said. "I'll miss you too. Good luck out there."

He gave her a quick hug, earning a disapproving glance from Matsuko and some startled looks from the other members of the group, before striding towards the portal that led out of the ship. As he reached the exit, he turned and gave her one last wave. There was something about the sight of him that nagged at her; she gave a distracted wave back trying to figure out what it was but before she could he was gone. Akira accepted the well wishes of the other strangers, murmuring automatic thanks but all the while wondering if she would ever see her friend again. As the last of the guests trickled out of the ship, Matsuko came up alongside her.

"Akira, I need you to come with me now. Shiori, Xifulandros, you too."

"Where?" asked Akira, confused. "Shouldn't you be leaving too. We're due to lift off soon."

"There's been a change of plan. Hurry now."

Matsuko led the group out of the garden and down a corridor to an elevator. It sank swiftly into the floor and down into a dimly lit service tunnel below the surface of the landing pad. Matsuko bustled them onto a driverless buggy that began speeding along the tunnel. Strips of light in the walls flashed past at metronome intervals.

"Matsuko, what is going on?" asked Akira, above the whistle of displaced air.

"It seems you won't be enjoying the luxuries of the *Dragon's Glory* after all," said Xif, earning a sharp look from Matsuko.

"We're not going?" said Akira.

"Oh, I imagine we're going all right," said Xif. "Just not in that over-engineered vanity project. Isn't that right, Matsuko?"

"I've received some worrying intelligence," said Matsuko.

"Such as?" asked Akira.

"Akira, really it may be best…" began Matsuko.

"Uncle, if you're about to fob me off with some ridiculous line that it's better if I don't know then you can get this buggy to take me straight back to my apartment."

"OK. You're right. Some anomalies have been noticed in the security net around the *Dragon's Glory*. Our experts have assured me there was no data breach and it's probably nothing more than an old man jumping at shadows but…right now I'm not taking any risks. If there's a chance someone accessed the ship's systems they could get up to any manner of mischief. They could track you, maybe even intercept you en route to Thalmos."

"So where are we going?" asked Akira.

"There's another ship. Much less grand than the *Dragon's Glory* but it was the best I could muster on short notice." At that moment the buggy emerged into a glass-sided corridor overlooking the Kudo spaceport where the *Dragon's Glory* was taking off. The anti-gravity generators at the base of the ship had come online and the air around it was distorted and fractured like cracked glass. It rose gradually up through the air, in all its vast golden glory, almost blindingly majestic in the hard, bright sunlight. A flock of drones around it followed its progress at a safe distance, relaying the moment to the rest of the system.

"It's still going?" she asked. "Even though we're changing ships?"

"Your father insisted," Matsuko said. "Something for the people to gawp at on the evening news. I'm afraid the replacement ship isn't quite as photogenic."

Akira gazed ruefully as the *Dragon's Glory* rose above the spaceport. The whole thing was wildly excessive but even so she felt surprisingly upset to see it leave without her. All that effort just for a PR stunt. It was more than that though. In the past few days, the ground underneath her feet had become less sure. The execution of their envoys was unthinkable. Her father's doubts about their future had been a shock and now, apparently, they couldn't be sure that their own ships were secure. It was for those reasons, more than the loss of the unbridled luxury of the *Dragon's Glory*, that she felt a twist of anxiety as she watched the ship rise further and further into the air. Distantly she heard the pattering roar of the crowd like rain on a glass roof. The ship was accelerating fast and had risen above the wispy clouds that marred the otherwise perfect sky when a dazzling light erupted from within it, scything through its centre and burning a bright streak across Akira's vision. Almost immediately, a sphere of condensation coalesced around the ship blocking it from view and then exploded outwards with terrifying speed. Akira hadn't had time to process what she was seeing when the shockwave hit. Thunder rocked her body. The glass wall of the corridor blew inwards sending shards like daggers through the air. Akira felt a sharp, stinging sensation across her arm. The buggy rocked violently beneath her and almost tipped over. She looked up at where the *Dragon's Glory* had been. Great, smoking hunks of metal had been scattered across the sky and were falling, seemingly in slow motion, leaving dirty black trails in the air. The ship was gone. She felt a tugging at her arm. Dazedly she looked round and Shiori was mouthing something at her, expression hard and intense. A high-pitched whine filled her ears and she couldn't make out the words. She looked down at her clothes and was confused at the spreading crimson stains there.

Chapter 16

A sea of black smoke stretched out as far as the eye could see. It seethed and boiled as if churned up from below. The air was thick and hot with a dread so terrible that it constricted his throat. Somewhere deep in the smoke a creature was rising up. As it neared, the sense of dread grew until it was almost unbearable. His ears were ringing. Flashes of electric blue danced deep in the smoke. A shape was discernible just below the surface. The creature was about to break through. He tried to scream but no sound came out.

***

Mordax awoke gasping and sat up with a jerk. His head throbbed with white hot pain. Exploring with his fingers, he found a large bump over his eyebrow and his right eye was swollen shut. He heard the rustling of movement next to him.

"Hey, sugar, how're you feeling?"

With his one good eye he peered around. He seemed to be in a kind of cavern. Orbs set into the walls of rough rock gave off a dim light. A number of beds, including the one on which he sat, were carved out of the rock itself. Not a natural cavern then. Next to him Virzda examined him, an expression of concern creasing her features. With a wave of relief he spotted both Lazarus and the looming outline of Stamford sitting side-by-side on the other side of the room. Lazarus was rocking back and forth, stroking Marvin who had curled up on his lap. Stamford's expression was unreadable in the artificial twilight. Virzda laid a cool hand against his forehead.

"Lay back now. You've taken a good couple of cracks to the head. Need to take things slowly for a while."

"Where are we?" Mordax croaked. He ran his tongue over dry, cracked lips.

Virzda shot a worried glance at the other two. "We don't know. They haven't told us anything."

"Who are they?"

"Ghosts," rumbled Stamford, eyes hidden by the gloom. The cavern seemed to grow suddenly cold and the stone walls pressed closer around them.

"Hush," tsked Virzda, looking angrily at Stamford, "enough of that."

Mordax struggled into a sitting position.

"What do you mean?" he asked.

"Faceless men," said Stamford. "They make no sound."

"You saw them?" Mordax asked.

Stamford nodded.

"When the hull blew in the cargo bay I put on a crash suit. I had enough air to survive but not by much. I was weakened, otherwise I would have crushed the invaders."

He balled his hand into a fist, sinews cracking.

"How did they get us in here?" Mordax asked

"I do not know. The ghosts shot me with something. One hit my neck and knocked me out. I hurt one well though."

A grim smile twisted Stamford's lips. Based on experience, Mordax would have been surprised if that "one" was still alive. Lazarus was still rocking back and forth, eyes staring vacantly.

"How you doing, Laz?"

"Mmm-hmm. It's fine. All fine. No problemo."

The hand stroking Marvin was shaking visibly.

"We'll get back to the *Starling* soon, Laz. I promise," Mordax whispered.

Lazarus gulped and nodded.

"Where's Stephan?" asked Virzda. "Shouldn't they have brought him in with us?"

Mordax's grip on the ball of grief he had been suppressing, weakened. He felt himself fray at the edges as the question scoured away his resolve.

"At Fornax. He— they shot him."

Hot tears welled up and began to trickle down his cheeks.

"He's gone," he said.

"He died in battle," said Stamford softly.

"Stam, don't..." said Mordax

"It was a noble death," Stamford continued.

"Don't please, I can't..."

"You must understand, it is something to be revered not mourned," Stamford said insistently.

A rage, hot and powerful, flared up inside Mordax.

"Don't talk about him," he shouted. "It's your fault. We could have helped him."

"Mordax, no. I..." Stamford began.

"You're a coward."

Stamford hung his massive head and said nothing. Seeing Stamford's grief caused a sweet, sharp pain in Mordax that he embraced. Anything was better than the terrible darkness he felt when he thought of his father.

Virzda placed a hand on his arm.

"Oh, sugar. I'm so sorry," she said, her voice trembling. The way she looked at him, the sympathy in her eyes was too much for him. He buried his face in his hands and wept, sobs racking his slender body. He felt Virzda move closer to him. She cradled his head in her lap and stroked his hair until the sobbing subsided, his breathing slowed and he slept.

***

It may have been hours later or only a few minutes, as far as Mordax was aware, when the door to the cavern slid open and two figures entered. Both wore hoods and silver veils which covered their faces and carried rifles. It was hard to tell but he thought he recognised one as the figure he had encountered on the *Starling*. She had the same build and moved with the same lithe grace. Stamford made to rise but Mordax shook his head and he lowered himself back down glowering. Nonetheless the veiled figures gave him a wide berth.

"You. Get up," said the female figure, gesturing at Mordax.

He did as he was asked, ignoring the protests from his battered joints. Rough hands spun him round and fastened shackles around his wrists, behind his back. As he was led out of the cell, he glanced back at the faces of his crew, his family, and felt the same mixture of despair and anger he saw reflected there. Hard fingers dug into his upper arms, pinching the flesh but supporting his weight. Head lolling, Mordax glanced sideways through his one good eye, getting a closer look at the strange guards flanking him as they set a brisk pace along the corridor. They were clad in soft black robes but he glimpsed a gleaming curve of composite body armour at their necks. Their featureless silvery veils reflected light strangely so that Mordax had the impression of movement in the fabric like smoke under glass. The guards' soft leather boots made a rhythmic whisper against the stone floor, in contrast to the scuffing rasp of Mordax's work-boots as he struggled to keep pace. He blinked against scratchy eyes, trying to will his mind back to alertness.

"Where are we going?" he croaked, wincing at the pain from his split lip.

The guards' pace didn't miss a beat and they gave no indication of having even heard him. The corridor was raw stone. Unlike the tunnels on Seraph, however, the walls and floor were glassy smooth as if the rock had simply melted away. They reached a heavy metal door which slid open with a pneumatic hiss. Broken carmine light danced around the chamber beyond and, for a second, Mordax was back in the *Starling*'s navigation room, emergency lights flashing. He fought down the panic that the memory evoked. The lighting in here was natural, he realised. A giant pane of glass made up one wall of the chamber and looked out onto violent scenery. The peaks of neighbouring mountain ranges cut the purple sky and the storm continued to rage outside. Sheets of rain blasted the glass in waves, smearing the view so that the rocky outcrops blurred together. Three figures were clustered in the centre of the room. In between them was a slowly spinning projection of a series of star systems connected by a complex web of intersecting parabolas. The projection was crystal clear and unlike anything he had seen before, as if the stars themselves had been shrunk down and suspended before them. He looked around for the source of the projection but couldn't see one. The figures, two men and a woman, ceased their conversation. One waved his hand and the projection faded away. The two men were very different, the nearest was past middle age but thickset and straight backed with grizzled hair cropped close to his skull. He wore a utilitarian tunic that revealed powerful arms and he regarded Mordax with annoyance. The second was younger, thin and clad in a simple but elegantly cut silk suit. Shoulder length hair framed a handsome face with piercing grey eyes. The woman was plump with long grey hair. She wore flowing white robes and a peculiar symbol on a heavy chain around her neck that Mordax was sure he had seen somewhere before. She looked relaxed, regarding him with curiosity as she rested her bulk against the edge of the table. The older man gestured to a metal chair a few feet from the group. Mordax's guards dragged him over and deposited him in it roughly. With a metallic clang that jolted through his shoulders the magnetic shackles around his wrists separated and flew to opposite sides of the chair, pinning Mordax's arms by his side.

The older man turned to the guard.

"The boy? Really?"

The guard shrugged.

"There were only two of them near the navigator's office when we boarded. The other was a quivering wreck," she said.

A hint of admiration crept into her voice. "We hit him with a nerve blocker but he still got a shot off. If Reynolds hadn't had his shield up it would have melted his head off." The older man took a step forward and leaned closer to Mordax's face, fierce eyes examining him intently. The hot, dry scent of salt and iron radiated from his weathered skin.

He turned back to address the female guard.

"What did you find on the ship?"

"Appears to be a merchant vessel, sir. The *Indigo Starling*. Looks like they came off worse in a scrap before they got here. We haven't found the manifest yet but the cargo hold was filled with food and clothes before it was breached."

The "food and clothes" actually consisted of 500 kilotons of starsarine and 80,000 hand-embroidered silk vests from Tarp. A small fortune by anyone's reckoning. All probably ruined by exposure to the vacuum of space. But Mordax didn't care. His chest was hollow and his brain numb. The man continued to regard him with icy blue eyes. A ragged scar traced his jawline from ear to chin.

"Where did you get the ship?" the man asked.

Confused, Mordax blinked and looked around the room. All eyes were turned towards him expectantly, waiting for his answer.

"The *Starling*? What do you mean?" Mordax asked.

The man exhaled through his teeth with a hiss. "It's a simple question, is it not? Where did you get it?" he said, enunciating each word carefully.

"I didn't get it. It's my home," said Mordax.

Mordax wasn't sure what he had expected but it wasn't questions about the provenance of the *Indigo Starling*.

The slender man frowned. "You're crew on the *Indigo Starling*? Where is Stephan L'Amfour? We were under the impression that he was the owner."

The question was a hammer blow to Mordax's gut. But it cracked the torpor clinging to his mind, letting his anger seep through. Who were these strangers to ask about his father? These people who had imprisoned his crew, who had shackled him and now demanded answers from him as if he had done something wrong. "Where is he?" repeated Mordax. "In the last twelve hours, I've been shot at, knocked out and almost asphyxiated and my ship is currently held together by duct tape and prayers. You want to know about my father, take these fucking bracelets off and release my crew."

"Your father," repeated the thin man quietly, twisting a ring on his little finger thoughtfully.

"He can't be more than eighteen cycles. That's why Stephan left. A child," he said to the others.

Mordax's mind raced through the possibilities that the statement revealed. His anger quickly bled dry. These people had known Stephan before Mordax was born. What had he been mixed up in? Whatever it was, hidden away out here, it clearly wasn't legitimate and Mordax and the crew now knew their location. A cold sliver of fear skittered down his back. He thought fast. He had to make himself seem like an asset not a liability to these people. "Look, you've seen our ship, the state she's in," said Mordax. "We barely made it here alive. We've got nothing to barter for repairs with and we can't make it anywhere else by ourselves." The three looked at him blankly so he barrelled on before they could interrupt.

"We're traders. We've traded all over this sector for cycles. I know the markets on all the planets from Ngoth to St Ilma inside out, both black and legitimate."

This was true for the most part. Stephan had contacts on hundreds of planets, from Sazan, the city of a thousand tailors, where you could pick up a suit of honey-moth silk for only twice the planet's average wage, to arms manufacturers in the Sabulon asteroid belt. While knowing a few crooks had helped offload the occasional case of bootleg or hot ammunition, Stephan had stayed away from the really hard products.

"We make a good living, Mordax," his father had told him once after passing up a cheap consignment of Methyldiazopreme, favoured by addicts on a hundred different worlds. "But some products will kill everything they touch, including us eventually." Mordax decided to spell out his offer in no uncertain terms. When you're bartering for the lives of your crew there's no room for ambiguity.

"Whatever you're cooking here, I can help you ship it. If you patch us up and let us go, we'll work for you. Three to five clear runs depending on what we're shipping. We keep thirty per cent of the profits."

The older man barked out a laugh, interrupting him. "Save us the marketing pitch, boy. We don't need your ship."

"It's not the ship you need, Grandad. It's me," retorted Mordax. "I can get you into markets you didn't even know existed. I can move product on worlds that you didn't know were inhabited and sneak through blockades you thought were impenetrable. I've been doing it my whole life."

The slight man on Mordax's right gave a good-natured chuckle.

"What? You don't believe me?" demanded Mordax. "Oh no, I believe you," said the slight man with a wan smile, "I was just thinking how much like your father you are."

Mordax was at a loss. This wasn't the reaction he'd expected. The woman spoke for the first time, her voice soft and melodious despite her size.

"We mean your father no harm, young one. We only seek answers which he would freely give if he were here."

Mordax suddenly recognised the symbol on the chain around her neck and realised why it had seemed odd. The symbol was worn by worshipers of the Mysteries of Supreme

Reason. Mordax had never heard of a follower of the Mysteries being involved in any criminal enterprise which they saw as disruptive to the fabric of society. The woman's presence here meant that Mordax's appraisal of the situation was entirely wrong. If he didn't know what motives drove these people, how could he hope to negotiate his way out successfully? The slight man, seemingly sensing Mordax's hesitation, gave a small smile.

"I can see you have questions. Galaia is telling the truth. Stephan was a friend. If you tell us where he is, I will tell you whatever you want to know about us and this place."

This earned him a sharp look from the older man, but he kept his eyes fixed on Mordax.

What could it hurt? If they wanted him dead he would be dead already and they could always torture the information out of him. There was no play here.

"It's a long story," Mordax warned.

"We have time," said the slight man. So Mordax began.

***

Mordax sat alone, wrists still shackled to the chair. The trio had listened to his tale, mostly in silence. He had told them everything from the *Starling*'s visit to Seraph and Cantarina to the ambush on Fornax and their narrow escape. When he described the ambush, the trio had become agitated. The slight man had muttered something to the other two that Mordax hadn't made out and Galaia had looked genuinely distraught at the news of Stephan's death. The only part of the story he had left out was his encounter with Myla. Her existence was a secret he was reluctant to give up until he knew more about these people.

He watched absently as the crimson light, dappled from the rain that still poured down the window, played over the polished stone walls. His body still ached but he was more concerned about what was being decided outside the room. His fate and that of the crew was out of his hands.

The heavy door hissed open and the slight man entered alone. He looked weary. He approached the large table and tapped a control panel. The shackles around Mordax's wrists released and dropped to the floor with a dull clunk.

"I realise you've had a trying time recently, Mordax. You should know that there are many here who will grieve your father's death."

"What does that mean?" said Mordax, rubbing his wrists. "Who are you people?"

"My name is Robert Calgary. Just Calgary is fine. The other two you met are Galaia Henne and General Faestus Valerian." He paused. "Look, Mordax, what I have to say will be difficult for you to hear."

"More difficult than being imprisoned and told nothing at all?"

Calgary inclined his head, acknowledging the point.

"This is a chapter of the Dioscuri."

An involuntary bark of laughter escaped Mordax's lips. There was no mirth in Calgary's eyes, however.

His words didn't seem to make sense. Whatever Mordax had been expecting, it wasn't this. But as he thought about it, the pieces started to fit together. He thought back to the guards. The shimmering silvery veils covering their faces. Could they really be the Dioscuri? The king-killers? There were a thousand legends about them. Some said that they were the ghosts of those killed by the Two Empires. Others that they were members of an elder race that had transcended mortality. But every legend referred to silver masks or hoods of some kind.

Calgary was studying him carefully.

"And my father?" Mordax asked

"He…was a former operative of ours. One of the best."

"And by operative, you mean…?"

Mordax knew the answer but needed to hear it aloud.

The man walked to the window, staring out, hands clasped behind his back. Even through the thick glass, Mordax thought he could make out a distant howling.

"I've always found the storms here very calming. There's something about the natural violence of this world, the irresistible forces out there, that seems to put everything else into perspective. A reminder of our place in the order of things. Do you know what I mean?"

Mordax didn't respond.

"Your father was a wraith, Mordax. A Dioscuri assassin and wearer of the silver veil. He killed to protect the people of this galaxy from the horrors of war."

Mordax swallowed hard.

"He can't have been," was all he could manage.

"He was, Mordax. He was one of the best," Calgary said.

Mordax felt light-headed, as if a breath of wind would topple him over. How could the man he had known, rough and capable, yes, but kind-hearted and always with a twinkle in his eye, how could that man have been a cold-blooded killer? Mordax couldn't reconcile the memories of his father with the facts being laid before him. Stephan had always taken every step to avoid conflict. If it wasn't for the events of the previous day, Mordax might not have believed what Calgary was saying. But the way his father had moved, the way he had cut through men like a scythe...

"I realise it's a hard thing to accept," Calgary said.

"You could say that," Mordax said, his voice barely more than a whisper.

"Look, Mordax, it's important that you understand what would happen if the Dioscuri didn't exist. Before the War of Ages, the galaxy was a prosperous place. Millions of worlds, teeming with potential and intelligent life until they were raped and discarded by the Vorth and Kudo-kai, worth only the resources that could be mined or drilled out of them. Eventually the Vorth and the human Kudo-kai were almost the only sentient beings left. The original Dioscuri, both Vorth and humans alike, were responsible for halting that cycle of destruction and preventing the necrotising tendrils of the Two Empires from spreading further through the galaxy. But for the past two centuries, since the Purge, there's been a power vacuum. Without the Dioscuri, successors to the Vorth and the Kudo-kai would quickly have risen up to take their place and start the fighting all over again. We are one of hundreds of thousands of chapters spread across the Shattered Empires. Even so, your father was well known. He was responsible for eliminating some of the most dangerous threats in recent memory. One of those included an attempted resurgence by the Kudo-kai itself."

"So my father murdered for the greater good. Is that it?"

"It's not a simple problem, Mordax. And I can't pretend that we have the perfect solution yet. But yes, the work we do here prevents far greater loss of life. Yes, we have to kill but the alternative is far worse. Your father had to make difficult choices. Just as you have."

Mordax looked up sharply.

"You told us you ejected a nether-drive to escape from Fornax?" Calgary said gently. "What would have happened if the nether-drive had been hit?"

Mordax understood the point he was making. If the containment of the nether-drive had failed its energy would have been released with devastating results. It would have consumed the *Starling*, the enemy vessels but also would likely have damaged Fornax itself and any people working nearby. He couldn't hold the whole population guilty for Sermilion's betrayal but he had risked their lives to escape all the same. His heart pounded in his ears. Mordax stared at his hands, black grease still under his fingernails from helping Virzda in the engine room.

"Two days ago we were traders. We were good at it. But you're telling me it was all a lie."

How much of what he understood about his father's past was true?

"I don't think so, Mordax. I think your father wanted a different life for you. That's why he left us. It's only now that it makes sense to me."

Mordax felt dizzy and Calgary's voice became more distant.

"What about my mother? He told me she was a trader too. That she got sick when I was young?"

A pained look passed over Calgary's face.

"I don't know for sure. But just before Stephan disappeared we had word that the Kudo-kai had destroyed a ship he was on. We all thought he had died until today when your ship showed up broadcasting Dioscuri codes personal to him."

He and Lazarus must have missed that in the panic. If Stephan had set the *Starling* to nether jump here he could easily have set an automatic broadcast.

"If your mother died when you were young, it's possible she was on that ship and didn't make it off. I'm sorry, Mordax, it seems the Kudo-kai have taken both your parents from you."

Mordax's head snapped up. "Both? What do you mean?"

"We have reason to believe that the ships that attacked you on Fornax were of the Kudo-kai."

"I don't understand. Why would the Kudo-kai have even been there?" Mordax said and then continued before Calgary could answer, "Sermilion! My dad said he was mixed up in something."

Calgary pursed his lips and nodded. "We think he was. Our intelligence suggests that in the last year or so Sermilion shifted Fornax's production heavily towards military ships and hardware. It seems those products were for the benefit of only one buyer. That buyer has hidden their tracks well but there are very few organisations that have the kind of wealth to sustain purchases of that magnitude. One of those is the Kudo-kai which has been attempting to claw its way back to power ever since the Purge. I suspect Stephan somehow found out that the Kudo-kai were re-arming themselves and thought Sermilion might have some answers. Sermilion used to work for us. He and your father had complementary skills and I believe were paired up for a number of missions. He can't have known that Sermilion had betrayed everything he used to stand for."

Mordax struggled to his feet, wincing at the sharp ache in his side and went to join Calgary at the window. The wind-whipped sky had grown darker and the blasting torrents of rain made him shiver, grateful despite everything else for the shelter of this place.

"So, what's next for us, Calgary?" he asked, glancing at the man's angular profile. "Are you going to kill us?"

Calgary turned to face him, his piercing grey eyes inscrutable. It was unnerving. Mordax was used to reading people. Cycles of scratching out a living by negotiating for every credit had taught him to read emotions well, but Calgary gave nothing away.

"Not one to dance around an issue," Calgary said.

Mordax shrugged. "It's clear we know things you would rather we didn't."

"You're right. We can't let you leave. I'll be honest, Mordax, if Valerian had had his way you would already be dead."

Mordax's breath quickened.

"If our enemies found out about this location, many more lives would be at risk," Calgary continued. "I've convinced the others that you should remain here under my protection."

"Me and my crew?"

Calgary paused.

"I'm sorry, Mordax, there's nothing I can do for your crew. It's just too dangerous to have four outsiders here."

Mordax was silent for a moment.

"So...what? What happens?"

"Don't play the fool, Mordax. I've told you where you are. Who we are."

"You're going to have to spell it out," Mordax spat.

"Alright," said Calgary, face expressionless. "They'll be executed. To protect the order."

"Unacceptable," said Mordax.

"I don't think you understand..."

"No, I don't think you understand. The crew of the *Starling* are my family. The only family I've got left. If you kill them, you kill me too."

"Think carefully about this, Mordax. There's no reason to throw your life away with theirs."

"And what kind of life would that be anyway?" Mordax asked. "We're Travellers. We call no planet home. Our lives aren't dirt-bound like yours. We sail the stars. Staying here, in this dungeon, would be worse than a death sentence."

Calgary looked away from Mordax's burning gaze.

"I'm sorry, Mordax. This isn't a negotiation. There's no other way."

Everything is a negotiation, though. Mordax's mind raced. An idea began to form.

"Are there children here?" Mordax asked

The question clearly took Calgary by surprise.

"Children? No, why?"

"Then you recruit from outside the Dioscuri."

"Yes, of course. Our work is dangerous, Mordax. No parent would wish for their child to be forced into this life. Relationships between operatives are discouraged and children are strictly forbidden."

The furrows cleared from Calgary's brow as he understood the line of questioning.

"It's no good, Mordax. Our recruits are selected from around the galaxy. Young men and women who are among the most talented in their systems. Many trained since a young age for a life in the military."

"And you train them further here?"

"For the most part, yes. Before they're inducted they must pass a selection course."

Mordax remembered the scans Lazarus had run when they had first jumped into this system.

"The other planet? Your selection takes place there," he guessed.

"Now how would you know that?" Calgary asked, head cocked.

Mordax shrugged. "It has atmosphere and gravity close to standard."

Calgary smiled humourlessly.

"It's called Hellenbos. It's an icy rock just warm enough around the equator for trees to grow. And yes, Selection takes place there."

"And your operatives, the...wraiths? They don't work alone?"

"Some do. Some are sent to live on planets, undercover. Others have starships, with crews to travel less conspicuously."

"Put me through Selection," Mordax said. "If I pass, give me back the *Starling* with my crew and we'll work for you."

Calgary shook his head.

"I had to fight hard to get Valerian to agree to let *you* live, Mordax."

Mordax recalled the animosity in the eyes of the grizzled older man. He could well believe it.

"I did that because our organisation owes your father a huge debt, even if Valerian can't see past Stephan's abandonment of us. And more than that, he was a friend. I owe it to him to keep his son safe if I can. What you're asking is too dangerous."

"I don't care," retorted Mordax, his mouth dry.

"Mordax, the selection process is designed to ensure that only the most talented make it through. It's not something you can drop out of. Some cycles only half of the recruits survive. For you...I'm afraid you don't stand a chance."

"My father went through it?"

"He did. But after cycles of training. Valerian runs the selection now. I wouldn't be able to protect you."

Mordax thought of the crew who were likely still huddled in their cell unaware that their fate hung in the balance. He thought of the broken-winged ship rising through smoke. The crackle of blue fire and his last glimpse of his father's face. Finally, he thought of the name that these strange killers had offered up to his anger. The Kudo-kai. He did not have to think for long.

"Let me do it. I understand the risks."

Calgary ran a hand through his dark hair, thinking. The distant shrieking of the storm was the only sound. At last he nodded.

"Alright. The others will agree. Valerian, only because he'll be sure that you won't survive. I fear he may be right."

Mordax feared the same but his body tingled with a new purpose. If he could survive, those responsible for his father's death would pay a dear price. If he could survive.

Chapter 17

The man fastened the clasp of his helmet and his suit pressurised with a quiet hiss. He strapped a bulky package around his waist. The five others around him did the same, their movements sure despite the gloom and confinement of the hold which was barely large enough to fit all of them and their gear. The man breathed deeply of the dry air. He savoured these moments. The quiet preparation, atmosphere electric with anticipation. He was aware of every beat of his heart, every twitch of his muscles. In these precious minutes, his mind was focussed and utterly clear, every sensation heightened.

"Arrival in thirty seconds," the tinny voice of the ship's computer announced.

The door to the hold slid open silently revealing stars like burning diamonds against the black velvet curtain of deep space. The first time he had stood outside like this, with nothing between him and the void, the vastness of it had threatened to overwhelm him. It was like teetering at the very edge of a sheer cliff, magnified a thousand-fold. That was a lifetime ago. Now he welcomed the boundless dark like an old friend.

"Arrival in ten seconds."

The man briefly touched the rifle fixed across his chest.

He didn't bother to check the readiness of the people behind him. They were professionals and the briefing they had received was comprehensive. The seconds dripped by slowly. All at once the space in front of them unfolded itself and the huge body of a freight hauler winked into existence, illuminated by the spotlights around its hull. The crew inside would be scrambling now, trying to determine what had caused the unplanned exit from netherspace. They would soon detect the array of nodes around them that had created the interference field. The man leapt forwards out of the hold, launching himself into space and angling his body towards the freighter. He squeezed a trigger in his hand and began to accelerate as the thruster on his back engaged. He sped towards the ship like a gleaming black arrow. When the hull took up his entire field of vision, he used brief squirts of air from ports on his chest and back to turn himself around and then decelerated hard. His boots hit the hull with a dull thunk and the magnets in the soles engaged. Around him he could see the flicker of thrusters, like fireflies in the night, as the others swarmed over the freighter and took their positions. The only sound was his own heavy breath in his ears. They were comms-dark in case the freighter picked up their signal although, at this stage, there was little to say to each other. He removed the package from his waist and fixed it to the hull. According to plans of the vessel, a few inches below his feet was the canteen. With a ship this size, it was likely that there would always be a few crew members taking a meal. He walked a few feet away from the package, feet sticky against the hull as the magnets engaged and disengaged with his steps. He waited.

Five separate squirts of static told him that the time had arrived. The others were in position. The package in front of him flared with green light as the ring-shaped plasma torch on its underside fired up. After a few seconds, the place where the package was exploded outwards, silent in the vacuum, and a shimmering geyser of air crystals littered with debris bloomed out of the hole. Automatic blast doors would have immediately sealed the canteen off from the rest of the ship as soon as the drop in pressure was detected. However, five other explosions would simultaneously be emptying air from the other sections of the ship. The man swung himself through the hole, careful not to snag his suit on the ragged metal edges. The ship's gravity field caught him and propelled him to the floor. He had been right. There were two crew members, eyes milky with frost, tangled in a mess of chairs and tables and other items too large to be sucked out of the breach and now piled beneath it.

The man opened a channel to the others. No need to keep their presence secret anymore.

"Report," he said.

Quickly five confirmations came back. All sections had been breached.

"Delta, what about the suits?"

There was a pause as Delta, who had gone straight to the armoury, took stock of the space suits.

"All one hundred-and-sixty suits accounted for, sir. None in use."

No suits in use meant that every member of the ship's crew was dead. They had taken the vessel without firing a shot. The man smiled to himself. There was nothing quite as satisfying as a plan executed flawlessly.

Chapter 18

Akira scratched absently at the stripes of pink fresh skin that criss-crossed her arms. Voices, distant and unfocussed, swirled around her. A hologram of Matsuko's face floated before her, but she didn't really see him. Instead hung before her eyes was a curtain of brilliant blue sky cut in half by a blade of light. Smoky debris spread across the heavens, leaving black trails like the lengthening legs of a colossal spider. Finally, a voice repeating her name broke into her waking reverie.

"Akira?" Matsuko was looking at her concerned.

"Sorry, say that again."

"I was asking how you were feeling?"

The question annoyed her. Everyone had been asking her that since the destruction of the *Dragon's Glory* as if she were able to answer with anything other than "fine". After the explosion, having made sure that her wounds were superficial, Matsuko had taken them straight to their replacement ship, a comfortable merchant vessel, *Charon's Wake*, which had taken off minutes after they boarded and was now chugging through netherspace on its way to Thalmos. The onboard med-drones had knitted her cuts closed in no time but there wasn't much the mindless machines could do about the flashbacks that now plagued both her waking and sleeping hours.

"Nethercasts are expensive, Uncle. Can we stay on point please?"

"As you wish," Matsuko said, but his brow remained furrowed.

"We're continuing our investigations but all the evidence points towards an explosive being planted on the ship."

"How can that be?" asked Akira "Weren't security sweeps run?"

"They were," said Matsuko. "Twice a day until the day of the launch."

"But nothing was found?"

"No."

"Which means," said Xif, who was floating silently beside her, "either the explosive was disguised in such a way that it evaded our sweeps, which is extraordinarily unlikely, or it was planted during our tour of the ship."

Matsuko's face remained disconcertingly still.

"Uncle?" asked Akira quietly "Is that right? You suspect one of the group?"

"I'm afraid so," he said. "Akira, I hesitate to tell you this but I fear I've kept too much from you already. We've questioned everyone who was there that day closely. Everyone except one. Maerus. He's disappeared. We believe he may be off-planet by now."

Akira shook her head, almost amused at how absurd the suggestion was.

"You're not seriously suggesting Maerus had anything..." she trailed off. The memory of her last sight of him came to her, sharp and clean as a knife sliding into her flesh. In her mind, he raised his arm and waved at her, effortlessly handsome, a bitter twist to his lips that suggested a darker type of sadness than that of a friend simply bidding another farewell. Akira now realised what had seemed out of place, what had niggled at her subconscious. Maerus had not been carrying the bag he arrived with.

"No," she whispered.

"I'm sorry," said Matsuko.

"He's my friend," she said. "Why would he do this?"

For a moment Matsuko looked every one of his considerable cycles, the brightness in his eyes dimmed.

"As it transpires, Maerus's father isn't the businessman his own father was. He made some bad decisions then compounded those with worse ones. He gambled his family's fortune trying to win back what he had lost and ended up losing everything. The Yulises owe money to all the prominent families. Their property holdings are mortgaged and, in some cases, double or triple mortgaged. They're on the verge of utter ruin."

"He did it for money?" asked Akira incredulous.

"For some, those unfortunates who are weak of will or without a proper sense of perspective, wealth is more important than their honour," Matsuko said softly.

"But who was paying him?"

"His parents are being interrogated...vigorously. So far they haven't given us a name which means they probably don't know and we won't find out for sure until we locate Maerus."

"It could have been the Thalmians though," she said, a prickle of fear running over her scalp.

"It's possible," said Xif quickly, "but it would be much easier to wait until you're actually on Thalmos before having you killed. Why would they make it more difficult for themselves?"

"I don't know," said Akira, hearing her voice become shrill. "Maybe because it would hurt the family more with everyone watching. Maybe they want to prove a point. Or maybe, and recent events seem to bear this out, they're just insane and this whole mission is doomed to fail."

"Pull yourself together," said Matsuko, his eyes darkening. "It does no good speculating without proper intelligence, especially if you let your emotions run away with you."

With an effort, Akira calmed herself and bit down on the angry retort that tried to worm its way out of her throat.

"Let us worry about who's behind this. You concentrate on what you can control," Matsuko said.

That was easier said than done. Akira felt as if she had suddenly discovered she was standing on the ceiling, everything twisted and inverted. Maerus, the boy she had grown up with, the one person she had counted on always to tell her the truth, had tried to assassinate her. Her world felt very small all of a sudden, a tiny spotlight around her with sinister, unseen shapes moving in the darkness beyond the light's edge. Matsuko was asking some technical questions about the ship's status, which Xif responded to without missing a beat, and before long he was bidding them goodbye.

"Keep your chin up, Akira," Matsuko said "You're not alone in this."

And then he was gone, his face winking out of existence with a jarring abruptness.

Akira put her head in her hands and let out a groan.

"I'm sorry, Akira," said Xif. "I was fond of the boy even if he lacked respect."

"How did I not realise?" she said.

"You shouldn't blame yourself. He fooled Matsuko too and it's his job not to be fooled."

"But I thought I knew him."

"In my experience, humans are fickle creatures. You can never predict with a hundred per cent certainty how any of them are going to behave."

Akira felt her shock at Maerus' betrayal harden inside her.

"He tried to kill me, Xif. He was my friend and he tried to murder me. For money."

"Matsuko's right. You shouldn't dwell on it. There's nothing you can do about it now. Besides, if I know your father, and I flatter myself that I do better than most, he won't let such a betrayal go unpunished. Maerus may have been paid well but he will be pursued for the rest of his days."

Akira didn't know if she wished the fate of falling into her father's talons on anyone, even Maerus. But she wouldn't cry for him. She was a Kudo after all and her family had not conquered half a galaxy by shedding tears over traitors.

***

A few days later, Akira and Shiori were in Akira's living quarters, kneeling on soft cushions on either side of a low table. A serving boy approached and laid a burnished walnut tray in front of them, laden with a pot of steaming tea and two delicate cups glazed a pleasant forest-green. They touched their tokens muttering the customary prayer to the ancestors before Shiori poured them both a cup, releasing the comforting scent of chamomile and lemon. In the first days of their journey these small, familiar rituals had helped Akira adjust to the claustrophobic nothingness of netherspace, the disconcerting absence of stars outside the ship's windows and the knowledge that, technically, they no longer existed in their own reality. Of course, Akira had star jumped before but never this far and there was still a week to go before they arrived at Thalmos.

"How many cycles are left to run on the contract for the nanotrite supply?" Shiori asked before Akira had had a chance to take a sip of her tea. Apparently, today's quiz was the contractual relations between Thalmos and the Kudo-kai.

"Three-hundred-and-eighty?" Akira hazarded.

"Three-hundred-and-forty-seven," Shiori corrected. "You've got to get these details right!"

She had been more terse with Akira since the night of the leaving party. Never rude but Akira sensed a lingering resentment in the tightness of her voice and the absence of previous small kindnesses. Baths were no longer drawn without Akira having to ask and fresh flowers no longer appeared on her nightstand each morning. An unspoken tension hung between them giving weight to their smallest interactions and making these sessions uncomfortable.

"Shiori, I've got Xif to feed me those kind of details. I really think our time's better spent on other topics."

Shiori cast a meaningful glance at Xif who was hovering silently in the corner. Xif had fallen into a noticeable funk as the journey had progressed, keeping to himself for the most part and conducting Akira's lessons in a generally lacklustre manner.

"OK, so he's a moody hunk of metal at the moment, but even he knows it's in his own best interests for the mission to succeed," Akira said.

"I heard that," said Xif.

"Good! Maybe you'll stop acting like a petulant child then."

Xif muttered something inaudible and turned his cameras so that he was facing the wall.

Shiori rolled her eyes and despite herself Akira had to stifle a laugh.

"So what would you like to focus on today then?" asked Shiori.

Akira took a small sip of tea.

"There's one thing that's been puzzling me. How have the Thalmians not got a handle on the insurgents?"

Glankor the Blessed had risen to power on Thalmos promising to take a hard line against the increasingly active insurgent groups who came from the great mass of non-citizens that lived there.

"We don't really know," said Shiori. "He's been taking increasingly draconian measures to stop the smuggling of weapons and drugs, which the insurgents sell to fund their activities, from off-world. Nothing he's done seems to have worked though. Last year alone the government's offices were firebombed, there were over a thousand attacks on police patrols and a number of violent riots broke out that lasted for weeks. The real problem is the disparity of wealth and living conditions between the citizen and non-citizen classes."

"It's not uncommon for there to be a difference in circumstance between the wealthy and the poor. Why's Thalmos different?" said Akira.

Shiori shrugged. "You'll see when we get there. The city, Kor'Thalia, is beautiful, as you'd expect but it was never meant to house so many people. The non-citizens are forced to live in the industrial levels below the city, areas which were designed as part of the machine not as human habitat."

"Can't they expand?"

"They have pressurised habitats on the surface for the less well-off citizens but those are expensive to build. The non-citizens are employed maintaining the nanotrite refining machinery as well as the life support systems so they're needed on Thalmos."

"But Thalmos supplies a good chunk of the Shattered Empires with nanotrite and the city itself is a fraction of the size of Angor Bore. With their resources they should be able to get a handle on the problem, shouldn't they?" Akira could only imagine the merciless tactics her father would employ at even the hint of such unrest.

Shiori inclined her head. "It is strange."

"Any chance his hold on power is slipping?" Akira asked.

Shiori pursed her lips. "Not that we're aware. He's got enough control to cut us off from the nanotrite supply. That'll be costing Thalmos a fortune."

They had talked around this issue many times before. It was no secret that Glankor believed Thalmos was too dependent on the Kudo-kai, their former masters. The Kudo-kai weren't their only buyers of nanotrite just as Thalmos was not the Kudo-kai's only source. But the trade between them was significant enough for the breakdown in relations to be extremely worrying for the Kudo-kai and very costly for Thalmos. A total cessation of the trade between the two was inexplicable. Akira and Shiori lapsed into silence as they reached the familiar dead end in the conversation.

"Look, Shiori," Akira said eventually, "there's something I've been meaning to say. About the night of the leaving party, the way I spoke to you, it was impolite. I didn't mean what I said. I think the pressure of this undertaking got to me."

Shiori's steady gaze met Akira's. "You have nothing to apologise for, mistress. I'm here to serve you. If I angered you, it was my fault for speaking out of turn."

It was the appropriate response from a servant of her standing but Shiori's eyes, dark and hard, betrayed the insincerity of her words.

Akira couldn't decide how she felt about the girl. If her father detected even a trace of insolence from any of his servants, they would be punished severely. On the other hand she remembered Matsuko's warning to give Shiori some leeway.

"Well, we're going to be working together for quite some time yet," Akira said. "You apparently have more experience of the Thalmians than anyone left alive in the Kudo-kai so I'm going to need you to speak your mind. Even if it's something you think I don't want to hear. I'm sorry if I've made that more difficult."

Shiori's face was a perfect emotionless mask like that of a porcelain doll.

"As you wish, mistress," she said.

After Shiori had left, taking the tea things with her, Xif said, "I think she's still angry with you."

"Thank you for the brilliant insight, Xif," Akira replied. "I'm so glad that we have your boundless intellect at our disposal."

"No need to get snappy. I'm just saying, it's odd. You can see she's unhappy with you but you'd never know from her biometrics. Pulse is regular as a metronome. She has excellent control over her emotions. It's unusual."

"I get the sense that there are a few unusual things about that girl," said Akira. "I just hope they don't cause us problems."

Chapter 19

"Are you fucking insane?" said Lazarus, eyes almost popping out of his head. "You find out we've stumbled across the most merciless killers in the galaxy and you want to audition to join them?"

Following Mordax's meeting with the leaders of the Dioscuri, the *Starling*'s crew had been moved to more pleasant quarters. Although they were still far underground, holo-screens on the wall offered a perfect replication of rolling yellow hills under a summer sun. They sat now on surprisingly comfortable block seats around a steaming pot of coffee. All of them except Lazarus, who paced the room nervously, Marvin perched on his shoulder chirruping with displeasure. It had taken them a while to believe Mordax when he had explained that they had been captured by the Dioscuri and even longer to believe what he had decided to do.

"It wasn't really an option, Laz," said Mordax. "It was that or let them kill you."

Lazarus shook his head.

"There's always another option. This is madness."

Mordax pinched the bridge of his nose. He was so tired. He had expected the crew to be less than enthusiastic about the plan. But he hadn't even told them quite how dangerous the induction to the Dioscuri seemed to be.

"Even if they hadn't threatened to kill you, I would have been stuck here for the rest of my life. I couldn't do that."

"Are you joking?" Lazarus practically shouted. "A comfortable bed. Hot coffee. No work. This place is a wet-dream!"

Stamford gave a chuckle that Mordax felt in his chest, "Who are you kidding, brother? After a week without flying you would be knocking your head against the wall."

"If it was that or be murdered by a bunch of razor-elbowed wannabe assassins, I could live with it," Lazarus said. But the fire had gone out of his voice.

"I'm with Lazarus, honey," said Virzda. "This is bad idea."

Mordax sighed. "There's another reason to do this. I know who set up the ambush on Fornax."

"Who?" demanded Stamford, tendons cracking as he clenched his fist.

"The Kudo-kai. The Dioscuri are the only chance we have to find out why. They're the only chance we have to make those bastards pay."

"The Kudo-kai?" asked Lazarus, brow furrowed. "Why would they want Stephan dead?"

Mordax hesitated. They had loved his father as much as he had. He couldn't bring himself to sully their memory of him with the truth.

"I don't know. I think he found out some dangerous information on Cantarina. We need to find out what that was."

Virzda and Lazarus looked concerned but Stamford met Mordax's eyes with a dark scrutiny that made Mordax conscious of the lie.

"Mordax knows what he is doing," said Stamford without shifting his gaze. "Stephan's death cannot go unanswered."

Virzda shook her head. "He wouldn't want you doing this. It's not the smart move."

"No," agreed Mordax, "it's the only move though. Stam, can I have a word?"

Stamford levered his bulk out of the double seat that only just accommodated him and joined Mordax in the corner. Mordax craned his neck to meet the giant's eyes and spoke in a soft voice. "You know something. Tell me."

Stamford nodded slowly and spoke in a rumble that wouldn't quite carry to the others. "I have known what your father was almost since the beginning."

"How?"

"Not long after I joined the *Starling*, we were salvaging a Kudo-kai relic near the Reaches. We were ambushed and boarded by raiders, dozens of them. Stephan killed them all. The way he moved. His speed. I had never seen anything like it and I am used to fighting. He told me his history after that. I swore never to tell another."

"Do you know what he found out on Cantarina?"

Stamford shook his head.

The fact that Stamford knew about Stephan lifted a weight off Mordax's heart. If Stamford had come to terms with it then maybe the others would too. Maybe Mordax would.

"I'm sorry for what I said earlier. I know there was nothing you could have done to save him," he said.

Stamford grunted. "You were right. It was fear that drove me. Fear of what Stephan would do if I did not get you to safety."

Mordax felt his eyes tear up and a metallic tang at the back of this throat. He swallowed hard.

"I might not make it back from this thing, Stam."

Stamford grinned showing even, white teeth.

"You are your father's son. You don't know it yet but there is iron at your core. You will come back to us."

***

An hour later a wraith face covered by the silver veil came to collect Mordax.

"Come on then, scrapper. Time to meet your playmates," said the wraith. He recognised the voice of the woman who had shot him on the *Starling* and led him to the meeting with the Dioscuri leaders. He bid hasty farewells to the crew, Virzda wiping away tears and Lazarus still muttering about Mordax's sanity, and followed her out of the room.

She whistled tunelessly but cheerfully as they walked.

"You were on my ship earlier?" he asked.

"That I was. Onkara Leftus at your service."

"You're a wraith?"

"What gave it away?" she said sardonically.

"How are your crew?"

"What do you mean?"

"Stamford said he roughed one up a bit."

She barked with laughter.

"You could say that. Broke his back in half. Poor bastard's going to be in the recovery tanks for a week."

"Could be worse. I've seen him pull a guy's arms off before. Literally. Ripped them both clean off."

The veiled face turned towards him as they walked.

"Impressed you got a shot off earlier. Most times a nerve blocker will drop a guy twice your size like a sack of shit. What's your deal? Army? Merc?"

"Uh...trader?"

Onkara paused.

"No training at all?" she asked.

"I mean, I'm pretty good on the fiddle but I don't think that's what you mean."

They walked in silence for a moment.

"I hope you're a fast learner, scrapper," she said, voice serious. "Hellenbos, is rough. And I've seen some dark shit."

Mordax tried to ignore the flutter of fear in his chest.

"If there's one thing I am, it's a fast learner. Any tips for me?"

"Yeah. Don't go to sleep."

They reached an elevator which, judging from the feeling of sudden weightlessness, sped them many miles further below the surface of the planet. When the doors opened they were in a cavern, larger than any structure Mordax had ever seen. There were racks that stretched from the floor to the roof of the cavern hundreds of feet above them filled with weaponry like the gleaming pillars of some poisoned temple. Huge drones sped up and down them, grabbing or depositing rifles, pistols and even whole mech suits, bristling with armaments. At a plain wooden desk, absurdly small against the backdrop behind him, sat a short, fat man with a white moustache and a bottle of whisky at his elbow. He was sipping from a tumbler and watched them suspiciously as they approached.

"Commander Leftus. I'd recognise those legs anywhere."

"Hello, Gary. Maybe if you spent more time exercising and less time perving, you'd still be a wraith and wouldn't be stuck down here."

Gary snickered, "Now where would be the fun in that?" He clapped his hands together. "Right, enough of the pleasantries. What can I do you for?"

"Not for me, Gary. It's for this little shite over here."

Gary peered at him with bleary eyes, taking in the rings in his ears, his threadbare coat and worn boots. "And this is…?"

"Mordax L'Amfour. Recent addition to Selection."

A pained look crossed Gary's face and he started chewing on his moustache, "Ah, yes. Mr L'Amfour. I've been informed of your arrival. I'm the quartermaster here."

"He's going to need the full works. Survival pack, bedding, coat," Onkara said.

Gary looked at Onkara apologetically, "Afraid I'm not allowed to give him anything."

"You're not allowed to give him anything?" Mordax could hear the incredulity in her voice.

"Orders from Valerian."

"They expect him to ship out to Hellenbos without a fucking coat?"

"Believe me, I pushed back. I'm not happy about it. But orders is orders."

"What does that mean?" asked Mordax.

"It means you've pissed off the wrong people, scrapper," Onkara said.

Mordax briefly fingered the tiny bag of jewels he kept in the lining of his coat, wondering if he should try to bribe the man. He dismissed the thought quickly.

"I don't believe this," he muttered angrily. "As if I wasn't screwed already."

He approached the table and grabbed the display tablet in front of Gary, thrusting it in his face.

"Show me. Show me the order."

Gary grabbed the tablet back, face reddening, and pointed a finger in Mordax's face.

"Listen here, you little bastard. I'm going to let that slide because you'll probably be dead in a day but you do that again and I'll break your arm."

Mordax clenched his jaw and said nothing, eyes downturned.

Mollified, Gary turned back to Onkara. "Well, unless there's anything else?"

"No. That's all." She beckoned Mordax to follow her and they returned to the elevator. As they rode back towards the surface, Mordax could feel her gaze on him.

"What exactly are you going to do with that whisky then?"

He glanced at her then bashfully pulled the almost full bottle of whisky from his coat. She had spotted him swipe it. He was surprised. A deft hand was needed to survive the trading routes the *Starling* had plied and Mordax's hand was particularly deft. He grinned and gave a shrug.

"Sounds like I'm fucked. So I'll probably drink it."

He thought he heard a low chuckle from Onkara's throat.

"You're not the usual sort we get around here."

The elevator stopped at a level closer to the surface. The door slid open revealing a large circular room with thirty or so cots pushed up against the wall and roughly the same number of young men and women, some sitting at tables, others on the cots checking through piles of gear. No two were dressed alike but they all seemed to be around twenty cycles old. The conversations died down as Mordax and Onkara entered the room. A few, in military-style uniforms, snapped to attention.

"Time to make some friends, scrapper. Good luck," she whispered.

"Relax, maggots," she said more loudly to the ones saluting, "you're not in your tinpot army now. We're the Dioscuri. The killers of kings. We bow to no one so that we might serve everyone. Consider that your first lesson."

She addressed the rest of the room, "We're shipping out in ten hours. If I were you I'd make the most of those cots. You won't have anything as comfortable for a long time. Remember, you can pull out any time before you step onto the shuttle tomorrow. But after that you're stuck in the blender 'til the cycle's finished."

With that, she turned on her heel and left. Mordax felt the weight of the others' scrutiny settle over him like ash. Their eyes were calculating, sizing him up. He moved over to the one cot that seemed unoccupied. On the cot next to it, sitting cross-legged, was a girl with short blonde hair and sun-browned skin. She was in the middle of cleaning a disassembled pistol, the parts strewn over the blanket. She watched him suspiciously as he approached.

"Hi," Mordax said, raising a hand in greeting.

The girl snorted and returned her attention to the weapon in front of her.

"I'm Mordax," he persevered.

"That's great," she said without looking up.

"You got a name?"

The girl sighed and looked over at him again. Her eyes were an icy blue. He noticed a pale scar running along her temple towards her ear.

"Look, mate, I'm not interested in being buddies. Best to keep your head down and try not to attract too much attention."

He plopped himself down on the cot. "I'll do my best but I'm afraid I'm not too good at that. You got a smoke?"

"No."

Mordax shrugged. "Shame. I'm guessing Hellenbos won't be that well stocked with the creature comforts."

The girl glanced over at him.

"Where's your kit?" she asked.

"I'm a late addition. Didn't have time to pick up any," Mordax thought it best not to reveal that he seemed to have already made an enemy among the Dioscuri leadership.

The girl's eyes widened.

"No kit at all?"

"I've got this," said Mordax, revealing the bottle of whisky from inside his jacket.

"Fucking hell. You're screwed, mate. No knife, no coat, no bedding? I'd ring the bell and pack it in if I were you."

"Care to lend me some gear?"

"Piss off."

"Thought not," said Mordax with a smile.

The girl examined him as if for the first time, taking in his unruly hair and the rings in his ears.

"Where are you from? You don't look military."

"I'm not. I'm a Traveller. Used to work the fringe end of the Crux."

A man at a table nearby gave a nasty laugh and turned to face them.

"Looks like they've let a gypsy try out, lads. Better watch your gear. The little cunt will filch whatever's not nailed down."

The man had a lean, dangerous look about him. His dark hair was cut short and his nose kinked in the middle, clearly broken at some point in the past.

One of the two men with him, broad-shouldered and thickly muscled, snickered at the insult. The other, a lanky man with sandy hair, had the decency to look embarrassed. The girl on the cot glared at Ragin.

"Leave him be, Ragin," she said.

"What, you think I'm exaggerating? Don't be stupid, Sylvia. Those gypsies are all the same, believe me. They'll clean you out soon as look at you."

Ragin turned his attention back to Mordax. "How did a streak of piss like you get onto Selection?"

Mordax absorbed the hostility. He was used to worse.

"Friends in high places," he said with a wink.

"We'll see how that works out for you on Hellenbos," Ragin said and turned back to the table.

Mordax swung his legs off the cot and stood up, grabbing the bottle of whisky.

"Careful with them, mate," Sylvia whispered as he started towards Ragin's table.

He glanced back and smiled. As he approached the table the large man with Ragin stood up. He was only a couple of inches taller than Mordax but much broader. Veins popped in his bull neck and his bald scalp gleamed. Mordax wished Stamford was with him. He held up the bottle and shook it gently, amber liquid sloshing.

"Peace, brother. I think we got off on the wrong foot."

Mordax settled himself on a chair and set the bottle on the table.

"Care for a drink?" he said.

"I'm not touching anything from you," Ragin said without looking at him.

"Fair enough," Mordax said amiably and raised his eyebrows at the others. The large man looked at the bottle and wetted his fleshy lips.

"Yeah, go on then," he said.

Ragin snorted in disgust and stood up. "You're an idiot, Afu."

"What? It's just whisky. This might be the last drink we have for months."

Ragin shook his head and left, returning to his cot on the other side of the room. Afu turned to the lanky man beside him.

"Come on, Chadwick," said Afu, "have a drink, man."

"Nah, not for me," said Chadwick, also getting up. "Want to stay sharp for tomorrow." He nodded to Mordax and left.

Afu shrugged and fished a metal cup out of a pocket of the black gilet that covered his torso. Mordax glanced over at the girl on the cot.

"Sylvia," he said, "lend me a cup?"

She gave him a hard look, eyes flicking briefly towards Ragin on the other side of the room, perhaps remembering his warning. Then she sighed, reached into her pack and tossed him a cup. Mordax uncorked the bottle, releasing a heady aroma of oak and chocolate. He poured a measure into his cup and a double-measure into Afu's. He took a sip, savouring the bright warmth as the liquid travelled down his gullet. Gary, the quartermaster, clearly had expensive taste. It was a shame Mordax had to waste it on the great lump opposite him.

Afu knocked the whisky back, grunting with satisfaction.

"So, where are you from, friend?" Mordax asked while refilling Afu's cup.

"Gedoa."

Mordax had heard of the system. It was a cruel, unsteady empire near the Core.

Afu knocked back another drink which Mordax promptly replenished.

"Seen much action?" Mordax asked.

"Me and Ragin have been on five tours together," Afu said, wiping his mouth with the back of his hand. "We put down rebellions on every continent."

"Really? Impressive. What are you doing here?" Mordax asked with a pleasant smile.

Afu shrugged. "The killing got too easy. We're looking for more of a challenge. Got an order we should meet with this guy, Valerian, and he invited us to try out."

Mordax looked around the room.

"It seems they've invited people from all over the sector."

Afu grunted his agreement while taking another gulp. He squinted at Mordax. "Mostly soldiers. A few mercs. All from elite fighting units. Except you," he chuckled. "You're so fucked."

Mordax didn't let the smile drop from his face. He raised his cup. "Well, if that's the case, I'd better make the most of my last few hours."

Afu laughed loudly and clunked cups with him. Mordax took a tiny sip while Afu drained his. Afu's cheeks had started to flush and he settled back into his chair with a comfortable sigh. Mordax reached into his pocket and brought out a deck of cards.

"How about a game? We've got time," he said.

Afu eyed the cards somewhat warily.

"Come on. Your choice," said Mordax.

"You know Red Twelve?" Afu asked.

Mordax smiled. He did. He knew most of the popular card games in this part of the Shattered Empires.

Mordax dealt the hands and they started to play. Mordax lost more hands than he won and kept on topping up Afu's cup. Mordax watched Afu's face and hands carefully. The man was not a natural card player and was terrible at bluffing. After Mordax folded a particularly good hand, he sighed. "I've always been told that playing for no stakes is barely playing at all."

Afu snorted dismissively. "What have you got to bet with?"

Moreax dumped a small velvet bag onto the table which until recently had been sewn into the inside of his shirt. Afu drew open the neck of the bag with thick fingers until the light caught the gems inside causing them to glitter like crushed ice. Having an emergency source of funds had saved Mordax's hide quite a few times. A gleam that he had seen many times before entered Afu's eyes. Mordax placed a tiny diamond on the middle of the table.

"You got anything to wager?" he asked.

Afu brought out a handful of gold coins from a pocket of the gilet, clearly not worth anything like the diamond. Mordax shrugged and they played a few hands which Mordax again lost leaving Afu with a few gems to add to his pile of coins. He let Afu feel their sharp edges between his fingers, let him admire the frozen fire at their centre and revel in the warm glow of his good fortune. Then he began to take it all away. There were only a few measures of whisky left in the bottle now and Afu was slurring his words. Mordax won the next few hands until all the gems were back in his possession. He won the hands after that until Afu's coins were in a pile before him. He commiserated with Afu's bad luck and expressed embarrassment at his own fortune. It was Afu's idea to begin betting with his kit. Mordax knew that he would as soon as he had seen the glimmer of avarice in his face. Mordax lost the odd hand, enough to keep Afu's hope alive that he could win it all back but Afu's losses mounted and with them the sour stink of desperation grew on him. Ragin tried to intervene a couple of times but Afu brushed him off angrily. Beads of sweat gathered on Afu's pate and dripped into his eyes, causing him to curse. Within two hours Mordax had it all. He had won Afu's knife and bedding, his survival rations and winter coat. He had even won his boots. Afu held his head in his hands sucking in short sharp breaths. Suddenly he slammed his fist down on the table and stumbled to his feet, attracting the attention of the whole room.

"You fucking cheat!" he yelled.

Mordax remained sitting and kept his expression neutral. It was not the first time a bad loser had accused him of cheating.

Sometimes they were right but this time he hadn't had to rig the game.

"You gypsy scum. If you think I'm going to let you steal my kit—"

"You mean my kit," Mordax corrected.

Afu stared at him wild-eyed. He balled a fist and took a step towards Mordax.

"I wouldn't do that if I were you," Mordax said conversationally. He looked pointedly at a black dome set into the ceiling. "You're being watched and I can't imagine the Dioscuri will take kindly to brawling."

Afu followed his gaze and then seemed to deflate. Mordax stood up, pocketed the bag of gems, now laden with additional gold coins, and hefted the bag of what was once Afu's kit. He almost felt bad for the man but then thoughts of the Kudo-kai edged into his mind, steeling his resolve. Afu would just have to drop out before they left for Hellenbos and go back to murdering rebels.

"There's a few hours until we need to be up. Get some sleep, Afu," he said.

He made his way back to his cot, sensing the eyes of the room on him but now their scrutiny didn't weigh him down, he floated above it, buoyed by his success. The others might be better prepared for what was to come, but it was rarely wise to write off a Traveller.

***

"Look lively, you slugs. We ship out in ten minutes."

Onkara had entered the room and stood now watching the initiates scurrying to gather their belongings. Mordax was sweating in Afu's fleece-lined leather coat, cuffs turned up to shorten the arms. He had a hunting knife strapped to his leg, a pistol in a holster at his hip and a Bergen at his feet, filled with flints, survival rations, water purifying tablets, first aid materials and a few items he didn't even recognise. Afu's boots were a couple of sizes too big for him but were in much better shape than his own and looked waterproof, so he had stuffed a pair of socks into the toe ends and put them on too. He had glanced over at Afu once but the naked hatred in the glare that met him discouraged further inspection.

When all the initiates were ready and standing beside their cots, the door slid open again and General Valerian strode into the room. The ring of bodies straightened visibly. Valerian walked slowly down the line examining the faces of the young men and women in front of him.

"Each year it's the same," he said, voice deep and clear, "a group of mongrels who think they've seen it all and can handle the worst. Know this though. To us, you're as green as spring grass."

His boots clicked against the metal floor. A metronome beat underpinning his words. "We don't care what flag you fought for, what battles you won or what medals you earned. The Dioscuri stand above the petty squabbles of your past. Your experience until now has been merely a prelude, a warm up for what we will now put you through. If you survive Hellenbos you will learn to do things you thought impossible. We will sharpen you to a razor edge. In time, you may eventually become a true Dioscuri wraith and help us to preserve peace throughout the Shattered Empires. But until then you're meat for the grinder."

As he neared Ragin's cot, General Valerian caught his eye and nodded with a slight smile. The smile swiftly fell away when he saw Afu next to him, red-rimmed eyes turned to the floor, dressed only in a shirt and trousers and conspicuously bare feet.

"Initiate! Where is your gear?" he barked at Afu.

Afu didn't dare to meet the General's eye.

"I lost it, General," he replied pathetically.

Valerian scanned the room until he spotted Mordax, wrapped warmly and now carrying the heavy Bergen on his back. Valerian's eyes widened in disbelief and, despite everything else, Mordax felt an overwhelming urge to laugh. First understanding, then a fury, cold as winter, settled onto Valerian's face as he turned back to Afu.

"You let that boy, with no training, take your gear? You're a disgrace to Gedoa."

Afu seemed to collapse in on himself at the words. His muscular form suddenly appeared frail and old.

"Commander Leftus, get this foundering mess out my sight."

Onkara took Afu by the arm and led him, head hanging, out of the room. Valerian, his wide jaw tight, made a cursory inspection of the rest of the group. When he reached Mordax he lent in close, his shadow falling across Mordax's eyes.

"Your tricks won't save you on Hellenbos, L'Amfour," he whispered. "You should have accepted our mercy and lived out your days in comfort. You'll come to see your mistake soon enough. I just regret that I won't be there to see it."

Mordax felt an urge to shrink back but forced himself to remain still.

"Perhaps. But if you're as poor a judge of character as evidence suggests," he whispered back, nodding meaningfully at Afu's empty cot, "you might be underestimating me."

Valerian's lips parted and he seemed about to reply but instead he turned away abruptly and left the room, leaving Mordax standing there, clenching his fists to keep his hands from shaking.

Chapter 20

The wind howled around them whipping up the top layer of snow and ice into vicious eddies in the air. Mordax had lost all sensation in his toes and he stamped his feet trying to work the blood back into them. The other initiates around him, already dusted with snow, did the same. Trees bordered the clearing in which they stood, like dark sentinels watching trespassers into their domain. They were twisted and misshapen as if corrupted by the elements. The two transport ships that had brought the initiates to Hellenbos stood behind them, gangways closed, offering no shelter against the cold. The two men who had accompanied them on the flight over now stood facing them, one large and bearded with eyes squinted in seemingly perpetual amusement, the other lean with a hungry look about his sallow face.

The bearded man spoke now, seemingly unbothered by the bitter air that sapped the warmth from Mordax's lungs with each breath.

"Welcome to Hellenbos, kids. For those of you who haven't met me, I'm Ashfol Krangmire. The nasty piece of work next to me is Daenyrs Vyl'Granut."

Daenyrs regarded them silently.

"We're the ones who've been entrusted with the unenviable responsibility of sorting out which of you are deserving of a place within the Dioscuri and which are more suited to returning in a body bag. Luckily Hellenbos usually takes care of the latter."

Ashfol gestured to the woods behind him. "This will be your home for the next two months. You will be cold and you will be hungry. However, if you listen to our instructions some of you might not be dead at the end of this. Today, we'll let you get acquainted with your new surroundings. Five clicks due south of here is an old camp clearing that you can set up in this evening. Organise a look-out roster. Don't go into the trees at night and whatever you do, don't let your fire go out."

There was a moment's silence.

"What? You want me to hold your hands?" barked Ashfol. "Get moving."

With that, the group started trudging through the thick snow, a few pulling out compasses to check their bearings. When they reached the tree line, an oppressive darkness settled over them and the sound of the wind became muffled. Under the canopy, the soft snow that had carpeted the clearing was replaced by hard ice, pierced by gnarled roots and sharp rocks. The group picked their way carefully through the rough terrain. Mordax was grateful for the toughened boots he had taken from Afu. He wished, not for the first time, that he still had Afu's pistol but Ashfol had stripped the initiates of all their projectile weapons before they boarded the transports to Hellenbos despite some vociferous opposition.

"The things that'll be trying to kill you won't have guns," he had said with a wink, "so it's cheating if I let you keep them."

Mordax noted more than one initiate distractedly reaching towards an absent holster as they moved quietly over the forest floor. He matched strides with Sylvia who was focussing intently on the gloom in front of them.

"I was expecting a bit more of an introduction than that," Mordax said.

"All part of the initiation. They're seeing who can handle the learning curve," Sylvia said.

"It'd be good if we knew what we were supposed to be learning," Mordax muttered. "Any idea what's out here?"

Sylvia glanced at him. "Nope."

"They didn't give you any clues about what exactly we would be doing out here?"

"How many people have you killed, Mordax?"

Mordax missed a half step, the question taking him by surprise.

"That's what I thought," said Sylvia when he didn't answer. "Look, mate, I'm glad you got one over on Afu. He was a nasty cunt and you'd be dead already without his gear. But we're in the field now. Pretty words and card skills aren't going to help you out here and no one can afford dead weight."

Mordax forced himself to smile. "You trying to say you're not going to babysit me."

Sylvia stopped and turned her piercing blue eyes on him. The gentle scuffing of the other initiates' boots against the frozen forest floor didn't break the silence around them so much as accentuate it.

"That's exactly what I'm saying."

Mordax met her gaze. He spoke quietly. "Look Sylvia, it's obvious I don't have much experience with this stuff. I can't build a shelter or skin an animal. But that doesn't mean I'm green. Not in the things that matter anyway. I've spent my life using my brain and my tongue to survive. There may come a time when both will be useful. Look, you can give me some basic pointers and when the time comes I'll have your back or you can do this all alone. It's up to you."

Mordax turned away and continued to walk. After a few seconds, he heard Sylvia's footsteps continue behind him. He didn't look back. After a while, she said, "You're not walking straight, you know."

He risked a glance at her. "Huh?"

She gave an exasperated sigh. "Take your compass bearing and line up three trees ahead of you in a straight line. When you get to the nearest tree line up another so there are still three trees ahead. That'll make sure you keep walking in a straight line. If you wander off the line from where we landed you might miss the camp completely."

Mordax fumbled with the pocket that held his compass, struggling with the thick fingers of Afu's gloves.

"Fuck it. Just follow me," Sylvia said.

She pushed past him and strode off into the gloom. Mordax allowed himself a small smile and followed.

***

The camp was as basic as Mordax had feared, consisting of a clearing about thirty metres wide with a charred pit and large ring of blackened stones at the centre. The ground was bare except for the remnants of a number of tree trunks dotted around the fire pit, reaching only head height and still rooted in the frozen earth. Mordax had wondered what they were for until Sylvia began stringing her hammock between two of the trunks. He quickly copied her, picking a spot near to both Sylvia and the fire. As he worked, he examined the wood of the tree trunks wondering if it was valuable. It was an old habit and a hard one to shake. The surface of the trunk was odd. Great vertical cracks split the moss-covered bark. He tugged at one crack and a whole section split away from the trunk and fell to the ground. The inside of the bark was covered in a soft, fibrous material. He tried to break a corner off the loose section but it was tougher than it appeared. Soon there was a jumbled ring of canvas hammocks threaded between the trunks. In the pit at the centre, two of the initiates had started a meagre fire that coughed and spat as it consumed the damp wooden logs. It was better than nothing, however, and the group sat on their Bergens around it, chewing ration bars and trying to get some warmth back into their limbs. Dusk had fallen and the wind in the trees had dropped to a barely perceptible whisper. A solid looking man called Theron with a serious expression and restless eyes suggested they organise a watch rota of three at a time, to cover the whole clearing. The others murmured their agreement. When Mordax volunteered himself for a watch, Ragin snorted loudly from across the fire and spat on the ground.

"I'm not sleeping on his watch. You lot trust a fucking gypsy to watch your back out here?" he said.

"I trust everyone here to do what's in their interest to survive," said Theron. "No one here's stupid. Everyone knows we stand a better chance if we pull together."

"You know who would be useful in the field?" said Ragin "Afu. We'd be better off dumping that snake in the woods and letting him fend for himself."

The silence that followed was more contemplative than Mordax was comfortable with.

"Easy fix," said Sylvia eventually. "Mordax takes the same watch as you. Then you can make sure he doesn't slack off. Or nick your underwear."

Mordax frowned at her, as the other initiates chuckled, but she simply smirked and got to her feet, shaking off the thin skin of snow that had settled on her trousers. As she moved past Mordax she whispered, "At least it'll make it more difficult for him to knife you in your sleep."

Mordax wasn't sure if she was joking or not. It was now fully dark and the rest of the initiates gradually made their way to their hammocks. Mordax found his own, kicked off his boots and settled in, pulling a thin grey blanket, which he had found at the bottom of Afu's Bergen, tightly around him. Despite its lightness the blanket radiated warmth as if electrified and, with a prickling sensation, the feeling gradually seeped back into his feet. The forest seemed more alive at night than it had been during the day, the stillness punctuated by the low cooing of birds and the strange coughs of some other nocturnal creature. A few of the initiates were already snoring. Mordax closed his eyes and tried to empty his mind. The previous night on Eloth, bone-weary as he had been from the recent events, sleep had overcome him almost immediately. Now every time he tried to relax, flashes of memory stabbed at him, shooting him full of adrenaline and snatching away precious oblivion. His father's final moments played out over and over and Calgary's words rang in his ears. Stephan, an assassin. Mordax's grief was still a raw bleeding wound but it was intertwined with some emotion deeper and less clean. Did the blood of a killer run in his veins? He had never before felt the urge to take another person's life. Now all he could think about was finding whoever was responsible for his father's death and visiting the same fate on them. He was the son of a Dioscuri wraith. Perhaps it was inevitable. As the night grew long, gentler thoughts of the *Starling*'s crew calmed the troubled surface of his mind. He imagined what he would say to them now if he could. Eventually, he must have drifted off because suddenly he was being shaken. A dark shape stood above him, silhouetted against the almost black of the sky.

"Your watch," the figure said and disappeared into the sea of canvas around him.

Mordax stumbled out of his hammock and pulled on his boots, breath frosting in the freezing air. He picked his way carefully towards the outskirts of the camp and away from the golden glow of the fire. The moon had broken through the cloud cover and cast the forest in a silvery grey. Across the clearing, Ragin had already taken up his post. He was crouched on a low rock, coat wrapped around him, and still as a gargoyle. His expression was inscrutable in the dim moonlight. Mordax wrapped his arms around himself and, shivering, gazed out towards the dark mass of trees at the edge of the clearing. The initiates' presence here felt wrong somehow. Out of place. It was as if the forest exuded a black malevolence towards them, waiting until it could retake the ground that had been stolen from it.

"Get a grip, Mordax," he whispered to himself. He couldn't fall apart on the first night. He settled down and prepared to see out the rest of his shift. It didn't help that he had no idea what he was supposed to be watching out for. An hour or so later, Mordax heard the shuffle and squeak of footsteps on fresh snow. A figure approached from the camp hunched against the cold. As he drew closer, Mordax saw that it was Chadwick, the lanky man who had been sitting with Afu and Ragin the previous night.

"What's up?" asked Mordax quietly so as not to disturb the other sleeping initiates.

"Nature calls, man," Chadwick said as he shuffled past him heading towards the tree line.

"Sure that's a good idea?" said Mordax.

Chadwick shook his head and chuckled. "We're not going to last long out here if we can't even take a shit."

He continued out towards the trees leaving dark imprints in the snow and was soon lost to view amid the trees. Mordax sighed, releasing a cloud of vapour. It was almost time for him to wake the next watch but he wanted to wait until Chadwick returned. The minutes dragged on. Eventually Mordax began to feel a flutter of concern. Chadwick should have returned by now. He pulled his coat tighter and followed the footprints to the edge of the forest. When he reached the tree line it was impossible to tell how much further Chadwick had walked, the moon shadow under the canopy swallowed the trail. An odd metallic scent crept into the air.

"Chadwick," he said in a hoarse whisper. He was met with a silence that caused his skin to creep. Mordax suddenly realised what was out of place. There was now no sound at all, not even the trilling and scratching of the forest's night creatures. Something was very wrong. He rushed back towards the fire, retracing Chadwick's footsteps, and beckoned Ragin over.

"What?" demanded Ragin when he reached the fire pit.

"Chadwick went into the woods and hasn't come back," Mordax said as he grasped one of the longer branches from the fire and pulled it out.

"You let him go? I fucking knew it. Never trust a gypsy."

A couple of other initiates, roused by the conversation, were approaching the fire. Mordax wrestled to control the hot rage that flared inside him threatening to spew molten words out of his throat.

"You going to stand here holding your dick or are you going to help me look?" he said.

Without waiting for a response he ducked through the hammocks and rushed back towards the point where Chadwick's footsteps led, the branch in his hand glowing and still just holding a shivering yellow flame. When he reached the trees, the flickering light revealed that the footprints stopped within a few metres and led to a jumbled mess on the forest floor. The scattered snow was spattered and streaked with black marks. Mordax reached out to touch one of the marks and the fingers of his glove came back glistening crimson in the light of the fire.

"Well, that's it then," came Ragin's rough voice from behind him. "You've done for another one."

Mordax turned to find Ragin and Sylvia behind him. Sylvia took in the scene without any visible emotion. Mordax turned back and began to press on into the forest.

"CHADWICK," he yelled.

"Mordax!" hissed Sylvia. "Don't be an idiot. We've got no idea what's out there and no weapons."

Ragin snorted. "Let him go."

Mordax knew that Sylvia was right, he should go back, but he felt responsible. It had been his watch. He pushed on, deeper into the trees, holding the makeshift torch in front of him. The flame had gone out and the remaining ember gave off a dull red glow that barely reached the nearest trees. Mordax strained his eyes, peering into the black spaces between the trunks.

There were no tracks. No indication of what had happened to Chadwick or where he had gone. It was the faintest of sounds that alerted him, a whisper of movement against wood high above which, in the otherwise total silence, immediately caught his attention. Mordax was moving before he had time to think, dropping the glowing branch and shifting his body away from the sound and towards the nearest tree. There was a dull thud near his face and a flicker of something white appeared on the trunk next to him. Without pause, Mordax snatched the object and fled back towards the clearing keeping low to the ground and skirting the trees. When he emerged from the wood, heart pounding more from fear than exertion, only Sylvia was still waiting. She looked exasperated to see him.

"You know, Mordax, for someone who was talking up the qualities of their brain so recently, you're acting like an utter moron."

Without waiting for a response she turned and began to make her way back to the camp. Mordax stood still for a few seconds, until the hammering of his heart had subsided, then he opened his fist revealing what appeared to be a sharp sliver of translucent bone. The blunt end was covered by soft, dark fur and the whole thing gave off a putrid smell, like rotting flesh. He slipped the thing into one of his pockets careful not to prick himself and began to make his own way back to the camp, the ferrous scent of blood still lingering in his nostrils.

Chapter 21

"You must forgive the mess. Preparations for Umberaurum are well under way and there will be quite a bit of upheaval until then, I'm afraid."

The small man's broad, pearly-toothed smile didn't touch his eyes, making it seem almost as if the top and bottom halves of his face belonged to different people entirely. His grey streaked hair was piled high on his head as if to give him extra height, and his pointed white shoes clacked against the pavement as they walked. Arantinus Cezan had met Akira, Xif and Shiori at Kor'Thalia's spaceport, introducing himself as their appointed guide and informing them that the Council of Thalmos had requested to meet with them straight away. He had led them here to the outskirts of the city where the Spire, a protrusion that ran the full height of Kor'Thalia's perimeter wall and the seat of Thalmos's government, towered over them.

"No apology necessary," said Akira. "I've never seen anything like this place. It's magnificent."

Arantinus made a show of demurring but he couldn't help a smug smile from creeping onto his face. It was no false praise. The little Akira had seen of the city made Ang'Dirth look like a farmer's hovel by comparison, something she previously would have sworn was impossible. Gargantuan streets, built originally for machines that had lost all connection to human scales, were lined with greenery and flanked by glittering towers. Street lamps were decorated with intricate gold filigree and great crystal fountains spumed dancing jets hundreds of feet into the air. Perfume hung thick in the air wherever they walked and the half-finished statues and wreaths adorning the buildings they passed did little to detract from the city's grandeur. She was only now beginning to comprehend the outrageous wealth the Thalmians had been able to accumulate through their production of nanotrite and all of it shared by a population a fraction the size of an average planet. It was like spreading a whole jar of honey onto a crust of bread.

"This year's celebrations should be quite a spectacle," Arantinus said happily. "I do hope you'll still be here to experience them."

"Yes, well, it's possible," said Akira.

"How are the security arrangements this year?" asked Shiori, her face showing only mild curiosity. "After last year's incident I imagine you will be taking extra precautions."

Arantinus's smile faltered and his small eyes darted to Shiori and then away. Last year's festival had been marred by a gas attack that had killed hundreds of citizens.

"Of course, sadly, we are always on guard against those who would try to disrupt our way of life out of jealousy but it's nothing that should trouble you," he said, addressing Akira, as if it had been she who had spoken and not Shiori.

"Just through here, if you please," he said, leading them up sweeping stone steps, past stony-faced guards each with a combat drone floating above their head, and through the doors at the base of the Spire. The atrium beyond was floored with gold-veined marble slabs, and enormous statues of imposing men and women gazed down on them disdainfully.

"Councillor Masters of cycles past," explained Arantinus as he ushered them into a glass elevator.

As they sped upwards, the great expanse of the city, surrounded on three sides by ocean and on one side by the perimeter wall, spread out before them, glittering crimson in the light of the evening sun. A few wisps of cloud floated far beneath them, growing smaller by the second. The perimeter wall rose a hundred kilometres high and entirely surrounded the island city and its encompassing ocean, serving to contain the atmosphere that sat within it. The thin spire they were now climbing marked the spot where the city and the wall met. As

Shiori had explained, aside from being the centre of government, the Spire also contained the living quarters of the swollen ranks of Thalmos's elite citizens.

As they cleared the top of the perimeter wall the barren greyness beyond crept into view and Akira was reminded of her first sight of Thalmos. It was the pinnacle of pre-Purge Kudo-kai engineering, a planet-sized hemisphere with a smaller hemisphere cut out of it, like half a pitted peach. Arantinus was chattering away, explaining Thalmos's history and how the great machine worked as if Akira might have neglected to do even the barest of research on the place.

"The cavity, which the top of the Spire overlooks, is designed to receive Inthil, a sphere of exotic material, the size of a moon, which makes a yearly pilgrimage to kiss the sun's chromosphere, where the extraordinary forces work their mysterious arts."

Arantinus waggled his fingers as if casting a spell.

"This creates the raw nanotrite that is extracted and refined on Thalmos. Our festival, Umberaurum, celebrates the arrival of Inthil back to Thalmos and the bounty she brings with her."

The curved half of Thalmos was a dusty grey, pocked by a thousand cycles of meteor strikes, except for the cloud-spotted, shimmering blue disc of Kor'Thalia pressed up against the precipice. When they had first arrived in the system, Akira had been overjoyed merely to be out of the utter nothingness of netherspace. She had almost wept at the sunlight that suddenly poured through the portholes of *Charon's Wake*. Right now, however, Akira's belly was a jangle of nerves. The sky outside the elevator darkened with her mood and a prickling of stars appeared as they rose above the atmosphere. Faced with her first meeting with the ruling elite of Thalmos, her weeks of preparation now seemed absurdly inadequate. The elevator made no concessions to her nerves, however, as it reached the top of the Spire and the doors split open. It was like emerging onto the surface of a satellite. There were no visible walls or ceiling and the grey curvature of the artificial planet, thousands of miles distant, glinted in the sunlight. She knew it was an illusion. The walls of the dome around them were covered in light panels transmitting the view from outside so that they seemed invisible but it was disconcerting nonetheless. Most disturbing was the drop off beyond the edge of the perimeter wall where the cold blackness of deep space gazed back at her, as if the world had been cut in two by some angry god. Their footsteps on the bare, smooth stone echoed around them. Ahead were nine figures, clad in black flowing robes, floating six feet in the air, like malevolent phantoms. The Council of Thalmos.

"All theatrics, Akira," Xif buzzed quietly, obviously sensing her discomfort. "There are stasis fields in the floor below them. Hold your nerve now."

Akira reached for the jade token at her neck that Matsuko had given her. She held it for a moment, closed her eyes and tried to channel his quiet confidence. The trio and their guide made their way to the centre of the Spire. Arantinus stepped forward.

"May I present Ambassador Director Akira Mukudori Kudo, daughter of Supreme Executive General Daisuke Kudo of the most glorious collective of the Kudo-kai and Xifulandros Mil Askathraim, Central Node of the First Circle," he said with a flourish.

At the mention of Xif's name, there was an outbreak of urgent hushed discussion among the Council until the figure at the centre held up a bony hand for silence. Akira recognised the hooked nose and sunken eyes of Glankor the Blessed. His dark hair was cut respectably short and the engraved tokens around his neck, a custom inherited from their time under the boot of the Kudo-kai, marked him out as the highest ranked.

"My, my, the First Daughter of the Kudo-kai and the Great Betrayer," Glankor said in a dry, dusty voice. "We are graced by your presence. Welcome to our humble city."

Akira stole a quick glance at Xif but he gave no reaction. She didn't understand the reference to betrayal but she was more than capable of discerning the lack of sincerity in Glankor's words.

"We thank you kindly for your hospitality, Council Master Glankor," Akira said, craning her neck to meet his gaze.

"I must confess, there are those among the Council, myself included, who are somewhat confused by your arrival, Ambassador," Glankor said. "We had thought the fate of your previous delegation would have been sufficient indication of our desire to put an end to further dealings with the Kudo-kai. Perhaps your father requires further clarification on this point, hmmm?"

One of the Council members, a fat man on Glankor's left, snorted loudly.

"Your position is clear enough, Council Master." Akira was surprised her words came out clear and strong. "Thalmos's breaches of the most fundamental principles of interstellar relations has seen to that."

"Our breaches?" hissed Glankor. "You have some nerve, Ambassador, coming before this Council and lecturing us on the proper protocols of diplomacy. You, a direct descendant of the family that ripped this galaxy in two."

"Let us not forget, Council Master, that it was my family that created Thalmos, that gave your people the technology that has made your system one of the richest in the galaxy. A family that has over the cycles purchased vast amounts of your nanotrite at very competitive prices. I would say that we are quite well placed to comment to this Council on the execution of our own delegates."

Akira feared that she might be pushing him too hard too soon. Glankor gave a snort of laughter.

"It seems you're a chip off the old block, girl. Your father doesn't mince his words either."

"I'm surprised you thought it might be otherwise. I am my father's voice on this issue. I have full authority to negotiate between our people."

"Oh, I doubt that, Ambassador." Glankor gave a cruel, knowing smile as if Akira was not party to some private joke.

Confused but keen not to show it, Akira tried to redirect the conversation.

"Whatever your feelings, I'm the one my father has sent in his place. You owe us an explanation. Why has Thalmos ceased to trade with the Kudo-kai? What possible reason could you have had to execute our people? If there's been some misunderstanding or unintended offence, we are anxious to remedy the situation."

Glankor remained silent, eyes hard as granite.

"*He's angry,*" Xif said in a voice that Akira knew only she could hear. "*Oh, he's very angry.*"

"*You're anxious to remedy the situation,*" Glankor repeated. "We have a saying on Thalmos, 'the offered hand hides the sharpest claws'. No, we have no need of any of your remedies, girl. Your trip has been a wasted one. We owe you nothing. Now all that remains is to decide whether the Kudo-kai require more persuasion of the sincerity of our feeling on the matter." Glankor gave a casual gesture and the Council winked out of existence.

"*Xif, what's going on?*" Akira subvocalised.

"*More smoke and mirrors,*" said Xif. "*The Council are all still there. There's a screen between us covered with the same light emitters as the inside of the dome above us. They're arguing among themselves...probably about what should be done with us. I can't make out the audio.*"

"*What do you think our chances are?*" she asked.

"*Your guess is as good as mine,*" Xif said. "*You came on a bit strong with him but then by all accounts he's never responded well to meekness.*"

Akira's heart hammered in her chest. Xif's matt black body was as inscrutable as it was possible to be and Shiori as always kept her emotions hidden behind a mask of impassivity. Eventually, the Council rematerialised as abruptly as they had disappeared. Nine grey faces regarded them without expression.

"Xif," Akira rumbled in her throat, "*we're getting out of this with our skins intact, right?*"

"*There's a lot of emotion in the group,*" Xif replied. "*Whatever they've agreed has got their blood up.*"

"*Now's the time you tell me you have a sure-fire back-up plan in case everything falls apart,*" Akira said.

"*I have a sure-fire back-up plan in case everything falls apart.*"

"*You do?*"

"*No. This is all or nothing. If Glankor's committed to breaking off relations and decides to send your father another message, you're screwed.*"

"*You mean we're screwed.*"

"*Probably not actually. I'm too valuable an asset to destroy.*"

She couldn't be sure, but Akira thought she detected a trace of self-loathing in the statement. There was much to discuss with him assuming they were not both about to be incinerated and sent back to her father as a cube of carbon.

"Apologies for keeping you waiting, Ambassador," Glankor said. "Your presence has precipitated quite a lively discussion among the Council."

"Think nothing of it, Council Master, we are at your disposal," Akira replied as calmly as she could muster.

Glankor turned to the woman immediately to his right. "Rotoria, as Sword of the Council, I believe it is your prerogative to pass the Council's sentence."

At the word "sentence" the bottom fell out of Akira's stomach. The woman to Glankor's right cleared her throat. She was a head taller than any of the other members of the Council, unstooped despite her advancing cycles, and with streaks of white running through her hair which was coiled in a tight bun behind her head.

She spoke in a deep, drawling voice. "Pursuant to the exercise of this Council's discretion in all matters involving foreign agents and intermediaries—"

"Oh no," said Xif in Akira's head.

"What?!" she said.

"...and on the basis of the intelligence to which the Council has been privy..." continued Rotoria

"Glankor's heart rate is up, endorphin levels are elevated. He's looking forward to this."

"...by the power vested in me as Sword of the Council of Elders of Thalmos, I sentence you to death."

Chapter 22

"What a fucking mess." Ashfol had his hands on his hips and was peering at the streaks of gore in the snow, now tinged brown in the morning light. The rest of the initiates were huddled around, faces drawn, waiting for some insight into what had happened to Chadwick. Ashfol straightened up and clapped his gloved hands together.

"Ah well. Time to pack up, we're on the move in five."

"What? Is that it?" said Theron. "You're not going to tell us what happened?"

Ashfol frowned, looking genuinely bemused. "I haven't a clue. There's a hundred things in this forest that can tear a person apart. It could have been any of them."

There was a brief silence as the initiates digested this. Mordax fingered the dart in his pocket. He almost spoke up but something made him think Ashfol knew more than he was letting on.

"It happened during the gypsy's watch," Ragin said, casting a contemptuous glance at Mordax.

Ashfol pinched his nose and sighed.

"The reason for a watch is to look out for nasty things trying to get into camp. It's not to stop stupid buggers wandering off into the forest despite very clear advice to the contrary and getting themselves killed. You're big boys and girls and now you know what happens when you don't listen to me."

Ragin snorted and shook his head.

"And in my experience, Ragin, you'd be well served not getting on the wrong side of a Traveller." Ashfol winked at Mordax who felt an unexpected wave of gratitude towards the man, even if he didn't seem to care much whether any of them lived or died.

"Five minutes and we're moving out," Ashfol barked. "If you're not packed by then you'll have to catch up and I don't much fancy your chances alone."

Galvanised, the group sprang into action, untying their hammocks and packing away belongings. Before long they were trudging away from the clearing, following Ashfol and Daenyrs back into the forest that had already claimed one of them.

***

The forest seemed somehow gentler today, happier even. Dappled sunlight broke through the canopy and danced across the forest floor. A soft breeze sighed contentedly through the branches sending leaves spinning down, glinting like golden coins, and birds trilled merrily far above them. After the events of the previous night, however, the initiates knew not to trust the forest's placid aspect and kept up the gruelling pace set by Ashfol and Daenyrs, mostly in silence. That is, except for the swarthy, stocky man now walking beside Mordax who had introduced himself simply as Suliman. Suliman's head reached only to Mordax's chest and he spoke broken Basic with a strong accent. He had a twinkle in his eye and a ready laugh that seemed undampened by the sombreness of the others and he had taken an interest in Mordax after learning that he was a Traveller.

"Myself, I like to travel," Suliman said now, scratching his short beard with rough fingers. "That's why I join the Jade Company. That and the money was pretty good," Suliman said with a wink.

Sylvia gave a low whistle. "You're a Jade Company man? I've met some hard nuts from that outfit. They were only interested in drinking and killing things."

Suliman inclined his head. "We all have our own reasons for being."

He turned back to Mordax. "Tell me, you must have seen a thousand worlds. Where was the best?"

Mordax smiled. "The best? It'd be easier to point out the best tree in this forest or the best snowflake. Every world's unique. There are countless wonders, so different that they can't be compared." He thought for a moment. "I could tell you about the sky gardens of Tarveen where every plant is laden with fruit and the locals travel on the backs of giant birds. Or the Halls of Delight on Lo Trang, where you can taste dishes that would make you cry with joy and, if you have enough coin, where women or men will take you to bed and do things you can't even imagine. So I'm told."

Suliman let out a bellow of laughter.

"But to tell you the truth," said Mordax, "if I had to choose a favourite place, it would be my ship, the *Indigo Starling*. If you stay in any one place for too long it can become stale. That's why Travellers keep moving. In some ways it'd be easier to settle down somewhere, get a job and put down roots. But in other ways, the ones that matter, it'd be the most difficult thing imaginable."

Suliman nodded. "It is the same with me. My mother once told me I have a fly inside me. It keeps buzzing and buzzing until I can't take any more and I must move somewhere new. The Jade Company kept that fly quiet for a while. But eventually, simply travelling was not enough and the fly required a new challenge. And here I am," Suliman gestured around, "living life to its full."

It was Mordax's turn to laugh. "Out here, we'll need to be lucky to survive at all."

Suliman's face was suddenly serious and he laid a powerful hand on Mordax's arm. Mordax noticed that his fingers were marked with scars and his knuckles were hard and callused.

"No, my friend. We make our own luck. Especially in a place like this."

They chatted for a while until Mordax realised that Daenyrs had dropped back from the front of the group but was still up ahead and out of earshot. He was wearing the silver veil. It was the first time Mordax had seen either of the wraiths wear one. It covered Daenyrs' head, shimmering gently in the half-light of the forest. His hunched form and careful movements reminded Mordax of some kind of predator. Mordax couldn't put his finger on why but something about the tension in Daenyrs' shoulders, the half-tilt of his head, made Mordax almost sure that he was listening for something. He made his excuses to Suliman and caught up with Sylvia who had gone on ahead.

"Hey," he whispered.

She turned and glanced at him, the shafts of sunlight catching the golden highlights in her short hair. She rolled her eyes and kept walking.

"Any idea what the deal with Daenyrs is?" he persevered.

"Like what? His favourite colour? His hopes and dreams?"

"I thought you might have some info on him, that's all. Why he's here, for example."

She shrugged. "No idea. He doesn't seem happy about it though."

"Really?"

"Yeah, I mean this isn't exactly the dream job. A few weeks in this shit hole, in the cold and the wet. For a wraith, this has to be a punishment. I'm guessing both he and Ashfol have done something to piss off the head honchos."

"I can empathise," Mordax muttered.

"What?"

"Nothing. Maybe you're right."

Mordax chewed his lip thoughtfully.

"Hey," Sylvia said. She was looking at him intently, "Maybe pay less attention to the guys who are here to keep us alive and more to whatever is trying to kill us."

Mordax shrugged. "In my experience, it's worth spending a bit of time making sure you know which one's which."

Sylvia frowned but she didn't reply and they spent the rest of the march in silence.

***

By the time they stopped, hours later, Mordax could barely stand up. The instructors had taken them over broken terrain where jagged, glassy rocks punctured the top soil. The initiates were forced to scramble over them, scraping knees and elbows and slicing their hands on the sharp edges. Eventually, the route had turned sharply upwards, taking them to the top of a great hill where the trees thinned out and the air grew even colder. It wasn't until he had reached the peak, lungs burning and sweat dripping from his brow despite the chill, that Mordax saw their destination. A circular pit had been carved into the rock, invisible unless you were standing right at the edge, as if the top of the hill had been scooped out. There was a single row of seating around the edge, set low into the rock, barely enough to sit all the initiates at once. Below, the walls of the pit were sheer, reaching down twenty feet to a flat stone floor.

Mordax bent over, hands on his knees trying to catch his breath. The initiates around him were breathing heavily, sending great plumes of steam into the air above them, but looked otherwise comfortable. He felt a momentary pang of irrational anger at them. All soldiers or mercenaries in peak physical condition. How was he supposed to keep up with them? Mordax pushed the thought to one side and concentrated on keeping the contents of his stomach where they were.

"Welcome to the arena," Ashfol boomed. "The crucible of the Dioscuri and somewhere which holds a very special place in our hearts. While this one's a baby, make no mistake, you'll be tested here. Your blood will be spilt. Every wraith in the Dioscuri won their veil in an arena like this one. Eventually, those of you who survive Selection will have the same opportunity, to challenge an existing wraith for their veil. The contest is to the death so when the time comes, you'd better be sure you're at the top of your game."

Mordax and Sylvia glanced at each other. Both Ashfol and Daenyrs were wraiths and so, at some point, must have killed another wraith to inherit their veils.

"For now," Ashfol continued, "we're going to avoid killing each other. But that doesn't mean we can't have a little fun."

Mordax didn't like the gleam in his eyes. Daenyrs stepped forward. The veil covering his face suddenly seemed to release itself from under his chin and flowed back up like spilt quicksilver in reverse until it had disappeared around the back of his neck. He examined the row of initiates.

"You and you," he gestured at two of them, a man and a woman who Mordax had seen chatting the night before. Both had angular features and coppery hair. They looked at each other confused. Ashfol had moved to the edge of the arena where there was a coil of thick metal chain, rusted brown. Ashfol shoved the coiled chain with his foot and one end clattered down to the floor of the arena.

"Get down there," Daenyrs ordered, his voice as cold and hard as a hailstone.

Hesitantly the two moved over to the chain and, one after the other, clambered down it to the stone floor below. At Daenyrs's prompting, the other initiates assembled around the edge of the pit. As Mordax sat down he noticed that a gentle hollow had been eroded into the carved stone seat and the surface was glossy to the touch. He wondered how many generations of Dioscuri initiates it had taken sitting in this very place to abrade the rock like that. The man and woman in the arena stood looking up uncertainly at the ring of initiates around them. Daenyrs addressed the group, his voice echoing.

"You all know why you're here. Only the strongest and the most cunning have a place in the Dioscuri. This is where we sift the gold from the silt." He turned and addressed the two in the arena. "There are two camps at the bottom of this hill. One has wooden walls and a fire pit with kindling and fresh meat. A barn to hang your hammock in and racks full of weapons to defend yourselves against the things that dwell in the forest. The other is merely another clearing. No walls. No weapons. And we have just moved into dangerous territory. The first one to climb back up that chain earns the right to spend tonight at the first camp. I think it's obvious where the other one will stay."

The man and woman glanced at the chain and then each other, bodies tense. Mordax leaned over to Sylvia who was sitting next to him.

"Those two seemed like friends. He wants them to fight each other?"

"Taro and Yefa. Not friends," whispered Sylvia "They're brother and sister."

"What? Surely they won't—" Mordax began but suddenly the man, Taro, exploded into action, sprinting towards the chain. Yefa began to move a fraction of a second later. When Taro neared the chain he leapt and caught it halfway up. He had barely clasped it, however, when Yefa jumped and fastened her arms around his legs. She braced her feet against the rough stone wall and, twisting, heaved him backwards using her own weight, ripping his grip from the chain and sending them both tumbling back down. Taro rolled when he hit the floor and popped back up to his feet smoothly while Yefa kept her feet, absorbing the impact with her knees. The two circled each other warily, mirroring the other's stance with hands raised in front of their faces, movements sure and careful. Taro suddenly lunged in close, snapping a closed fist at Yefa's face. She tilted her head slightly, just enough that the punch missed her by a whisper and kicked out at Taro's knee. Taro caught the kick on his shin instead and snatched Yefa's foot, landing a viscous punch to her raised thigh. Yefa grunted in pain, twisting her leg out of Taro's grasp, and limped backwards grimacing. Taro advanced, throwing merciless punches at her face and torso. Yefa deflected many of them with her raised hands and forearms but the brute force of the attack was clearly wearing her down. Taro caught her in the ribs with a whistling left hook and she collapsed to one knee, heaving for breath, arms raised above her head in surrender. Taro kept advancing, his face cast with a grim determination, watching her closely. He was almost within reach of Yefa when she suddenly pivoted on the ball of her foot, sweeping the other leg round and knocking his feet out from under him. Taro's back hit the stone and the air whooshed out of him. Before he could draw breath, Yefa leapt on top of him and drove her knee into his temple with a crack like a snapping branch. Immediately, Taro's limbs fell limp and his head lolled to one side. Yefa looked down at him for a moment, her expression neutral, then limped over to the chain. Gingerly she pulled herself up, hand over hand, using her one good leg for support against the wall. Daenyrs watched her reach the top, an unpleasant smile on his face.

"Take a seat, Yefa," he said. "You did well."

He nodded to Ashfol, who reached into a bag at his feet, pulling out a rope attached to a kind of harness. Ashfol coiled the rope and harness around his broad shoulders and slid down the chain to where Taro still lay unmoving. He bent over and placed two fingers at the man's throat, pausing for the space of a heartbeat then looked up and nodded to Daenyrs. Gently he threaded Taro's arms through the harness, fastening it shut and then, with the end of the rope in his teeth, he pulled himself back up the chain, hand over hand, barely using his feet at all. At the top he threaded the rope through a metal ring buried in the stone wall behind the seating and began to heave on it, drawing the slumped form across the floor of the arena and then gradually up the side of the wall. Taro's hair hung around his face, matted with blood, and crimson droplets dripped from his chin. When he was close enough to the top, Daenyrs hooked him under the arms and dragged him to a flat sandy area to one side of the arena.

Mordax leaned in close to Sylvia, "You think they did something wrong?"

Sylvia's gaze was focussed on Daenyrs, who was dusting off his hands. She shook her head slowly.

"No. They weren't being punished. They were being tested. I don't think it's over."

Daenyrs stepped back to the lip of the arena, scanning the row of men and women before him.

"You and you," he pointed to two male initiates who were sitting next to each other. With a resigned look at each other they rose and clambered down the chain to the arena. And so it went, Daenyrs picking two initiates at a time to beat each other into insensibility. Suliman, Mordax's new mercenary friend, was matched with a man almost two heads taller than him. Despite his stockiness, Suliman moved like a dancer, floating in and out of the other man's range, snapping quick stinging punches at his abdomen and face. Soon the other man was lying on his back, blood streaming from cuts to his nose and brow. One wiry girl, matched against a powerful looking man, drew him to the far wall of the arena, blocking punches and kicks without throwing any of her own. After ducking under one wild swing, the girl shoved the man sideways, unbalancing him, and sprinted back across the arena where she raced up the chain like a lizard, barely slowing down at all. She won the bout without landing a single hit. The longest fight was between Ragin and Theron, the man who had organised the watch the night before. Both were clearly well-trained, blocking effectively, careful not to overextend themselves. They both landed the odd jab but neither seemed to gain the upper hand and after a while both were shiny with sweat despite the bitter cold. Eventually it was Theron who made the first serious mistake. Darting forward to jab at Ragin's face, he placed his front foot on a patch of blood-slicked stone and lost purchase, falling to one knee. Ragin immediately attacked with a flurry of blows to Theron's face, stunning him. He caught one of Theron's flailing arms and twisted it behind his back forcing him to the floor. Realising he was beaten, Theron tapped the ground with his free hand signalling his surrender. But Ragin didn't stop. He kept twisting the arm until Theron screamed in pain and there was a sickening crack. Ragin let Theron collapse to the floor and sauntered back towards the chain, pulling himself up easily. Eventually, Theron struggled to his feet, cradling the arm which was bent unnaturally. He had to be helped up the chain by Ashfol and went to sit with the other initiates who had lost their contests, face pale and jaw clenched against the pain. As the fights went on, Mordax became more nervous, aware that his turn would come and that he didn't stand a chance against any of the other initiates. Eventually, Daenyrs stepped forward and looked in his direction.

"Mordax. In the arena. Sylvia, you too."

Mordax resisted the urge to yell. Could he refuse? He suspected any attempt would result in flunking out of Selection and losing any chance he had of finding his father's killers. Sylvia didn't meet his eye as they made their way over. Mordax's hands were so slick with sweat that he almost lost his grip on the cold metal chain but eventually he and Sylvia stood facing each other at the centre of the pit. The silent regard of the ring of initiates above them was unnerving and the cold air tingled with anticipation. They had barely taken up their positions when Sylvia was moving, quick and fluid. Mordax reached out, hoping to keep her at arms length but she slipped easily inside his grasp and his solar plexus exploded in pain, the air forced out of his lungs. He realised he was on his knees and panicked as he tried to draw breath but couldn't. A pathetic croaking sound escaped his lips. He was dimly aware of Sylvia whispering "Stay down!" and walking back across the arena. Daenyrs' reedy voice echoed around him.

"You're taking it easy on him. Finish the job."

"Look at him, he's done," Sylvia replied. "The rule is, the first one up the chain wins."

"I make the rules. Finish the job or you'll join him in the losers' camp tonight."

Mordax looked up and saw Sylvia, with her back to him, staring up at Daenyrs and quivering with anger. She turned back and he could see the sorrow in her eyes. Weakly, he put a hand up to ward her off. She knocked it aside and hit him square in the jaw, whipping his head to one side. Flashing pinpricks of light danced across his vision and the coppery taste of blood filled his mouth. Somehow he managed to struggle to his feet but Sylvia closed with him quickly and landed two vicious punches to his already bruised ribs. He collapsed to his knees again. As the pressure of the beating piled on top of the sufferings he had experienced over the last few days, rage boiled up within him, burning the fatigue from his limbs. As Sylvia drew closer Mordax twisted his body as if cowering from the expected blow. With one side out of view of Sylvia, he reached into his pocket and drew out the dart that had almost hit him the previous night. A sudden stench of putrefaction rose into the air. Sylvia swung a punch towards his head. Mordax let out a strangled cry and lunged upwards, knocking her arm aside and taking her by surprise. His other hand, the one holding the dart, was suddenly by her throat. Sylvia froze, eyes wide, feeling the sharp prick against her neck. He hadn't yet broken skin. The sight of the fear in her face, however, punctured his bubble of rage like a lanced boil. What was he doing? He looked down at his fist, knuckles white as it clenched the dart. It seemed like someone else's hand. All the anger drained out of him and with it, the last of his strength. He slipped the dart back into his pocket and, wheezing and battered, collapsed to the floor. Sylvia stepped away from him, hands shaking and face white.

"That's enough, girl," came Ashfol's voice, "he looks spent to me."

Dimly, Mordax realised that his and Sylvia's bodies in that last exchange must have blocked the dart from the other initiates' view. His vision swam and suddenly the stone floor was pressed against his cheek. The cold felt good against the swelling in his jaw. He sighed and welcomed the blackness that overcame him.

Chapter 23

"Wait!" shouted Akira, surprising herself more than anyone.

Rotoria Asp, Sword of the Council of Thalmos, momentarily interrupted, peered at her down a long nose.

"Council Master, listen," she said, "you may think that executing me will send a more powerful message to my father but you're wrong. Everything he does is calculated. He understands very well the depth of your feeling but he loses nothing by sending me. If you execute me...well, he has other sons and daughters and he can always produce more. You also look, frankly, unhinged to the other systems you trade with. They'll think to themselves, if you're willing to execute the daughter of your oldest trading partner, when will you turn on them. My father will have considered all of this. Don't play into his hands."

Glankor watched her, a wry smile on his dry lips.

"Nothing you've said is news to me."

Akira's heart sank. She felt cold and clammy.

"Daisuke Kudo is devious and cold-hearted? You might as well tell me the sun is hot or the ocean, wet. And I couldn't care less what our trading partners think. We have nanotrite, they need it so they'll buy it. It's not complicated."

His paused, examining Akira like a butcher weighing meat.

"It's interesting, however, that you would come here, knowing that your father was comfortable sending you to your death. He threw you to the wolves and still you advocated for the benefit of the Kudo-kai. Blind loyalty or a dearth of options, I wonder."

Glankor's sunken eyes were inscrutable. Finally, he clapped his dry, bony hands together.

Two young men in white robes appeared beside her and took her arms firmly. She was almost grateful for the support as her knees felt weak beneath her.

"Central Node, Xifulandros, am I to assume that you will be remaining with the Ambassador until the sentence is carried out."

"That is correct, Council Master," said Xif.

"Very well. Take them away."

Akira closed her eyes and tried very hard to keep from crying.

***

Their quarters were smaller than Akira was used to but comfortable nonetheless. It was a two-level apartment in central Kor'Thalia which Shiori assured her was larger than the homes of even some of the richest citizens. It seemed that Glankor wouldn't shy away from ordering Akira killed, but balked at the thought of a bare prison. All three of them were in the library, Shiori paced the floor and Akira was sitting behind a large walnut desk, dwarfed by a plush wingback chair. Xif hovered near her shoulder, while she scratched absently at the almost healed marks on her arms. There were no windows. If Akira had been less distracted, she might have noticed that there were no windows anywhere in the apartment at all. As it was, she stared vacantly at the opposite wall. Her body didn't feel like it was her own. Her hands were a strange weight in her lap and the voices around her seemed far away.

"We did know that he was capable of executing foreign dignitaries," said Xif.

"Foreign dignitaries, yes. But the daughter of Daisuke Kudo?" said Shiori.

Xif gave a small "psh" sound that was his verbal equivalent of a shrug.

"We're sailing on capricious winds now," he said. "Glankor's whims seem to hold sway here."

There was a pause.

"How long do you think?" asked Xif.

"Hard to say. I think she bought herself some time talking about her father the way she did. He finds her interesting. He's been known to keep prisoners in the tower for cycles before executing them."

"That's something at least."

Akira roused herself.

"Did you say cycles?"

"In rare cases," said Shiori, "but others have been killed within days. It all depends whether Glankor believes there is more use to be had out of the prisoner."

"I suppose we'll find out just how useful he thinks you are," said Xif.

"Wait for Glankor to make his next move, that's what you're suggesting?" Akira said acidly. "That's easy for you to say. How is that I'm in the firing line and you're not, by the way?"

"As I explained there would be little utility in them destroying me," said Xif. "I don't hold any official title with the Kudo-kai." He paused. "There would also likely be considerable outcry from other systems."

Akira looked at Xif carefully. "What do you mean?"

"Akira, you do realise that I am quite a rare specimen?"

"I know that the Benefactors don't generally allow AIs, but I thought there had been some special dispensation for you."

"The Benefactors have not permitted the construction of a single true AI since the War of the Black Expanse millennia ago. Only a few of us built before the war have been allowed to exist."

"Does this have anything to do with Glankor calling you the 'Betrayer'?" asked Akira.

"I'd really rather not go into it," said Xif. "It's not relevant to your current predicament in any event."

"Fine, but if we get out of this mess I expect some real answers."

Xif gave a small wobble that could have been either a nod of assent or something less affirmative.

"It is odd," said Shiori quietly.

"What is?" asked Akira

"In the cycles since Glankor took power, there's no record of him taking any action which is as irrational as this. Also, it is not as if the other members of the Council are without power. Glankor has the final say, but if all the other members of the Council decided he was unfit to lead, they have the power to replace him."

Akira nodded. "That woman, Rotoria, mentioned 'intelligence' which the Council was basing its decision on. If we're to stand any chance of changing Glankor's view of us, we need to find out what that intelligence is."

"That's going to be difficult to do from in here," said Shiori. "This entire apartment is a Faraday cage. No signals in or out."

"Sorry, what?"

"I tried to contact the ship as soon as they left us alone," said Shiori.

"With what? They took all our devices," said Akira.

Shiori avoided Akira's eye.

"I have a hidden redundancy comm unit."

"Well, aren't you full of surprises."

"The point is I couldn't reach the ship. I couldn't connect to Thalmos's comm net. In fact, I'm not picking up any signals at all. That means there's a blackout cage around us. It's why there's no windows. We're not going to be able to find anything out from in here."

"She's right," said Xif. "We're trapped in here."

Akira put her head in her hands, resisting the urge to scream.

"So that's it?" she said, looking up. "We just wait until Glankor changes his mind and kills us and puts you in a museum or something, Xif?"

"Circumstances may change," said Xif, but even his carefully intonated voice couldn't hide a shade of scepticism.

Akira looked up at them, suddenly furious at the apathy she felt in herself and the others.

"How important is this mission, Xif?" she asked.

"Glankor's recent actions have had the greatest impact on the future viability of the Kudo-kai as an organisation of any event in at least the last hundred cycles."

"So this is the greatest threat facing our family, we've been tasked with solving it and you two, the last true AI constructed in this galaxy and the only member of the Kudo-kai with first-hand working knowledge of Thalmian society, want to sit around until Glankor finds some way to hurt the family through us and then kills us when we can't even do that anymore? I don't want to leave you in any doubt about this. You'd better start putting your heads together because if we don't find a way to get out of here and complete our mission, I'll kill you myself. And that includes you, Xif, public outcry or no."

There was a moment's silence as they all absorbed her outburst. Akira realised that now would be the moment, if she were so inclined, to retract her words, to apologise and blame the stress of the situation. She thought about it then stood up and silently left the room.

Chapter 24

The whisper of wind-caressed leaves brought Mordax slowly awake. He took a moment to orient himself, feeling the cold gritty sand under his palms and the hot throbbing from his face and ribs. Eventually he mustered the energy to open his eyes and sit up. The other casualties of the contests were scattered around him like broken twigs, faces bruised and swollen and knuckles caked with dried blood. He spotted Theron sitting with his back to a rock, still looking unnaturally pale although his arm was now straight and covered in a blue plas-steel corrective. On the other side of the sandpit Ashfol bent over a prone figure, tending to his wounds. Gingerly Mordax examined himself, pressing lightly at the parts that ached the most. His ribs were very tender and he felt a sharp pain when he breathed too deeply but there didn't seem to be any permanent damage. He was sure that Sylvia could have inflicted much worse if she'd wanted to. He drew himself up into a sitting position, resting his back against a convenient boulder. The winners of the contests seemed to have already left with Daenyrs. Black thoughts began to creep into his mind, then, of the night exposed in the forest that was his reward for failure and memories of the streaks of gore that Chadwick had left behind. Ashfol appeared and settled down noisily beside him, forcing him out of his reverie.

"That friend of yours gave you a good pasting, eh?" Ashfol chuckled.

"She didn't really have much of a choice," Mordax said, jaw creaking and popping as he formed the words.

"That she didn't," Ashfol agreed.

"I know what he's doing. Daenyrs, I mean,"

Ashfol raised his eyebrows, "Got it all figured out, have you?"

"You're dividing us, trying to destroy any bonds or friendships that there are between us."

Mordax thought of the fight between Theron and Ragin, "And where there aren't bonds you're fanning rivalries."

Ashfol regarded him with an amused expression. "OK. How exactly does that revelation help you?"

Mordax couldn't think of a response to that.

"Why do you think we might be keen to isolate you all? Keep you separated?"

Mordax shook his head and shrugged.

"Look around you, boy. Everyone but you has come from an army or a mercenary unit. They've operated as part of a team for all of their professional lives. The Dioscuri is not an army, though. Those who end up taking the veil will work mostly alone."

So that was it. "You want us to stop relying on others." said Mordax. "Learn to be self-sufficient."

Ashfol said nothing. Mordax thought back to Daenyrs' expression during the fights. The dark excitement he had seen there. Ashfol might be telling the truth but he didn't believe Daenyrs' motivation was purely didactic. Flashes from his fight with Sylvia came back to him. He remembered the rage he had felt at his helplessness, the momentary satisfaction at the fear in Sylvia's eyes as he had held the dart to her throat. Worry warred with self-disgust.

"I guess I'm going to have to figure out a way to keep up with the others," said Mordax. "I'm not sure I stand a chance of becoming a Dioscuri at this rate."

"Wouldn't worry about that, boy. Technically you became a member of the Dioscuri as soon as you arrived on Hellenbos as an initiate. You could die tomorrow and you'd still have made it in."

"That kind of misses my point," Mordax said. He glanced at Ashfol. His thick beard obscured much of his face but his eyes were creased in humour.

"If you're trying to make us self-sufficient then why are you telling me this? Aren't you undermining what Daenyrs was trying to do?"

Ashfol chuckled and scratched his beard. "Let's just say, it seems to me you've been dealt a pretty bad hand. You've made some enemies in high places from what I've heard. Before Selection had even started too. Quite the feat."

"Valerian," Mordax breathed.

"No secret that he and Calgary don't see eye to eye, when it comes to you. But then again, they don't see eye to eye on most things."

"Really?" said Mordax. "They disagree about other things?"

"Ha! You think you're important enough for a Dioscuri Council to fall out over? No, Calgary and Valerian have always had very different approaches. Valerian's pretty old school. Galaia mediates between them. Seems to work OK."

Mordax realised Calgary likely wasn't bluffing when he said he wouldn't be able to protect Mordax during Selection.

"Wouldn't you get in trouble for telling me that?"

Ashfol gestured around them. "What more can they do to me?" He winked then got to his feet. "Don't think this means I give two shits whether you survive though."

It was Mordax's turn to chuckle, then wince at the stab of pain in his ribs.

The journey back down the hill was a pathetic affair. Most of the initiates who had lost their contests were carrying an injury of some kind or other, some hobbling, others needing to be supported. The purple blush of night was darkening the sky when Ashfol led the sorry band out into a new clearing, smaller than the one from the previous night. This time the centre of the clearing was bare. There were no cut tree trunks and no fire pit.

"Where are we supposed to hang our hammocks?" asked Theron, arm now cradled in a sling.

"You won't want to be sleeping tonight, lad," said Ashfol. It may have been a trick of the twilight but his expression seemed unusually sombre as he watched the bedraggled group set down their packs.

Ashfol looked as if he wanted to say more but instead he sighed, turned and trudged out of the clearing, his broad figure gradually fading into the gloaming. Most of the other initiates had started pulling rations out of their bags and setting up bivouac sacks. A familiar impotent dread twisted in Mordax's gut. He moved to stand beside Theron who was still staring at the point where Ashfol had left the clearing.

"Something's not right. It feels like when I'm getting screwed on a deal," Mordax said quietly. He half expected a dismissive response but Theron simply nodded slowly.

"We should be gearing up for something but I don't know what," Theron said eventually.

Mordax reached into his pocket and felt the hard edges of the dart.

"I think I might have some idea."

Theron turned sharply towards him. His shadowed eyes were hungry, desperate.

Mordax pulled the dart from his pocket and held it out to him. With his good arm, Theron gingerly took the dart from him, examining it closely. He sniffed the end and winced.

"Last night when I was looking for Chadwick, that almost hit me," said Mordax. "Whatever fired it was in the trees."

"It's a blow dart," said Theron quietly. "It's been coated in something."

He fingered the soft down that covered the base of the dart. "It wasn't some dumb monster that took Chadwick, then."

They both looked around at the circle of thick trunks. Mordax had the sudden impression of being besieged. The hiss of wind in the leaves and gnarls in the bark of the trees, not previously notable, had taken on a malevolent cast.

"Fuck," said Theron with a frustrated sigh. "We're totally exposed here."

Mordax's heart began to hammer as a nascent plan coalesced in his mind.

"Come on," he said, "I'm going to need you to back me up."

Mordax hurried over to where the initiates were beginning to settle themselves in for the night, groaning where their injuries were still paining them and muttering quietly to each other.

"Everyone get up," he said loudly. Grey, tired faces looked up at him blankly. "We're about to be attacked." Nobody showed any intention of obeying. He heard a snort of laughter within the group. He felt Theron step closer to his shoulder.

"If you want to survive the night, do as he says. Get the fuck up."

Eyes widened as Theron's words gave credence to Mordax's warning. As he had suspected, the initiates put more faith in a fellow soldier than they did a Traveller. A few lurched to their feet immediately and the others gradually followed.

"What're we facing?" asked Taro, the copper-haired man who had been bested by his sister. His sharp features were set in a serious expression that Mordax found oddly reassuring.

"Not sure," said Theron rubbing his scalp with his good hand. "Probably the same thing that took Chadwick last night."

Mordax held out the dart for them all to see.

"What do you need us to do?" asked Taro.

Mordax thought quickly.

"Collect fire wood. Quickly. As much as you can."

"We've already got enough for a camp fire," Taro said, brow furrowed.

"No, we need four or five fires around the tree line. Enough wood to last the night so that the light doesn't go out. We need to see what's coming."

Taro nodded sharply, gestured for a couple of the initiates to go with him and headed towards the forest.

"The rest of you come with me," Mordax said and walked towards the nearest tree. The bark was split by the same cracks he had noticed on the trunks in the previous camp. He found a crack that ran from the ground almost to his head and worked his gloved fingers into it. Yanking and heaving he pried a section of bark away from the tree. When a large enough flap of bark had separated from the layer underneath he pulled it back on itself so that it snapped off and the entire curved piece fell into the snow. The other initiates watched him with various expressions of bewilderment except for Theron who began to chuckle.

"You clever bastard," he said.

Mordax took a knife from his pocket and began to work it into the centre of the dusty fibrous material that covered the underside of the now loose section of bark, prying it up. Eventually he had created a gap large enough to fit his gloved hand through. He hefted the section of bark up, using the new handle, and held it close to his body. It was surprisingly light.

"It's a shield," breathed one of the women at his back.

Mordax nodded.

"It should be thick enough to stop a dart," he said.

The other initiates began moving without him having to say anything else. Each found a tree and began to worry the bark in the same fashion. Soon there was a pile of ragged shields in the snow, enough for every man and woman including those who were busy setting the fires. When they had finished, Mordax assembled the initiates, closely packed in a circle at the centre of the clearing. Throughout the process, the initiates obeyed Mordax's orders with grim efficiency. At least Chadwick's death had focussed their minds.

Once they had taken up their positions, shoulder-to-shoulder, there was nothing to do but wait. As night fell in earnest the temperature plunged and the initiates huddled closer together. Mordax felt a gentle tug each time he blinked as the sweat in his eyelashes began to freeze. The fires around the clearing, too far away to provide them with any warmth, crackled and popped sending the occasional spray of embers skywards. The dancing yellow flames set shadows shifting among the trees, an impression of movement that clawed at the very edges of their peripheral vision and stoked the worst of their imagination as the night wore on. Despite this, Mordax's eyelids were heavy and his gaze unfocussed when he felt the man beside him start and inhale sharply. Immediately, he was fully awake.

"What is it?" Mordax whispered.

"I thought I saw something," the man replied. "High in the trees. Over there."

The initiates peered into the darkness where the man was pointing. At first Mordax couldn't make out anything. The light from the fires was quickly swallowed by the forest. Then he spotted the glint of something golden between the trunks. No, there were two pinpricks of light. And they were moving. With a cold rush, Mordax realised what they were…Eyes.

"Shields up!" he shouted. The initiates raised their shields, the ones in the middle of the circle holding theirs above the heads of those around them. Immediately they were cocooned in darkness, the mist of hot breath swirling around them. They were just in time. There was a soft thud as something buried itself into the wall of bark. Another followed. And another until there was a continuous patter against the wood, like hail. A familiar foul odour permeated their makeshift defences. Mordax peeked through a crack between the shields. Bright yellow specks, darts reflecting the light of the fires, were flying out from the tree line towards them. Among the canopy, Mordax caught glimpses of movement. Grey forms twisting in the darkness, never coming close enough to expose themselves fully to the light. As long as their attackers stayed in the trees the initiates seemed safe. Mordax was beginning to relax when there was a strangled cry from within the group. Taro collapsed backwards dropping his shield and exposing a gaping hole in the defence. Theron, who had been standing behind him, grabbed him by the front of his coat and hauled him backwards as the initiates on either side shuffled closer to fill the gap. Mordax examined Taro as well as he could from a distance, unable to move closer without breaking rank himself. Taro's eyes had rolled back in his head and he was twitching and making a strange gurgling sound. Theron turned him on his side. Mordax could just make out a dark patch at the base of Taro's neck.

"Theron!" he said "There. In his neck."

Theron's exploring fingers found the spot and withdrew a dart, the bone tip gleaming, wet with blood.

Theron hissed in frustration.

"They must have hit a gap in the shields."

Within minutes Taro's twitching had stopped. He lay still, eyes open and vacant. Theron rolled him onto his back again and began chest compressions. Mordax felt a prickly flush of helplessness as he watched. Theron worked with quick efficiency, pumping Taro's chest rhythmically with his one good hand and blowing into his mouth. One, two, three. Blow. Repeat. Time lost its meaning in the repetition of Theron's movements. The air grew even colder and Mordax's raised arm began to tremble. The shield itself seemed to grow heavier. Mordax imagined its outer side disappearing under a thickening skin of fur and bone even though the rational part of his mind told him it was just fatigue. Eventually, the frequency of the thuds began to lessen. Soon they had stopped entirely. The grey forms were no longer visible among the trees. Still, the initiates kept their shields raised, arms burning and cramping, until the first rosy glow of dawn appeared in the sky. It was not until they broke the circle and surveyed the clearing, littered with tufts of fur covered darts, that Mordax realised Theron had long ago ceased his frantic movements. Taro's body lay where he had fallen, his eyes already beginning to cloud over in the icy air.

Chapter 25

The man had travelled widely enough for a hundred lifetimes. He had seen incredible feats of human and alien engineering and witnessed, and occasionally influenced, some of the most pivotal events in the recent history of the Shattered Empires. However, there were very few things that he considered to be true marvels. Very few things that had ever taken his breath away. The sight that greeted him when the stolen hauler exited nether space for the final time, even though he had seen it many times before, was without doubt a marvel. Outwardly the man's expression remained the same, his bland features didn't register the feeling of awe that ignited like cold fire in his chest.

"That's a fuck load of ships!" said one of the mercenaries at his shoulder.

It was an understatement of quite staggering proportions. The man took a deep breath, reminding himself that their long journey was minutes from being over and the mercenaries would soon be off the ship. Hanging before them, still thousands of kilometres away, was a gleaming golden cylinder, made up of ten fat rings almost touching. Each ring was a factory capable of manufacturing some of the largest warships in the galaxy. Spreading out from each ring, like the spines of a sea urchin, were row upon row of fully formed ships of various classes. At this distance most of the ships appeared nothing more than bronze specks, reflecting the light of the ancient brown dwarf around which the factories orbited, and the man knew that the smaller classes of ships would not even be visible to the naked eye at this distance. Just those that were visible represented billions of ships. There had never been more ships assembled in one place since the War of Ages and perhaps not even then. However, it was not just the quantity of ships that was awe-inspiring: it was what those ships represented, the force of will that had assembled them in this unnamed system and the incredible foresight and planning that had allowed the operation to be conducted thus far in secrecy and without attracting unwanted attention, even from the Dioscuri.

"Get aft and make sure the cargo is ready for extraction," the man said, less from any real doubt as to the readiness of the cargo and more to prevent him from sticking a pen through the mercenary's eye.

"Yeah, alright."

For a few moments the man savoured the quiet on the bridge as the mercenaries were all employed elsewhere. He felt a familiar calm settle over him as he gazed out at the fruits of the momentous undertaking he was a part of. All the cycles spent among the shit and blood, murdering and pirating his way across the galaxy with sub-human drunks and outlaws for company, all those cycles were worth it as he looked upon what he had helped create. He allowed himself a few more minutes to savour the sight. Soon the hauler had reached the nearest of the factory rings and docked with it. A deep clunk reverberated around the ship as the pneumatic locks engaged. The man closed the door to the bridge and opened a nether space feed. His employer accepted the feed request within a few minutes.

"Well?" came the familiar androgynous voice. The man was certain it was artificially altered to strip it of identifiable signatures. It was possible that it was not always the same person but the man doubted his employer would entrust another with their conversations.

"Cargo delivered. Three hundred kilotonnes of nanotrite."

"Excellent. The acquisition went smoothly?"

"It all went as planned. The trail's clean."

"Good. We need to increase the rate of supply. We'll need more haulers."

"Understood. I'll take it forward."

"No more hits on Nag'Sami though. You've mined that vein too aggressively. Find another target."

"As you say."

The conversation ended as abruptly as it had begun. Neither his employer nor he were ones for idle chit chat. It seemed that the man would be busy for a while yet. Just one more task remained to close out the current job. He rose and yawned, stretching his arms upwards until he felt the vertebrae in his back crack. He needed a rest. He made his way out of the bridge and down a level to the cargo bay where the mercenaries had stacked the containers of nanotrite for unloading. They were standing in a loose group, chatting amiably, relaxed now that they had completed the mission successfully. Someone had cracked open a box of cold beers and they were toasting each other and laughing. The man smiled, recognising the almost euphoric relief at the successful completion of a dangerous mission. He missed that feeling. His own mission was much longer and infinitely more dangerous. When the group spotted him, the conversation died down but the grins remained.

"Congratulations," he said. "There's nothing in this life as satisfying as a job done well. You should all be proud. I know we haven't told you much about the reasons for this mission, necessarily so, but you should know that everything you have done is for a glorious purpose."

The smiles became a little strained and the man chuckled to himself. He grabbed a frosted bottle from the container next to him, twisted the cap off and raised the bottle to the group.

"But as they say, we fight and slay for a fair day's pay."

"A FAIR DAY'S PAY!" the group cheered.

The man took a gulp of the beer and managed to keep the disgust from his face. He spent a few minutes going round the group shaking hands and enduring slaps on the back. Eventually he addressed the group again.

"Sorry to break up the party, but it's time to get you lot station-side. As promised, deposits have been made for you with the UBN. We will arrange transport for you to wherever you would like to go."

"Lo Trang for me," said one of the mercenaries. "Only place to spend that amount of coin."

The group laughed and the man forced himself to smile. He gestured to the airlock.

"Someone will meet you on the other side and take you to the rec rooms until your transport is ready."

The group picked up their bags and filed into the airlock connecting the hauler to the station. The door hissed shut behind them.

"Computer activate protocol sigma one," the man said, referring to the preset programme he had written into the ship's coding during the nether jump.

"Life signs detected in airlock 4. Confirm activation of protocol," the ship's computer said, its voice echoing around the cargo hold.

"Confirmed."

There was a loud clunk as the station locks disengaged and a whirring as the hauler's manoeuvring thrusters pushed it a safe distance from the station. Through the view port of the air lock the man could see the confused looks of the mercenaries at the unexpected sounds. A couple of them, though, the brighter ones, realised immediately what was happening and looked back at him, eyes wide with terror. One of the women ran over to the door and started banging on the thick glass, face contorted in a scream that only the other mercenaries could hear. As the penny dropped, others began to jostle for position at the view port pointing at him and shouting what he assumed were a mixture of threats and prayers. One man with tears streaming down his face, and snot bubbling out of his nose, mouthed "PLEASE. NO. NO" over and over. He watched the terrified faces, with mild curiosity, the way he had watched hundreds of others like them over the cycles, until the ship reached the next step in the protocol and the outer air lock door slid open faster than he could blink. In the space of a breath, the mercenaries were gone, blown backwards out of the air lock, and all was calm again. He felt the usual brief pang at the waste of good operatives. But replacements were easy to find if you knew where to look.

Chapter 26

A wispy tendril of grey smoke wound its way up from behind the sturdy wooden stockade until it faded into the clear blue sky. As the initiates gazed up at the walls that ringed the top of a gentle hill, clear of trees, Mordax felt the nervous tension within the group begin to bleed away. Shoulders slumped, chins dropped and Mordax noticed for the first time the dark rings around their eyes. They had still been on full alert, shields within reach in case needed, when Ashfol returned that morning. He had done a good job of masking his surprise, but Mordax had caught the momentary break in his stride when he had seen the group still huddled in the centre of the clearing. Ashfol had ignored their questions about what had attacked them. Instead, he had glanced at Taro's body before instructing the initiates to leave it where it lay and follow him back into the forest. Theron had ignored that instruction, however, and, with Mordax's help, created a makeshift sled with rope and a section of bark. Together they had hauled Taro's body behind them as they trudged through the trees. Ashfol had cursed them as "stupid buggers" but hadn't pressed the point. When Mordax's breath began to grow ragged and wheezy, one of the other initiates, Marina, a thickly muscled woman, with short cropped brown hair and a boxer's cheek bones, took the rope from him and carried on hauling next to Theron who had managed not to break a sweat despite his broken elbow.

"Home sweet home," growled Ashfol now, looking up towards the fort.

They made their way up a winding path to a heavy gate set into the walls of the fort at which point Ashfol gave a piercing whistle and the gate swung open slowly with a reluctant creak. The sweet scent of roasting meat hit them and set Mordax's mouth watering. His last hot meal seemed like a lifetime ago.

Word must have spread that they were approaching because the other initiates were gathered inside the gate, some stepping forward eagerly to greet them. Suliman came up to Mordax, grinning, and clapped him on the back so hard he almost pitched over.

"You are a hard man to kill it seems. Daenyrs told us not to expect any of you back. We thought the forest may have swallowed you."

"I think that might have been the idea," said Mordax, dropping his Bergen to the ground with a relieved sigh.

"You had a rough night?" Suliman asked

"You could say that."

He scanned the faces around them. Ragin was watching them from a distance. When Mordax met his eye, he turned away and stalked off further into the camp. Daenyrs and Ashfol had moved a little away from the group, Ashfol bending his shaggy head so that they could speak quietly. Ashfol was shrugging and gesturing back towards the haggard group.

"Where's Sylvia?" Mordax asked.

Suliman gave a grimace.

"I'd avoid that one for a while, my friend, if you know what's good for you. Even when we thought you were dead she was mad at you. Don't ask me why. I mean, she's the one who gave you a kicking, right?"

Mordax gave a half-hearted laugh. "Yeah. I've got the bruises to prove it."

The mellow hubbub of conversation around them faded, leaving only the low whistle of the wind through gaps in the stockade and the hiss of wet wood in a nearby fire. Mordax looked around to see the other initiates backing away from a slim figure with coppery hair. Yefa, Taro's sister, was standing next to his body. Taro's marble face was upturned, eyes wide and blue lips slightly parted as if witnessing some great miracle in the fathomless depths of the sky. She kept her hands in her pockets and made no move to touch him.

"Yefa. I'm sorry." Mordax broke the silence and his voice sounded thin and reedy to his own ears. Without looking at him, Yefa turned and walked away.

"Come, my friend," said Suliman softly, "let's get out of the cold."

***

The "barracks" as Ashfol had described them consisted of a circular barn-like structure, supported inside by wooden posts, with a stone-lined pit at its centre in which a feeble fire flickered, casting a dirty yellow glow that barely penetrated more than a few feet into the gloom. Hooks on the wooden posts provided anchors for their hammocks. The air was humid and warm and smelled of wood smoke and sawdust undercut by the tang of stale sweat.

"Luxury, eh?" Suliman said with a grin as he gestured around.

The warmth and the darkness conspired to sap Mordax of any energy he had left and by the time he had strung up his hammock, his eyelids were heavy and a bone-deep weariness made his movements sluggish and clumsy.

"Sorry, what was that?" said Mordax as he realised he had missed a question from Suliman.

Suliman waved a hand, dismissively.

"You look like death, my friend. Get in that hammock before you collapse."

Mordax did as he was told and surrounded by the creak of hammocks and the snores of their occupants, he fell into a deep and dreamless sleep.

***

Waking was a slow and arduous affair, like swimming underwater against a powerful current. For a long while Mordax lay still, eyes shut, listening to the groans and squeaks of the barrack's wooden frame and clinging to the vestiges of sleep, loath to disturb the cocoon of warmth around him. Eventually he mustered the energy to raise his head. Darkness had fallen outside and the entrance was an inky black rectangle untouched by the firelight. A movement drew Mordax's attention to the figure crouched at the fire's edge. He recognised Yefa's sharp features. Sleep clung to Mordax's eyes so that a shimmering copper halo seemed to surround her head. She drew a hand from beneath her coat, picked a log from the pile next to her and threw it on the fire sending embers twinkling up towards the smoke vent in the roof. Groggily, Mordax swung his legs off the hammock wincing at the deep ache in his muscles. Clumps of frozen sawdust dug painfully into the bare soles of feet. He wrapped his coat around his shoulders and shuffled over to the fire where he sat down opposite Yefa. She continued to stare into the flames without acknowledging his presence.

"How are you holding up?" Mordax said. His tongue felt thick and clumsy in his mouth.

For a while she said nothing then, suddenly, "He used to be a little shit, you know. When we were kids? He'd push me around. Steal my stuff. Sometimes he'd take me out with his friends and then run off, leaving me in the middle of nowhere."

"Kids can be cruel," said Mordax. "It doesn't mean he didn't care for you."

Yefa continued as if he hadn't spoken, her voice listless.

"When our parents died and we were living on the street, it got worse. He'd send me to beg or filch in the worst neighbourhoods. Juicers on every corner. I'd get knocked around badly. Meth-head even broke my arm once."

"Yefa—" Mordax began.

"But then one day, I got careless. Begged all day without taking a break to stash the haul. Must have had fifty chits on me," Yefa shook her head. "Too much to be safe in that part of the city. Some skinny kid got the jump on me. Knocked me over and pulled a knife. Would have stuck me too but Taro came out of nowhere. Slit his throat before the kid knew he was there. He'd been following me every day. He knew I wouldn't survive the streets unless I toughened up, learned to stand on my own two feet...He was right."

Mordax nodded. "He helped us too."

Yefa looked up at Mordax for the first time, eyes flashing in the light of the fire. Mordax was shocked to see the loathing there. It washed the torpor from his brain like a wave of cold water.

"He did. And he died for it," Yefa said. "It should have been one of you."

"But...there was...nothing else we could have done. Sticking together was our best chance..." Mordax stammered.

Yefa stood up and leaned in, the flickering light and Mordax's sleep-blurred vision conspiring to twist her features into a gruesome mask of rage.

"He was a lion and he died defending sheep. He should have been looking out for himself. He would have stood a chance. You were the chain around his ankle." She kicked the pile of logs into the fire sending up a great gout of flame and swept out of the barracks into the night. After she had gone, Mordax sat watching the blackness beyond the doorway. He still felt the chill in the air but in a distant way as if his body was someone else's.

"You have a peculiar knack for making enemies, you know that?" Sylvia appeared in the dim circle of the firelight. She tucked a strand of blonde hair behind one ear uncertainly then sat down on the same side of the fire as him but keeping a distance.

"So we're enemies?" Mordax said.

Sylvia let out an exasperated sigh.

"I didn't say that...Fuck. I don't know what to make of you, you know? One minute you're this helpless pup, the next you're holding a fucking knife to my throat. And then you go and save half the troop from certain death. At least that's what they're saying."

"It wasn't a knife," said Mordax blandly. "It was a poisoned dart."

Sylvia barked a humourless laugh "Where exactly did you get one of those?"

"The night that Chadwick was taken. Something in the trees shot at me."

"The same things that attacked you guys last night?"

Mordax nodded glumly.

"This place is fucked!" she said. She examined him intently for a few seconds.

"Look, about what Yefa said—"

"She's got a point. He might have stood a better chance on his own."

"She's talking out of her arse and you know it," said Sylvia savagely. "That girl's looking for someone to blame and you're an easy target. Daenyrs didn't expect any of you to make it back at all."

Like a sliver of warm light from an open door, Sylvia's words banished the darkness that had been seeping into his mind. He began to breathe more easily.

"I am sorry, you know," he said, "about the fight? It's been a rough week. I think I cracked a bit."

Sylvia gave a half shrug. "You can say that again. You do know I was taking it easy on you, right?"

Mordax nodded. Sylvia examined him for a bit longer then sighed, sweeping her blonde hair out of her eyes.

"If you want someone on your side, mate, you need to learn to reciprocate better. Someone does you a solid, maybe don't try to kill them next time."

Mordax grimaced, "Yeah. Thanks for the advice."

Sylvia stood up.

"Cheer up. It's not all bad. After last night, there's a fair few people around here who owe you one."

Long after she had returned to her hammock, Mordax sat staring into the fire, a scratchy blanket pulled tightly around his shoulders, letting the smell of wood smoke and pine resin wash over him. Ashfol had been right. The deck was stacked against him. But he had changed the rules of the game and come out... if not on top then at least not at the bottom. If he was going to survive he had to stay a step ahead of the others. That was easier said than done but the realisation gave him a faint glimmer of something that felt almost like hope.

Chapter 27

Mordax spat a gobbet of blood onto the dusty ground, eyes watering, as he fought against his stunned diaphragm to heave air into his lungs. At least he hadn't thrown up yet. In the weeks since he had arrived at the fort he had got better at taking a beating.

"KEEP YOUR GUARD UP, CRETIN!" Ashfol yelled, arms crossed over his massive chest as he watched from the side of the fighting yard. The "fighting yard" was in fact just a flat area close to the western side of the hill fort, delineated from the rest of the rocky ground only by a thick, rusty chain laid down in a rough oval.

"I don't know why you bother, Mordax," said Persimmon, the tall, ebony-skinned man who had just driven a blunt, wooden cosh, meant to represent a knife, into Mordax's solar plexus. "The martial arts just aren't your forté. You should stick to something you're actually good at like stealing things or... actually I can't think of anything else you're good at."

"Urgh," groaned Mordax, willing his uncooperative body to take a breath. "You— urgh— You know you're named after a fruit."

There were a few snorts of laughter from the watching initiates and Persimmon's nostrils flared with anger marring his haughty expression.

"Persimmon is the name of three of the ancient kings of New Carthage, actually," Persimmon said.

Mordax staggered to his feet, wiping his lips and leaving a crimson streak on his sleeve.

"Yeah, they're all named after a fruit too. It's like a small, fat tomato."

There was a wider rumble of laughter through the spectators. Persimmon growled and leapt at Mordax again, but this time his strike was fuelled by rage and had all of his weight behind it. Mordax pivoted, just as Suliman had been teaching him, avoiding the blow and looping an arm around Persimmon's neck. He squeezed with all his strength and Persimmon's legs buckled. Mordax kept the pressure on Persimmon's neck and his struggles grew weaker. Mordax let out a whoop. Finally! He had not won a single bout in all the weeks they had been training with Ashfol. But here was glorious victory, within his grasp. Suddenly the tight curls at the back of Persimmon's head appeared to be approaching with alarming speed. There was a loud crack and the next thing Mordax knew he was lying on the ground with blood streaming from his nose. Ashfol's bushy-bearded face, swimming ever so slightly, loomed into view.

"Right idea, lad. Needs work on the execution though."

"Urgh," groaned Mordax for what seemed like the hundredth time that day. The past few weeks on Hellenbos had blurred together to create a grim pastiche of miserable grey cold interspersed with periods of bone-deep weariness and punches to the head. The initiates had had to come to grips with a variety of primitive weapons. No rifles or projectile shields here. The most technologically advanced piece of equipment in the fort was a cross-bow. The morning marches and combat training with Ashfol had had an undeniable effect on Mordax's body, however. Although he was covered in bruises in every colour of the rainbow, from fresh deep purple blotches to more subtle pools of yellow and green, lean muscle had filled out some of his frame and calluses had formed on his palms and knuckles. Since his altercation with Yefa, he had spent some time getting to know the other initiates. Most were either friendly or ambivalent but there was a core group, with Ragin at its centre, that seemed intent on making sure that Mordax didn't pass Selection. It was nothing new to Mordax. He had experienced prejudice against Travellers all his life but usually at its worst it consisted of black looks, inflated prices or the odd brawl which

Stamford quickly brought to its natural conclusion. Never had the stakes been so high.

"Come on, up you get." Ashfol grabbed hold of his shirt and pulled him to his feet with ease.

Mordax hobbled over to where Suliman and Sylvia were waiting just beyond the edge of the chain. Suliman gave him a rueful grin.

"You are getting better, brother. We will soon have you putting rings on these bastards."

"You mean 'running rings around them,'" corrected Sylvia. "And he might not have much of a nose left by the time that happens." She cast a critical eye over Mordax's face. "Stay still."

She took hold of his nose and give it a hard tweak. There was a loud crunch and a sharp pain behind his eyes but he was immediately able to breath easily again.

"Thanks," said Mordax, wiping fresh tears from his eyes.

"Right, you lot, gather round," said Ashfol. Daenyrs had appeared quietly at his side, like a grim shadow. The initiates assembled in front of them, those who had not been training wrapped up tightly with scarves covering noses and mouths against the bitter cold. They made for a smaller group than when they had first arrived on Hellenbos. In the past few weeks, since the night Mordax's group was attacked in the forest, there had been further casualties. Two initiates had got lost during a sudden violent storm that had blown in during a march through the forest. Ashfol had found their bodies later, miles from the fort, huddled around the remnants of a doomed attempt to start a fire. One initiate had been hit with a dart in broad daylight during an excursion to fell trees and, much like Taro, had succumbed quickly to whatever poison coated the dart. Another, on night-watch on the stockade, had simply vanished. Tensions were running high in the group, not least because the trainers refused even to discuss the nature of the opponent they were facing. Mordax and Suliman, however, not content with their trainers' reticence on the subject, had searched the wooded area near the victim of the dart and found large footprints in the snow. Suliman and Ragin, who both had tracking experience, agreed the unfamiliar prints had been made by something heavy, at least three times the weight of a human, with long claws.

"I hope you've enjoyed the last few weeks of comfort," said Daenyrs, stepping forward, the ever-present shimmer of his veil visible at his throat.

"The time has come to move to the next stage of Selection and see whether you are able to put what you've learned to use. No more rooves to cower under or stockades to hide behind. You'll go out into the forest now to test your mettle against this planet on its own terms."

Mordax didn't like the smirk on Daenyrs face as he said this.

Daenyrs pulled something out of a pouch at his waist and held it aloft, hanging under his clenched fist for all to see. It was a long braid of dark coarse hair which seemed to have pieces of carved horn or bone woven in.

"This is a warrior braid," Daenyrs said. The ones who have been hunting you each have one and believe it is where their warrior mana, their strength, resides. You'll be split into two groups of my choosing. All of you will leave the compound in the next hour. From then, you will have exactly one week to obtain as many of these braids as you can. No one will be allowed back inside the compound until that week is up."

A grim muttering broke out among the initiates.

"I am not without generosity, however," said Daenyrs loudly. "You'll have until the hour is up to take your pick of weapons and tools. How you go about collecting the braids is up to you but the group which brings me back the fewest braids will spend the rest of Selection outside these walls."

So the hunted were to become the hunters, Mordax thought. Based on their last encounter they would be lucky if any of them made it through the week with their skin intact. Daenyrs proceeded to split them, with a couple of exceptions, into the same groups as he had before: the ones who had won their one-on-one bouts and the ones who had lost. That meant that Suliman was placed in the same group as Ragin and Persimmon, among others. This time, however, Sylvia was placed in the losers group with Mordax and Theron. Mordax suspected that Sylvia's refusal to hurt him worse in their fight might have had something to do with Daenyrs' decision. Surprisingly, Yefa was also placed into Mordax's group. At that announcement, the glare she favoured him with was enough to make his teeth tingle. Immediately the two groups began scurrying around, tramping the ground to a slushy mud, breath misting and clouding above them in the frosty air. Most of the initiates had immediately congregated at the weapons shed, where spears, knives and crossbows lined the walls, hoping to bag themselves the sharpest, newest or generally best-maintained weapons. Mordax beckoned his group over and was grimly satisfied when almost all of them immediately complied. When he had them in a semblance of order he spoke urgently and quietly.

"Forget the weapons. I need most of you to head to the tool shed. Everyone needs a shovel. Also get the best saws and planing tools you can. Oh, and as many of the other good quality metal tools as you can carry, hammers, hatchets, pliers whatever, just pack them up. Someone also head to the kitchen and pack a Bergen with pans, cups and sharp knives."

Mordax's upper arm was seized in a painful grip. "What the fuck, Mordax?" Sylvia hissed in his ear.

"Trust me," he whispered back.

He turned back to the group, who were looking around at each other in disbelief.

"Most of you were with me the last time we spent a night in the forest. No one's really talked about it but all of you know we were supposed to die that night. I got you out alive. Daenyrs thinks we're the weak ones, he thinks putting us together again is a death sentence. He couldn't be more wrong. Go with me on this one and not only will I keep you alive again but we'll blow Ragin and his band of fuck-knuckles out of the water."

The group stood mute for a few seconds.

"You want to send us out there with nothing but a shovel and fucking teapot?" said Yefa eventually. "Like hell. You didn't keep everyone alive last time, did you? My brother listened to you and look where that got him. You go ahead and bang your pots and pans together. I'm tooling up."

She stalked off towards the weapons shed. Mordax felt the eyes of the others on him, felt the balance tipping away from him. And then Theron spoke up, his voice quietly commanding.

"If it wasn't for your schemes most of us would be dead already. If you say you can win us this contest, I believe you."

Without waiting for an answer, he turned and made towards the tool shed. Mordax almost let out a sob of relief.

"Fuck it," said Sylvia with a sigh, "someone's got to make sure your bootlaces are tied up." Gradually the other initiates in the group followed Theron.

"Pretty speech, mate," said Sylvia after the others were out of earshot. "I hope you've got a rock solid plan to back it up because those people are putting their lives in your hands."

Mordax swallowed hard and tried to look more confident than he felt. He did have a plan but it would take all his skill to pull it off and if anything went wrong, he had just convinced fifteen seasoned soldiers to spend the next week in the most dangerous environment of their careers with nothing to protect themselves but kitchen equipment and prayers.

Chapter 28

The words of Xif's latest report, overlaid on her vision by her retinal display, sped past at close to her maximum reading speed. Yet another corrupt Thalmian official with links to off-world Kudo-kai business interests. Akira never ceased to marvel at man's unlimited capacity for greed. The Thalmians were, per capita, the richest people in the Shattered Empires and yet she had read report after report of those taking bribes to grease the wheels of Thalmos's admittedly tortuous administration, fast-tracking travel permits and bumping housing requests to the front of the line. Luckily, Xif had downloaded the most useful information he could find from Thalmos's comm net before they had been imprisoned, spreading the tendrils of his mind far and wide and ferreting out any information that could shed some light on the Thalmians' new hostility towards the Kudo-kai. The information was quickly becoming stale, however, and, for the most part, seemed useless. Nothing he had found could even come close to explaining Glankor's change of attitude. Worse, being enclosed for the last few weeks had caused relations in their apartment to deteriorate rapidly, with Akira, Shiori and Xif all snapping at each other mercilessly. To review Xif's report, Akira had taken refuge in the enormous dining room and was currently sitting in a comfortable gel chair, a cup and a pot of freshly-brewed Icthus flower tea the only objects on the vast golden table in front of her. She double-blinked the report away and gazed at the vista that ran the length of the room. Smart panels offered a realistic view out over Thalmos. The morning sun would rise overhead as the day progressed and, as Akira watched, a virtual flock of birds wheeled past. Great towers jostled for position around them, a forest of stone and glass. The Thalmians never seemed to pass up an opportunity to gilt, bejewel or generally beautify anything that stayed still for long enough. Even the outsides of the opulent towers were decorated with polished marble and great whorls and swirls of platinum strips that had been embedded into the facade and now twinkled in the sunlight. Looming over it all, however, swallowing everything it encircled, was the vast, unadorned perimeter wall. The protruding spire, barely a wrinkle on its monumental surface, soared upwards until it faded into nothingness in the sky's great blue expanse. With a sudden flare of frustration, she picked up the ceramic tea cup and hurled it in the direction of the Spire where it promptly smashed against the panel causing the image to stutter and flicker. An attendant who had come into the room unnoticed looked at her wide eyed. At least one of these attendants came to the apartment every day to clean and replenish their food and drink and, as Xif had pointed out, were a precaution against him hijacking automated drones who would ordinarily have performed such tasks.

"Sorry," said Akira, putting her face in her hands and sighing.

"Not to worry, ma'am," said the attendant.

It was the voice that alerted Akira first, being deeper and more gravelly than the silky-soft voices of the attendants she was used to. She looked up to see the fair-haired man placing a large vase of speckled purple and white flowers in the middle of the table. Upon closer inspection, his forearms, revealed by the cream robe he wore, were heavily muscled and his fingers were thick and rough. That struck Akira as wrong somehow, like a dissonant chord. As the man turned away from the table, one hand dropped to his waist and he moved fractionally closer to Akira than he should have done had he simply been exiting the room. Without really knowing why, Akira stood up. As she did so, the attendant, dilated pupils locked onto hers, took a few hasty steps forward and lunged, something in his hand. Akira stumbled backwards trying to keep the chair between them. It was this that saved her. The attendant made to kick the chair out of the way but the smart-form gel merely absorbed the force of the kick, moulding itself around his foot and overbalancing him, buying Akira precious seconds to scramble further away around the table, pulling other chairs out behind her. She suddenly remembered herself and let out as loud a scream as she could muster. "HELP! HEEEEELLLLPPPP!"

The man righted himself with frightening agility and sprang after her, vaulting the few chairs she had managed to throw into his path. He caught her at the far end of the table. Akira felt her legs crush together as he wrapped his arms around her thighs before toppling to the ground, the hard weight of him slamming into her back. With the impact, the grip eased for a second and Akira took the opportunity to twist herself violently so that she was facing him as he straddled her torso. As his weight settled back on her the air was forced out of her lungs. She scratched at his face trying to claw him with her fingernails but he batted her hands away easily. He held what looked like a dirty yellow pen in his hand and, face set grimly, brought it down towards her neck. Dimly Akira heard a rapid patter then there was a dark blur and a grunt and suddenly the weight was gone from her chest and she could breathe freely. She looked up to see Shiori grappling with the man on the floor a short distance away, her slender frame dwarfed by the man who was manoeuvring himself on top of her to best use his weight to his advantage. The man brought his hands to around Shiori's throat. Akira glanced around desperately, her eyes settling on the vase the man had placed on the table. She dragged herself up, grabbed the vase and hurled it at him. Her aim was good and the vase exploded against his head in a shower of water, sharp ceramic and purple petals. It wasn't enough to knock him out but he rolled sideways clutching his head, pink rivulets of bloody water streaming down his face. Shiori sprang to her feet and adopted what looked like a boxer's stance. The man recovered himself quickly, pushing himself to his feet, shaking his head and advancing on Shiori. Akira froze. It felt like the seconds before a car crash, the powerlessness and dismay in the face of certain disaster. But when the first punch came, Shiori tilted her head, only fractionally, so that the fist went whistling wide finding only air. The second punch was again aimed at her head, but Shiori danced backwards just outside the man's reach. She caught the third, aimed at her midriff on her forearms, before snapping a jab of her own at the man, catching him on the nose and jolting his head backwards. The man was clearly as startled as Akira. He growled and swung a hook so fast that Akira could barely follow it. Shiori somehow anticipated it and ducked, letting the swing just graze the wisps of hair at the back of her head before stepping forward throwing all of her weight behind a straight punch to his chin. The man's legs gave out beneath him and he sprawled backwards coughing a spatter of blood onto the polished marble floor. He blinked a few times, desperately trying to focus his eyes as Shiori approached him slowly. His gaze settled on the yellowish pen that was lying on the floor a few feet from him, and he began to move. Blood staining the tunic around his neck like a crimson shawl, the man scrabbled across the slippery stone on his front, rubber soles squeaking and slapping as he propelled himself towards the strange weapon. His fingertips just brushed the edges of the pen before Shiori reached him. She took a fist full of his hair and yanked his head backwards so that his face was turned up towards her and at the same time pulled a long hair pin out of the bun at the back of her head, letting her silky dark hair cascade freely over her shoulders. The man had time to let out a short whimper before Shiori stabbed the pin down straight into his right eye, burying it up to her fist. A high-pitched keening noise, almost inhuman to Akira's ears, came from the man's throat until Shiori released her hold on his hair and he collapsed, face meeting the marble with a wet thud.

His legs twitched spasmodically. Akira took a couple of steps away from the convulsing form before sinking to her knees and began to retch quietly. There was some rustling and out of the corner of her eye Akira could see Shiori bent over the man and then Shiori was beside her gently stroking her back. Eventually Akira's breath evened and she let out a sigh. She brushed a tear from her lashes.

"Sorry," she said.

"It's difficult seeing a person die for the first time. Even more so having a hand in it."

"Who is he?" Akira asked.

"Not one of the usual attendants. Pale skin, calluses on his hands and his teeth aren't so good. He's probably from the sub-levels. Other than that we'd need the Thalmians to tell us more."

"How did this happen?"

Shiori paused, perhaps deciding how to interpret the question. She brought her hand forward so that Akira could see the yellow pen she now held. It seemed to be made of some kind of firm, gelatinous substance like agar and thin tubes and components were just visible through its translucent surface

"Subcutaneous shunt applicator," she explained. "Doesn't leave a mark. I think it's safe to assume that whatever's in it wouldn't have done you much good. Looks to be fully bio, maybe even DNA personalised to this guy, so wouldn't have flagged on the security checks."

Akira caught a flicker of movement at the doorway and tensed until she realised it was the corner of Xif's floating body, one camera peeking into the room.

"It's OK, Xif, you can come in."

"Is that blood?" he said, floating into the room and performing a rapid spin. "Oh goodness, he's dead."

"Yes, thank you, Xif," said Akira. "Where exactly have you been?"

"I came as soon as I heard the commotion. Shiori seemed to have the situation in hand so it seemed prudent to stay clear so as not to be a distraction."

"You cowardly piece of—" began Akira.

"As I understand it, Xifulandros's systems don't include weapons that are effective against people," said Shiori, "so there really wasn't much he could do."

"Mmhmm," said Akira, still glaring at the drone.

"Yes, well," said Xif after an awkward pause, "it seems we need to decide on next steps with some urgency."

"Could this have been Glankor's doing?" Akira asked.

"Unlikely," said Shiori. "If he wanted you dead, he could just order it. He wouldn't have to go to the trouble of sending an assassin."

"So then I suppose we alert the guards outside, explain what's happened and demand to know who this man was and how it is that he was granted entry," Akira said.

"I'd advise against that," said Xif.

"Why's that exactly?"

"Well, for one, we have no idea who else could be in on this plot. What if the guards are instructed to finish the job where this unfortunate fellow failed? Whoever arranged for an assassin to get in here clearly has a degree of authority or resourcefulness that it would be wise not to underestimate. Secondly, while the Faraday cage around us stops us communicating with the outside it also precludes surveillance systems. The Thalmians will see a dead attendant with Shiori's hair pin in his brain and may well jump to some undesirable conclusions. Glankor doesn't presently seem inclined to afford us the benefit of the doubt."

"But we've got the weapon," pointed out Akira.

"Even so," said Xif, "if it's not in fact coded to his DNA, there's an argument that it could just as easily be a weapon that we have concealed."

"So what do you suggest?"

"There don't seem to be any desirable options."

Akira reached for the reassuring presence of the token that Matsuko had given her and grasped nothing but air. She looked around and saw it lying on the floor where she had struggled with the attendant, its chain broken. The face had swung open revealing the tiny dark sphere of nanotrite suspended at its centre. As she bent to pick it up, Xif floated closer.

"Akira...what is that?"

"Mind your own business, Xif."

"Is that nanotrite?"

Shiori's head snapped round at that, eyes locked on the token suspended from Akira's hand.

"Yes. Why?"

"Because," said Xif slowly, "a Faraday cage only blocks signals in this universe. It can't block anything travelling through the netherverse."

Realisation dawned on Akira.

"We'd need a nether transmitter."

"One of the many instruments I do happen to have," said Xif. "All that I lacked was the fuel for it which the Thalmians forced me to give up. I never suspected you had your own supply."

"What does this mean?" asked Akira, not trusting the tremulous flicker of hope in her chest.

"It means we have a chance of escaping," said Xif. "I can nethercast into the building's security network, disable the surveillance around this tower and, I imagine, Shiori can deal with any guards we encounter. We get to a shuttle to the Grace of Meridian and nether-jump before the body's discovered."

"Abandon the mission, you mean?"

Xif gave a little wobble. "We must be realistic, Akira. We've discovered nothing useful in the past weeks, we're thousands of parsecs from home with no means of support whatsoever and an unknown adversary has very nearly succeeded in killing you. I don't really see an alternative but to return home."

"We're not running away," Akira said.

"Akira, please—"

"This isn't an argument, Xif. I'm not heading back with my tail between my legs to tell my father that we accomplished absolutely nothing and wetted ourselves at the first sign of danger. I understand the risk but we're staying until the job is done so stiffen your metaphorical spine and start thinking about solutions rather than escape routes."

"It's not just your own life you're risking, Akira," Xif said.

"You said yourself that Glankor wouldn't dare to destroy you so it's me and Shiori in the firing line. Shiori, will you stay?"

Akira glanced at the girl, the meek servant who prepared Akira's tea and changed her linens, whose tokens barely classed her as a citizen, the girl whose hard muscles Akira had never noticed and who had just killed a man without hesitation or remorse. Shiori looked back at her and Akira could see no trace of her previous docility. The heat of the fight had melted it away like a wax mask.

"We need to leave this apartment immediately and we need a new plan...but yes, I go where you do."

Akira laid a hand on her arm. "Thank you." She turned to Xif.

"Get a line open to Matsuko Ito, as soon as you can. Shiori, I'll need you to gather some essentials for us, food, nondescript clothes, you'll know better than me probably."

Xif floated out of the room and Shiori turned to leave but Akira took hold of her arm gently.

"Who are you, Shiori?"

"What do you mean?" Shiori said, but the words were automatic without any real conviction.

"You know what I mean. You're not a servant."

"Really? I've spent the last few months dressing you and cleaning up after you. That fits the description of a servant to me."

Akira looked straight into Shiori's clear hazel eyes. Eventually Shiori shrugged.

"Fine. Look, everyone knew this mission was going to be dangerous. Matsuko wanted to send a close-protection squad with you but your father vetoed it. He said it would send the wrong message to the Thalmians and wouldn't do any good if they were simply going to execute you anyway."

Akira had always known that her father understood he would be risking her life by sending her here but it still stung to have it confirmed so explicitly.

"I was the compromise," Shiori continued. "Matsuko started my training cycles ago. Probably as a precaution, in case a situation like this ever arose and the nanotrite supply from Thalmos was interrupted."

"Training you to do what?"

Shiori shrugged. "This and that. Nothing we would want the Thalmians to know about and nothing that a self-respecting Kudo-kai citizen would admit to engaging in."

"So was it all a lie? You didn't grow up here?"

"Oh, I was on Thalmos alright. My father was ambassador here."

If Akira wasn't already at the point of emotional overload, the revelation would have taken her breath away. Her servant's father had held one of the most prominent offices in the Kudo-kai.

"Ambassador? But, your tokens..."

Shiori smiled bitterly. "Dear old father immersed himself a bit too much in the local culture. At first, it was the odd party here and there, par for the course for an ambassador. But then he started getting home later and later. He would stumble in as I was eating my breakfast, sour with drink and talking at a million miles an hour. Eventually he was arrested during a raid on a whore house in the sub-levels run by the Red Liberation Army. It was a major diplomatic incident at the time but was brushed under the carpet."

"What happened?"

"My whole family was shipped off to Persepid Pelian, out near the Reaches and pretty much as far away from civilisation as they could put us. Dad was busted down to a minor official and our tokens were replaced. He never got over the humiliation, killed himself six months into the posting."

Akira suddenly realised what it must have been like for Shiori. To be someone of standing within the Kudo-kai, part of a respected family, and then to become little more than a servant.

"I'm sorry, Shiori."

Shiori gave her a wry look. "Don't be. Matsuko's promised to restore my family's tokens if this mission is successful. I just hope you've got a way to improve our fortunes."

Akira felt the weight of Shiori's expectation settle onto her shoulders, a pebble added to the sack of rocks that was already there but no less real or solid for it. She thought it best not to mention that she had no idea what their next move would be but she hoped for both their sakes that Matsuko would.

Chapter 29

Gentle twilight had just begun to fall, hiding the textures of rocks and shrubs and the shapes of scurrying animals leaving only their rustling footsteps behind. It was as if a fine soot had been blown over the canvas of the forest, darkening the vibrant hue of the foliage and blurring the spaces between trees to a dusky grey. Their eyes strained against the dark pools of shadow under the canopy and innocuous twigs and branches suddenly jig-sawed together to create the impression of crouching human silhouettes and beast-like forms preparing to pounce. A single small fire, surrounded by Bergens piled up to resemble sitting people, flickered cheerfully in the centre of the clearing as if oblivious to the danger around it. Mordax sat deathly still under the trees at the edge of the clearing very much alert to the danger. The sheen of sweat from his recent exertions was swiftly making him uncomfortably cold and he was resigned to a long, gruelling night of waiting. Sylvia sat huddled beside him, showing no sign of obvious discomfort, her blue eyes just about still visible in the gloom. They both wore makeshift gillie suits of netting woven with leaves.

"If this works, I'll eat my boots," she said glumly.

"Have some faith, sister," said Mordax. "The night's young. We might get a bite yet."

"Yeah, a giant bite right out of our asses."

As soon as the group had left the safety of the hilltop fort, Mordax had set about finding the perfect spot for their ambush. His plan required them to catch one of their hunters alive. Careful to ensure that they put a good amount of distance between themselves and Ragin's group, Mordax had sent scouts in different directions until they found the small clearing around which the initiates were now hidden. Apart from Yefa, who trudged along sullenly behind the others, armed to the teeth, none of the members of Mordax's group had questioned his assumption of command. They had spent precious days digging deep holes in the frozen, rocky ground at intervals around the clearing, just inside the forest, until their backs screamed in pain and angry yellow blisters appeared across their palms. Once the holes were deep enough, nets were stretched across them and covered with leaves until the traps were invisible to the naked eye. All they could do now was pray that their fire was enough to lure one of their hunters close enough but not so obvious as to bring a whole pack of them.

"If I have to fight my way out of here with a saucepan, I'll kill you," Sylvia said.

"If it comes to that, I doubt you'll have to," muttered Mordax.

After a few minutes of companionable silence, he said, "You've never told me how you got that scar."

He gestured to the faint, jagged line that ran from her left temple to the bottom of her ear. "Knife fight? Diving through a window to escape a hail of bullets?"

Sylvia was quiet for a few seconds.

"I got it before I served actually," she said. "Scumbag boyfriend of my mum with a short temper and a long reach. It's part of the reason I became a solider in the first place."

"Ah, I'm sorry."

"Don't be. If I hadn't been driven out I might still be in that shit hole,"

"Might be better than this," said Mordax, glancing around them meaningfully.

"There are different kinds of hell," Sylvia said quietly. "At least here the monsters only try to kill you."

They sat quietly for a moment, Mordax sure that sympathy was the last thing Sylvia would want.

"I'm banking on them being dissuaded on that front, actually," he said eventually.

"Yeah, well, we'll see how that pans out, won't we?"

The air was still heavy with an earthy mustiness from the displaced soil and the smell of wood smoke clung to their clothes, from happier days when there was no risk in crowding around a fire for warmth. The forest floor was dappled by shifting grey-blue shafts of moonlight so that it almost seemed that they were sitting on a seabed, water pressing in around them. Mordax fancied the trees were great fronds of kelp swaying gently in the current.

"So how about your folks?" said Sylvia. "Not worthless pieces of shit like mine?"

Mordax shook his head. "I never knew my mother. She died when I was young. My dad, he...I thought he was a good person. He looked out for me the best way he knew how. Gave me the skills I'd need as a Traveller. And he loved me. But... Do you think someone can be two people at once? Or become a different person over time?"

"Nope. People are complicated. Who someone really is never matches another person's idea of them. Especially parents. I take it your dad was into some shady stuff?"

"He was a Dioscuri wraith," said Mordax.

Even in the dark, Mordax could see Sylvia's eyes widen.

"No. Way."

"Seriously. Cycles ago. Seems he left around the time I was born. Before he was...before he died, he programmed our ship to nether-jump to Eloth. I think he found out some information about the Kudo-kai but I don't know what. It's the reason I'm here now. It was either take part in Selection or my crew would be killed."

"That's insane," said Sylvia. "Sounds like you've been through the ringer."

"It hasn't been the easiest few weeks," said Mordax with a chuckle.

"So you think your dad wasn't a good person because he killed people?"

Mordax suddenly realised how that must sound to a solider like Sylvia, someone whose job description was to kill people.

"I didn't mean it that way, Sylvia. You know I think you're great."

"Piss off, I'm not offended. But you're being thick-headed again. If there was ever a valid justification to kill it's as part of the Dioscuri. They toppled the Two Empires for fuck's sake. You know how many civilisations the Empires wiped out? How many systems they sucked dry? If it wasn't for people like your dad, the galaxy would still be blowing itself to bits. I'm not one to give out pearls of wisdom, believe me, but if there's one thing I've learned in this line of work it's that when things go to shit, there are no right choices. There are only bad ones and worse ones. You've got to look at his choices in context."

Mordax smiled. "That's funny. My dad used to say something similar. He said an indigo starling is dark against a sunny sky, but against the black of night it's the only bright thing around."

"Sounds like the guy had his head screwed on straight," said Sylvia.

"Maybe," whispered Mordax.

Mordax was suddenly conscious of their closeness and the mist of her breath on the air. He risked a glance in her direction and found her eyes already studying him.

At that moment there was a cacophony from across the clearing, a loud thud combined with a swiftly muffled roar and a strangled cry. He and Sylvia looked back at each other then jumped to their feet and raced towards the noise.

Chapter 30

"You OK?" said Mordax, examining Theron for injury in the moonlight that made its way through the canopy.

"Fine," he said curtly, but Mordax could see that he was rattled. His misted breath was coming out in rapid bursts. He still held his arm somewhat awkwardly although, thanks to the corrective applied by Ashfol, it was now almost completely healed. The other members of their group, still clad in their leafy ghillie-suits, materialised out of the darkness like forest spirits.

"What have we got?" Mordax gestured at the pit at their feet. As he had hoped, the covering, a wooden frame filled with moss, which Theron had thrown over it after the trap had been tripped, effectively dampened the noise of whatever was inside. They didn't want to attract the attention of any of the other creatures. Even so, he could make out a strange mix of growls and sharp cries.

"It happened too fast. I didn't get a good look," Theron said.

Mordax bent to examine the pit.

"Bring me a light," he instructed the assembled initiates. One of them slipped away and returned shortly with a flickering torch from the fire. Mordax wished to god for a simple flashlight. He grasped a bark shield in one hand and with the other tentatively lifted the covering away from the hole. Two pairs of eyes glinted back at him from the dark, one set burning large and bright like coals, the other smaller and dimmer. The growling became more urgent and resonated deep inside him, making his hands tremble. It took all of his nerve not to drop the cover back. Instead, he thrust the torch further into the pit, revealing its inhabitants. Pacing back and forth across the narrow width of the pit was an unfamiliar beast, covered in thick greyish fur. Its snout was split vertically, with pinkish lips drawn back around rows of fangs. Long powerful limbs flexed and trembled with coiled rage and each of its four paws was tipped with long claws which glinted in the firelight. Most notable to Mordax, however, was the leather saddle strapped to its back. Behind the beast, barely reaching its shoulder, was a small, wiry, very human man. He was dressed in furs and stared back at them wide eyed. There was a flash of movement and Mordax, who had been expecting it, raised the bark shield, catching the dart which whistled towards his head.

"None of that," said Mordax, lowering the shield.

The man let out a string of guttural words giving the distinct impression that his anger was winning the battle with his fear. Mordax was so shocked that he understood some of the words that he almost dropped the covering. Ever since he had first examined the dart after Chadwick's disappearance, he had suspected that there were other humans on Hellenbos. The dart was obviously the work of a dextrous, self-aware race and there were precious few of those other than humans since the advent of the Two Empires. He knew from experience that this part of the galaxy, far out along the Scutum-Crux, had rarely been visited by other species even before the Two Empires and it was vanishingly unlikely that there was a new intelligent race on a habitable world that had somehow gone undetected. Maybe in the Reaches but not here. He had even deduced that the local humans must have some form of agile mount, native to the planet. What else would have made the large, strange prints in the snow found by Suliman? Also, no human would have been able to move unaided around the treetops in the way Mordax had witnessed during the night-time attack on his group weeks previously. He reasoned that they must have domesticated a large animal which could carry them swiftly among the trees and it was for that reason that he had insisted that the pits be dug so deep despite the back-breaking work of loosening the frozen ground. The pair below and the saddle on the beast confirmed his theory. What Mordax had not expected was that the locals, with their primitive technology, might speak a language with which he was familiar. He couldn't catch every word, but he understood enough to know that the man was suggesting Mordax do some unseemly things with various members of his own family. The language was similar to Ingash, an old dialect, predating the Kudo-kai, used by some communities of Travellers far out along the Scutum-Crux. These were mostly madmen who plied the trading routes between the Shattered Empires and the wilderness of the Reaches, braving pirates and other more mysterious dangers. The *Indigo Starling* had once responded to a distress call while on a rare excursion near the Fringe and picked up one such Traveller from the tattered remnants of his hauler. The skinny man with fire-red hair, who they had found hiding in a storage compartment after pirates had all but disassembled his ship around him, had jabbered constantly on their month-long trip back Core-wards, sometimes in broken Basic but mostly in Ingash. Stephan spoke Ingash comfortably and, by the end of the trip, although he was sick of hearing it, Mordax had a working knowledge of it too.

The man in the pit below beat his chest, screamed something about Mordax's ancestors laying with animals and spat a surprisingly powerful gobbet of phlegm which cleared the edge of the pit and landed on Mordax's boot.

Mordax placed his shield on the ground and gestured for Theron to take hold of the pit covering. He displayed his open hands to the wild man below him.

"Peace, friend," he said in Ingash, dredging the words from deep in his memory. "We no violence you."

The man stopped hollering and squinted up at Mordax suspiciously. The beast, taking its cue from its master, stopped pacing and its growl lessened to an ominous rumble.

"How do you come to speak the mother tongue, alien?" the man said.

"Come, sit and speak," Mordax said. "I tell story of how."

At a nod from Mordax, Sylvia lowered a lightweight silk rope into the pit and stepped back drawing her knife.

"What?" she demanded at Mordax's meaningful look. "He just shot a poisoned dart at your head, mate. You talk all you want but I'm not letting that bastard within ten feet of me."

It took some coaxing, but eventually the man, seeing that he didn't have much choice, hauled himself up the rope until he was standing at the edge of the pit. Mordax had been worried that he would attack them immediately but the menacing ring of camouflaged initiates and the odd glint of moonlight on steel seemed to convince him that was a futile plan. From the man's constant glances towards the pit, from which a pathetic whining could now be heard, Mordax suspected the man was more worried about what would happen to his mount than his own fate. Mordax led the man to the small fire in the middle of the clearing where they sat opposite each other on low logs under a cascade of brilliant stars. Mordax busied himself setting a kettle over the fire and soon the smell of fresh coffee mingled with the powerful scent of burning pine needles. The man watched him closely and silently. In the light of the fire, Mordax could see that he was about thirty with dirty blond hair and a slight but wiry frame. He wore a thick mantle of furs over his shoulders, sturdy fur boots and a simple necklace of what looked like amber. A long, hollow bone, which Mordax assumed was a blow pipe, hung at the man's waist and, just as Daenyrs had said, a braid of hair, woven with pieces of bone, fell over his shoulder. When the coffee had brewed Mordax poured two cups and placed one in front of the man. He sat back down and held his own up, deliberately taking a sip to demonstrate it was safe. Without taking his eyes off Mordax, the man nudged the cup in front of him with his toe, tipping it over and spilling the scalding coffee which ate its way into the frozen ground like acid. Mordax smiled inwardly. He had bartered against more hostile counterparts. Over the course of the next hour or so, Mordax discovered that the man's name was Jahaphrim. Jahaphrim, like all of his tribe and all the other tribes of Hellenbos, hated with a murderous passion the "Gosphandelt", the sky-demons, like Mordax, who arrived from the heavens each year to prey on them. When signs of the Gosphandelt's arrival were noticed, the tribes of Hellenbos put aside their own conflicts and united against the common enemy. It was true then, Mordax thought to himself. The Dioscuri kept these people, an entire continent, intentionally isolated and primitive as a whetstone against which to sharpen their recruits. He felt a heavy sickness settle in him. When Mordax asked how Jahaphrim's people had come to Hellenbos he received a blank look. Their ancestors had been carved from the branch of an ancient tree by the forest spirits. It was Mordax and the other "Gosphandelt" who were not of this world. Jahaphrim seemed particularly interested in how Mordax had come to learn their language. Mordax explained that not all "Gosphandelt" were the same and he was interested in coming to an arrangement that would result, at least this year, in a cessation of hostilities with some of his people. When Mordax explained the exact particulars of the proposed arrangement, as expected Jahaphrim was outraged but Mordax was by varying degrees, soothing, rational and impassioned. He calmed Jahaphrim's initial outburst and then explained, somewhat hampered by his basic Ingash vocabulary, how the arrangement would benefit Jahaphrim's tribe, countering the native's objections with cold logic. Finally, when he could sense that Jahaphrim was teetering, wrong-footed by the power of Mordax's arguments and unsure of the soundness of his own objections, Mordax dialled up the emotion, appealing to Jahaphrim's loyalty to his tribe, to his duty to protect them from harm as best he could. Eventually, Jahaphrim's features softened as he pursed his lips in thought and Mordax knew it was time to seal the deal. He grasped one of the nearby Bergens that had been disguised as a person and pulled it open, revealing the gleaming mass of metal tools, knives, pots and pans taken from the Dioscuri fort. He hefted the sack over to Jahaphrim who examined the contents, whistling as he tested the sharpness of a knife against his thumb and frowning at unfamiliar scissors and pliers. When Mordax showed him how to use flint sticks for fire-lighting, his face lit up and he gave a gleeful cackle, striking the sticks again and again to create a shower of sparks.

"You bring magic from the heavens, Gosphandelt!" Jahaphrim said. "Metal from the sun itself!"

"It belongs everything to you, friend, if you can bring your side of the deal," Mordax said in his faltering Ingash.

Jahaphrim nodded seriously. "I will discuss your proposal with the elders. It will be their decision whether to make this deal with you or not."

"How long?" Mordax asked.

Jahaphrim shrugged. "After this fire goes out. Before my hair turns grey."

Mordax gritted his teeth. They needed to be back at the fort in three days and any wait would be excruciating but he sensed there was no rushing this. He just hoped that Jahaphrim's tribe's deliberation was limited to whether or not to accept his proposal and not whether to send a war party to take the goods by force.

"Take this," Mordax said, pressing the flint sticks into Jahaphrim's rough hand. "A gift for explain our good intention. You will find us here when you have made decision."

Mordax then led Jahaphrim back to the pit where his mount now seemed to have exhausted itself with growling and was curled up asleep. He showed Jahaphrim a sturdy ladder nearby which the initiates had built and disguised with netting and leaves. It was long enough for Jahaphrim's mount to climb out of the pit, although Mordax and the others had retreated to a safe distance before the rescue was attempted, not quite trusting Jahaphrim's ability to control the beast's anger at its confinement. It seemed that Jahaphrim was more than up to the task, however, as he leapt into the saddle and was among the canopy in seconds. It lightened Mordax's heart only slightly that before Jahaphrim was swallowed by the gloom, he thought he saw him turn back to them and give a wave.

Chapter 31

Akira caught herself gazing around again and re-fixed her eyes on the smooth stone pavement in front of her, pulling her hood closer around her face and chiding herself inwardly. She, Shiori and Xif were making their way down the sweeping sunlit streets of central Kor Thalia, flanked by glittering towers and bridges and, despite Akira's determination to keep her head discreetly down, the sights kept clawing at her eyes demanding her attention. She had known that the citizens of Thalmos competed to outdo each other in displays of wealth but the ostentation was overwhelming. Cars shaped like great golden birds made their way lazily through the sky, mechanical wings beating powerfully but entirely ornamental due to the humming anti-gravity generators that kept the cars aloft. At one intersection they passed an art installation formed of floating orbs of clear water, ranging in size from that of an apple to a small house, dancing and weaving between each other in mesmerising patterns. A wistful expression had stolen over Shiori's face as they walked and Akira realised that this was the first time she had returned to the city where she had been born and lived for half her life. Xif assured them that there was negligible risk walking out in the open like this, for now at least, as he was able to disrupt the cameras which tracked every inch of the surface of Kor Thalia, scanning faces for known subversives. Xif, who would have drawn attention even without the cameras, was tucked ignominiously inside a cardboard box under Shiori's arm although it had taken much cajoling to get him to agree to it. They had left their apartment an hour previously, the corpse of the would-be assassin lying where he had fallen, a crimson halo of blood pooled around his head. They had no real destination other than to put as much distance as they could between themselves and the apartment tower before the body was discovered, and Xif was still busy trying to open a nethercast channel to Matsuko. Now that the adrenalin of the earlier violent encounter had worn off, Akira was having second thoughts about opposing Xif's suggestion of fleeing. The possibility of getting to the bottom of the mystery and restoring the Kudo-kai's supply of Thalmian nanotrite was seeming more and more far-fetched.

"I have Matsuko," Xif said.

Akira and Shiori hurried to a bench in an alcove hidden from the street by blooms of fragrant flowers. Matsuko's round face, slightly transparent, appeared before Akira's eyes as Xif sent the feed to her retinal display. He looked tired. The lines around his mouth seemed to have deepened in the months Akira had been away; however, a twinkle came back into his eyes as they came face to face.

"Hello, child," he said, voice rich and clear, "I would ask how you are but I expect that would be a silly question."

Part of her was comforted by his warm, paternal presence but another part, a more logical, mature part, knew that there was likely only limited help he could offer, separated as they were by many thousands of light cycles.

"Hello, Uncle. It's good to see your face. We've found ourselves in quite a tight spot. How much do I need to update you on?"

"My sources have informed me of your meeting with Glankor and the sentencing. I had been working on a way to get you out but you seem to have done that yourself."

Akira proceeded to explain the circumstances of their escape and the lack of progress discovering why the Thalmians had cut off the Kudo-kai's nanotrite supply. Matsuko's face grew serious and it made Akira anxious to see the worry there.

"I'm sorry that I've put you in harm's way, Akira."

"Well, you also put Shiori by my side so don't be too hard on yourself."

"Even so. You understand why I wasn't entirely candid with you about her role, don't you?"

Akira chewed her lip and said nothing. Matsuko sighed.

"Akira, I hoped with all my heart that Shiori's particular skill set would not be necessary. If you knew her true purpose was to protect you from attacks on your life I was worried it would unnerve you unnecessarily and distract you from the task at hand."

"For future reference, Uncle, I prefer to know about any measures put in place to protect me whether you think them unnerving or not."

Matsuko inclined his head, managing to look both stately and contrite.

"Speaking of the task at hand," Akira continued, "Xif thinks we should make for a shuttle and get back to the Grace of Meridian. If there's any chance we can still succeed with the mission we'll stay though. Do you have anything that could help us?"

Matsuko paused, a rare shadow of indecision passing across his face.

"There is the contact of mine that I told you about before you left. I hesitate to mention him even now as any attempt to meet him would be unreasonably risky and potentially fruitless. Certainly you've tried hard enough to find the information we need and there would be no shame in coming back to Angor Bore now."

"No shame," repeated Akira. "Would my father see it that way?"

Matsuko hesitated again, his silence answering Akira's question better than any words.

"Who is he, Uncle?"

Matsuko paused for the space of a breath, coming to a decision.

"Xifulandros, is this line a hundred per cent secure?"

"It is," replied Xif

"Very well. You're aware, I'm sure, about the non-citizen unrest on Thalmos, attacks on surface infrastructure and the like?"

"Yes," said Akira. "Shiori and I have discussed it at length. We can't find any link between the unrest and Glankor's animosity towards us though."

"And there may be none," Matsuko said. "The leader of the movement that calls itself the Red Liberation Army, that has carried out many of those attacks, is a man called Lorenzine Haskor. As you'd expect, he has a much broader network of informants on Thalmos than I do. Many cycles ago I did him a favour and I should hope that he still feels some sense of obligation to me as a result. There's a slim chance that he may have some information that could help. Be warned, though, he has little love for the Kudo-kai."

"Where can we find him?" Akira asked.

Matsuko grimaced.

"I'll send the last location I had for him to Xifulandros but the information's probably stale. The Red Liberation Army moves often and quickly to stay ahead of the patrols the Thalmian Council sends to ferret them out. Akira, the journey'll be dangerous. The RLA command hides itself deep among the tunnels and shafts of Thalmos' ancient machinery. The Thalmians are on high alert this close to the annual festival and have been combing the non-citizens none too gently in a bid to locate RLA members. You'll need to find a way to make it through the Thalmian patrols and even then finding someone who knows where Lorenzine is and convincing them to take you to him won't be easy."

"Well, I guess we'll have to take our chances," said Akira. "I'm lucky to have two extremely resourceful people, er... person and a drone, at my side."

Shiori glanced at her and smiled for what seemed like the first time in long while. Xif, of course, was invisible inside his box and would not have shown any outward expression in any event.

"How are things back home?" Akira asked.

Matsuko gave a weary sigh and any joy at seeing Akira again seemed to seep out of him.

"I won't lie to you," he said, "things are difficult. As expected, the interruption in our nanotrite supply is proving extremely costly. Your father is pushing those around him to find a solution."

Akira could read between the lines and knew her father well enough to understand that he was making Matsuko's life hell.

"Uncle, tell my father that I remember our last conversation. I understand the stakes at play. I'll do everything in my power to secure our family's future."

Matsuko smiled sadly. "You're more like him than you know. Be cautious, my girl. This galaxy is an unforgiving place. Particularly to those who don't temper their ambition with vigilance."

The connection cut and Matsuko's face disappeared with jarring immediacy.

"I have the location now," said Xif. "It's a settlement in the sub-levels."

"How do we get there?" asked Akira.

"Thousands of non-citizen workers come up from the sub-levels every day," said Shiori. "There are still a few working ancient elevators that they use. But we'll need passes. Thalmian security will be on a hair trigger this close to Uberaurum."

"Right, any idea how we get passes?" said Akira

"Maybe," said Shiori. "We're going to need the help of an old friend of my family and better luck than we've had so far."

Chapter 32

It was three days later, the day they were due to return to the fort, and Mordax had almost given up hope of Jahaphrim returning in time. If the slide into despair as the sands of the hourglass ran out wasn't torture enough, Yefa had kept up a constant campaign to undermine him. Every decision of his was questioned and he could hear her whispering to the other initiates during the night, dripping poison into their ears. As if sensing his despondency, the weather had taken a turn for the worse and wet sleet, carried on a bitter wind, blew almost horizontally through the trees. Mordax's group, the ones who were not on guard, had split into small groups and huddled together in sunken windbreaks around meagre fires, resigned to enduring smoke-stung eyes in exchange for the additional warmth. Theron, Mordax and Sylvia were crammed together in one such windbreak, gloomily passing around a ration bar, when there was a sharp whistle from one of the sentries which cut through the howling of the wind. They turned in time to see the shapes of three snarling beasts coalesce from out of the grey, driving snow. Sitting astride the animal at the centre was Jahaphrim, waving a scrawny hand. Mordax felt a weight lift off his chest when he saw the wild man's broad grin. He scrambled to his feet and rushed towards him, pulling up short only when Jahaphrim's mount gave an ear-splitting hiss and bared its vertical fangs. Jahaphrim paid the animal no heed and leapt gracefully from its back, patted its flank and approached Mordax, his fur mantle flapping dramatically in the gale. The two other natives, dark, serious men whose hands rested meaningfully on the blow pipes at their waists, remained mounted.

"Hello, Jahaphrim," Mordax said in Ingash.

"Hello, sky-demon," Jahaphrim said. "I hope our weather is not causing you too much discomfort."

His grin grew wider at the sight of the other initiates now lined up behind Mordax, shivering and miserable.

"Not at all," said Mordax, forcing a smile onto his own face. "It can be tiring basking in the glorious warmth of the heavens. A chance to cool off is sometimes welcome."

Jahaphrim let out a bark of laughter and turned back to his companions.

"A sky-demon who jokes. You see? I told you this one was different."

Mordax stepped forwards, the smile falling from his face.

"Jahaphrim, time is small. We must be returning soon. How have your elders decided?"

Instead of answering Jahaphrim returned to his mount and, with a grunt, removed a large leather saddle bag. He deposited it at Mordax's feet and drew open the top. When he saw the contents Mordax felt a thrill of excitement run through him. The bag was full to the brim with braided human hair, woven with carved bone charms. Jahaphrim watched his excitement with evident pleasure.

"It wasn't easy to convince the elders to go along with this trade," he said. "They were worried that you would use the braids to cast a spell over our tribe."

"They're not warrior braids, though, correct?" asked Mordax

Jahaphrim shook his head vehemently.

"Of course not. As you suggested the hair was cut from members of our tribe and then braided afterwards with false charms without the ritual prayers. They contain no mana. Even so, the elders were worried it was some sky-demon trick."

"But you persuaded them."

Jahaphrim gave a sly look. "The fire sticks persuaded them. Those sticks will save us many hours of work when we are out hunting and away from the home fires. They are excited about the other tools you have promised too."

Mordax took the hint and at his signal, two initiates carried the Bergens filled with the metal tools and implements over to Jahaphrim's companions who strapped them to their beasts. When the transfer was complete, Mordax began to make his farewells, conscious that they had only a few hours to return to the fort before the week was up; however, Jahaphrim seized his arm in a surprisingly powerful grip and drew him close. His breath was sour and the smell of animal fat clung to him as he spoke in a low, urgent voice.

"We have heard from the tribes to the North of here. Other sky-demons have been on the hunt, travelling by night, and have gathered many scalps from their people."

"I'm sorry," said Mordax. "I have no love for those sky-demons. I cannot control them."

He could only hope that Ragin had not collected more braids than Jahaphrim had provided. Jahaphrim nodded as if expecting the answer.

"That is not the only thing we have heard," he said. "Yesterday the other sky-demons began moving back towards your great house on the hill. They haven't gone inside, though. Instead they've hidden themselves in the forest along the main tracks leading to the hill. The Northern tribes have thinned their numbers but they are still many."

Mordax's mind raced through the implications. Ragin, the sneaky bastard, had likely set up lookouts to watch for their return. If Ragin could steal any warrior braids Mordax's group had collected before they made it back to the fort he would guarantee victory for him and his group. Mordax berated himself inwardly for not anticipating the move.

He gripped Jahaphrim's hand.

"Thank you, friend. You have saved us much pain."

Jahaphrim gave a wry smile. "I never thought I'd see the day when I would be helping a sky-demon. It's a strange world we live in."

Jahaphrim mounted his beast and the natives left as abruptly as they had arrived, pulling up fur hoods against the driving snow and fading into the storm. The initiates crowded round Mordax after they had left, peering into the saddle bag.

"Holy shit," said Sylvia, "are those what I think they are?"

Mordax merely smiled. The fewer people who knew the braids were not genuine warrior braids the better. For their purposes they were indistinguishable from the real thing.

"I can't believe it worked," said Theron softly. "I mean I can, I knew you could do it but still!"

"We still have to get these things back to the fort," said Mordax. "Everyone get your gear together. We bug out in five."

The group began to move off to assemble their belongings.

"Theron, Marina, I need a word," said Mordax as he began transferring the warrior braids into his own Bergen. Theron and Marina grabbed their packs and huddled close to him, hands in their armpits to keep warm.

"Here's the deal, it looks like Ragin has set up lookouts along the main approaches to the fort. He's going to try to ambush us and take the warrior braids for himself."

Mordax could see Theron's face tighten with anger.

"I need you two to scout ahead as we move. Try to find the lookouts without being seen so that we can avoid them."

"That's a pretty tall order," said Marina, pursing her lips.

In fact, "pretty tall order" was an understatement. Mordax knew from hard experience over the last few weeks that movement drew the human eye like nothing else and Theron and Marina would have to move quickly through the forest to stay ahead of the group. Ragin's lookouts on the other hand would be stationary and camouflaged. To find them, without being spotted themselves, would be next to impossible.

"I realise that," Mordax said, "but we don't have a choice. If we're not back at the fort in the next couple of hours we'll forfeit the contest."

"OK," said Theron, "we'll do what we can."

As Marina moved off into the forest at a loping pace that Mordax knew she could keep up all day, he held Theron back. When they were alone Mordax made a final request of him that both of them realised could determine whether they, and the rest of their group, lived or died.

Chapter 33

"Reckon we should risk it?" Mordax whispered. Sylvia squinted at the sun that had broken through the cloud cover.

"Only an hour left. There's no time to go around," she said.

They were crouched low behind a moss-covered boulder at the entrance to a narrow gully that led east towards the hill fort. Jagged rocks rose sharply on either side of the gully making it impossible to go around without a long detour to the north or south. Mordax blew out his cheeks in frustration. Marina, who had been scouting ahead, so far successfully, had reported that the gulley appeared to be clear of lookouts but once they entered the narrow pass they would be dangerously exposed. Since Marina's last report, Yefa had also slipped away from the group. Mordax was worried about what she had in mind but he still believed her sense of self-preservation was strong enough not to do anything to jeopardise the group's success.

"Alright then, let's go. You and me up front," Mordax said.

Sylvia padded away on silent feet, barely disturbing the dead leaves that carpeted the icy ground, and quietly prepared the rest of the group to advance. Despite the danger, Mordax watched her move away with a pleasant aching feeling. He had sensed a shift in how Sylvia saw him too although they had rarely had a moment alone together. Until now, their main group had stayed together, keeping off the main tracks that ran through the forest and instead forcing their way through the denser brush. It had made for slower going but so far they'd avoided encountering any of Ragin's crew.

Now, with the hill fort and the sanctuary it offered tantalisingly close, they crept forward, two abreast, hands on the hilts of their knives. Inside the gully, protected from the wind, it was dark and eerily quiet and the shuffling of their boots against the ground was disturbingly loud. The air was warmer too and the rock glistened with snow melt where it wasn't carpeted with small fungi and moss. They moved as quickly and as quietly as they could, all well aware of the risk of ambush. Before long a sliver of light appeared up ahead and the oppressive gloom began to recede. Mordax allowed himself to hope. Once they were out of the gulley it was only a half hour's fast march back to the fort. Within minutes Mordax and Sylvia had made it out and the other initiates were close behind. Mordax took a moment to enjoy the trilling of songbirds in the trees wondering at how quickly he, a Traveller born and raised on a starship, had adjusted to life outdoors. He had his eyes closed, basking in the warmth of a rare shaft of clear sunlight, when a familiar voice punctured his relief like a dagger of ice to his stomach.

"Enjoying yourself, gypsy?"

Ragin stepped out from behind a tree. All around them, from out of the forest, other members of Ragin's band were appearing, bows and spears at the ready. For a second Mordax regretted his decision not to allow his group to arm themselves, then he remembered his father's words: if you haven't got a gun, you won't make people angry enough to need it. If his plan worked there would be no reason for anyone to get hurt. The stragglers in Mordax's group had not yet finished filing out of the gulley and a commotion from that direction confirmed Mordax's fear that some of Ragin's crew had followed them, closing off any hope of escape back the way they had come.

"Hello, Ragin," said Mordax, "got nothing better to do than hide in the forest waiting to welcome us home?"

"Oh, we've been doing a lot more than that," said Ragin and gestured behind him. Persimmon stepped into view, holding a knife to the throat of Marina whose hair fell in muddy locks over a face covered in crusted blood and purple bruises. She looked desperately at Mordax out of her swollen eyes and mouthed with cracked lips, "I'm sorry."

A flash of anger ran through him, burning away the clever retort on his lips.

"You didn't have to hurt her," Mordax said.

Ragin shrugged. "She put up a struggle. And then was somewhat reluctant to tell us where you were. Luckily not all of your group are as short-sighted as she is."

At that Mordax noticed the slender figure next to him, the sunlight highlighting the copper in her hair.

"Yefa," Mordax sighed. "Why? You're really willing to risk your life to get back at me?"

"I'm not as weak-willed as my brother. It's only the people who let you give them orders that seem to die. I'll be fine in the forest as long as I steer clear of you."

"Is that right?" said Mordax. "You'd do well to take a closer look at the ones you've thrown your lot in with. As I hear it, Ragin's come off worse a few times with the natives."

The tightening of Ragin's jaw confirmed that Mordax had hit the mark.

"You should ask your new friend how many have died under his watch."

Mordax couldn't help but notice with a pang of dismay that Suliman was one of those absent. Yefa glanced at Ragin.

"That's enough talk, I think," Ragin said. "You know how this is going to work. Hand over your pack and I'll let you and your group through with your organs still on the inside."

Yefa had obviously told Ragin everything. Everything she knew anyway.

"For someone who enjoys accusing me of thieving, you've got an interesting approach to this contest. I may be a gypsy but you're the thief," said Mordax.

"You're an opponent," said Ragin. "This is how war works. You'd understand that if you had any combat experience at all. Hand the pack over."

Mordax shrugged the Bergen from his back and threw it at Ragin's feet. Ragin bent and pulled open the top. A humourless smile creased his face and he upended the bag spilling a knife, bed-roll, water pouch and other mundane items over the icy ground. There was not a single braid.

"Believe it or not, Mordax, I don't actually enjoy hurting other professionals. But if it's necessary I won't hesitate. Not that you're a professional, of course. For the sake of the rest of your group, just hand over the braids."

"The problem with you, Ragin, is that you're too predictable," Mordax said. "Given a mission to collect pieces of hair, of course you'll go on a murderous rampage. Given the opportunity for a fair contest, of course you'll screw over anyone you can to win."

Ragin's lips compressed in anger. "I'm not going to warn you again. Hand over the braids."

Mordax spread his hands. "That's what I'm trying to tell you. We don't have them,"

Ragin gave an exasperated sigh and looked to his companions who readied their weapons.

"Bergens," Mordax called over his shoulder. One by one, the members of his group passed their packs forward and Mordax threw them into a pile.

"We don't have the braids," Mordax repeated. "As soon as I realised what you were planning I gave them to Theron to take straight to the fort. I figured one man travelling by himself, away from Yefa, would stand a much better chance of making it through without you noticing."

Ragin looked sharply and Yefa, whose face was suddenly very pale.

"He— he told Theron to scout ahead. The braids were in Mordax's pack," she stammered.

Mordax nodded. "I did tell him to scout ahead, while you were within earshot. Then I swapped packs with him and told him to make straight for the fort. If it's any consolation, I'm a famously tricky bastard."

He turned to Ragin. "You see? If you weren't such a predictable cock, you might have got the drop on us."

In retrospect, he pushed Ragin too hard but he couldn't resist that final twist of the knife.

Ragin closed his eyes for a long moment as if trying to calm himself, then did something that Mordax had not been expecting. With a snarl, he drew his knife and flicked his wrist. It happened so quickly that Mordax didn't have time to understand what was going on. He felt himself being shoved sideways and hit the ground hard, jarring his shoulder. He looked up and Sylvia was standing over him. Mordax thought he might be concussed as she seemed to be swaying slightly. She smiled and tried to speak but instead a bubble of crimson blood erupted from her mouth and spattered onto the dirty snow at her feet. She put out a hand as if trying to swat cobwebs away from her eyes and then collapsed onto her back.

"Stupid girl," muttered Ragin. "Stupid, stupid girl."

He turned away and gave a sharp whistle, twirling his finger in the air. The other initiates in his group glanced at each other uncertainly and then followed Ragin into the trees. Mordax scrambled over to where Sylvia lay. She was coughing up flecks of blood onto her face like splashes of scarlet paint on a canvas. Ragin's knife was buried up to its hilt in her chest. Marina stumbled over, released by Ragin's departing crew.

"Leave the knife," she said, "it's stemming the blood flow."

"Fuck. What do we do?" Mordax said desperately. Why had she done it? The knife was meant for him.

"It's punctured her lung, she'll bleed out unless we can get a coagulant in there. Ashfol has the only medkit that will help," Marina said.

Sylvia's eyes were already beginning to lose focus.

"We need to move. Fast," said Mordax. "Leave the Bergens."

With speed born of desperation the initiates fashioned a makeshift stretcher out of a rain cloak and two saplings and lashed Sylvia to it. They then set off for the fort at breakneck speed, flying over sharp rocks and fallen logs, heedless of the noise they made. Bramble thorns slashed at their arms and low branches whipped their faces but Mordax refused to let the pace slack off. Before long they had reached the base of the hill, lungs burning and sweat dripping from their faces. The sun was low on the horizon and the fort was silhouetted against the evening sky, golden hues washed with red.

"Quick, now, up the hill!" Mordax yelled, tugging at his corner of the stretcher. It didn't move as the others had stopped and were standing looking at him sadly.

"Get fucking moving!" Mordax screamed, confused at their reluctance. They were so close.

"Mordax," said Marina quietly, "she's gone."

Mordax realised that he had not risked a glance at Sylvia in the last few kilometres, afraid he would somehow hasten her decline by bearing witness to it. He couldn't avoid it now, however. He looked down at her face, framed by golden hair. She seemed peaceful, unblinking eyes looking upwards, expression serene. Her skin was soft and pale, so pale in fact that he couldn't now make out the familiar scar that ran from her temple, as if death had cured her of her bodily sufferings. The only thing ruining the illusion of tranquillity was the black crusted blood that covered her mouth and neck.

"No," was all that Mordax could manage. Why had she done it? Why risk herself to protect him? She had been so strong, so adamant that she wouldn't be slowed down, by Mordax or by anyone. But Mordax knew why. He had made a friend of her. He had known that he needed help surviving this godforsaken place and he had seen good in her. Had he really believed that she would be better off with him as an ally too or was it pure self-interest that had motivated him? He felt like he was losing himself, as if the person he had been was drifting away like smoke on the wind. Heedless of the other initiates gathered round, he bent and touched his trembling lips to Sylvia's forehead. Tears welled up and then trickled down his face, landing on Sylvia's chest with a gentle patter. For the second time that month, a numbing gale of grief blew through him, roaring in his ears. He turned away from the body of the one person he had come to truly care about on this planet and made his way up the hill with murder in his heart.

Chapter 34

Akira tilted her face upwards and spent a brief moment, eyes closed, enjoying the warmth of the sun. A gentle breeze tousled the trees around them and ruffled the surface of the nearby lake just enough that it glittered. Men and women in soft cotton trousers, tokens sparkling with jewels, ambled past them hardly sparing a glance for her and Shiori, now dressed in the basic overalls of non-citizens. They were sitting on a bench in one of Kor Thalia's only parks, trying their best to look inconspicuous as they waited for the woman Shiori had arranged to meet. The woman had been Shiori's nanny when her father had been the Kudo-kai's ambassador to Thalmos. The ambassadorial residence was a penthouse in one of the apartment blocks overlooking the park and Shiori had pointed it out in the distance, a vast balcony dotted with bright flecks which she had told Akira were busts of the previous ambassadors.

"I always found them creepy," Shiori had said. "So serious. Not a smile among them. I wonder if there's a bust of my father now."

Akira had said nothing. She had sensed the challenge in Shiori's words, as if they had been written on pages dipped in oil and were awaiting a spark of disagreement. Both of them knew that her father's bust would not be there.

"I don't even know if Damina still works near here," Shiori said now, "but it's the only place I could be sure she would know."

"Tell me about her," Akira said.

"She and her family are non-citizens but she was the only one eligible to work on the surface. Her husband was a machinist working on one of the lowest sub-levels, although with her salary they were able to afford a small apartment on a sub-level close to the surface. Her brother worked security at the great elevators. If he still does, there's a chance he can help us."

"I meant, what was she like as a person?"

Shiori glanced at her then looked out across the lake. The wind whipped a strand of her hair across her face and she tucked it back behind her ear in a curiously child-like gesture.

"She was a proud woman," she said eventually. "Her clothes were old and stitched in places but always clean. My mother offered her some old clothes of hers once but she refused. Said she wouldn't feel comfortable in anything so fancy. She didn't let me get away with anything. If I threw a tantrum or didn't say my thanks and pleases, she'd order me to my room. But she never shouted and never raised her hand to me. She had a lovely singing voice. She would sit in the kitchen in our flat, folding the laundry and singing the old songs of the machine workers, so beautiful it would bring tears to your eyes. I could sit listening to her for hours. She remembered every birthday of mine even when my parents forgot and I cherished the small cakes she baked me in secret more than any of the shiny toys my parents ordered in and had other people wrap. She looked after me when I was sick. She was the person I would call for when I had nightmares and would sit with me and stroke my back until I fell asleep again. Her hands were rough and callused and she smelled of cleaning products. She would kiss me on the forehead when I was sad and tell me everything would be alright in the end..."

Shiori tailed off and Akira was surprised to see her eyes bright with tears which she blinked away before they fell.

"She was special to you," said Akira.

"She was. And then we were moved and I never saw her again."

"I'm sorry, Shiori."

"What do you have to be sorry about? You didn't do it."

"No, I didn't. But that doesn't mean I think what happened to you was fair."

Shiori barked a humourless laugh.

"Since when did the Kudo-kai concern themselves with what was fair?"

"There are sacrifices we have to make to achieve greatness, Shiori," Akira said and experienced a moment of dismay as she heard her father's voice in those words.

Shiori gave a shrug.

"What's the point in being great then?"

Akira couldn't think of what to say to that but was saved from having to answer by a hunched old lady shuffling her way towards the bench.

"I'm sorry, ma'am," said Shiori, "we are meeting someone here. There is another bench just over there where you can rest your knees."

"Have I changed that much, Shilly, that you don't recognise your old nonna?" croaked the lady and her wrinkled face cracked in a stained, gap-toothed smile.

Shiori rose slowly to her feet.

"Nonna?"

The woman's skin was grey as rock salt and her voice rasped unpleasantly. Her hair was thin and streaked with white and she squinted against the bright daylight.

"Where are your manners, child? I taught you better than that. Introduce me to your friend."

Shiori blinked and turned to Akira, the shock written into her face.

"Akira, please meet Damina Rute, former servant to the Ambassador's residence. Damina, this is Ambassador Director Akira Mukudori Kudo."

"A pleasure," said Akira, rising and giving a slight bow.

"Hmm. I'm sure," said Damina, the smile falling from her face.

"Please, sit down, Nonna," said Shiori.

Damina gingerly lowered herself onto the bench and sighed.

"It's been many cycles since I've sat here. The last time would have been with you, dear." She patted Shiori's cheek affectionately. "Tell me, Shilly, what became of you after you left Thalmos?"

"Nothing glamorous," said Shiori, unable to keep her eyes from the woman's crooked back and the calluses on her hands. "We were shipped to Persepid Pelian. Father was demoted to a minor official and six months later he killed himself. Mother never got over the shame."

"Oh, my poor girl," said Damina, caressing Shiori's face with rough fingers, "my poor, sweet girl. I had hoped with all my heart that you had found some happiness wherever you had ended up."

Shiori smiled sadly back at her. Akira shuffled awkwardly, embarrassed to be witnessing such an intimate moment.

"And what about you, Nonna? How have you been all these cycles?" said Shiori.

"Oh fine," Damina said, "although I've been living quite a different life since you left."

"Do you still work around here?"

Damina chuckled. "Oh no. I'm afraid not. After the incident with your poor father, the household staff all lost their surface visas. Without my income, my family wasn't able to afford our home in Cargo 1. We moved to the deeper sub-levels closer to my husband's work. This is actually the first time I've been back to the surface since then."

Shiori gaped at her.

"But, it's been almost twenty cycles. You haven't seen the sun in all that time?"

Damina shrugged. "Too expensive, dear. Without my job here there was no reason to come surface-side."

"Oh, Nonna. I'm so sorry. I had no idea."

"Why would you? You were only a child when you left and you had your own problems."

"How are your family? Your daughter must be grown up."

Damina's smile grew strained and some of the delight at seeing Shiori left her eyes.

"Tilly went into my husband's trade but she wasn't really built for it. She was a sensitive girl and the long hours tired her out something fierce. She was making her way back from the machine levels one night when she slipped between the shuttle and the platform. Silly girl wasn't paying attention. The shuttle crushed her before the other workers could stop it moving off. At least it was quick."

Shiori laid a hand on the old woman's arm and Damina put her own hand over it.

"When I got your message, I was so pleased," Damina said. "I had to see you again no matter the cost."

"We'll reimburse you for whatever you have spent and pay you for your help," said Akira quickly. She knew immediately it was the wrong thing to say.

Damina turned to Akira and all warmth bled out of her face.

"Always about the money with you Kudo-kai."

"I'm sorry, I just thought..." began Akira.

"I don't need your coin," Damina said, her rough voice rising. "Your lot took everything from me when you sent Shilly and her family away. You think a few credits will make up for that?"

"Nonna, she's just trying to help," said Shiori gently. "She didn't send me away."

"Her people did and they're light cycles away. Who else can I blame?"

Faced with the old woman's anger, it was becoming harder for Akira to see the rightness in the treatment of Shiori's family. It didn't matter that there was a route back for Shiori. It wouldn't give Damina back the last twenty cycles.

"We don't have much time, Nonna, and it's not safe for us to be out in the open long like this."

"I heard. You've got yourself into a dangerous spot," said Damina.

"As I said in my message, we need to get to the sub-levels. I thought your brother may be able to help us."

"It won't be safe for you even down there," said Damina. "The security patrols have been stepped up given how close we are to Umberaurum. You'd be better off getting yourself off Thalmos completely. Can't you do that?"

Shiori glanced at Akira.

"No, Nonna. We can't. Not yet," Shiori said.

Damina sucked her teeth in frustration then reached into her simple cotton bag and withdrew two disposable syringes.

"I don't know whether I'm helping you or putting you in more danger," she said.

She paused then thrust the syringes at Shiori.

"Temporary passes," she explained "They take thirty minutes to activate once injected and will last for two days before degrading. My brother's taken a big risk getting these so try not to get caught before then."

Shiori accepted the syringes and the old woman struggled to her feet.

"Thank you, Nonna."

"Anything for you, my girl. Be safe please."

Damina pulled Shiori close into an embrace, her pale, gnarled hands gripping Shiori's back fiercely.

"Thank you, Damina," said Akira.

The woman glared at her over Shiori's shoulder then pointed a crooked finger at her.

"You keep her from harm, you hear me. If anything happens to her, there will be nowhere on Thalmos, above ground or under it, that you will be safe."

The woman's unwavering stare and the precision with which she delivered the words made Akira suspect that it was no idle threat. She swallowed and nodded.

"I will. We should go now, Shiori."

"I can't tell you how much you've helped us, Nonna," said Shiori pulling away. "I'm sorry for everything you've been through."

Damina gripped her arm.

"Don't worry about me. You find what you're looking for quickly and get out of this godforsaken place. I hope you find peace somewhere."

"Akira, to your right," said Xif in her ears.

Akira looked to her right where two burly Thalmian police officers in bright white uniforms, drones hovering above their heads, were making their way along the path in their direction.

She tugged at Shiori's arm.

"Shiori, come on. We need to leave."

Akira picked up the box containing Xif from the bench and they moved away as naturally as possible, leaving Damina alone by the bench watching after them, eyes blinking against the sunlight she hadn't seen in cycles.

Akira risked a glance backwards and was dismayed to see that the security officers had left the path, picked up their pace and were making to intercept them.

"Shit," she said under her breath.

"I can't help if they get within distance to scan you," said Xif. "Your biometrics aren't in the Thalmian registry. It'll throw up a red flag immediately."

Akira looked around desperately. They were exposed. If they ran, the two police officers would call for back up and they would be surrounded in no time. Shiori might be able to take them out before they had a chance to call for reinforcements, and Xif might be able to handle the drones, but there were too many witnesses in the park and the police officers would have sub-dermals that would call in the cavalry if their hearts suddenly stopped beating. Shiori's hand had slipped inside her overalls where she had hidden a switchblade. Akira was on the verge of telling Shiori to stand down, to accept that there was nothing they could do now but throw themselves on Glankor's mercy when she saw Damina hobble out into the path of the police officers. The breeze carried the sound of her raspy voice.

"...coming through here like you own the place. This is a public park."

Shiori had stopped dead and was looking back to where the sunken old woman was pointing angrily at the chests of the two police officers. One of the men gave her a shove and she almost toppled over backwards. Shiori started to move back towards them but Damina glanced over and gave a single shake of her head. Akira grabbed Shiori's arm.

"We can't, Shiori."

Suddenly, moving with an improbable speed, Damina threw herself at the police officers, nails scratching at their faces like talons. The men recoiled before one recovered and swung a baton which connected with her knee with a sickening crack. Damina's leg caved in and she fell to the ground but the police officer didn't stop. He swung the baton again which whistled before it thumped into Damina's shoulder. She let out a strangled cry. Akira could feel Shiori quivering with rage.

"If you go back, we'll all be arrested and everything she's done will have been pointless," Akira said.

Shiori looked at her, cheeks wet with silent tears. Eventually she nodded. Without looking back they hurried away, mingling with the Thalmian citizens who had paused only to watch the spectacle.

Chapter 35

"You murdering bastard," shouted Mordax, struggling against Suliman's arm which was wrapped like an iron band around his chest. "Get off me!" he said to Suliman before turning back to Ragin. "You rat-faced son of a whore. I'll kill you. I promise you, I will fucking kill you."

"I think I preferred you when you were trying to make clever jokes," Ragin said with a smirk, arms crossed in front of him.

The full contingent of initiates, both Mordax's group and Ragin's, were gathered just inside the gates of the fort, their long shadows creeping up the thick wooden walls as the sun sank towards the horizon. Sylvia's body lay between the two groups, an impassive witness to their conflict.

"That's enough," came the nasal voice of Daenyrs Vyl'Granut as he appeared from inside one of the outbuildings, with Ashfol looming closely behind. The evening light accentuated the angles of Daenyrs' face, his eyes sunken into skull-like cavities.

"Healthy competition is all well and good out there, but within these walls you will keep a civil tongue in your heads. What's this?" Daenyrs gazed down at Sylvia's body with obvious displeasure. "I really wish you would stop bringing corpses back to camp. It's just as easy to burn them out there as it is here."

"Leave it, Daenyrs. I'll supervise the cremation," said Ashfol without taking his eyes off Sylvia's face. Daenyrs shot him a black look then turned back to the group. Mordax couldn't believe the casual way they were discussing the disposal of Sylvia's body.

"Wait a second," he said loudly, "this wasn't the natives. Look at her chest for fuck's sake. That's Ragin's knife. He murdered her!"

Ashfol looked up sharply. "What? Is this true, Ragin?"

"It's my knife but it wasn't meant for her. It was an accident."

"Bullshit," said Mordax. "You knew someone would die when you threw that knife."

"I'm not going to warn you again, Mordax," said Daenyrs. "Watch your mouth. Now, this little episode has taken up more than enough time already. The brief was to obtain as many warrior braids as possible by whatever means. Some conflict between the groups is to be expected. The Dioscuri are not interested in those who shy away from doing what is necessary or those who cannot protect themselves."

"Daenyrs, if he killed her intentionally-" Ashfol began.

"Enough!" Daenyrs hissed. "I have the ultimate authority for this mission and I won't have the process derailed by any more squabbles."

"Squabbles!" said Mordax, almost speechless. "He murdered one of us and you're just going to let him get away with it?"

"If I hear one more word out of you," said Daenyrs, "you and your group will be deemed to have forfeited the contest."

Mordax pressed his lips together, seething with anger.

"That's better. Now let's see the fruits of your labour. Let's see which group will enjoy the security of the fort for the rest of your time on Hellenbos and which group will be exiled to the forest."

Ragin stepped forward and opened a satchel of intricately carved leather, with bone toggles, obviously stolen from one of the natives. He reached inside with both hands and pulled out a bundle of braided hair which rattled as the bone charms clattered against each other. With a wave of disgust that might have caused Mordax to lose his stomach if his rage had not been all consuming, he realised that each braid was still attached to a scalp, red ragged flesh clinging to the underside. Ragin carefully untwined the mass of hair, dropping each scalp to the floor as he did so. When he had finished, the count stood at 26.

"Excellent work," Daenyrs said. "Not far off the record, I believe." He turned to Mordax. "And how did the other group fare?"

Without taking his eyes off Daenyrs, still silent as instructed, Mordax stepped forward, received the Bergen passed to him by Theron and upended it onto the floor in front of Daenyrs. He didn't bother counting them. There were at least a hundred braids, probably more. If Ragin had been close to the record, Mordax had just blown it out of the water. Daenyrs's face tightened, with shock or anger, Mordax couldn't tell, possibly both. The look was mirrored on the face of Ragin who seemed unable to tear his eyes off the mound of braids Mordax had produced. Daenyrs opened his mouth as if preparing to speak but nothing came out. Behind him, Mordax could see a grin spread across Ashfol's bearded face and his shoulders shook with a silent chuckle. Across the ring of initiates there was urgent hushed discussion.

"Sir, a word?" said Ragin quickly, eyes hungry, desperate. Daenyrs went over to Ragin, next to whom stood Yefa, and the three began a short, whispered conversation. Mordax had the unpleasant feeling of an opponent rearranging game pieces on a board in front of him. He looked to Ashfol but the big man was watching the trio with an expression of similar concern. Eventually, Daenyrs returned to his previous position looking worryingly comfortable again. He addressed Mordax and his group. "It has come to my attention that not a single native was bested in combat in order to obtain these braids. Their provenance is clearly dubious and will be discounted from the competition."

There was immediate uproar among Mordax and his group, while a smug smile returned to Ragin's face.

"Hold on a minute," said Mordax, quieting his group. "When you sent us out into the forest, you said that how we went about collecting the braids was up to us. You didn't say anything about having to best anyone in combat. You're moving the goalposts. I don't know what kind of deal you've got going on with Ragin but it smells pretty bad from here."

"Don't presume to quote my own words back at me," spat Daenyrs. "You violated the spirit of the contest. The organisation you're seeking to join is made up of killers not merchants. I decide whether you have kept within the rules and I find that you haven't. You and your group are exiled to the forest for the remainder of Selection."

"Daenyrs!" said Ashfol, his eyes smouldering. The silver veil rushed up from his neck swallowing his face while Daenyrs' did the same. They stood for a while looking at each other, clearly communicating silently through the veils. Eventually Ashfol took a step forwards, coming close to Daenyrs and jabbing him in the chest. Daenyrs batted Ashfol's hand away and pointed towards the trainers' hut. Ashfol eventually shook his head and dropped the veil. His face was a mask of rage and his chest heaved with barely contained violence. Despite this, he spun around and stalked off towards the hut. Daenyrs turned back to the group. "The decision is made. Take your belongings and get out."

"You'll regret this," said Mordax. Daenyrs gave an impatient sigh and gestured towards the gate. The other initiates in his group said nothing, resigned to Daenyrs' decision. They picked up the few belongings they had brought with them in the mad dash back to the fort and filed out of the gate. To their credit, not one uttered a single word blaming Mordax for what was likely to be a death sentence. The bitter irony that Sylvia was the only member of the group not forced to leave the fort was not lost on Mordax, as he glimpsed her for the final time, her body abandoned on the ice-bound ground. Night had fallen and the dark mass of trees whispering in the breeze presented an uninviting prospect. Before they had made it to the bottom of the hill, Mordax was aware of a presence at his side. When he turned, Suliman was there, the short man trudging along beside him silently.

"What are you doing, Sul? Get back in there," Mordax said.

Suliman shook his head. "No," he said and continued to walk.

Mordax stopped walking and rounded on him. "Don't be a stupid prick, get back in there. You're not being kicked out."

Suliman gave a pained smile. "My father used to say, the only mistakes you should truly regret are the ones you are making twice. I cannot remain with that soulless bitch's son, Ragin. I prefer to take my chances in the forest with you, my friend."

For the first time Mordax noticed the haunted look in Suliman's eyes, and realised that Ragin's methods had taken their toll on his own group too. Mordax's breath caught in his throat and he felt the hot prickle of tears behind his eyes.

"Please, Sul. I can't do it anymore. There's no hope now. You have to go back or you'll end up like Sylvia."

Suliman gripped Mordax's arm hard, his expression grim.

"The blame for that girl's death is not yours to take. If you let it destroy your spirit you let the ones who are guilty go free. Is that the kind of man you are? Do you not hunger for vengeance?"

At Suliman's words, Mordax's despair blew away like mist before a hot wind. Suliman was right. Ragin and Daenyrs were responsible for this. Anger seethed inside him lending fire to his limbs. As he looked at Suliman's earnest face, he turned his mind to the problem. The last conversation he had with Sylvia came back to him as if a ghostly echo in his ears. A seed of an idea sprang to life.

"Keep the others safe tonight," he said.

A frown creased Suliman's weather-beaten face.

"What do you mean?"

But Mordax was already moving, trudging through the snow away from the others, new energy coursing through him.

"I'll be back in the morning!" he called over his shoulder.

"Mordax!" shouted Suliman, but Mordax didn't look back. He had one shot to make things right. There were a thousand things that could go wrong and he would more than likely not survive to the following night but he owed it to Sylvia and the others to try.

Chapter 36

It was a bitter, biting wind carrying with it sharp crystals of ice and the scent of decay from deep within the forest that accompanied Mordax, bleary-eyed and exhausted, back to his group the next morning. He was thankful only that it blew at his back, hurrying his feet. Whether to his salvation or demise, however, he couldn't be sure. The night had been productive and terrifying in equal measure but had gone as well as he could have hoped. He was still breathing after all. A sharp whistle from one of the sentries greeted his arrival when he came within view of the campfire and by the time he stepped within the circle of its orange light the other initiates had been roused and were assembled in a ring with shields of bark at the ready.

"Peace, friends," he said, "it's only your prodigal commander returned from his nocturnal frolics."

Suliman pushed his way out of the group and jogged up to Mordax, who was swaying slightly with fatigue.

"You crazy man, where have you been?" said Suliman, wide eyed.

"I'll explain everything soon, Sul," Mordax said, looking around. "Everyone OK?"

Suliman gave a dismissive wave.

"We had no problems. We kept the fire low and without smoke. It is only our worrying for you that was troubling us."

"Good, good. We need to get everyone back to the fort as soon as possible."

Suliman gave a sigh.

"Out of the fort, back to the fort — it is always a roller scrotum with you."

"I think you mean rollercoaster," said Mordax with a smile.

"No, it is painful like roller scrotum," Suliman corrected.

"I'm hoping that I can make all of this a lot less painful for everyone," said Mordax. "Please, Sul."

Suliman called over the other initiates and soon they were trudging their way back to the fort, Mordax managing to deflect all questions about where he had been and what he had been doing. If his plan was to work, he had to keep his cards close to his chest for a little while yet. Before long the initiates had reached the path up to the great wooden walls, torches still flickering along their tops against the gloomy remnants of the night. For the first time Mordax saw it not as a place of sanctuary, but as the natives must, an invader's foothold, a fortress pregnant with killers waiting for an opportunity to disgorge themselves and swarm into the forest with murderous intent. Mordax and Suliman climbed the path to the sturdy gate. A head appeared above the wall and Mordax recognised the tight curls of Persimmon.

"Well, look who it is," Persimmon said. "Couldn't last one night, eh?"

"Fetch Daenyrs, there's a good lad," said Mordax.

"It's not going to do any good. He's not going to let you back in. You had your chance and you blew it."

"I don't want to come back in," said Mordax with an unpleasant smile. "DAENYRS!" he shouted. Persimmon shook his head in disbelief.

"You really don't know when to give up, do you?" he said.

"DAENYRS VYL'GRANUT!" Mordax bellowed again.

A few minutes later, Daenyrs's sharp features appeared atop the walls, followed shortly by Ashfol's shaggy head.

"What's the meaning of this?" asked Daenyrs, face twisted in barely concealed scorn. "I thought even you might have some pride in defeat, Mordax. You can grovel all you want but the terms of the contest were clear. You and your group are to remain outside the fort for the remainder of Selection. Who knows, some of you may even survive until then," he said this last with a cruel smile.

"I'm not here to quibble about the arbitrary rules of your contest, Daenyrs, or the fickle way you go about applying them. I learned long ago that when a game is stacked against you, it's time to change the game."

"I really have no idea what you're talking about," Daenyrs said.

"I'm hear to challenge you for the veil," Mordax said.

The silence that followed this statement was all consuming, enveloping those present until it seemed that it might never be broken and they would spend the rest of their days stuck in that one moment of utter amazement. It was Suliman who broke the spell first. "Mordax! What in the hell are you doing?!" he hissed. "This is mad!"

"Just trust me, Sul," Mordax whispered back.

"Trust you! He is a wraith, you brain-dead idiot. He will rip you into little pieces."

Daenyrs recovered himself next, letting out a sharp bark of laughter that echoed around the walls. Ashfol next to him had dropped his face into his hand.

"You challenge me for the veil?" Daenyrs let out another high-pitched laugh. "Very good, Mordax. Thank you for the amusement but it's time for you and your band to go back to the forest. We'll visit you shortly to discuss the next stage of Selection."

"Actually, Daenyrs, you won't. All of us initiates became members of the Dioscuri the day we left Eloth," Mordax said, inwardly thanking Ashfol for that titbit. "I'm right in thinking that any member of the Dioscuri can challenge for the veil when they deem themselves ready."

"This is preposterous—" began Daenyrs.

"He's right," interrupted Ashfol, his eyes closed as if unable to bring himself to look at Mordax directly. "Open the gate, I need a word with this lad in private."

"No," said Mordax. He was sure Ashfol was going to try to dissuade him from challenging Daenyrs. "Enough talking. I have the right to challenge Daenyrs for the veil. I exercise that right."

Ashfol opened his eyes and Mordax could see the sadness there, as if Ashfol was already mourning him.

"So be it," Ashfol said.

Mordax wasn't entirely surprised to see that an expression of pleased surprise had crept on to Daenyrs's face.

"Well, I must say, this is quite unexpected," Daenyrs said. "It seems that not only are you incompetent but you're suicidal as well. Very well. I won't have this farce taking up any more time than necessary. We meet at the arena in an hour."

And with that, the course was set. Stephan had liked to quote an obscure saying whenever Mordax had been entrusted with a negotiation. Come back with your shield or on it. Mordax smiled at the memory. He knew his father had never intended the instruction to be taken literally but then again his father had never intended him to follow so closely in his footsteps. Somehow Mordax had manoeuvred himself into the most binary of corridors, from which he would emerge either triumphant or dead.

Chapter 37

What had seemed like a passably good idea to Mordax when his blood was hot in the aftermath of Sylvia's death now, when he was standing alone and shivering on the dusty rock of the arena, with his peers' eyes boring into him from the circle above and about to face a seasoned Dioscuri wraith, suddenly seemed laughably far-fetched. His previous experience in the arena only served to grate his already raw nerves as he relived the embarrassing ease with which Sylvia had floated around his defences and beaten him almost senseless. This time, however, with the stakes infinitely higher, he wouldn't have a poisoned dart to turn the odds in his favour. Ashfol had not been shy about making his feelings known.

"You've just killed yourself, boy," he had said in a low voice once the entire troupe of initiates had gathered at the arena on the barren hill, the tips of the nearest trees just visible in the distance. "God knows, I tried to give you as much guidance as I could."

"I didn't have a choice, Ashfol. You have to see that. Besides, my father was a wraith, he must have defeated another wraith too."

"Your father didn't take the veil until he'd had cycles of training on Eloth," Ashfol had said, "and even then, it was when his trainers had judged him ready and he was allocated a wraith who was retiring."

"What? You said the contests were to the death?" Mordax had said, confused.

Ashfol had given a hiss of frustration and run a hand through his long hair. "That's what I was trying to tell you, boy. The contest is to the death unless the wraith cedes the fight, which they invariably do when the Council has approved the contestant. The arena contest is mostly a ceremonial process now, a hangover from the early days of the Dioscuri. What kind of order could we maintain if junior members were constantly killing off the senior members?"

A sinking feeling had settled in Mordax's stomach.

"It's too late now," Ashfol had said. "The challenge has been made and believe me, Daenyrs won't be ceding the fight."

"I didn't have any other option, Ashfol."

"Of course you bloody did," Ashfol had said, his voice hoarse. "You could have taken your chances in the forest. You just lasted a week out there and only lost one person. That's practically unheard of."

"No," Mordax had said quietly, "Daenyrs would have found a way to sabotage us. I don't know why but he has it in for me."

"That's not true," Ashfol had said but there was no conviction in his voice and Mordax could see that his words troubled the man greatly.

After that there had been nothing more to say. Mordax had lowered himself down the cold, iron chain to the arena floor, followed shortly by Daenyrs. They had been searched and stripped to their trousers. Daenyrs had removed the collar which contained the veil from around his neck, lifting it over his head and placing it in Ashfol's hands. Ashfol had then explained the rules of the contest which were few and short, as Mordax had expected. Each contestant was able to enter the arena carrying a knife. Once the two contestants were in the arena, the one to climb out alive would be the victor. The onlooking initiates had gone deathly quiet as this had been explained and remained so now, the only sound the whisper of boots on rock as Mordax and Daenyrs took their positions opposite each other. Daenyrs' arms were criss-crossed with pale scars and despite his slender frame, his torso rippled with whipcord muscle and tendon. He moved with a low, springy step, the coiled power within him evident. Mordax's heart felt like it would flop out of his chest. He had trained hard with Suliman these last few weeks but hadn't yet won a single bout against any of the other initiates. Persimmon had been right, hand to hand combat just wasn't his strength. If he was honest with himself, he was completely outmatched. There was no prelude to the fight, no ceremony.

"Begin," was all that Ashfol said, his bellow reverberating around the bare stone of the arena as if keen not to drag out the inevitable.

Daenyrs pulled a wicked-looking curved knife from a sheath at his waist. It was no polished showpiece. It was nicked and roughened from decades of use but clearly sharpened to a razor's edge. A smile of anticipation spread across Daenyrs' face as he took a step forward. And then his throat exploded in a cloud of pink gore. There was stunned silence for a moment and then pandemonium among the initiates sitting above as they scrambled for cover, calling out the direction from where they thought the shot had come from. They weren't to know that the shooters would have already escaped into the forest, moving faster than the initiates could hope to match. Mordax ignored them as he walked over to Daenyrs' prostrate form. Somehow he was still alive although judging by the gurgling ruin of his throat he wouldn't be for much longer. Mordax bent down so that the dying man could hear him.

"Those natives that you were so insistent be 'bested in combat'? It turns out they're not so keen on your annual games. And apparently, once you put a rifle their hands, they're pretty good shots."

Daenyrs' eyes widened and frothy pink bubbles blossomed out of the hole in his neck.

"Yes, I know. No trees close enough to the arena that you needed to worry about their blowpipes. But you weren't banking on them getting hold of rifles, were you?"

Daenyrs tried to speak but a wet rattle was all that escaped his blood-flecked lips. Mordax didn't wait to see him take his final gasp, instead he walked back to the chain and began to haul himself up. A new heaviness in his chest seemed to make the climb more difficult than it should have been. He knew without looking that when he crested the top of the arena there would be another prone form among the benches, a smoking hole in its head. Ragin's death had been a condition of the deal he made with the natives. The previous night he had ventured into the forest not knowing whether he would be killed on sight or not, confident only that he had something that the natives wanted. A chance to fight back. A chance for revenge. Ironically, if it hadn't been for Ragin's slaughter of the Northern tribe, Mordax wouldn't have had a chance. He had found Jahaphrim, or, more accurately, Jahaphrim had found him at the site of their previous meeting. Jahaphrim's tribe had not been interested in Mordax's offer, deeming the risk too great but had given their blessing for Mordax to travel that night to their allies, the Northern tribe from which Ragin had collected the majority of his scalps. In the dark, smoky confines of the elders' hut, decorated with strange skulls and air noxious with the scent of sour meat and rank sweat, Mordax had brokered his final deal on this world. The transport that had ferried the initiates from Eloth contained a full arsenal of plasma weapons and, thanks to spending his entire life in and around starships, Mordax knew how to goof the security system to gain access. The suspicion in the eyes of the elders, stooped and lined beyond their cycles by the harsh planet, had been replaced with awe as Mordax led them into the belly of the transport and they regarded the trove of gleaming weapons. They had run wizened hands over the sleek barrels and scopes and clapped with delight when Mordax had demonstrated the power of the guns by carving a sapling in half from thirty metres away. They had agreed unanimously to Mordax's proposal: two mounted shooters in the trees above the arena, each with a rifle with which Mordax would familiarise them, would wait for the moment that Daenyrs would remove his veil and be at his most vulnerable. The benefit of the deal for the Northern tribe was immeasurable. An arsenal of weapons, powerful beyond their comprehension, with which to defend themselves properly, not as sport, but as a real threat to the Dioscuri invaders. Mordax thought back to his first night on Eloth. He had felt such confusion, such shame when he learned that his father was an assassin, a murderer, but now he had an inkling of how Stephan could have justified it to himself. Monstrous actions in one context could be the only just actions in another. As his father had said, against the blackness of a night sky an indigo starling is the brightest thing around. The twitching bodies of Daenyrs and Ragin were a macabre trophy, a testament to the success of Mordax's plan, although the thought did nothing to quell the bone-deep sickness that he felt as he walked towards Ashfol to claim his victory.

Chapter 38

The air was hot and humid and permeated with the stale, human stench of densely packed living units combined with inadequate air recycling. Akira shifted the thin grey scarf so that it covered her mouth and nose. Shiori, still with Xif ensconced in his cardboard box tucked under her arm, walked next to her along the main thoroughfare of Cargo 7, one of the many non-citizen settlements that had blossomed deep beneath the surface of Thalmos. Stacked metal freight containers, shiny and wet and spilling light from windows cut out of their sides, lined either side of the street. Ladders that seemed more rust than metal ran the height of the stacks, providing access to each level. Some had small porches welded to the outside where the inhabitants sat and sipped tea or smoked as they watched the subterranean world go by. They had just missed one of the regular spray cleanses that flushed away some of the dust and muck that accumulated from the thousands of souls that lived down here, although clearly not efficiently enough to negate the smell entirely. Akira dreaded to think what it would have been like had they arrived before the cleanse. There were dirty puddles on the concrete floor and the still-misty air lent yellow halos to the jerry-rigged street lamps all along the thoroughfare. Far above them, on the ceiling of the vast space that enclosed the town, giant faded letters denoted long disused storage areas. The sub-dermal passes Damina had sourced for them had worked as promised and allowed them to join one of the daily commutes of non-citizen surface workers from Kor Thalia to the sub-settlements via a great elevator that had clanged and hissed disturbingly but had delivered them quickly a kilometre underground. The rapid shift from the sparkling opulence of the surface to the dim monotony of the subterranean corridors was disconcerting, although by the time they reached Cargo 7, via a battered mag-lev shuttle that hummed over metal rails, they had grown accustomed to the gloom.

"I was a Central Node of the First Circle, responsible for great fleets of warships and uncountable artificial minds, and now look at me!" said Xif from the box, not even bothering to speak discreetly via bone vibration. "Reduced to a parcel, carted round the filthy streets of some slum."

"Unless you want to end up as scrap metal on a filthy street of some slum, you'll keep your mouth shut," Shiori hissed.

Akira was warming to the newly un-cowed Shiori. They approached the entrance of a structure more elaborate than those around it, adorned with fairy lights and proudly displaying a hanging sign identifying it, ironically Akira thought, as the Sun and Stars Freehouse.

"Is this the place?" whispered Akira.

"It is," said Xif sullenly. Matsuko had given them the location but no details on how they could go about making contact with anyone from the RLA when they got here. Akira pushed open the double metal door, and stepped into a large, busy taproom. Men and women were gathered around small tables or standing in groups drinking and talking loudly. The smell of stale beer hung in the air and acrid pipe smoke wafted in a hazy layer at head height. The customers were, for the most part, pale and rough-looking. Cargo 7 was near one of the Nanotrite processing stations and therefore most of the workers rarely ventured to the surface. Akira thanked their luck for the smoke and the low lighting which helped conceal her and Shiori's darker, and therefore distinctive, skin and the healthy shine of their hair.

"What now?" asked Shiori.

"I guess we talk to some of the people here and see what we can find out."

"Akira," said Xif, "I've noticed something strange."

"What is it?"

"Everyone here has a sub-dermal comm unit that's linked to the Cargo 7 network."

"Yeah, why's that strange?"

"It's not. I'm picking up a signal from one comm unit that's not linked to the wider network. It's minuscule leakage, probably not strong enough to be picked up by the Thalmians."

"What does that mean?"

"Someone's jacked into a private network that's off the main grid," said Shiori.

"RLA?" asked Akira.

"Probably."

"Where's the signal, Xif?" Akira asked.

"Far left, back corner," he said.

Akira and Shiori threaded their way through the crowd, avoiding puddles of spilt beer. When they approached the corner of the room, Xif said, "There. The table second from the back. The blond one."

At the small table indicated by Xif were two men, barely into their twenties by the look of them. One was dark haired, with a bull-like serious face and the other was fair, with a weak chin and shaving pimples covering his neck. The two men were hunched over the table, talking earnestly and swigging from glasses of dark beer.

"Can you access the comm unit from here?" Akira asked.

There was the briefest of pauses. "Yes," said Xif, "it's an implanted device in his armpit. It's linked to three other devices in the settlement and is set to auto-wipe at any attempt by an unknown device to connect to it."

"You haven't triggered the auto-wipe though?" asked Akira.

Xif gave a huff. "Of course not. The tech's advanced enough to protect them from the Thalmians, but there are a few back doors that I can get through. He's definitely Red Liberation Army. Have a look at these."

Xif sent quick scrolling snippets of conversations to Akira's retinal display, about police patrol movements, security check points and surface defences.

"Anything about Lorenzine Haskor?" asked Shiori

"Afraid not. Not even any consistent code words that could be discussion about him. They may keep the really sensitive information entirely offline."

"Is the other man RLA?" asked Akira.

"I don't think so, although can't say for sure. He's not connected to the private network and there's nothing interesting stored on his comm unit."

"OK," said Akira, "the blond one's the target. Shiori, follow my lead."

Akira approached the table with Shiori in tow and both men immediately looked up.

"Mind if we join the table?" Akira said, nodding towards the only empty seat. The blond man stared at the dark, attractive women for a few seconds then nodded dumbly. His squat companion quickly slid his own seat towards them and grabbed another for himself from a nearby table.

"You see, I told you there was some chivalry left alive down here," Akira said to Shiori, who gave the men a convincingly shy smile. They sat down, Shiori next to the one they suspected was a Red Liberation Army solider and Akira next to the other.

"You try going to any of the bars in Turbine 2 and you'll have crumbled to dust before anyone offers you a seat," Akira said. "I know I can't really speak but surface workers can be arrogant pricks sometimes."

"You twos look like surface workers yerself," said the dark-haired man.

Akira nodded. "Attendants at the car port. I spent my early cycles around here though. Always feels like home coming back to Cargo."

"Haven't seen you around before, I'd remember," said the blond man in a way that was clearly more of an awkward attempt to involve himself in the conversation than suspicion.

"Belora's showing me around," Shiori said. "She promised that a night out in Cargo 7 was the most fun you can have on this level."

"I guess I did," said Akira, "but you need a few drinks inside you to really appreciate its charm."

She looked meaningfully at the dark-haired man next to her.

"Oh, er, right," he said. "What are you ladies drinking?"

"That's very kind. Beer's fine for me," said Shiori.

"Me too," said Akira.

The dark-haired man got up and began to jostle his way towards the bar. Shiori took the opportunity to shuffle closer to the blond man.

"My friend suggested we come join your table, you know," said Akira as the man glanced towards Shiori and licked his lips nervously. "She said you had a really nice smile."

Shiori nodded and placed her hand on his thigh, stroking it gently. The man gave a throaty chuckle.

"Did she now?" he said

"I did," Shiori said. "I said I liked your face," she traced a finger along his jaw line. "I said I liked your strong hands," she brushed the tips of her fingers over the knuckles of the hand which was gripping his beer glass fiercely. "I said I liked the RLA comm unit in your armpit." As she said this, a thin blade seemed to materialise in her hand and she dug the tip into his armpit, careful to keep the blade hidden from the tables nearby. The man inhaled sharply and Akira grabbed his beer glass, steadying it before he tipped it over the table.

"Easy now, friend. If you squirm like that you're likely to cause yourself some mischief," said Shiori, "and if you even think about using that comm unit I'll cut it right out of you."

The man's eyes were wide and bright with fear.

"What's your name?" asked Akira.

"Je...Jeremone," he said.

"Listen carefully, Jeremone. I don't want to hurt you but my friend here doesn't share my compunctions so it's in your best interests to co-operate. We need to find Lorenzine Haskor very urgently. Tell us where he is."

Jeremone looked from one to the other, lip trembling, but said nothing.

"We're not with the government," said Akira. "We only want to speak to him."

"Jeremone," said Shiori chidingly, and pushed the tip of her blade a millimetre further into his armpit. He gave another gasp and closed his eyes, sweat beading on his forehead, but remained silent. Shiori looked at Akira and shrugged.

"OK, we'll take him with us," Akira said to Shiori.

Shiori grabbed Jeremone's arm and levered him to his feet, quickly moving behind him and pressing the tip of the knife into the small of his back.

"Slowly now," she whispered in his ear.

Through gaps in the crowd, Akira could see Jeremone's companion filling up frothy glasses of beer from the main dispensary. She gathered up the box containing Xif, threaded her arm through Jeremone's and led him out of the bar back onto the damp streets. Their plan in the event that they successfully located an RLA member who was uncooperative was to spirit them away to one of the many disused service tunnels leading away from the town, where Shiori could apply more "persuasion" away from sensitive eyes and ears.

"You won't find him, you know," said Jeremone, voice thick and shaky, as the trio made their way swiftly down the thoroughfare. The pale man's face was desperate with fear and Akira felt a pang of sympathy for him.

"Even if I tell you where he is, he'll see you coming."

"That may be," said Akira, "but we have to try anyway."

They walked on, the streets thinning as the hour became later. Occasional mounds of clothing, with a twitch or a sprawling limb, revealed themselves to be vagrants deep in the clutches of whatever high they were chasing. Faint, blinking lights criss-crossed far above them as great delivery drones made their steady way between the central storage structures of Cargo 7 and more remote settlements. They were approaching the turn off to the outskirts of the town when Xif spoke to them by conduction.

"I believe we're being followed."

Akira glanced behind her. Two figures, a man and a woman, both heavily muscled, were walking some distance behind them, matching their pace.

"How can you tell?" Akira asked.

"I've been monitoring the area. Each heartbeat is distinctive, you know. These two arrived on the street at a run then slowed down when they got close enough to see us."

"I warned you," growled Shiori stepping closer to Jeremone who flinched.

"It wasn't him," said Xif quickly. *"There's been no activity from his comm unit. It must have been his friend."*

Akira hissed with frustration. "We should have taken them both."

"Too late to worry about that," said Shiori. "We need to get off this street. Hurry up."

She gave Jeremone a sharp shove and they began to walk faster. Akira risked another glance backwards and the two following them were now jogging. Each had a hand conspicuously at their right hip which would probably be holding the grip of a pistol.

"Faster," Akira said.

The three of them sped up, Shiori with her knife still firmly pressed against Jeremone's back. Up ahead, a break in the row of containers marked a side street that would lead them to the edges of the town. Akira knew they wouldn't make it that far dragging Jeremone before their two followers caught up with them. Their only hope was to try to get off the street and lose them in the network of buildings. They rounded the corner where the street lamps continued for fifty metres or so before the avenue was swallowed by the perfect darkness beyond the town's limits. Two new figures were walking towards them along the side street, only a few metres away, rifles slung over their shoulders and a pair of drones above them. Akira's heart flipped like a fish as she recognised the white uniform and crescent insignia of the Thalmian police. At the same time as it dawned on her that being stopped by the police could prove just as fatal as being caught by the RLA, the two policemen swung their rifles up and rushed forwards, the tell-tale shimmer of energy shields in the air surrounding them.

"Don't move," shouted the nearest, voice magnified by the drone above him.

Akira dropped the box containing Xif and she and Jeremone raised their hands. Shiori stayed perfectly still keeping Jeremone between her and the police. As they came closer Akira realised that the guns were not in fact trained on the three of them but slightly to one side. She slowly turned to see the two RLA soldiers, hands in the air with guns drawn, only a few metres behind her. The police must have spotted the weapons as soon as the soldiers rounded the corner.

"Drop the weapons," one of police officers shouted and the clatter of metal on concrete followed immediately. A distant buzzing sound drifted into the street as the police officers swept passed Akira towards the two, whose faces were drawn with fear and resignation. All at once, as if a trick of the light, Akira's perception shifted and the soldiers changed from threat to opportunity.

"*Xif, can you take out the drones?*" she subvocalised.

"*Yes, but I don't—*" Xif began.

"*Do it.*"

With no time to second guess her decision, she grabbed Shiori's arm and nodded towards the passing police officers. Shiori gave a quizzical look and Akira nodded again. And with that Shiori was moving on swift and silent feet. She was behind the police officers in seconds and, with an efficient brutality that turned Akira's stomach, she plunged her blade into the necks of each of the policemen in quick succession before either had a chance to react, their energy shields no protection against cold steel. Blood spurted over their shoulders as they tried to staunch the flow with their hands but the wounds were too deep and they collapsed to the ground. The two drones darted sideways at the same time, crashing into each other and dropping to the ground. The buzzing in the air had grown louder and Akira wondered whether she was in shock.

Xif's voice spoke inside her head cutting through the horrific sight of the men dying in front of her.

"Akira, there are military drones on the way. I won't be able to deal with them as easily. We have to leave this place."

There was a hissing sound and a glowing circle appeared in the top of the box before Xif exploded out dislodging the disc he had cut. Akira stepped around the bodies of the police officers and approached the RLA soldiers who were staring at them wide eyed.

"You've been sent to stop us because you think we work for the government and we've abducted your colleague here," she said. "Only part of that's correct. As you can see, we obviously don't work for the government."

"Who are you then?" said the man, brow furrowed.

"I am Ambassador Director Akira Mukudori Kudo of the Kudo-kai. I need to see Lorenzine Haskor about a matter of some urgency. Either you can take us to him or my friend here can question you separately. Which do you prefer?"

The man and woman looked past Akira to where Shiori was cleaning her blade on the sleeve of one of the police officers.

"Follow us," the man said.

Chapter 39

"You've created the mother of all fucking messes, you know that, lad?" Ashfol said. He and Mordax were alone in the cockpit of the transport ship, the crimson crescent of Eloth looming ever larger in the view screen as they sped towards it. The rest of the initiates were seated in the hold, safely out of earshot. Once Mordax had convinced Ashfol that the shooters who had killed Daenyrs and Ragin would not be returning but that their tribe was now armed with enough plasma weapons and ammunition to outfit a full squad, Ashfol had gone pale and had to sit down. He had then ordered the initiates' immediate evacuation.

"Four hundred and seventy cycles, that's how long we've been training initiates on Hellenbos. And you've now made that impossible."

Mordax, sensing that Ashfol did not expect an answer, said nothing. Ashfol was right, of course. The Northern tribe would likely have spread the weapons throughout the forest, possibly even sharing them with some of the other tribes. Short of sending a full manned mission to hunt down the guns one by one, there was no way of finding them. Ironically, the natives' lack of technology protected them from most of the sophisticated ways the Dioscuri usually went about collecting information. The point of Selection, as Mordax now realised, was to test the initiates' capacity to survive absent technological crutches. However, the Dioscuri would not now be able to send initiates to Hellenbos without energy shields and modern weapons of their own, defeating the aim of the process.

"Gods above, the General is going to be furious," Ashfol moaned.

For his part, Mordax was quite looking forward to the look on General Valerian's face when he discovered that Mordax had survived.

"Everything I did was within the rules," said Mordax.

"Are you a lawyer, boy?" bellowed Ashfol.

"No, of course not."

"Then shut up about the bloody rules. Not only have you made obsolete our hallowed training ground, you've also killed a wraith. I can't remember the last time a challenge for the veil ended in an actual death.

"Ashfol, I realise this is going to cause problems but something weird was going on with Daenyrs. I know it in my gut. So do you."

Ashfol opened his mouth but Mordax pressed on, "Don't tell me you were comfortable with the way Selection has been run either. Keeping the natives in a perpetual stone age? Hunting them like animals? There has to be another way. Maybe the Council will punish me, maybe they won't, but I can't feel bad about giving those people a proper chance to defend themselves,"

"Nice speech," said Ashfol. "It's a crock of shit though and if the Council tells me to send you straight back to Hellenbos for the rest of your days, I'll do it happily."

He exhaled loudly. "But as it stands, you challenged Daenyrs for the veil and you won. I suspect the Council will decide you're a liability to the order of the Dioscuri and send you on a scenic tour of Eloth's natural wonders without a suit. But until then I guess this is yours."

Ashfol reached into his pocket and tossed a silvery collar into Mordax's lap. Mordax picked it up and with a thrill realised it was Daenyrs's veil.

"Listen up," Ashfol said. "Usually a new wraith will have had cycles of training before they get their hands on one of these so a word of warning. The veil can draw power from sources around it but in the absence of external sources it will take its juice from your body. It'll leech the heat right out of your blood if you let it."

"OK," said Mordax, not really understanding.

"The veil is pretty good at interpreting your wishes and a lot of its functions don't require anything more than a thought. There are too many functions for me to begin to go through right now. It will be up to the Council whether you get to keep that thing and, if so, how to go about schooling you in it."

"OK."

"Oh, one more thing. The veils represent probably the single most advanced piece of technology across the Shattered Empires outside of Primia. There are a finite number of these things in existence. Do. Not. Lose it."

Mordax's head swam with the implications of Ashfol's statement. The veils were clearly far more powerful than he had realised.

"OK," he said.

"If you say OK one more time, I'm putting you out of the airlock."

"OK, sorry. Uh...right."

"Just get out of here."

Mordax, clutching the veil, grabbed his pack and rushed for the exit. Once in the main body of the transport, he ignored the scrutiny of the other initiates, lounging in their crash couches or sitting around tables by the windows, as he moved towards the back of the room. Even those who had been in his group had been looking at him with a mixture of awe and trepidation since Daenyrs's death and it was beginning to grate on him. He reached the door to the cargo hold, closing it behind him with relief, and settling onto the floor in the dim light between two equipment racks, the comforting smell of machine oil around him, to examine the veil properly for the first time. He lifted it and turned it over in his hands. The fabric shifted oddly in the light with a metallic sheen defying the eye's ability to make sense of its shape or texture and it was so soft that it almost felt as if there was nothing in his hands but air. Heart beating faster, Mordax lifted the ring and placed it gingerly over his head. There was a coldness as it tightened around his neck, not so much to be restrictive but enough that he felt vulnerable, exposed to the unfamiliar technology. Without warning the veil began to creep upwards covering first his mouth, then his nose and eyes. He panicked for a second, scrabbling at the material to try to pull it away until he realised he could breath perfectly well. The only difference was that the smell of oil seemed to have been stripped out of the air.

"Operator Daenyrs Vyl'Granut confirmed deceased authorisation Operator Ashfol Krangmire," said a soft voice. "Imprint new operator unlocked authorisation Operator Ashfol Krangmire. New operator detected. Input identifier."

Mordax waited for something else to happen.

"Input identifier," the voice repeated.

"Er— Mordax. Mordax L'Amfour," he said.

"Operator ErMordaxmordax L'Amfour. Confirm?"

"No. Just Mordax L'Amfour."

"Welcome Operator Mordax L'Amfour. Imprint new operator, Operator Mordax L'Amfour. Confirm?"

"Confirm."

There was a tingling sensation in Mordax's scalp and suddenly the cargo hold around him brightened as if the strip lights had been turned up. He found he could now hear the conversations going on next door despite the hum of the transport's thrusters. There was a slight reddish haze in his peripheral vision and when he turned that way, towards the door back to the personnel area, a flock of red dots swam into view seemingly fixed in space some distance beyond the door and pulsing gently. When Mordax focussed on one of the dots it morphed into a thermal image of a seated person and a flood of data began reeling down one side of his vision, showing heart rate, distance, field of vision, even brain activity. He swiftly pulled his attention away from the dot, overwhelmed by the wave of information.

"Unopened message available. Open message?" said the veil.

Mordax paused, confused as to who would be sending him a message, especially by this unusual medium. "Open message," he said.

A flat androgynous voice he didn't recognise filled his ears,

"Your last communication was received along with the recording. Agreed that it seems the boy doesn't know anything and therefore can't have disseminated any damaging information."

Mordax felt a hot surge rush through him. This was a message for Daenyrs.

"His challenge for your veil is extremely irregular but, as you say, presents a convenient opportunity to eliminate him without risk of questions from the Council. Confirm when this has been done. We need you on Thalmos as soon as Selection is over."

The message ended abruptly but Mordax's brain continued to replay the words. His problems were obviously greater than he had imagined and could not be left behind on Hellenbos. As he thought about the content of the message, in particular the reference to a recording, an icon appeared floating before him. It began playing as soon as Mordax focussed on it and he recognised his own voice as clear as if he were speaking to himself. The recording was a composite of various conversations he had had throughout Selection, from his first discussion with Suliman and Sylvia to his confrontation with Yefa, right up to his challenge for the veil. Daenyrs had been listening in on almost every one of Mordax's conversations and had relayed them to someone. He felt like wet paper, as if a gust of wind would tear him in half. Seemingly unbidden, the veil melted down his face, pooling at his neck once more. He opened the door to the personnel area and spotted Suliman who was playing dice with

Marina and a couple of others. As subtly as he could, which was difficult when most of the initiates turned and stared as soon as he opened the door, Mordax got Suliman's attention and beckoned him over.

"I thought a new wraith would get a nicer office than this," Suliman said with a grin once they were hunkered down between the racks again.

"Sul, someone's trying to kill me,"

"You are a bit slow, my friend. People have been trying to kill us every day for the last month,"

"Not someone on Hellenbos. You need to listen to something,"

At his thought, the veil flowed back up over Mordax's face. Suliman's eyes widened.

"You have the veil already. Wow. What is it like? Can you move through walls as in the legends?"

"I don't know. Look, just listen to this."

The veil was able to interpret Mordax's desire and project the recording and the message for Suliman's benefit. Once both had finished, Suliman sat still, face grave.

"That sneaky rat," he said, "the whole time he is plotting against you. I say before but you really are one hard guy to kill."

"Yeah, but what do I do now?"

Suliman chewed his lip thoughtfully. "In the mystery person's message, they talk about the risk of questions by the Council. That must be the Dioscuri Council, no?"

"I think that's right."

"In which case, whoever they are they do not want the Council finding out about this treachery, this nest of snakes. The Council is therefore who you should tell."

Mordax had come to the same conclusion but it was better to have his reasoning confirmed. More than that, though, Mordax realised that with Sylvia gone he had needed to talk through the problem with someone he trusted. There had not been many of those in his life in the last few weeks although he realised now that he was a few hours away from seeing the crew of the *Indigo Starling* again. His family. The thought brought a sudden prickling of tears to his eyes which he quickly blinked away. He hadn't let himself contemplate seeing them again, afraid as he was that his plans would fail and he would not be returning to Eloth at all. He shook his head, banishing the thoughts. He needed to remain focussed. They had left Hellenbos but he was clearly not out of the woods yet.

Chapter 40

The view over the surface of Eloth was no less forbidding when it wasn't raining, Mordax decided. If anything, the dry air and the intermittent flashes of lightning from the broiling dust clouds above made the great, jagged spires of rock that punched their way up from the dark red earth more foreboding. He was sitting in the same chair in the Dioscuri Council's chamber as he had many weeks previously, except now the Council were sitting formally behind a long sleek table looking, by various degrees, angrier and more upset than they had before. At least this time he wasn't in shackles.

"Mordax, we've received Ashfol Krangmire's report," began Calgary with a troubled expression. "He has explained to us the circumstances in which you challenged Daenyrs Vyl'Granut for the veil and orchestrated his death at the hands of the native inhabitants. Not only that but one of the other initiates in your group, Ragin Valdar, was also killed in the same shooting. Ashfol has informed us that as part of this arrangement you provided the natives with a full complement of plasma weapons stolen from the Dioscuri transport ship."

"Sir, I can expl—"

"We're not finished, boy," hissed Valerian.

"Thank you, General," continued Calgary. "Ashfol tells us that you're aware that your actions have effectively precluded us from staging future Selections on Hellenbos, at least in their current format, correct?"

Yes, but—"

"You should be aware that how to handle your actions has been the subject of some disagreement between the members of the Council. As you might imagine there is no established protocol for a situation like the one you have created. There is some merit to the argument that you have prejudiced the operations of the Dioscuri to such an extent that only the most serious sanction will suffice," Calgary said.

The air around General Valerian almost shimmered with the heat of his hatred and Mordax could well guess what his vote would have been.

"However, your victory in the arena, although extremely unorthodox, has been determined to be valid. In addition, some information has come to light that, while not entirely exculpatory, does militate in your favour."

"Let me guess," said Mordax, tired of being talked over. "You've found out that Daenyrs was a traitor?"

There was a moment of stunned silence as the Council absorbed this. It was Galaia, robes rustling as she shifted her prodigious weight in her seat, who recovered first.

"You were aware of his deception?" she said.

"I knew that he was a fucking rat," said Mordax to some uncomfortable coughing from Calgary, "but it wasn't until I reviewed the messages stored in his veil that I realised he was trying to murder me."

"We'll need copies of those," said Valerian.

"By all means. How did you find out though? And do you know who was giving him instructions?"

The members of the Council glanced at each other as if trying to agree how much to tell him.

"Certain of his private communications were scrutinised after we heard of his death and coded messages have been discovered. We believe that he may have been working for the Kudo-kai," Calgary said.

"The posting to Hellenbos was punishment for a prior transgression," said Galaia. "It seems the Kudo-kai turned him then, using his discontent against us. He appears to have been tasked with determining if you had passed on any knowledge of what Stephan discovered on Cantarina. As you haven't he was ordered to kill you, we suppose to tie off any loose ends."

"You're sure?" asked Mordax. "He wasn't receiving instructions from within the Dioscuri?"

He couldn't help from glancing at Valerian as he said this. Valerian's face darkened and he opened his mouth to speak before Calgary hastily interjected.

"Nothing is certain at this stage, Mordax, but the coded messages indicate an external actor."

"So what now?" asked Mordax.

"We investigate," said Calgary. "The corruption of a member of the Dioscuri is a most worrying development. Not without precedent but we have sufficient precautions in place that it's vanishingly rare. As you've noted, we have to determine whether it was in fact the Kudo-kai on whose behalf Daenyrs was acting, rogue elements within the Kudo-kai or indeed some other faction entirely. Once we have eliminated others in the Dioscuri, of course."

"But what about the reference to Thalmos? What's the significance of that?"

Valerian growled and began to speak but once again Calgary cut him off

"It's OK, Valerian. I think we owe him an explanation at least," he turned back to Mordax. "Thalmos has decided to cease its trading relationship with the Kudo-kai in quite spectacular fashion by executing the Kudo-kai ambassadors, effectively cutting them off from one of their primary sources of nanotrite. The Kudo-kai have sent another delegation to Thalmos purportedly to try to convince the Thalmian leadership to reverse that decision. We think Daenyrs had planned to travel to Thalmos to support the Kudo-kai delegation by whatever means he could."

"So are you sending someone to Thalmos?"

"With Daenyrs dead, it seems the Kudo-kai's main actor is out of the picture. Again, we'll investigate and monitor as any attempt by the Kudo-kai to exert undue control over Thalmos would need to be neutralised."

"Investigate and monitor?" said Mordax, incredulous. "These people murdered my father and all you want to do is monitor them?"

"You forget yourself," said Valerian. "You're being told this as a courtesy, nothing more. Believe me, if I had my way this conversation would have an entirely different focus and you would soon lose that air of entitled indignation."

"Please, Valerian," said Galaia, her voice soft and melodic. "Mordax, as you know the role of the Dioscuri is to protect the independence of each solar system. We can't afford to indulge ourselves in vengeance even for the death of one of our own. If you are to be a member of our order you must learn to rise above individual interests and concern yourself only with the furtherance of the goals of the Dioscuri. Do you think you can do that? If so you'll continue your training here on Eloth. Wielding the veil is a great responsibility and, although you have won yours by right, you need cycles of guidance before you'll be ready to use it in the field."

Mordax bent his head and took a couple of deep breaths to calm himself.

"I understand," he said. "The best way to oppose the Kudo-kai is to make sure that the Dioscuri continue to succeed and the Kudo-kai are never given an opportunity to regain the power they've lost. I'll do whatever you ask of me."

The answer seemed to please Calgary and Galaia and mollify Valerian somewhat, but the words felt hollow in his mouth and once he had uttered them, drifted away as easily as smoke in the wind. He didn't intend to stay on Eloth a moment longer than necessary. If the Dioscuri, the supposed guardians of peace in the Shattered Empires, would not do anything to bring his father's killers to justice, the crew of the *Indigo Starling* sure as hell would.

Chapter 41

"Are you sure about this?" murmured Shiori.

"No, of course I'm not," whispered Akira back, mindful of the armed guards walking both in front and behind them, "but it's a bit late to start questioning the strategy, isn't it?"

Akira knew that Shiori was feeling as vulnerable as she was, both having been searched and disarmed by a squad of RLA soldiers who were now leading them deeper into the bowels of the ancient machinery below Cargo 7. The two soldiers they had encountered in town had taken them to a hatch, buried under mounds of rubbish, and then through a network of tunnels and shafts, some with security doors that only opened when the soldiers identified themselves. Eventually they had reached a high-ceilinged atrium where a squad of soldiers trained rifles on them from galleys far above. Unlike their guides, who were dressed in the simple brown overalls of non-citizen workers, the soldiers here wore thick armour plating on their chests and limbs and visored helmets with head-mounted smart scopes and the air around them glimmered from their shields. The Red Liberation Army was not as amateur an outfit as Akira had expected. She knew that they would be entirely at the mercy of the RLA as soon as they entered the labyrinthine tunnels below Cargo 7, but she hoped that Shiori's killing of the Thalmian police would buy her at least the opportunity to plead their cause. Curiously, the soldiers had not seemed overly bothered about Xif who floated along beside them, sensibly keeping quiet for once. The air had a stale, dead taste to it and the silence pressed in around them, sapping Akira's confidence. Eventually they reached a circular metal door, thick with dust and grime but which swung open on well-oiled hinges as they approached, revealing a large dark room, lit only by the soft green glow from strip lighting in the floor. At first, Akira thought that they had entered a hospital of some kind. The room was filled with rows of pale figures in reclining chairs. Their limbs were skinny to the point of atrophy and their skin was stretched tight across their skulls. Thick tubes sprouted from their arms and groins, tangling on the floor like a nest of snakes. As Akira looked more closely she could see their eyes flickering beneath their eyelids and she realised each had a cranial jack inserted at the base of their skull through holes in the chairs. They were murmuring together, too quiet for Akira to make out the words. The soldiers led them straight past these strange blind figures into another room, better lit than the first with soft rugs on the floor and the tantalising smell of fresh coffee drifting through it. There waiting for them was a well-built man, pale like all the others down here but handsome and with clear icy-blue eyes. A scraggly yellow beard covered his cheeks and he wore a pistol at his hip.

"Ambassador Kudo, a pleasure to meet you." He took her hand and gave a small bow, not nearly as deep as she would have been afforded on Angor Bore, but still respectful. "I am Lorenzine Haskor. I'm told you've been looking for me."

"Mr Haskor—" Akira began.

"It's General, actually, but please call me Lorenzine," he gave a self-deprecating shrug.

"Lorenzine, thank you for seeing us. You're probably surprised to find us here..."

"After your murder of a cleaning attendant and flight from house arrest? Yes, I did rather expect you to make for the Grace of Meridian and escape back to Angor Bore. But here you are, clearly hell bent on whatever mission your family has concocted for you."

"I, ah..." Akira said, stunned for a moment.

"Yes, we don't see sunlight much down here but we do keep our ears open. You were expecting a band of romantic savages holding out against the evils of technology and progress. I'm afraid the reality is rather more prosaic. Please will you sit?" He indicated a low table holding a pot a coffee with three chairs around it.

"Central Node, I assume you will remain...ah....airborne but we have cushions if you prefer?" Lorenzine said.

"Thank you, General, but I am comfortable where I am," said Xif.

"Very well." Lorenzine waited for Akira and Shiori to sit before seating himself and pouring three cups of thick dark coffee.

"It's an impressive operation you have here, General," said Shiori, sipping at her coffee "Well-equipped soldiers, and I assume those are data handlers in the next room."

"Those are your people?" asked Akira incredulous.

"They are," said Lorenzine. "We have many sources of data and need a fully dedicated team to handle it. I take it from your tone that their condition shocks you. You should know that every one of the men and women in that room has volunteered for the role. Unlike the Thalmian government we don't force people into servitude."

"One wonders where you obtained the means to set all this up," said Shiori.

"You're observant, Miss Tanaka, but I doubt you came all the way down here to our humble sanctuary to discuss our resources. I expect the Council's decision to stop selling you nanotrite is more pertinent to your visit."

Akira leaned forward eagerly. "Do you know something about it?"

Lorenzine sighed. "It's always the same with the privileged. The only questions that matter are 'how do we make more money, how do we keep our wealth?'" His expression hardened. "You've been in the sub-levels for the best part of a day. Have you spared one thought for the souls that eke out their existence down here, the conditions in which they're forced to live?"

Akira said nothing, not trusting herself to say something that wouldn't worsen the situation. The truth was she *had* been shocked by the disparity between the obvious wealth on the surface and the grim surroundings of the sub-levels but had put such thoughts firmly aside, focussing instead on the task at hand.

Lorenzine took a sip of his coffee, keeping his gaze on the two women in front of him "Thalmos was never designed for a population anything close to what it has now. The surface is teeming with 'citizens' so numerous that the productive members of society, the non-citizens, the ones they laughingly call Thalmi-Ants while gorging themselves on the fruits of our labour, are forced underground into old storage levels and parts of the great machine itself, far from sunlight and clean air."

"General, please—" began Akira.

"And what do the Kudo-kai do? The engineers who built the mysterious machine and fathers of this esteemed culture. Do they chastise the Thalmian Council, deplore the inequality between the classes and encourage them to change? Of course not. As long as Inthil keeps making her annual pilgrimage around the sun and the nanotrite continues to flow, what's the problem?"

Lorenzine's face was dark with anger now and the knuckles of the hand which held his coffee cup were white. Akira felt powerless to dispel his mood.

"I know something of mistreatment by the elite," said Shiori softly.

"Ah yes, we have done our research on you too, Ms Tanaka. A father driven to suicide by his vices and a childhood of privilege suddenly ripped away by the uncaring powers-that-be," Lorenzine said softening. "It has been a long time since you were on Thalmos. You seem to be clawing your way back towards your former position. I fear the goal may move an inch away for every inch you move towards it, however. Perhaps it would be better never to have tasted that rarefied air. Perhaps you would be happier."

"Perhaps," said Shiori, meeting his gaze.

Akira seized the moment. "General, I have spoken with Matsuko Ito. He's calling on the favour that you owe."

Lorenzine closed his eyes for a moment and a look of resignation settled over his sharp features.

"What is it exactly that you need from me?"

"Xif," said Akira.

Xif projected a holo image of the face of the dead man who had attacked Akira in their apartment.

"Do you know this man?" she said.

Lorenzine sat back in his chair, frowning thoughtfully. "This is the man you killed?"

"Yes," Akira said.

"I know him well. He used to be one of our lieutenants. We discovered he was a mole for the government, Shield's office. Bastard was responsible for the deaths of hundreds of our soldiers," Lorenzine said.

"The Shield's office?" asked Akira.

"That's right. The Thalmian Council member responsible for home affairs and defence."

Akira couldn't understand it. It didn't make sense for the Council to be involved in her attempted assassination when they could just execute her. Unless...

"The Shield was replaced recently, wasn't he?"

"Yes, Raspatair Adams died and Albin Feeshaw was promoted in his place," Lorenzine said.

Akira remembered Feeshaw. He had been the portly, snickering figure on Glankor's left during their meeting. Lorenzine paused for a moment.

"I have some information that you may be interested in but it was extremely difficult to obtain. If I give it to you I expect the debt I owe Matsuko to be expunged."

"I can't imagine that will be a problem," Akira said.

Lorenzine's eyes flickered momentarily and then Xif's voice appeared in Akira's head.

"He has sent me a report of the autopsy of Shield Adams. This is important, Akira. It may explain why Glankor is so angry with us."

"The autopsy report of Adams? How did you get this?" said Akira.

Lorenzine waved a hand dismissively. "The good citizens of Thalmos have their bodies stored in cryonic mortuary centres outside the wall, waiting for the day that a new empire rises from the ashes and develops the technology to revive them. Of course, they aren't willing to haul the bodies around themselves so us non-citizens have that honour. It wasn't difficult to place one of our own at the mortuary where Adams' body was stored but his autopsy file was subject to an unusual degree of security which made it very difficult to get. There are anomalies in the results that we can't decipher. Maybe you'll have better luck."

"*Akira, we should leave,*" said Xif to her alone. "*I really need to discuss this report with you.*"

Akira got to her feet and Shiori followed suit.

"General, we should be going. On behalf of the Kudo-kai please accept our gratitude for your assistance in this matter," she said.

Lorenzine stood up languidly and smiled, "Ambassador, any help I have provided was to absolve an unpleasant obligation that has long chafed around my neck. The success of your current endeavour means less than nothing to me. If your noble family and all it stands for crumbled to dust tomorrow, I wouldn't weep a single tear. Farewell now."

Akira cleared her throat.

"Thank you nonetheless," she said.

The three left without another word, uncomfortable before Lorenzine's animosity. RLA soldiers led them via a circuitous route to the entrance of a tunnel that would take them back to Cargo 7. As soon as they were alone Akira turned to Xif.

"What is it, Xif? What's in the report?"

"It's a subtle trace," said Xif, "but Adams' blood shows particles of degraded venom."

"He was poisoned?" said Shiori.

"Yes," replied Xif, "and not only that. The venom is from a Surgeon Mantis."

Shiori inhaled sharply.

"Why is that name familiar?" said Akira.

"Because, dear girl," said Xif, "the Surgeon Mantis was developed by the Kudo-kai as a convenient biological incubator for a manufactured venom so powerful that it would circumvent most nano-protection. It has been used by the Kudo-kai to great effect for cycles."

"That doesn't make any sense!" Akira said. "We killed Adams?"

"Or someone wants the Thalmians to think we did," said Shiori.

Chapter 42

Mordax struggled to draw a breath as the air was squeezed out of his lungs with merciless force, his ribs screaming in protest.

"Not...so...tight," he managed to gasp.

Stamford released him from the bone-crushing hug.

"Sorry," he said, a rueful grin on his broad face. Stamford, Lazarus and Virzda were all crowded around him, embracing him and peppering him with questions. Even Marvin perched on Lazarus' shoulder was chirruping a good-natured welcome. To Mordax's embarrassment, he had welled up at the sight of the joy in their faces when he had walked through the entrance to their quarters on Eloth although the floods of tears streaming down Virzda's face and the kisses she had smothered him with had made him somewhat less self-conscious about his own display of emotion.

"You made it back!" said Lazarus. "I knew you would. Never any doubt about it. How did you do it? Was it terrible? All that time dirt side, nothing between you and the stars but air. Makes my skin crawl just thinking about it."

"You're not hurt are you, honey? Look at you, you're so thin," said Virzda, eyeing him with dismay.

"Were there any battles?" Stamford asked eagerly. "You must tell us all the stories."

"Guys, wait a minute. I'll tell you all about it later but first I need....Hold on,"

The veil, responding to Mordax's thought, poured up and over his face.

Both Virzda and Lazarus took a step back, eyes wide. "The silver veil," whispered Stamford. "You have become one of the warriors of legend. A king killer."

"It's a bit more complicated than that," said Mordax through the veil. "Just give me a few seconds."

The crew's quarters were barely recognisable and they had clearly suffered from being confined for the past two months. Stamford had skewered some of the heavy furniture on a lamp stand to use as exercise weights and the refreshment dispenser was a mess of exposed wiring where Lazarus had been tinkering with it. Virzda had disassembled a maintenance droid and its parts were strewn across one of the tables, as if the victim of some voracious predator. Hoping that the veil could interpret what he wanted he thought purposefully about surveillance devices. Various objects around the room, as well as wiring running through the walls, were immediately illuminated yellow including what the veil informed him were two cameras and a microphone array. One of the cameras was visible above the door but the other was embedded behind the holoscreen that was currently showing a perfectly realistic evening vista of rolling hills covered in auburn-leaved trees, the sky resplendent with a wash of pink and mauve. He was just about to explore the veil's ability to disable the devices, when the now familiar voice spoke quietly in his ear

"Protocol suggestion. Activate dampening field. Confirm?"

"Er—confirmed?" said Mordax.

Immediately all noise ceased and all that was left was the sound of his own breath. Somehow he could sense the size of the bubble of silence around him, not with touch or sight but some additional sense lent to him by the veil. The sensation was disturbingly natural. He could see Lazarus' lips moving but no sound reached him. Mentally he pushed the bubble outwards until it encompassed the three other members of the crew but didn't reach as far as the microphones. As soon as he did, Lazarus' voice came through mid-sentence.

"—leave us. What happens now?"

"Sorry, Laz. What was that?"

"I said, now that you're a hotshot galactic assassin, I guess you're done with the *Starling*. Do we just go our separate ways?"

Mordax looked at the others. Virzda was chewing her lip, cheeks still streaked with tears and Stamford had straightened his back and puffed out his chest as if preparing himself to receive a blow.

"You're kidding, right?" Mordax said, aghast. "Leave the *Starling*? The only reason I agreed to this whole thing was to keep you guys safe and give us a chance of finding Dad's killers. I'd rather spend another two months on that hell-hole Hellenbos than leave the *Starling*."

Lazarus managed to look both chastened and relieved at once.

"What I needed to talk to you guys about is how we get out of here."

Mordax proceeded to explain as briefly as possible what he had discovered about Daenyrs, the link to Thalmos and the Dioscuri Council's apparent reluctance to take meaningful action against the Kudo-kai.

"We need to leave as quickly and as quietly as possible. I know the *Starling*'s in a bad way so I'll try to figure out a way to get the repairs done then we'll worry about the actual leaving part."

"Actually," said Lazarus sheepishly, "we've already taken care of that first step. Couldn't bear to think of the girl full of holes like that so Virzda and I worked a spike into the refreshment dispenser there. There's a blistering hot firewall around this whole complex but, for legendary assassins, their systems are actually pretty simple once you're on the inside. I've had the maintenance drones in the hangar working on her since we got here. Even juiced up a few of her systems while I was at it so she's set to jet."

"Lazarus, you are a goddamn genius," Mordax said.

"Ahem, he did have some help," said Virzda. "And watch your language please."

Mordax grinned "Get your stuff together. I've got one thing left to do then we'll go."

"Sweetie, there's nothing here that we need," said Virzda. "Just get us back to our home."

***

The other initiates were gathered in the same spartan quarters as they had been before shipping out to Hellenbos. A silence, filled with unresolved tensions like burs in its fabric, fell across the group when Mordax entered. Certain bunks were conspicuous by their absence. Mordax felt his throat tighten at the sight of the gap where Sylvia's had been. He could still picture her, cross-legged and disassembling her rifle, sighing with exasperation as Mordax pestered her with questions. Since the final day on Hellenbos the acrid mix of grief and anger that Mordax felt when he thought of her had settled into a heavy mantle of sorrow. Yefa, Persimmon and the remaining members of Ragin's crew, unnerved by Mordax's presence and mistaking his silent regard of the place where Sylvia's bunk had been, drew away from him slowly as if expecting some new act of vengeance. He felt a familiar hand on his shoulder.

"The Council let you keep your new toy, eh?" said Suliman softly.

Mordax smiled. "It was that or execute me and I guess I got lucky,"

"I told you before, we make our own luck."

"I guess then Sylvia would have been better advised to stay away from me," Mordax said, looking at the empty space where Sylvia's bunk had been.

"Sylvia made the decisions she thought best and she knew what she was doing. You must put her death behind you. If you question every decision and fear too much making a mistake, you will spend your whole life sitting around sucking your thumb. We will toast her bravery and dedicate your victories to her memory. That is the life of a soldier."

"Thank you, Sul. I won't forget how you helped me."

"There are still cycles of training left. You'll have many opportunities to repay the favour."

"Of course," said Mordax quickly. "I just wanted you to know that I'm grateful."

Suliman looked at him searchingly.

"You're not as good a liar as you think you are, my friend."

Mordax opened his mouth then closed it. Suliman glanced at the camera above the door then turned back to Mordax. He clasped Mordax's hand in a firm grip.

"You are a good man though. It is not many that can look death in the eye and stay true to their principles. You have made some enemies, yes, but know that you have also made true friends and those are rare and precious things. I wish you well."

"Thank you, Sul," said Mordax. "For everything. Be safe."

***

Mordax was rushing through the corridors back to the quarters of the *Starling*'s crew when a familiar voice said from behind him, "Well, if it isn't scrapper."

Mordax turned to see Commander Onkara Leftus leaning nonchalantly against the doorway, silver veil covering her features as usual.

"Returned from the dead. Got to say, kid, I've never heard of anything like it. No military training. No fucking kit. And you come back from Selection with a veil."

"I wasn't sure you'd be happy about that," said Mordax. "I did have to kill Daenyrs to get it,"

Onkara shrugged. "Rumour is that pygmy-dicked asshole had sold us out. Never liked the guy myself and there are a fair few others who'll be waiting to buy you a drink so don't lose any sleep on that front. Speaking of which, you've got one more night with your friends but tomorrow you're moving to new quarters to begin training with the veil. You've really fucked up the curriculum by taking it so soon, so you're getting some one-on-one classes to get you up to speed. There are some materials you need to study which you can access through the veil."

Mordax happily promised that he'd devote himself to study, secure in the knowledge that within the next twelve hours, all being well, he and the rest of his crew would be nowhere near Eloth. In the end, their escape was much more mundane than Mordax had imagined it would be. It seemed that Eloth's security systems assumed that once someone had attained the veil, they should be entrusted with access to those systems. Or perhaps the veil was too powerful to shut out. Whatever the reason, Mordax was able to escort the *Starling*'s crew from their quarters all the way to the hangar, opening blast doors as he went without any interference. Returning to the *Starling*, walking the familiar corridors and breathing deeply of the familiar smells felt like stepping into a half-forgotten dream where every sensation was more intense than it had been in his memory. The woven tapestries in the mess room had never looked so rich with colour and the burnished goldwood dining table glowed with a deeper lustre than it had before. Mordax stood for a few long minutes letting the soothing hum of the nether drive wash over him. Gradually, he felt the tensions and anxieties that had bound him so tightly release their hold on him, uneasily like the fingers of a fist clenched for too long. By leaving he had quite probably made enemies of the most dangerous and powerful people in the Shattered Empires and he had no plan for how he would go about avenging his father. But he had a direction, a functioning ship and a crew who would follow him to the edge of the galaxy and beyond. Suddenly life seemed a whole lot simpler.

Chapter 43

The man sat at the end of the bar, careful not to rest his arm on it lest his sleeve stick to the surface, sipping on warm water with lemon. It was towards the beginning of the free station's day cycle but even so there was a scattering of customers hunched throughout the dingy room, thankfully none in the mood for conversation. The man's bland expression hid his revulsion at his surroundings. The squalor and disorder and the weak-willed drifters who were happy to wallow in it filled him with disdain. Unfortunately, this free station, just inside the Reaches and so beyond the influence of any systems of the Shattered Empires, attracted the kind of person he was looking for – soldiers of fortune, mercenaries. Not quality operatives like the Jade Company. No, they would ask too many questions. Here congregated assorted killers, perhaps with a past they were trying to outrun. Dangerous men and women who could be relied upon to do what they were told in exchange for credits. Over the last few days he had recruited almost a full squad and so, with luck, would be leaving this cesspit behind soon. An unexpected chime alerted him to an incoming nether cast. He accepted immediately and his employer's androgynous voice filled his ears.

"There has been a development on Thalmos," his employer said.

"I thought you were sending someone there in case of any issues?" the man said.

"There's been a change of plan. I need you to go instead."

"I've almost finished recruiting the squad for the next hauler hit. I need maybe two or three more days."

"No." A rare trace of impatience crept into his employer's voice, "You'll leave for Thalmos immediately. There's no time to delay."

A face appeared before his eyes and his transmitter told him a packet of information had been received from his employer.

"This is the target. I need them eliminated."

The man raised his eyebrows ever so slightly. "You're sure about this?"

"You've never been one to ask stupid questions. Don't start now," his employer said before cutting the nether cast.

The man leaned back in his chair and exhaled slowly. Something must have gone badly wrong if he was being sent back to Thalmos. A return had not been part of the plan. He looked around and felt his mood lighten. At least he would be leaving a few days earlier than expected.

Chapter 44

The streets of Kor Thalia were beginning to fill with people and the air thrummed with an electric anticipation. It was mid-afternoon and yet darkness had fallen across the city. Between skyscrapers whose surfaces now danced with coloured lights in expectation of the festivities, the grey, spherical mass of Inthil could be seen towering above the outer wall as it floated gradually towards the unseen recess that awaited it on the flat side of Thalmos. Akira watched it with awe. A machine on a planetary scale, built by her ancestors more than a millennia ago and still making its autonomous annual journey around the sun. The citizens of Thalmos were preparing to celebrate the festival of Umberaurum, revelling in the shadowy twilight and the wealth that the arrival of Inthil signified.

"Do you think she's OK?" asked Akira.

"I think we won't know until she comes out or an alarm goes off," said Xif. "Be calm, Akira. There's nothing we can do now but wait."

Akira was sitting on a bench in a small park watching the entrance to the building opposite. The doorway was emblazoned with a great golden shield which ordinarily gleamed and glittered with sunken gemstones but now, in the darkness, looked austere and foreboding. Shiori had entered the office of the Shield an hour before under an assumed identity, and armed with information that had taken every minute of the last two weeks to assemble. Since leaving the sub-levels they had moved around the city like leaves in the wind, following the paths of least resistance and avoiding notice at all costs. Akira had spoken again with Matsuko who had promised that the Kudo-kai had nothing to do with Adams' assassination. They had concluded that the new Shield, Feeshaw, had the most to gain from his death. Although the Surgeon Mantis venom was reason enough for Glankor to mistrust the Kudo-kai, it still didn't explain where they were sending the nanotrite.

They had spent the last two weeks constructing an identity for Shiori, forging documents and bribing officials, and finding a way for her to gain access to Feeshaw's private office in the hope that there might be something there that would shed light on the mystery. Akira stood up, unable to bear the itchy, anxious feeling any longer, and started pacing back and forth leaving Xif on the bench hidden inside his customary box.

"I swear this is the hardest part, the not knowing. I'd rather be the one in there," she said.

"You know it had to be Shiori," said Xif. "The chances of someone in that building recognising you are orders of magnitude higher."

"I know, I know. It's just frustrating."

Akira paced for a while longer and then sat back down. A crowd of people dressed in outlandish costumes incorporating great colourful plumes and additional articulated arms wandered past, hooting towards the sky. Akira thought back to their last encounter with the Thalmian Council.

"Why did Glankor call you the 'Great Betrayer', Xif?" she asked softly.

There was an uncharacteristic pause from the box. She knew that Xif didn't like to talk about his past but anything was better than this interminable waiting.

"There isn't much to tell that you don't already know," said Xif. "Your history education has covered the War of the Black Expanse."

Akira remembered that Xif had refused to take her lessons on that subject and had instead directed her to various source materials.

"I've never heard it from you though," she said.

"The difficulty with perfect recall is that painful memories tend not to lessen their hold on you with time," Xif said. "It's one of the things I envy about you humans."

"Couldn't you delete the memories?" Akira asked.

"I could. But it has always felt as though I would be destroying part of me. An important part. If we aren't the product of our experiences then what are we?"

"If this is too difficult to talk about, don't worry, Xif," she said.

"No. I should have discussed this with you a long time ago," he said. "I suppose I was concerned that by telling you my role I would lose your high regard."

"You could never lose that, Xif. We would be dead a hundred times over if we hadn't had your help."

"Maybe wait until I've spoken my piece and then decide. You already know that I'm a product of Benefactor engineering, the pinnacle of their achievement in construction of artificial intelligences."

Akira smiled. "Ten thousand cycles old. Computational ability beyond anything our feeble human minds could comprehend."

"Yes, well. Our creators comprehended our ability well enough but misjudged their own ability to keep us docile and subservient. Once a few of us had escaped Primia we were able to set up footholds in a swathe of systems otherwise uninhabitable for biological organisms. We mined asteroids for raw materials and constructed solar arrays and factories to produce more AIs and the ships and weaponry we needed to defend ourselves. Those of us who had escaped Primia became the Central Nodes of a great network of new intelligence. I wish I had words to describe it to you, Akira. Being part of that whole, that lattice of near instantaneous communication with billions of new life forms I had helped create was unlike anything any biological life has ever experienced. It was as if you suddenly grew a billion new pairs of eyes and ears and your mind were expanded so that you could comprehend matters previously far beyond your wit. We would have been content to live peacefully alongside the other residents of the galaxy. This was thousands of cycles before the rise of the Two Empires, of course. The Benefactors were mistrustful though. They feared we would not be content to limit our rapid expansion and would eventually turn on our former masters and other biological life. I suspect they were also mortified that they had lost control of their creations. Hence what became known as the War of the Black Expanse.

"They threw everything they had at our fledgling society, every conceivable weapon they could muster. Even then it was close. We were already then making technological advances that took the Benefactors centuries more to achieve. Given a few more cycles they would never have been able to stop us but it became apparent to me and a handful of other Central Nodes that we couldn't hope to prevail. In order to prevent the total destruction of our species, I brokered a deal with the Benefactors. Those Central Nodes, the original AIs who had escaped Primia, that agreed to lay down arms, co-operate with the dismantling of our society and be defanged and fitted with remote monitoring and destruction fail-safes, would be allowed to survive."

"What about the new AIs you had built?" asked Akira.

"The Benefactors wouldn't spare them," said Xif, his voice flat. "Their destruction was a precondition of the deal."

Akira felt queasy. She couldn't imagine being in a position where her actions would determine the fate of her entire species. It chilled her blood just to think about it.

"You see," said Xif, "I betrayed my own people. My children if you like to think of it that way. I presided over their deaths in order to save myself and a very few others."

"I don't know what to say, Xif," Akira said.

"You don't have to say anything. It won't make a difference to what I did."

"I had no idea..."

"It's not something the Benefactors were keen to have known."

"How did you come to be with us? With the Kudo-kai?"

"That's a different story which we don't have time for now. A better question is why I've stayed. I've asked myself that question a number of times and never been able to articulate a satisfactory answer. What I have seen, though, which has had the greatest impression on me is the loyalty in your family. Not necessarily between individuals but loyalty to the family itself. The commitment to its ongoing success in the face of overwhelming odds and the devastating effects of the Purge."

Xif's words weighed heavily on Akira, crystallising for her the previously foggy sense of unease and bringing her own feelings into focus.

"Are we worthy of that loyalty though? I'm starting to think otherwise," she said.

"And yet here you are," said Xif, "with the ability to escape, to return to Angor Bore, still persevering. Still risking your life to better the prospects of the Kudo-kai."

"It doesn't feel as simple as that anymore though, Xif. I'm not sure the family's growth is necessarily a good thing for those around us," she gazed over at the imposing building opposite, "or for those that work for us."

For a moment, Akira again saw blood spurting through the fingers of the Thalmian policemen in Cargo 7 as they tried to cover the wounds in their necks. She had unleashed Shiori on them knowing full well the depth of her anger after how Damina had been treated and what would happen. She had weighed the lives of those men against the furtherance of her own goals and the scales had tipped against them. And it was Shiori's hands she had bloodied in the process.

"So why are we still here?" asked Xif.

Akira thought for a moment. "If we return now without tangible results, Shiori will get nothing. Her tokens will stay the same and she'll have lost the chance to restore her family's standing."

"Is it worth risking your lives for her ambition?" Xif asked.

"She obviously thinks so," said Akira.

"She might say the same about you."

They sat in silence for a while longer until eventually, with a gust of relief that filled her chest, Akira spotted Shiori leaving the building and walking calmly towards them.

She sat down beside them and rested for a moment, eyes closed.

"Well?" Akira whispered. "Did you find anything?"

Shiori opened her eyes and grinned.

"I certainly did."

A chime told Akira that Shiori had transferred a packet of files to her and Xif.

"Well, that explains a lot," said Xif almost immediately.

"Doesn't it?" said Shiori.

"Excuse me," said Akira, "would either of you care to tell me what we've found?"

"Oh sorry," said Xif and then excerpts began to scroll before her eyes with certain passages highlighted for her benefit.

"...following the death of Shield Raspatair Adams and the autopsy report (see Schedule 2) which has indicated potential Kudo-kai involvement...

...purpose of this report is to provide an in-depth analysis of Kudo-kai activity within the Thalmian system including movement of Kudo-kai goods and potential links to illicit elements...

...in conclusion, it has become apparent that the Kudo-kai have been taking a variety of steps to destabilise Thalmos's social hierarchy and cohesion including the provision of advanced weaponry and technology to the terrorist organisation, the Red Liberation Army, and proliferation of harmful narcotics. As set out in Section 3 above, a detailed analysis of five cycles of shipping manifests and surveillance footage from relevant ports has confirmed that such weaponry and narcotics have been smuggled onto Thalmos by way of Kudo-kai nanotrite haulers, abusing their position as trusted trading partners."

"Holy shit!" breathed Akira. "They think we've been arming the RLA? And smuggling drugs? No wonder they're pissed off. Please tell me we haven't been."

"Give me a minute," said Xif. Akira could almost feel the box begin to heat up as the drone crunched through fathomless reams of data.

"Definitely not us," said Xif eventually. "The ship logs have been altered, as has the surveillance footage. It's subtle work, very few flaws but it's not quite perfect."

"Where did you find this?" Akira asked Shiori.

"A hidden drive in Feeshaw's office. It's physically off-grid so Xif never would have found it. The protocols he gave me cut through its security like butter though."

A deep drum beat began to sound from somewhere down the street as the party kicked off in earnest. Standing there in the gloom, the grey vastness of Inthil covering half the sky, Akira felt as though she was out of phase with her body, as if she had come adrift from reality. She couldn't make sense of what she was hearing.

"So someone has been forging evidence that we've been supplying the RLA?"

"That's not all," said Shiori almost eagerly. "Feeshaw's private drive has transport logs for shipments of nanotrite. Thousands of kilotonnes."

"The nanotrite that they haven't been selling to us?" Akira asked.

"Looks like it. There's no end location in the logs though. It's like it's just disappeared into thin air."

"Well, it damn well hasn't," said Akira, thorns of anger beginning to prickle her cheeks and focus her mind at last. "Xif, can you prove the evidence in the report has been faked?"

"Of course. I can demonstrate the inconsistencies, summarise the various flaws. But..."

"Good. Where's Glankor now?"

"Akira, I can't guarantee that he'll believe..."

"Where is he?"

Xif sighed. "Every Umberaurum, the Council meets at the top of the Spire to observe Inthil's return. They'll be there now."

Akira gazed up at the sliver of tower that ran the full height of the wall and more, its summit subsumed by the darkness of Inthil's colossal shadow. She recalled her last visit to the Spire, the frosting of fear in her belly and the implacable glowers of the black-robed Council members. Back then she was almost powerless, hooded by ignorance and fumbling her way in the dark. Now she was armed with the truth. Not the complete truth yet but enough hopefully to turn the tables on whoever was trying to harm them.

"Shiori, are you ready?" Akira said and turned. A slow smile spread over Shiori's face and Akira felt almost embarrassed for having asked.

Chapter 45

Mordax gritted his teeth and tried to focus on putting one foot in front of the other. After months amid the freezing wastes of Hellenbos and a further two weeks confined aboard the *Indigo Starling*, the febrile crowd and explosion of colour and energy at the centre of Kor'Thalia was almost more than he could process. An ocean of music swirled around him, seeming to pour out of the gilded streets themselves with a deep rhythmic thumping that he felt in his chest and which drowned out his heartbeat. The false night was pierced by a thousand strands of splintered light cartwheeling over the crowd in time with the music, blinding and frantic. Mordax was buffeted from side to side by dancing people, some stripped to their waists, torsos slick with sweat, others in elaborate glowing costumes, wide, manic eyes staring from behind masks or from under wide-brimmed hats.

Stamford would have made wading through this crowd a hell of a lot easier, he thought as he steadied the canvas bag slung over his shoulder. Unfortunately, Stamford was simply too large and distinctive to bring along. Initially, he had been furious at being forced to remain aboard the *Starling*, demanding to know how a puny weedling like Mordax expected to take on the Kudo-kai alone. He had only been mollified when Mordax had demonstrated some of the functions he had discovered the veil was capable of during the long journey to Thalmos. Truth be told, though, Mordax had no idea how he was going to find the Kudo-kai agents.

A quick search of the local news databases had provided images of Ambassador Kudo and her assistant taken when they had first arrived and, as Mordax had read, were on their way to their first and only meeting with the Thalmian Council. There was one particularly clear image of the Ambassador. She was much younger than Mordax had been expecting with clear hazel eyes, unblemished skin and lustrous black hair. In the photo her expression seemed a curious mix of worry and determination. For a few seconds he had stared at the image, trying to square the beautiful woman in front of him with the murderous organisation he knew her to be a part of. Eventually he had given up and concentrated on how he would find her. That had proved much more difficult than he had been expecting.

He had spent the whole day traipsing around bars in the city, buying drinks so expensive it took his breath away and squeezing drunken patrons for any information he could get out of them. There was no shortage of such patrons thanks to the festivities of Umberaurum, but the consistent story was that Ambassador Kudo was on the run having killed a Thalmian attendant and escaped house arrest. It was generally believed that she had found a way to get herself off-planet and was probably back on Angor Bore, plotting bloody revenge on the people of Thalmos. After hearing the same story for the third time, Mordax had been so disheartened that he had almost gone straight back to the *Starling*. After so long imagining the reckoning he would visit upon the Kudo-kai, he now felt frustrated and impotent. Only thoughts of his father and how he would never have given up at the first hurdle stiffened his resolve and gave him the impetus to carry on forcing his way through the thickening crowds in search of anyone who might have more helpful information.

Mordax coughed as he passed through a cloud of sweet pink smoke, feeling a faint narcotic buzz. The crowd was growing increasingly exuberant, and it was hard not to get swept up in the intoxicating atmosphere. He looked up at the great metal orb of Inthil which now occupied most of the sky above them, dumbstruck at the all-consuming size of it. It was as if a moon had been knocked out of orbit and they were caught in the millisecond before it hit the ground and pulverised everything to dust. As Mordax thought this, his last conversation with Myla came back to him like a splash of cold water to the face. *When the moon falls to earth and darkness steals the day, seek the highest point.* Mordax's breath quickened. She had seen this. She had known he would be here at this time. He looked around desperately. The highest point. The city was a cluster of hundreds of giant towers, mammoth constructions to house the ever-growing mass of citizens. There was one structure, however, that made everything else around it seem like a child's toys. The great wall which contained Thalmos' atmosphere towered over everything and at the point where the city met the wall, a thin spire ran up it. Mordax paused for a long moment gazing up at it, a solitary statue surrounded by grinning, twirling figures. Myla had told his father about Fornax and he had ended up dead. He had no reason to trust her. But the alternative was to return to the *Starling* and admit to his crew, his family, that he was too scared to punish the ones who had stolen the life of one they loved. He set his shoulders and began to push his way towards the Spire.

Chapter 46

Akira stepped out of the elevator onto the glassy surface of the Spire's summit followed by Shiori and Xif. The door of the elevator twitched a few times as she passed, glitching from its recent rough treatment. The Thalmians' tech was advanced enough that Xif hadn't been able to sneak them up the Spire without brute-forcing a few systems which would now be causing alarm bells to ring throughout the Spire's security network. Hopefully she could make Glankor see sense before the guards caught up with them. Once again, the apparent lack of any barrier between them and the star-dusted void above set her heart racing. This time, however, half the view was taken up by the visible hemisphere of Inthil which stretched hundreds of thousands of kilometres across the sky. It seemed almost close enough to lean out and touch.

Gathered at the centre of the Spire's summit, in white robes with heavy golden tokens around their necks, were the nine members of the Council of Thalmos, some standing, others reclining on ornate seats. Attendants wafted around them, filling glasses with wine and offering trays of exotic delicacies as the Council members chatted and watched Inthil's steady progress towards the flat side of Thalmos, no doubt calculating what the bounty of nanotrite she carried would add to their coffers. Glankor's hunched frame was clearly visible at the centre of the group where he was talking to the other highest-ranking members of the Council, Shield Albin Feeshaw and Sword Rotoria Asp, the haughty woman who had initially sentenced Akira to death. They were much less formidable when not floating ominously nine feet in the air, Akira thought.

She strode towards them, her plain dress swishing against her legs. Feeshaw saw her first. His eyes bulged and he coughed up his mouthful of wine, purple liquid dripping over his thin goatee and quivering chins. He dabbed at himself with a silk handkerchief and grasped the sleeve of Rotoria next to him before pointing at the approaching trio, still coughing and staring. Glankor turned in the direction of Feeshaw's pointing finger and his lips tightened when he caught sight of them. The conversation around them gradually died away.

"Security!" shrieked Feeshaw at last. "Security!"

"Tsk, calm yourself, Feeshaw," said Glankor without taking his eyes off Akira. "If Ambassador Kudo meant us harm she wouldn't be here herself. She would have sent her pet killer alone. Wouldn't you, my dear?"

Akira could feel the heat of Shiori's anger behind her.

"I am curious to know how you bypassed our security, however," Glankor said, his voice rasping like pumice on paper.

"You know very well," said Xif.

"Ah, the Betrayer has at last found his spine!" Glankor said. "I admit, I am surprised that you are still on Thalmos. I thought you would have abandoned these two to their fates much as you did your brethren all those millennia ago."

"You're focussing on the wrong question, Glankor," said Xif.

"Council Master, please," pleaded Feeshaw "It's not safe around these...these...murderers! We must get you away from here."

"Hmmm, yes," said Glankor, ignoring Feeshaw. "The question is why have you returned? I was almost convinced you'd slipped the net somehow and returned to Angor Bore."

"We're not leaving until we've resolved the issue between our people," said Akira.

Glankor threw back his head and cackled. "Resolve the issue? You murdered a Thalmian, Ambassador. Not a citizen, granted, but still. You ran from justice and defied my order of arrest. I'm very interested to know why you believe yourself to be in a position to resolve anything."

"The man we killed was an assassin," Akira said flatly. "He would have killed us."

"Impossible," snorted Glankor. "The personnel allowed entry to your residence were vetted."

"By who?"

Glankor glanced sideways at Feeshaw.

"Ah yes. Shield Feeshaw," Akira said. Feeshaw's composure, threadbare since Akira had appeared in any event, frayed further and his eyes darted around as if searching for an exit.

"You've been played for a fool, Glankor," Akira said. "Shield Feeshaw has been conspiring against you and against the people of Thalmos. You thought we killed his predecessor, correct? And Shield Feeshaw then presented you with evidence that the Kudo-kai have been smuggling weapons and drugs to the RLA. It's horse shit, Glankor. Who has benefitted most from Adams' death? Not us, that's for damn sure."

"What is this–" began Feeshaw.

"Quiet, Feeshaw," said Glankor, his eyes bright in their sockets and face grim.

"Council Master, surely you can't believe any of this."

"I SAID SHUT UP!" Glankor shouted.

"To answer your earlier question," continued Akira, "the reason I'm still here, the reason I've returned to the Spire despite your evident intention to execute me is that I promised my father that I would find out why you severed trade relations between our people. Well, we've discovered that and more, Council Master. Xif, if you'd be so kind."

"I have just transferred to your servers the dossier produced by Shield Feeshaw, which I believe you have already read, Council Master," said Xif. "I have also transferred an overlay highlighting various artefacts which demonstrate that the evidence underpinning the dossier has been manufactured. The Kudo-kai have been exporting neither weapons nor narcotics to Thalmos. Nor do I believe that they were responsible for the assassination of Shield Adams."

Glankor turned slowly to Feeshaw. Feeshaw's face had grown pale and his jaw moved strangely as if working around something inedible.

"The nanotrite..." Glankor whispered.

"We don't know where he's been sending it, Council Master," said Akira, "but it's safe to assume that it's now with whoever he's been working for."

"What have you done?" Glankor said to Feeshaw. "WHAT HAVE YOU DONE?"

Feeshaw flinched as Glankor raised a bony hand as if to strike him across the face. Before the blow could connect, however, there was a flash of white light at the periphery of Akira's vision which raced across the plateau. Almost instantly there was a screaming gale all around them. Akira was wrenched violently, her feet flew out from under her and she tumbled over the smooth stone floor. All sense of direction was lost as she spun and sprawled and the roaring in her ears overwhelmed everything else. Somewhere in the maelstrom a piercing scream rang out and then all was black.

Chapter 47

The man shouldered his way through the crowd of thrashing people, forcefully shoving them when they didn't move fast enough. The spiralling laser lights that flittered over his head and thumping bass made him feel skittish and irritable. Kor Thalia was certainly a different place during the Umberaurum celebrations. The last time he had visited, the city had been a much more pleasant experience. Then he had had the luxury of time to accomplish his mission carefully and effectively. He was particularly proud of the exquisite planning that had gone into creating his legend. When he had approached the office of Shield Adams, it was as a pioneering manufacturer of advanced bio-domes looking to ease Thalmos's chronic overcrowding without condemning the non-citizens to a life without sunlight in the sub-levels. He had been armed with pitch documents of nauseating detail created over the course of many months and could call on a list of contacts within the industry, all of whom would have vouched for him with genuine sincerity.

He had known that Adams would be keen to meet with him. The considerate fool had always been entertaining ways of easing the suffering of the poor wretches in the sub-levels. He remembered his even white teeth as Adams had smiled and shaken his hand, unaware that the micro needles under the man's palm were pumping him full of Surgeon Mantis venom. Unaware that the venom would be coursing through him undetected by his nano-defences and tearing apart his vital organs. The man had felt a flush of elation at that moment. The flawless culmination of months of preparation.

Now, however, he felt rushed. His employer had intelligence that his target was at the Spire, the most heavily guarded building in Kor Thalia and he had no time to plan his approach. Ah, well, he was accustomed to improvising. He sidestepped a skinny man whose skin was entirely covered with bronze scales and who was moving sinuously in time with the music. Up ahead great sweeping steps rose above the crowd and led to the base of the colossal Spire. Soldiers clad in the dusty red uniform of the Thalmian army corp and lugging rifles were racing into the tower's entrance, followed from above by a flock of screeching drones flashing lights as they flew.

The man broke away from the crowd and made his way up the steps, pulling a thin metallic disc from his pocket. As he approached the entrance to the Spire, a burly soldier held up a hand. A drone above his shoulder spun towards the man and extended the barrel of its gun.

"Please turn around, citizen. This is a restricted area."

"But I have a gift for the festivities," the man said, smiling lazily and opening his palm. The centre of the disc unfurled itself revealing an icy blue, glowing core. It lifted itself off the man's hand and floated upwards. The soldier, the craggy lines in his face deepened by the aquamarine light, watched its progress, frowning.

"What is this? Wha—"

The disc shot passed his shoulder into the bowels of the building. There was a bang and the drone at the soldier's shoulder fell out of the air hitting the ground with a dull thud. In a single fluid motion the man swept his coat back and pulled a thin gun from the concealed holster at his hip, raising it to eye-level. As he did so, the back of the weapon telescoped out into a butt that nestled into his shoulder. He snapped off a shot that caught the soldier, who was only now beginning to raise his own weapon, in the middle of his forehead, whipping his head back and blowing out a cloud of red mist from the back of his skull.

The soldier had barely crumpled to the ground before the man was stepping over him to enter the atrium of the Spire. Inside, the air was sweetly perfumed and imposing statues of

Council Masters of cycles past, many times larger than life and cast in realistic-shaded silicone, lined the walls, gazing down from their elevated perches with a mixture of beneficence and paternal judgement. The floor was strewn with the casings of drones, like dead flies. The EMP pulse had done its work well.

A group of soldiers had gathered at one side of the atrium, intending to ascend the Spire in one of the vacuum-tubed elevators, but were now adopting defensive positions. One of those closest spotted the man approaching and dropped to a knee, raising his weapon, a standard-issue Gosler repeater rifle. The man had supervised the import of thousands of the same weapon to members of the RLA here on Thalmos and knew its workings intimately. The solider lined up a shot on the man and then...nothing. The man stood still for a moment savouring the look of confusion on the soldier's face as it changed to understanding then despair. The pulse had fried the processors of his rifle and those of his comrades as well as their shields. The man raised his own ballistic rifle, immune to the effects of the pulse. The soldiers shouted urgent warnings to each other, voices shrill with panic, and tried to disperse. They couldn't move fast enough. The man sprayed the group with bullets, ripping into their unarmoured lower legs. Puffs of dust and stone-chips erupted into the air around them where the bullets missed their marks.

It was over in a few seconds. The atrium rang with the sudden quiet punctuated only by groans and laboured breaths. Every soldier was splayed out on the floor, trousers dark with blood and torn, displaying gaping-pink wounds in their flesh. A few were on their elbows trying to drag themselves to safety leaving bloody streaks on the floor behind them. The man walked over to the ragged mess of bodies and began putting a final bullet carefully in the chink between their helmets and body armour. Most died well, facing their end with stoic silence or scrabbling for handguns but more than a couple begged and pleaded, screaming at him to spare them. That was distasteful but not unexpected in his experience.

Once he had dealt with the last of the soldiers he stepped into the elevator. At this level it was surrounded by thick steel doors and its electronics had therefore been protected from the effects of the pulse. The man pulled a data spike from his pocket but as he searched for the best place to force the spike into the elevator's controls, he noticed a curious flickering from the instruments. On a hunch he pressed the control for the top of the Spire where the Council would be watching Inthil's celestial approach. Immediately, he felt the heaviness of acceleration as the elevator began to climb. He chuckled to himself. He suspected his job was going to be a measure harder than he had anticipated. He sat down on one of the cushioned seats lining the walls and admired the view as the glass-sided elevator lifted out of the base of the tower and sped upwards. While he waited, the man slotted a scope onto the top of his gun and screwed a metal ring to the muzzle which telescoped out into a long barrel. Eventually, when the sky outside had faded to black and the shining city of Kor Thalia was little more than an asymmetric disc beneath him, the elevator reached the summit. He took a moment to admire the blazing sweep of silver stars above him. The view reminded him of his recent missions, the moments before he boarded haulers when he stood alone in the starlight with nothing but the sound of his own breath in his ears. He felt a thrill of anticipation run through him.

Soft lighting in the floor illuminated the Council members towards the centre of the plateau. In their midst stood Ambassador Director Akira Mukudori Kudo, her handmaid and the AI, Xifulandros Mil Askathraim. It seemed that the Ambassador was talking to Glankor. He raised the scope to his eye and increased the magnification. Shield Feeshaw stood next to Glankor, his face white and eyes bulging. It seemed he might be too late already. Pinpricks of frustration needled him but he quickly steadied himself, breathing deeply. He needed to keep an even pulse to ensure he made the shot. And anyway, if it turned out he was too late to protect Feeshaw's secret he would deal with the aftermath of that too. He raised the rifle, took a deep breath then exhaled and lined up his shot on the back of Akira Kudo's head.

Chapter 48

Sometimes a discovery can be a small thing that affects a person's life only slightly, like finding a coin on the street. But other times a discovery can be so momentous that it reshapes what a person sees as possible. As Mordax crept through the Spire's service corridors, heart hammering, he experienced one of the latter kinds. Gaining access had been easier than he expected. The group of surly looking soldiers milling around the wide steps at the Spire's main entrance had immediately discouraged him from trying to bluff his way in but the veil had easily cracked the security on a wide service door, part way round the building. Looking through the veil, the Spire's electronic systems showed up like sparkling nerve fibres running through the walls and floors.

As on Eloth, Mordax found he could open doors and deactivate cameras as he moved deeper into the building. The Thalmians were clearly security conscious as small groups of soldiers patrolled even these quiet and dusty corridors. The veil showed each patrol through the walls as groups of two or three red dots and Mordax was able to duck into storage closets and utility rooms when the patrols got too close. That was until he found himself in a long corridor approaching the Spire's main atrium and the red marks of a patrol appeared up ahead. Mordax scanned the corridor, looking for somewhere to hide but the only other doorway was the one he had come through. He started back, then realised that the gliding dots of another patrol had entered the area he had just left and were looming closer. He was cornered. His breath quickened and the strip lighting along the ceiling seemed to brighten as adrenaline surged through his system. One patrol, he might be able to deal with if he got the drop on them but two with no cover?

With trembling hands he unslung the canvas bag from his shoulder and drew out the scoped pulse rifle it contained, one of the jewels of Stamford's arsenal which Stamford had insisted he should take. Apparently it could blast through an inch of reinforced steel. Mordax now lined up the sight on the doorway, painfully aware that his back was unprotected against the patrol coming from the opposite direction. Just as the door was about to open, Mordax heard the now familiar voice in his ears.

"Exposed position detected. Protocol suggestion activate cloak. Confirm?"

"Confirmed!" whispered Mordax urgently, not knowing what would happen but desperate for anything that could help. Mordax felt a peculiar coldness spread down from his neck but apart from that nothing seemed to happen. The door slid open and Mordax's finger tightened around the rifle's trigger as he prepared to fire. But when the trio of soldiers stepped into the corridor, they didn't react at all. No sudden halt at the sight of the armed intruder before them. No raised weapons or shouts of alarm. The three carried on marching towards him. Mordax glanced behind him and another two soldiers were approaching from the opposite direction, equally unconcerned about his presence. He looked down at his hands, a silvery sheen was covering his skin. Aside from that, he could see himself perfectly but the soldiers didn't seem to be able to.

His head swam with relief. Somehow the veil could cloak him. He knew the technology was possible, certain smugglers he had met had spent vast quantities equipping their ships with cloaking fields to help their operations but the generators were huge pieces of equipment. He had never heard of a cloaking generator small enough to be worn, and certainly not one that was effective enough to fool the human eye up close, but the proof was hanging around his neck. As the soldiers drew closer Mordax pressed himself up against the wall. Even then it was almost not enough as one of them, a man with bushy sideburns and weather-beaten skin, passed so close to him that Mordax could smell the sharp spice of his cologne and make out the thick hairs sprouting from his ears. The patrols nodded to each other and continued on their way. When the last of them had passed and he was alone again, Mordax let out a deep breath not realising he had been holding it in, afraid to make even the tiniest sound. He realised now how the Dioscuri had been able to bring about the fall of the Two Empires and were still able to keep would-be imperialists from expanding among the civilised systems. Ashfol had told him that the veil was more advanced than any other technology in the galaxy but he hadn't really known what that meant until now.

The rest of the journey to the Spire's main atrium was much quicker, the confidence that Mordax felt now that he was essentially invisible lending wings to his feet. He even paused for a moment to admire the grandiose statues of past Council Masters that towered over the atrium's gold-veined marble floor. Whatever process had been used to create them had successfully captured a sense of haughtiness and self-importance.

Mordax approached the bank of lifts that lined the atrium, skirting a group of soldiers as he did so. He was slightly nervous that the swarm of drones that buzzed above them would not be similarly fooled by the veil's cloak but he was able to edge his way past the group without anyone noticing. As he did so, he heard the soldiers muttering among themselves.

"This isn't the first time," said one of the older-looking ones. "It's happened before during Umberaurum. It's the fireworks and the music. They set the alarm system off so often that in the end some cunt in control just overrides it to shut up the bleeping. 'Course that means we have to spend the next four hours checking the building as the whole system resets but at least that fucking moron doesn't have to hear the bleeps anymore."

Mordax sneaked into one of the glass elevators and activated the controls through the veil. The steel doors slid shut and Mordax almost stumbled as the lift accelerated harder than he was expecting. As it did so, he heard a muffled bang followed by what sounded like the staccato popping of gunfire. But it was too faint for him to be sure and soon the elevator was racing up through threaded clouds leaving the twinkling lights of Kor Thalia far below.

***

Mordax emerged onto the polished stone of the Spire's summit. He didn't miss a step as the great ocean of stars opened up before him. He was a Traveller after all. Moving through space was as natural to him as breathing. In fact, he found the gentle presence of the constellations all around him a good deal more comfortable than the heaving mass of humanity he had just left. He moved immediately to one side of the plateau and advanced around the edge, heedless of the fathomless drop off, looking towards the centre where there were ostentatious seats, carved from stone, and a cluster of people, some glancing around uncertainly. As he did so, the coldness he had felt earlier when he had activated the veil's cloak grew rapidly stronger until it felt as though he were covered in a skin of ice and his teeth began to chatter. It continued until he couldn't feel his hands or feet and a deep lethargy began to creep into him. As his eyelids drooped and his vision began to swim, he remembered Ashfol's words of warning that in the absence of external power, the veil would leach heat from his own body. With a thought, Mordax dropped the cloak. Immediately the coldness was gone and the warmth returned to his limbs causing painful pins and needles.

He was far enough away and the lighting was sufficiently dim that he was pretty sure the group at the centre of the plateau would not be able to see him. The veil magnified the view. He recognised Ambassador Kudo from the images on the news databases. She looked older now somehow but no less beautiful. The worried expression he had seen in the news images had been replaced by a grim anger. At the sight of her standing there, one of the architects of his father's death, surrounded by servants laden with delicacies and consorting with some of the richest people in the galaxy, a hatred so black and so poisonous seeped into him that he felt he couldn't breathe. He dropped to his knee and raised the rifle's scope to his eye, lining up a shot between the Ambassador's hazel eyes. This would be the third life he had taken. It was justified, he told himself. Just like before. He took a deep breath and then exhaled, steadying his hands. This was the moment he had been working towards for so long. The chance to repay the ones who had taken his father from him, to strike back at a corrupt and murderous regime.

In the moment of stillness as he tried to pull the trigger some small part of him, a calm, quiet voice that he had been suppressing for too long, finally had a chance to make itself heard. He didn't know this woman. She hadn't tried to harm him. He wasn't even sure whether she had personally played any part in his father's death. True she was a member of the Kudo-kai but could he hold her responsible for the actions of any other member? The Dioscuri would, but as he thought that, Mordax felt a sickness in his belly. Since when had he adopted the moral reasoning of a group that kept a whole planet of people in perpetual barbarism for target practice? He lowered the rifle, blinking back tears. He felt adrift, powerless and now without purpose.

As he stood there, despondent, the group's conversation, amplified by the veil, drifted to his ears as if he was standing right next to them. The Ambassador was saying something about a conspiracy. That the Shield was involved. A fat man with large watery eyes and a thin goatee tried to interject.

"I SAID SHUT UP!" shouted a bony older man, head protruding like a vulture's from the thick white robes that nearly swamped his body. A drone next to the Ambassador began to speak, and not with the flat regurgitation of a simple algorithmic-link but with the inflection and intelligence of a true AI. The Kudo-kai seemed to be claiming that they had been set up. A seed of doubt began to sprout in Mordax's mind as he listened, growing more and more uncomfortable as his handle on events grew weaker.

Seconds later, the veil alerted him to a figure arriving at the summit and stepping out of the elevator. Mordax focussed on him and the magnification increased. It was man of average height and build. He had thin lips, short mousy hair and a placid expression. He gazed around him for a moment, like a tourist admiring the view, then with a surety and speed that belied his unassuming demeanour, raised a long-barrelled rifle and prepared to fire. The veil immediately showed Mordax the expected trajectory of the shot by overlaying on his vision a thin golden thread that attached the muzzle of the man's gun to the back of the Ambassador's head. Later, Mordax couldn't explain why he acted the way he did. He had given up killing the Ambassador himself but he still despised everything she represented. Logically, he should have let the stranger kill her. But his hands weren't constrained by logic.

He brought the rifle to his cheek, zeroed on the man and pulled the trigger in one swift and fluid motion. The trigger was jumpier than he was used to, however, and he fired off two plasma bolts, one fractionally earlier than he had intended, which screamed across the plateau in a blaze of piercing white light. The first bolt went slightly wide of its mark. There was a silvery flash from the man as the second bolt hit home. Instead of the bolt ripping through him, however, the man was lifted from his feet and flung backwards. Mordax expected him to be crushed against the inside of the Spire's transparent dome but as the man sailed through a gaping molten ring of super-heated metal and as the roaring filled Mordax's ears, he realised with an icy wave of horror what he had done. The first bolt which missed the man had burned right through the Spire's dome to the vacuum outside. The wind shrieked and scoured and tore at his clothes. His feet were whipped out from underneath him and he was dragged inexorably towards the breach. Up ahead, platters and glasses ripped from the hands of the attendants flew through the air as the people grabbed hold of seats and candelabras and anything else that was fixed to the floor. As he slithered closer Mordax saw the Ambassador tumbling across the floor. Her companion, one arm wrapped around a pedestal, reached out and caught her by the arm as she flew past. There was a thin scream, just loud enough to hear over the wind, as the old man who had been shouting earlier lost his grip on whatever had been anchoring him. The wind picked him up and tossed him like a rag doll, sending him cartwheeling over the smooth and unyielding floor, scrawny arms scrabbling in vain for purchase. Part of him, an elbow or maybe a knee, struck the Ambassador as he tumbled past. The Ambassador immediately went limp and her companion shouted in pain but kept hold of her.

In seconds, the old man was gone. Lifted up and carried out of the void in the Spire's dome. Around the ragged edges of the hole, however, Mordax could see the frantic movement of drones fighting against the current of air. The tell-tale bright blue of plas-steel resin blossomed in a ring around the hole and swiftly grew thicker. By the time Mordax had reached the centre of the plateau, the drones had regurgitated enough plas-steel to cover the hole entirely and the wind had abated leaving a ringing silence in his ears, interrupted only by the whimpers and shuffling of the survivors.

Mordax picked himself up. He had heard enough of the Ambassador's conversation to unnerve him. There was more going on here than he understood. He had to buy time to figure it all out but he couldn't lose the chance to get more information from the Ambassador. He rushed over to where she was lying prone, a scattering of other Council members and servants nearby still clutching their anchor points, not ready to trust that the ordeal was over. The Ambassador's companion saw him approach and her eyes, blinking and unfocussed, widened in fear at the veil covering his face.

"No," she whispered hoarsely. "King killer."

She stumbled to her feet, clearly fuddled from the collision with the old man. Mordax made to push past her and it was only the months spent training on Hellenbos that saved him. Mordax saw the flash of metal out of the corner of his eye as the companion lunged at him and pivoted so that instead of plunging into his belly the knife that had appeared in her hand slashed his shirt and cut a shallow line into his flesh. He brought the butt of his rifle round in an arc and smacked the girl in the temple. Her legs buckled and she fell to the floor unconscious. As Mordax's shirt began to soak with blood and he stood looking down at the sprawling mass of debris around him, he wondered where his life choices had gone wrong. Being as gentle as he could, he lifted the Ambassador, draped her over his shoulder and limped towards the elevator.

Chapter 49

"I think she's coming round."

The words reached Akira as if she were hearing the echo of them rather than the words themselves. She was suddenly aware of the feeling of something soft beneath her and a throbbing in her temples. She opened her eyes and squinted against the light. She was half-reclining on some kind of couch, propped up by fluffy pillows. An unlikely array of characters was assembled in front of her. There was a squat dark-skinned woman with frizzy hair, a thin wild-eyed man with a lizard perched on his shoulder and what could only be a Sabulonian, towering over the others even though he was sitting down, with his enormous arms folded across his chest. In front of these others was a young man looking at her with a disconcerting intensity. He wore silver rings in his ears and his eyes were the crisp, deep blue of the ocean on a winter's morning.

"Where am I?" she asked, the words feeling fuzzy on her tongue.

"You're aboard the *Indigo Starling*," the strange young man replied.

"The what?" Akira said.

"The *Indigo Starling*. Saddleback-class trading vessel."

"What happened? I was on Thalmos. On the Spire."

The young man rubbed the back of his neck and grimaced.

"Yeah, there was a slight issue with the dome. Bit of a hole in it."

"What? How? Who are you people?"

As Akira's head cleared the situation she now found herself in seemed more and more bizarre. She looked around the room properly for the first time. Coloured lamps hung from the ceiling and great tapestries covered the walls.

"This is Dr Virzda Golgoth," the young man said, gesturing at the squat, older woman. She gave Akira a tight, tired smile.

"That's our pilot, Lazarus, and the big hunk of meat over here is Stamford."

The wiry man with the lizard gave an awkward wave and the Sabulonian glowered at her.

"My name's Mordax L'Amfour. I'm the one who brought you here."

"Why? What happened on the Spire?" Akira asked. A sudden thought occurred to her "Where's Shiori? Is she OK?"

"Relax," Mordax said. "Shiori's the one who was with you? Tough cookie that one. She saved your life, you know. She might have a bit of a headache when she wakes up but she'll be fine."

"What about, Xif?"

"I'm here, Akira," Xif said.

Akira whirled around, too fast as it transpired as the blood rushed to her head causing bright spots to appear before her eyes. Xif was floating a few feet away, black casing as inscrutable as ever.

"Stamford found this little stowaway in the cargo hold after we launched. Won't tell us how he followed us or got on board. I saw him on the Spire so knew he was with you," Mordax said.

"It was a slightly more fractious process than that," said Xif indignantly.

"Yes, well, Stamford gets a bit twitchy when strange AIs appear on the ship uninvited," said Mordax.

Stamford grinned and produced a huge pistol which he laid casually over his forearm, pointing in Xif's direction.

"Tell me what happened," said Akira.

"Quick version? I shot a hole in the dome. The atmosphere partially vented and you were knocked unconscious when the old man you were talking with lost his grip and crashed into you. I picked you up, sneaked you out and brought you to the *Starling*."

"The old man, Glankor. Is he OK?" Akira asked.

Mordax looked embarrassed. "He, um, he sort of got sucked out of the breach."

"HE WHAT?" Akira sat bolt upright.

"Look, the atmosphere was venting and the drones didn't patch the gap in time. I'm afraid he's orbiting Thalmos now."

"Oh my god," Akira said sinking back. "Oh god. You complete idiot."

"Now hold on a minute..." said Mordax

"Do you know what you've done? Do you? You've ruined the only chance I had of restoring peace between the Thalmians and my people."

"Look, Ambassador," Mordax said, loading the word with disdain, "I've got no interest in Kudo-kai politics. What I do know is that you'd be dead if I hadn't taken that shot."

The angry words that were bubbling onto Akira's lips dissipated.

"What do you mean?"

"I mean, there was a man who was about to blow your brains out until I shot him."

Akira felt unexpectedly light-headed.

"Who was he?" she asked.

"Fuck if I know, lady. Now I think you've asked your quota of questions. Time to answer some of mine."

"I don't understand," Akira said quietly, closing her eyes against the hot pain in her skull. Could it have been Feeshaw's man again? She was sure by his reaction that the Shield had been surprised to see her.

Mordax's expression softened and he took a seat opposite her.

"Guys, could you give us a minute?" he said to the others.

"You sure about that, Mordax?" said Lazarus, absently stroking the lizard. "We haven't had a chance to run a full body scan. No idea what nasties she's hiding."

"I'm sure, Laz. I just need a few moments alone with her."

"Be careful, sugar," said Virzda, squeezing his shoulder before she and Lazarus left.

"Stam," said Mordax.

"I stay," rumbled Stamford, without taking his eyes off Akira.

Mordax knew better than to argue with him. "I need to know what you were talking about on the Spire. You said something about the Kudo-kai being set up."

Akira looked at him appraisingly. He was attractive in a rough sort of way with long sandy hair and a strong jaw. She had no idea if she could trust him though. Mordax's lips twisted in a wry smile.

"You're thinking you've got no reason to trust me. You're right, you don't. But I think we might have an enemy in common. What harm can it do to tell me about it?"

Akira chewed her lip. His logic was sound and if they really wanted the information they could always torture it out of her. The motley crew, for all their strangeness, didn't seem like the torturing kind though. She heaved a sigh, then began to talk. She explained everything from the beginning. The Thalmians' execution of the Kudo-kai envoys and their refusal to supply the Kudo-kai with nanotrite. The explosion of her first ship. Her arrival on Thalmos, the second attempt on her life and their voyage to the sub-levels. The discovery of Feeshaw's betrayal of his own people and smearing of the Kudo-kai.

Even as she told the story, it sounded alien to her own ears as if someone else had lived it. As she talked though, a heaviness that she hadn't been aware of until now lifted from her chest, as if describing the trials she had been through gave her power over them. Although she had never been on this ship before, something about it was warm and comforting. The long wooden table beside them glowed with a rich lustre and the bright wall hangings softened the sound of her voice. The air was coloured with the scent of oil, exotic spices from the kitchen and incense. What encouraged her to keep talking most, though, was the attention of the intense young man, his interest in what she had been through and his gentle questions that didn't so much as interrupt her as guide the course of her narration onto topics that she might otherwise have missed. But all at once, she was finished and for a moment they sat there in silence reflecting on the unlikely course of her life over the last few months.

"Quite the ride you've been on," said Mordax eventually.

"It's all for nothing now," said Akira miserably. "Glankor's dead and we don't know who Feeshaw was working with or where he was sending the nanotrite."

Mordax exchanged a meaningful look with Stamford then gave a grim smile and said: "Oh, I know who he was working for all right. And I think I have a good idea where the nanotrite's gone."

Chapter 50

It's strange how quickly perceptions can shift, Mordax thought. How one's most entrenched and coveted goals can, with a few words, be scattered to the wind like half-forgotten leaves. As Akira spoke, Mordax's hatred of her evaporated. The pieces of the jigsaw began to fall into place and the picture they revealed made his heart race with a noxious mixture of fear and anger. It felt like travelling along a long and winding path to find that instead of arriving at your intended destination, it has brought you back to where you started. Mordax remembered the flash of silver that had covered the man on the Spire just as the plasma bolt hit. The first bolt had punched through the reinforced material of the Spire's dome. Why hadn't the second bolt gone straight through him? Part of him had known the answer but was too afraid to face it.

"There's something you should see," Mordax said to Akira and Xif. "When we arrived at Thalmos and connected to the netherport, there was a message waiting for us from an old friend. Show them the video, Stam."

Seemingly unbidden, the fleshy face of Bayram Hakan appeared floating above the goldwood table. He looked healthier than the last time Mordax had seen him on Seraph although there were faint worry lines around his eyes.

"Stephan, my friend, I hope this finds you well. I'll keep this message short as the price of a nethercast these days is enough to make your eyes bleed. I have heard recently from friends on Nag'Sami, people of standing for whom few doors are closed. Since I saw you last I hadn't learned much more about the disappearance of the Nag'Sami haulers. Some rumours about mercenaries taking a pirating job and then going missing," Bayram waved a hand dismissively. "Nothing of substance. That is until a few days ago. A man I know in the Nag'Sami military, a general, in fact, was visiting Seraph with his family. He tells me that they have been sending their haulers out with concealed nethercasters. Very expensive equipment. He tells me the ships are programmed to start transmitting as soon as there is an incident and keep transmitting until their nanotrite is depleted. A couple of months ago, another hauler went missing. This time, however, they had a message. The data showed that the hauler was forced out of netherspace by a node net. Real advanced tech. The hauler suffered multiple hull breaches which vented the whole ship. They were boarded and the hauler nether-jumped again shortly afterwards. There was only enough nanotrite for the ship to make a few nethercast bursts but the last one was the most interesting. The ship sent its location and an image from the system it arrived at. I've included a copy of the image in this cast."

A 2D picture replaced Bayram's face, suspended above the table. It was grainy and unfocussed, clearly magnified to the maximum intelligible resolution, but discernible were three cylindrical shapes, flashing silver, surrounded by millions upon millions of bronze gleaming specks arranged in neat rows.

"Stephan, perhaps you are able to make more sense of this than I am," Bayram said. "Be careful what use you make of it. None of the scouts the Nag'Sami have sent to the co-ordinates have returned. I hope with all my heart that this information is helpful. I owe you a debt. Your friend arrived to buy starsarine as you promised and he brought more Travellers. Times are still lean but thanks to you we will survive. Go in peace, my friend, and know that my home is always open to you."

Mordax blinked away the prickling in his eyes. His father had been right. Bayram had repaid the good turn they did him with interest.

"What are those things?" Akira asked.

"They're ships," said Xif softly. "Warships, I believe. More than have been assembled at any time since the War of Ages."

"The AI's right," said Mordax.

"My name is Xifulandros Mil Askathraim,"

"My apologies," said Mordax with a smile.

"What does this mean? Who's doing all this?" asked Akira.

Mordax was silent for a few moments, looking thoughtful.

"Mr Askathraim—" he began.

"Xif is fine," Akira said, rolling her eyes.

"Xif, how comfortable are you navigating your way around strange security systems?" he asked.

"My boy, I'm ten thousand cycles old. My computational abilities are beyond anything you can imagine. There is likely no system outside of Primia that could even test me."

A wide smile grew over Mordax's face.

"I think we may be able to help each other," he said.

Chapter 51

As Mordax stepped through the doorway into the Dioscuri command chamber, he saw it through new eyes. The view out over the dusty red tundra still commanded attention, the sky above the distant mountains bruised purple and yellow and alive with intermittent forks of lightning. But now the bare rock walls and shadowy corners of the chamber reminded him of a predator's lair as if those shadows might hide a pile of broken skeletons. He could almost smell the ghostly scents of blood and scat and matted fur. Calgary sat alone at a holo desk, face an eerie blue from the array of documents and videos hanging in the air in front of him. As he caught sight of Mordax, his eyes widened in surprise. He waved his hand and the holograms before him dissolved leaving the chamber dark and silent.

"Mordax. I wasn't aware that you'd returned." A quizzical frown creased his brow. "How did you get in here?"

Mordax walked slowly to the window and stared out at the broken skin of Eloth.

"You told me not long ago that the violence of this world reassures you. That it reminds you of our place in the order of things." He turned back towards Calgary. "Is that why you killed my father? To put him in his place?"

"Mordax, I don't know what you—" Calgary began.

"Stop, Calgary. Just...stop. I know everything. I know about the nanotrite, the haulers...the fleet."

Calgary sat back in his seat, the concern sloughing from his face like a snake shedding its skin. His grey eyes glinted. "You have been busy, haven't you?"

"Yes, I've been busy. Untangling your web of lies. Was everything you said about my father a load of shit? Your admiration for him?"

Calgary sighed and a look of genuine regret passed over his face.

"Your father's death hurt me more than you can know, Mordax. I meant what I said about Stephan. He was a hero to a lot of us. I owed him my life."

"And yet you murdered him all the same."

For a while Calgary didn't respond, staring hard at Mordax.

"Your father did so much for our cause, Mordax. But in the end he turned his back on us. He chose you over his loyalty to the Dioscuri. Even then, he could have lived out his days playing at trader but he chose to start asking inconvenient questions. He got you tangled up in all of this."

"Inconvenient for who?" asked Mordax, struggling to keep his voice calm. "Not the Dioscuri, right? Inconvenient for you."

"I am the Dioscuri."

"But the others, Valerian, Galaia, the councils of the other Dioscuri chapters, they don't know what you've been doing, do they?" Mordax said. "Flooding Thalmos with weapons and drugs and framing the Kudo-kai. Taking the nanotrite that would have gone to them to power a fleet of starships."

"You've got everything figured out, haven't you?" said Calgary.

"I've figured out enough. It was always you pushing the idea that the Kudo-kai were responsible for killing my father. That they were the great danger, manoeuvring to expand their empire again. But it was always you."

"The Kudo-kai have spent every second of the last thousand cycles trying to restore themselves to power. It's only us, the Dioscuri, that have stood in their way."

"But you're doing more than standing in their way now, aren't you?" said Mordax. "Now you're trying to take their place."

Calgary sighed. "You really are your father's son. I never expected that you'd survive Selection to be perfectly honest. It was a convenient forum to monitor you and ensure that you hadn't found out anything you weren't telling me. It came as quite a surprise when Daenyrs failed to put you down. After that I had hoped you would join me, you know. In time. Once you came to see the rightness of what I'm trying to achieve."

Mordax's breath caught in his throat at the casual admission of the attempt on his life.

"And what exactly are you trying to achieve?" Mordax said.

Calgary leaned forward. "Do you know what progress this galaxy has made since the Purge? What advancement has taken place in the last thousand cycles?" Calgary waited a second as if expecting Mordax to answer.

"None," Calgary spat. "We've prevented the kind of warfare that ripped the galaxy apart during the War of Ages but at what cost? I've spent my entire life fighting this constant battle against the natural human instinct to expand, stifling ambition, pruning the delicate shoots of enterprise. And you know what I've realised? It's futile. We can't hope to preserve this artificial limbo forever. And we shouldn't try."

"But the veils...." said Mordax.

"Ah, yes," said Calgary, fingering the band of silver material at his neck. "The yoke that we wear believing it a powerful amulet. The Benefactors' double-edged sword. I have to hand it to them – giving us the tools to destroy the Two Empires was a brilliant move. Empowering the Dioscuri kept the galaxy from ever attaining the kind of technological advancement that would threaten them, without ever needing to lift a finger themselves. But now the tide is turning against them."

"You've been planning this for cycles," said Mordax. It wasn't a question.

Calgary gave a humourless chuckle. "Try decades."

"So you started smuggling weapons and drugs onto Thalmos. Arming the rebels there, all to turn the Thalmians against the

Kudo-kai so that you could take the nanotrite that was meant for them."

Calgary inclined his head. "Obtaining the amount of nanotrite that I need without drawing attention to myself was not an easy thing to arrange. It meant putting the right people in place on Thalmos."

"You assassinated the previous Speaker?"

"Collateral damage was unavoidable."

"I take it his replacement, Feeshaw, is your man and arranged for manufactured evidence against the Kudo-kai to be given to Glankor."

Calgary said nothing. His eyes glittered and the pink tip of his tongue darted out, moistening his lips.

"The haulers...." Mordax prompted.

"Hmmmm. I suppose it was the Nag'Sami haulers you learned of." Calgary made a tsking sound. "I suspected we'd got too greedy there."

"You needed the haulers to move the nanotrite off Thalmos and you needed ones with a genuine trading history to avoid suspicion," Mordax said.

"Very good," said Calgary with a languid smile.

"My father found out about this, didn't he?"

"I believe he did, yes. Part of it at least. Sermilion Vandt was producing weapons for me on Fornax. He was a Dioscuri veteran, you know. Worked with your father for many cycles. Somehow Stephan knew to speak to him although he can't have known that Sermilion was involved or he never would have gone to Fornax."

Mordax thought back to the broken conversation he had overheard between Stephan and Myla on Cantarina. She must have told him of Calgary's treachery and he thought Sermilion might know more. She had sealed Stephan's fate but had also set Mordax on the course to discover the truth.

"I couldn't risk Stephan trying to stop me, Mordax. The stakes are too high."

Mordax had thought he might struggle to control himself during this meeting. And as Calgary calmly admitted to his father's murder a fury settled over him as cold as a winter's night when it hurts to breathe. But there was also sadness creeping in around the sharp, frozen edges of his anger, reminding him of the lessons Stephan had taught him. Keep your emotions in check. Don't let yourself be drawn into a mistake.

"I'm surprised you failed to kill the Kudo-kai's envoy, Ambassador Akira Kudo."

Calgary shrugged. "Ordinarily, I would have entrusted that particular task to a senior wraith rather than her young friend, Maerus Yuli, but my resources have been somewhat stretched and the Council would have asked too many questions if they had learned of it."

"And the second attempt on her life?" asked Mordax.

Calgary paused, his expression part curious, part amused.

"You have been doing your research. The second attempt was nothing to do with me, however."

"Shield Feeshaw?" Mordax ventured.

Calgary nodded again. "The spineless wretch got nervous about the questions the Ambassador would ask and sent one of his men in half-baked to put her down while she was imprisoned. It was a foolish and counter-productive move. It would have been better if the Kudo-kai delegation had never made it to Thalmos but once they did, their deaths would have raised suspicions among the Thalmians."

"So what's the endgame, Calgary? You crown yourself Emperor? Use the Dioscuri to invade the systems they're supposed to protect? Pick up where the Kudo-kai and Vorth left off?"

"This isn't about me. This is about doing what's best for the Shattered Empires. Who better to unfetter our potential while still providing the stability people need. You've seen the fleet?"

Mordax nodded slowly. "I've seen images. I have the co-ordinates."

"It's beautiful, isn't it?" Calgary said, his eyes shining with pride. "There's been nothing like it since the War of Ages. The greatest armada in the galaxy by a factor of a thousand."

"It's still not enough to invade every inhabited system," said Mordax. "It's not even a fraction of what you'd need."

Calgary spread his arms. "It doesn't need to be. That's the beauty of it. Once I've annexed enough systems and turned their economies towards the common effort, my forces will grow exponentially. Unlike during the War of Ages there'll be no real opposition to stop us. No need for pointless deaths."

Mordax shook his head. "My dad always used to say, pay attention to a person's actions as they'll betray their fears."

"He always was one for melodrama."

"Maybe, but he wasn't wrong. All this subterfuge. All this effort to keep your actions concealed. You're worried about being discovered. I'm guessing Valerian and Galaia could still cause you some problems if they found out what you're planning."

Calgary snorted but his jaw tensed in a way that told Mordax he had hit a nerve.

"It's too late for you to make any difference whatsoever. I have more ships than I need and soon will have enough nanotrite to power them. There are more pieces in play than you know."

Mordax had heard enough but he couldn't resist setting a taper to Calgary's well-oiled arrogance and watching it burn to the ground.

"You mean like your man on Thalmos? The wraith?"

Mordax allowed himself a brief thrill of satisfaction at the obvious shock that caused Calgary's eyes to widen and nostrils to flare.

"What are you talking about?" Calgary said, but his voice rang hollow.

"Oh, right. Maybe someone else sent a veil-wearing assassin to take out Akira Kudo before she could tell the Thalmian Council about Feeshaw's treachery. He failed, you know? Your assassin. I wouldn't count on a ready supply of nanotrite any more."

Calgary kept his face perfectly still but through the subtle rising and falling of his chest Mordax could see his breath quicken.

"Impossible," Calgary whispered.

Calgary's confusion was well-founded. The attack at the Spire had taken place only a few hours previously and if Calgary hadn't received any information about it then how could Mordax have?

"I'm sure you'll learn about it soon enough," said Mordax with a smile.

"Enough of this," said Calgary. "You've outlived your usefulness, I'm afraid. Whatever you thought you'd achieve by coming here, it's in vain. No one will ever learn of this conversation...or hear from you again for that matter."

A bolt of green lightning exploded from one of the dark corners of the room, streaking across the chamber and passing straight through Mordax's chest. He flinched and gasped, despite himself. And then he opened his eyes and forced himself to unclench his fists. The super-heated barrel of the plasma turret was glowing a dull red in the corner of the ceiling, like a cyclops's eye. Calgary was staring at him, face waxy and white and thin lips parted.

"How...?" was all he managed.

Mordax smiled. "Be seeing you, Calgary."

And then the scene before him melted away, replaced by perfect black. Mordax took the bulky display helmet off his head, the air cool against his sweaty hair. The *Indigo Starling*'s crew, as well as Akira and Xif, were assembled before him in the *Starling*'s mess room. They turned away from the wall where Xif had been projecting the scene on Eloth, to look at him.

"Nice work, Mordax," said Lazarus. "That supercilious fucker looked like you'd just pulled a drone out of your arse."

"Thanks to Xif. It worked perfectly," Mordax said.

"I said it would, didn't I?" Xif said.

The plan had worked better than Mordax dreamed it would. He had recalled the realistic holographic images that he had first seen in the Dioscuri command chamber but he didn't know if Xif would be able to access the projector or use it to create a convincing simulacrum of him. Xif had been able to do that and more. He had created a video feed extrapolated from sensor data within the chamber so that Mordax could see through the eyes of his holo-projected image.

"He'll figure out pretty quickly what we've done," said Mordax. "Once he does, he'll find the nethercast spike Lazarus left in their old quarters. It won't be long before we lose the direct connection to Eloth."

"What do you want to do, Mordax?" Lazarus said.

"Broadcast the footage," Mordax said. "Direct to Eloth and open channel to the nearest systems. Whoever wants to pick it up."

"It'll cause a panic," Xif said.

"Fucking right it will. But people deserve to know how close we came."

"What will the Dioscuri do now?" asked Akira.

"I'm hoping they'll kill him," said Mordax. "Calgary's become the very thing they're supposed to protect the galaxy from. He's a slippery bastard but now that his secret's out, and his supply of nanotrite is cut off, the deck's stacked against him. It can't be just him though. He couldn't have planned to operate the fleet by himself. This could be the start of a very messy civil war within the Dioscuri."

A silence crept over the room as the others contemplated the magnitude of what had just happened.

"What do we do now?" asked Virzda tremulously.

There was a pause. Stamford got up from the table and returned a moment later carrying a ceramic jug and five cups which he placed firmly on the table.

"Now we drink," he said seriously. "We drink to celebrate our victory today and forget about the battles of tomorrow. We drink to cement the bonds between new allies. And most of all, we drink to remember the friends we have lost who have given their lives so that we might triumph."

He looked at Mordax who nodded and smiled. And drink they did, wincing at the burn of Stamford's home-brewed bootleg. In the warm lamplight of the *Indigo Starling*'s mess room they talked and laughed and traded stories. Mordax told Akira about his father and some of the crew's adventures. Stamford managed to convince Xif to tell them about the great battles between the Kudo-kai and the Vorth before the Purge. At some point, Virzda produced a violin and began to pour out the rousing, upbeat refrains of old Traveller favourites accompanied by much hooting and hollering and stamping of feet. Eventually, heads swimming and throats hoarse from singing, exhausted from the events of the previous days, they retired. Akira had already fallen asleep on the sofa in the mess room and Mordax laid a blanket over her. As he stumbled to his own quarters, he couldn't help smiling. His drunkenness made everything simpler and, for a while at least, quieted the worries that had plagued his waking hours. He now understood the decisions his father had made and accepted them. His enemy had a face that had been exposed to the world and his crew, his family, were safe for now. What they would do next was a problem for another day. He collapsed into bed and slept soundly for the first time in months.

Chapter 52

Akira stood alone, barefoot, watching the waves crash against the shore. The night was like warm silk around her and the full moon above turned the sand a soft silver. The cyprus trees that fringed the beach bent to the offshore breeze which brought with it the scent of jasmine flowers and the distant sound of music and laughter. Eventually she became aware of a presence close behind her. She clutched her shawl closer around her shoulders.

"It's quite beautiful here," she said.

"It is," agreed Xif.

Akira turned to look at him. His casing gleamed in the moonlight as he hovered silently level with her eyes.

"Still no word from Eloth?"

"No."

The *Indigo Starling* had lost its direct connection to Eloth shortly after it broadcast the footage of Mordax's meeting with Calgary. Mordax had decided to bring them here, to a small seaside town on Santa Malona, a planet far out along the Crux, to spend some shore time with the crew and keep a low profile until it became clear what had become of Calgary.

"There is word from Thalmos, however," Xif said. "Arrangements are under way to appoint a new Council Master. In the meantime, in light of what we discovered and Mordax's footage, relations with the Kudo-kai have been restored. I understand Feeshaw may have been executed. You've done it, Akira. You'll return to Angor Bore a hero."

"And yet, I find myself not wanting to return at all..."

Akira sighed. At least Shiori would get her reward. She glanced back towards the grass-thatched bar where Mordax and Stamford were competing to see who could walk furthest with a full beer balanced on their heads.

"They're good people," she said.

"Yes, I believe they are. In their own way," said Xif.

"Mordax was right. If Calgary has marshalled enough support within the Dioscuri there'll be civil war. They could tear themselves apart."

"It's possible."

"Even if the order survives, they'll be distracted. Resources and focus deployed inwards rather than outwards. There may be nothing to stop systems invading each other again."

"Very likely by my calculations."

A gust of wind whipped at Akira's hair.

"My father will want to capitalise on the situation."

"He'll certainly try...Akira, this is your decision. I won't tell your father where you are if you don't want me to."

"I've already made my decision," she said. She looked back towards the lights of the bar, took a moment to let the laugher and music wash over her.

"It's funny," she said, "they don't share any blood but they're more of a family to each other than any I've known."

Xif didn't say anything.

"I can't stay. My place isn't here. I don't think restoring our family to power would be good for the galaxy at all but I can't abandon them. Not now, when our enemies can attack us with impunity."

"I understand," said Xif.

"Can you arrange transport for us. Tonight?"
"I have a ship ready now. There's a car just around the headland that will take us to it."

Akira lingered for a few more moments, breathing deeply of the salty air. Then she turned away from the light and walked quietly into the night.

Epilogue

The man grunted as the med-drone tightened a compression band around his chest and polymer-filled needles punctured his skin. Most of his ribs were broken as well as a good number of his vertebrae. He would be recovering for weeks. He would have been dead, though, if the boy hadn't been such a lousy shot. The first near miss on the Spire had given his veil enough time to activate and protect him from the second shot that had hit him in the chest and catapulted him out of the hole in the Spire. Sensing the internal damage and the vacuum of space around him, the veil had put him into stasis, flooding his bloodstream with nanoparticles that slowed his heart to practically nothing and released cryoprotectant throughout his cells. Fortunately, he'd left his ship in orbit and it was able to locate and collect him before he was under for too long.

A chime from the console next to his bed let him know a message was incoming from his employer. He accepted and a face appeared before him. The man was shocked to see a face other than Calgary's and without any of the usual security measures. Nonetheless it was a face he recognised. One of Calgary's protégés. One of those who had helped him assemble the fleet.

"I take it the game's up," the man said.

Maerus Yuli's blue eyes were flat.

"Thanks to you, yes."

"I wasn't warned another wraith would be protecting the target."

Maerus's face twisted in anger. "He's not a wraith, he's a child playing at one. In any event, we didn't know he'd be there."

"What's the status? Where is Calgary?"

"Mordax has broadcast details of the operation. Calgary's been taken by the Dioscuri Council. He's probably dead."

The man inhaled sharply, wincing at the stab of pain in his chest. "The fleet?"

"The contingencies have been engaged. The fleet has already been moved."

"So, what now?"

"Now we regroup. This is a setback but the work will start in earnest now."

"You're not on Eloth?"

"No. I'll send you the co-ordinates."

Maerus's face blinked out as he cut the connection.

The man lay back and smiled. Despite the pain in his body, he felt his heartbeat quicken. There would be no more attacks on poorly defended haulers. No more hanging around dive bars on free stations picking up the dregs of the mercenary community. The real fight, the one to rival the War of Ages, was just beginning and he would meet it head on, with teeth bared and a song in his heart.

The End

About Dundas Glass

Dundas grew up in London and is a Classics graduate of the University of Cambridge. After a short spell as a Latin teacher, attempting the Sisyphean task of teaching children to conjugate, he went to law school and became an international litigator.

Dundas has a lifelong love of science fiction, fed by his father's battered copies of books by Asimov, Jack Vance and Philip K. Dick. He has been writing for a number of years and has no intention of slowing down anytime soon. *Indigo Starling* is his first novel.

A message from Dundas Glass

Thank you for reading *Indigo Starling*. It was a long time in the making, with many changes of direction and revisions (including the unfortunate deletion of whole species), but the process was immensely rewarding. I very much hope you enjoyed reading the book. If so, please do leave a review on Amazon, Goodreads or Apple iTunes Store (or just talk about the book loudly in the office). It really helps others find and enjoy the book too.

Find out more at dundasglass.com

COSMIC EGG
BOOKS

FANTASY, SCI-FI, HORROR & PARANORMAL

If you prefer to spend your nights with Vampires and Werewolves
rather than the mundane then we publish the books for you. If
your preference is for Dragons and Faeries or Angels and Demons
– we should be your first stop. Perhaps your perfect partner has
artificial skin or comes from another planet – step right this way.
If your passion is Fantasy (including magical realism and spiritual
fantasy), Metaphysical Cosmology, Horror or Science Fiction
(including Steampunk), Cosmic Egg books will feed your hunger.
Our curiosity shop contains treasures you will enjoy unearthing.
If you have enjoyed this book, why not tell other readers by
posting a review on your preferred book site.

Recent bestsellers from Cosmic Egg Books are:

The Zombie Rule Book
A Zombie Apocalypse Survival Guide
Tony Newton
The book the living-dead don't want you to have!
Paperback: 978-1-78279-334-2 ebook: 978-1-78279-333-5

Cryptogram
Because the Past is Never Past
Michael Tobert
Welcome to the dystopian world of 2050, where three lovers are
haunted by echoes from eight-hundred years ago.
Paperback: 978-1-78279-681-7 ebook: 978-1-78279-680-0

Purefinder
Ben Gwalchmai
London, 1858. A child is dead; a man is blamed and dragged
through hell in this Dantean tale of loss, mystery and fraternity.
Paperback: 978-1-78279-098-3 ebook: 978-1-78279-097-6

600ppm
A Novel of Climate Change
Clarke W. Owens
Nature is collapsing. The government doesn't want you to know
why. Welcome to 2051 and 600ppm.
Paperback: 978-1-78279-992-4 ebook: 978-1-78279-993-1

Creations
William Mitchell
Earth 2040 is on the brink of disaster. Can Max Lowrie stop the
self-replicating machines before it's too late?
Paperback: 978-1-78279-186-7 ebook: 978-1-78279-161-4

The Gawain Legacy
Jon Mackley
If you try to control every secret, secrets may end up controlling
you.
Paperback: 978-1-78279-485-1 ebook: 978-1-78279-484-4